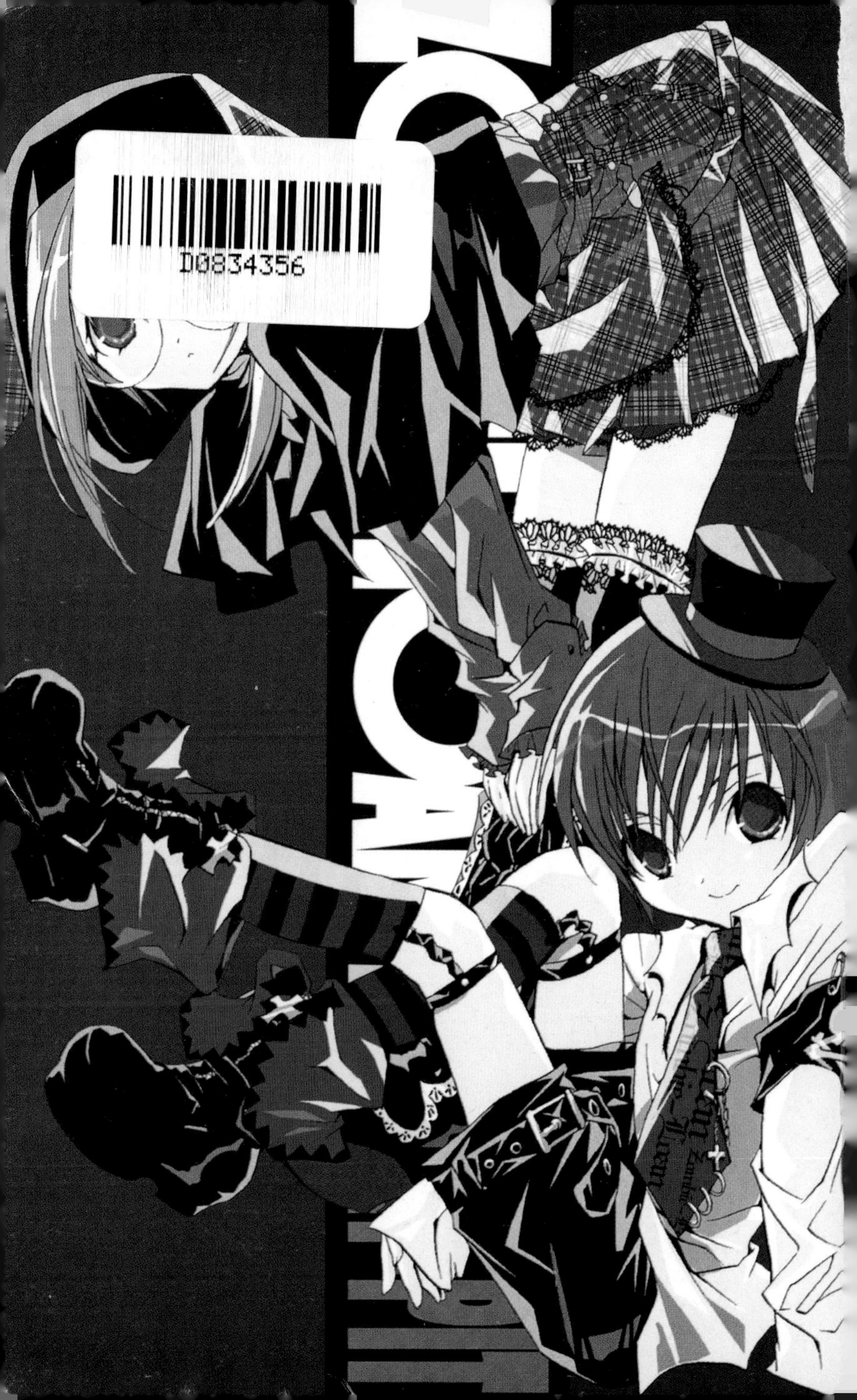

CONTENTS

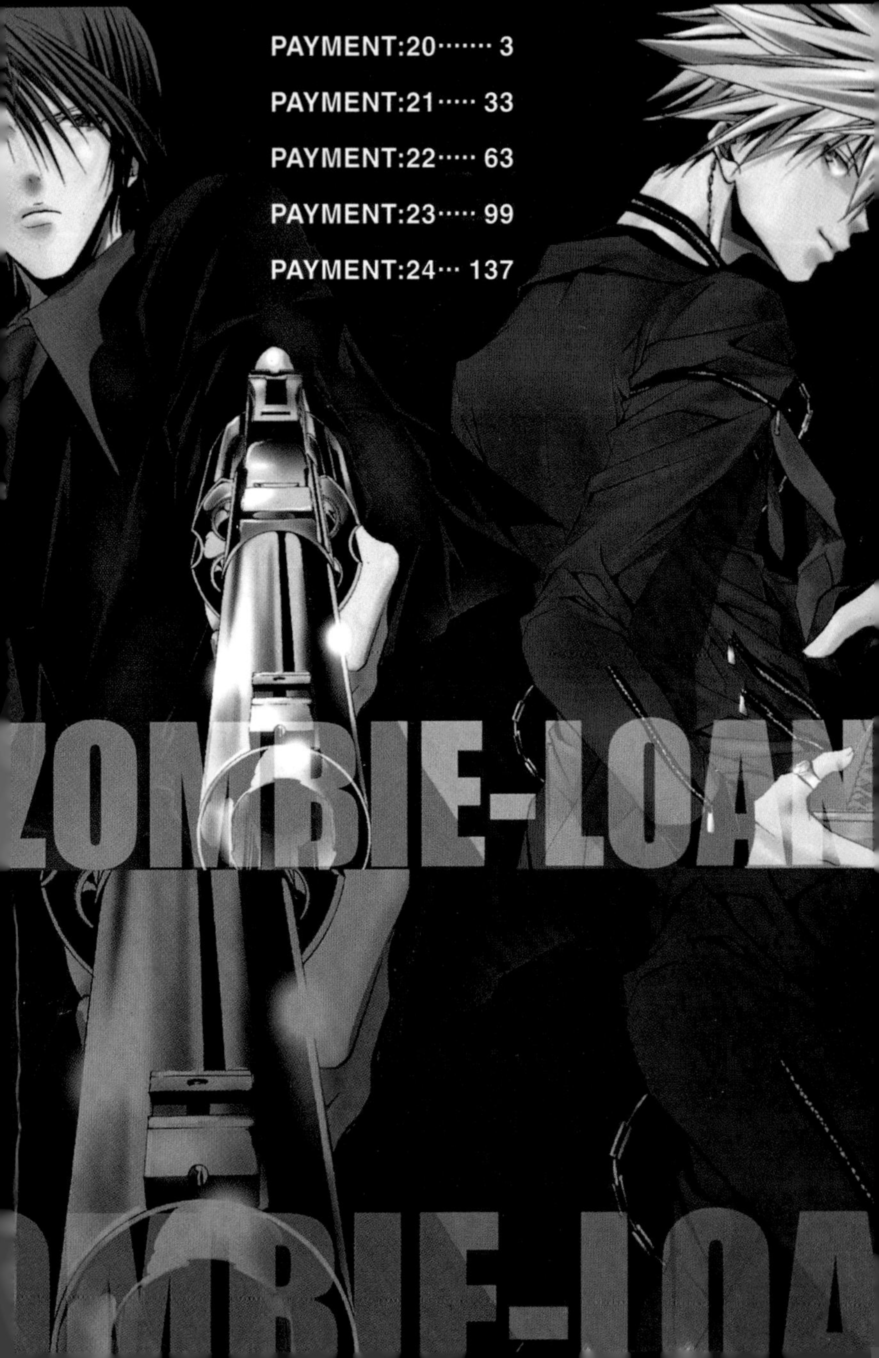

ZOMBIE-LOAN

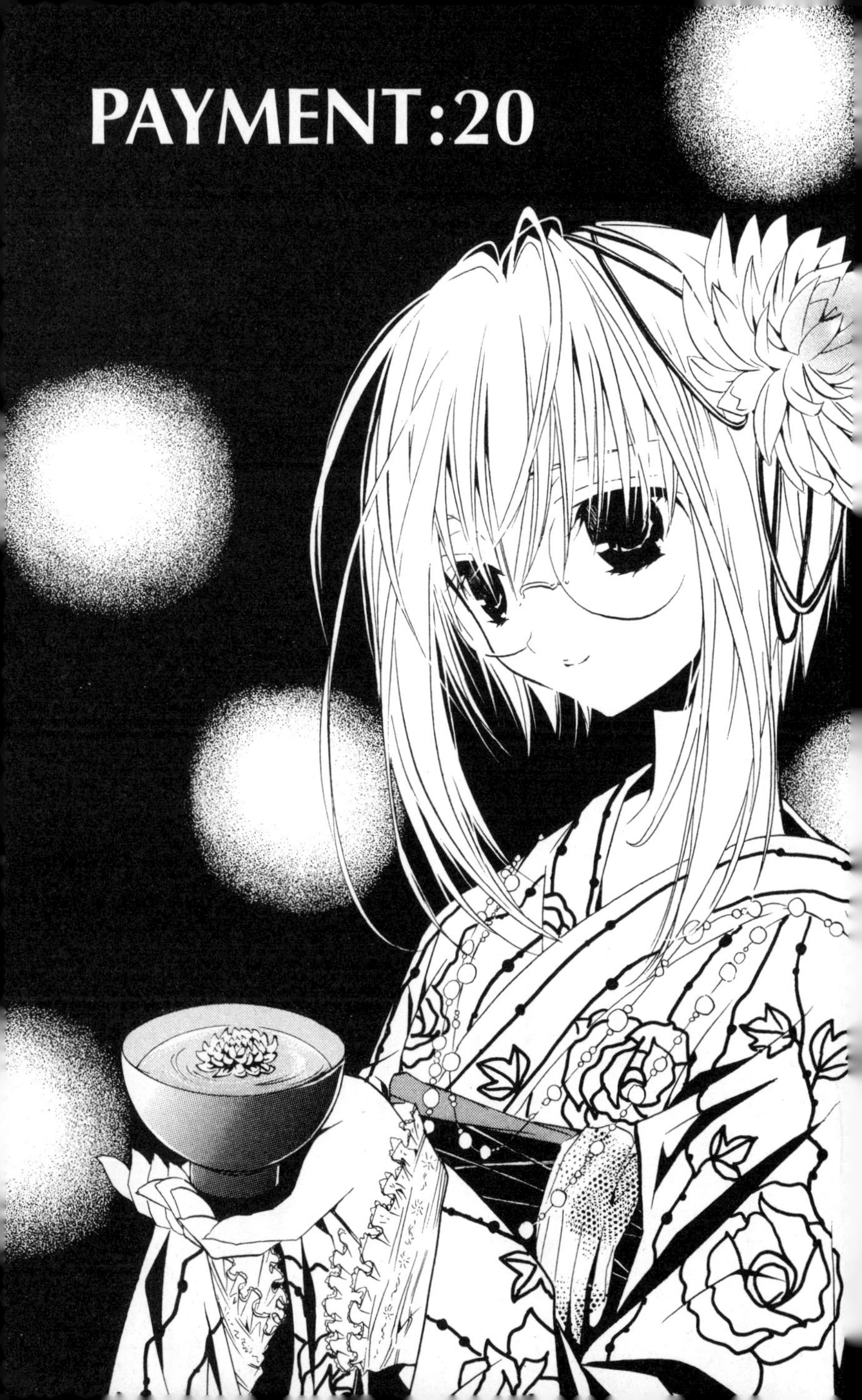
PAYMENT:20

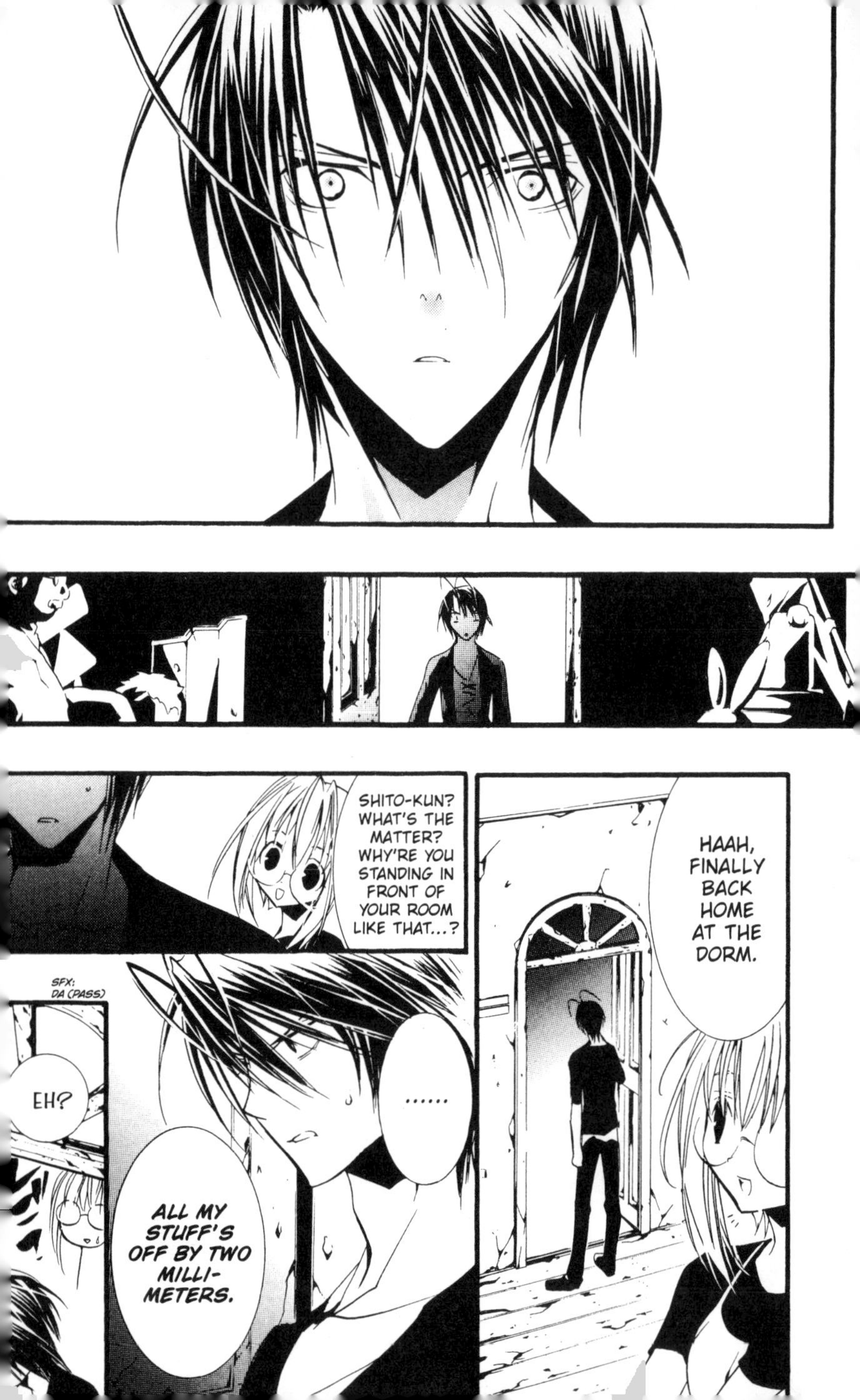
HAAH, FINALLY BACK HOME AT THE DORM.
SHITO-KUN? WHAT'S THE MATTER? WHY'RE YOU STANDING IN FRONT OF YOUR ROOM LIKE THAT...?
SFX: DA (PASS)
......
ALL MY STUFF'S OFF BY TWO MILLI-METERS.
EH?

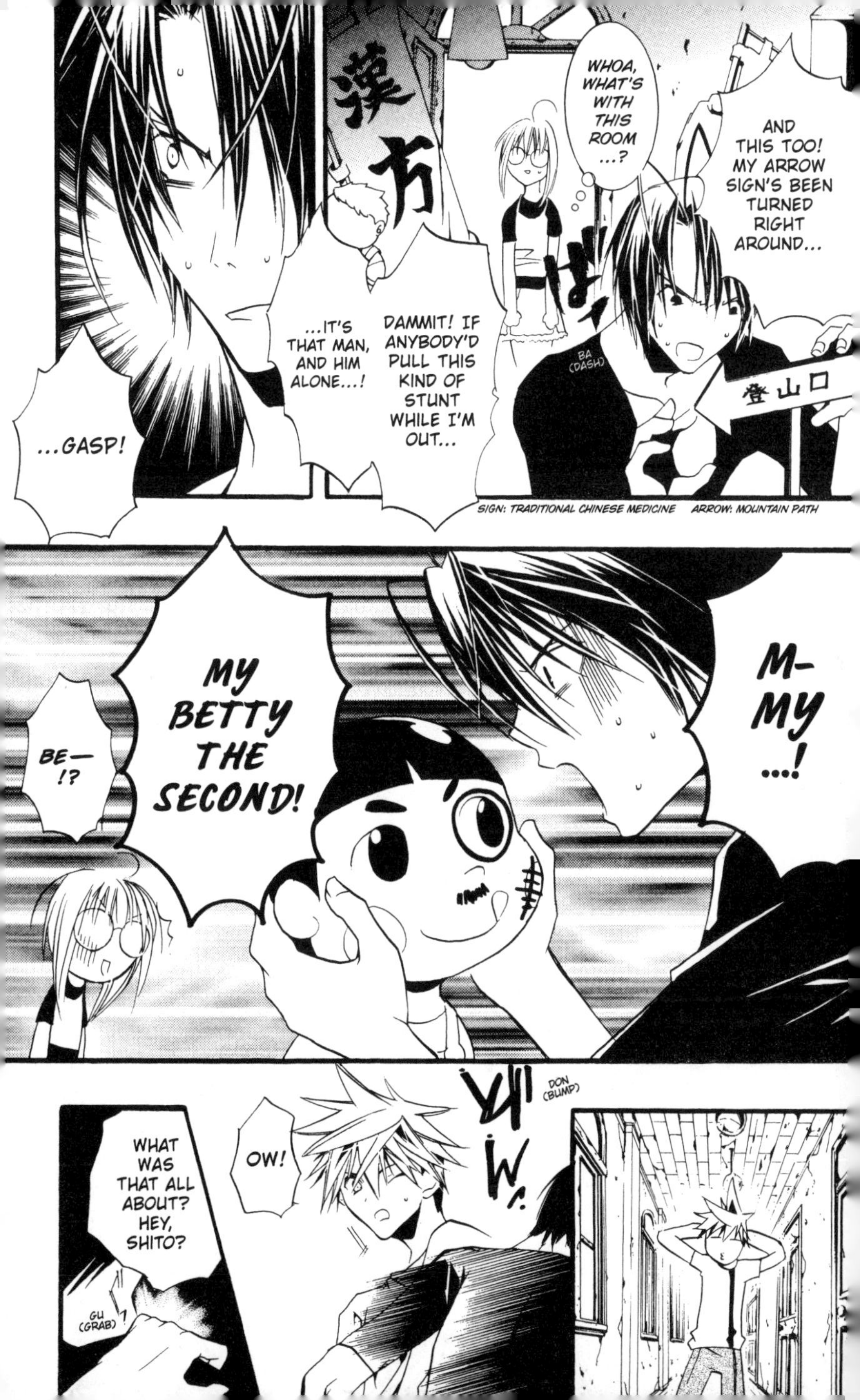
漢方
WHOA, WHAT'S WITH THIS ROOM...?
AND THIS TOO! MY ARROW SIGN'S BEEN TURNED RIGHT AROUND...
BA (DASH)
登山口
DAMMIT! IF ANYBODY'D PULL THIS KIND OF STUNT WHILE I'M OUT...
...IT'S THAT MAN, AND HIM ALONE...!
...GASP!
SIGN: TRADITIONAL CHINESE MEDICINE ARROW: MOUNTAIN PATH
M-MY...!
MY BETTY THE SECOND!
BE—!?
DON (BUMP)
OW!
WHAT WAS THAT ALL ABOUT? HEY, SHITO?
GU (GRAB)

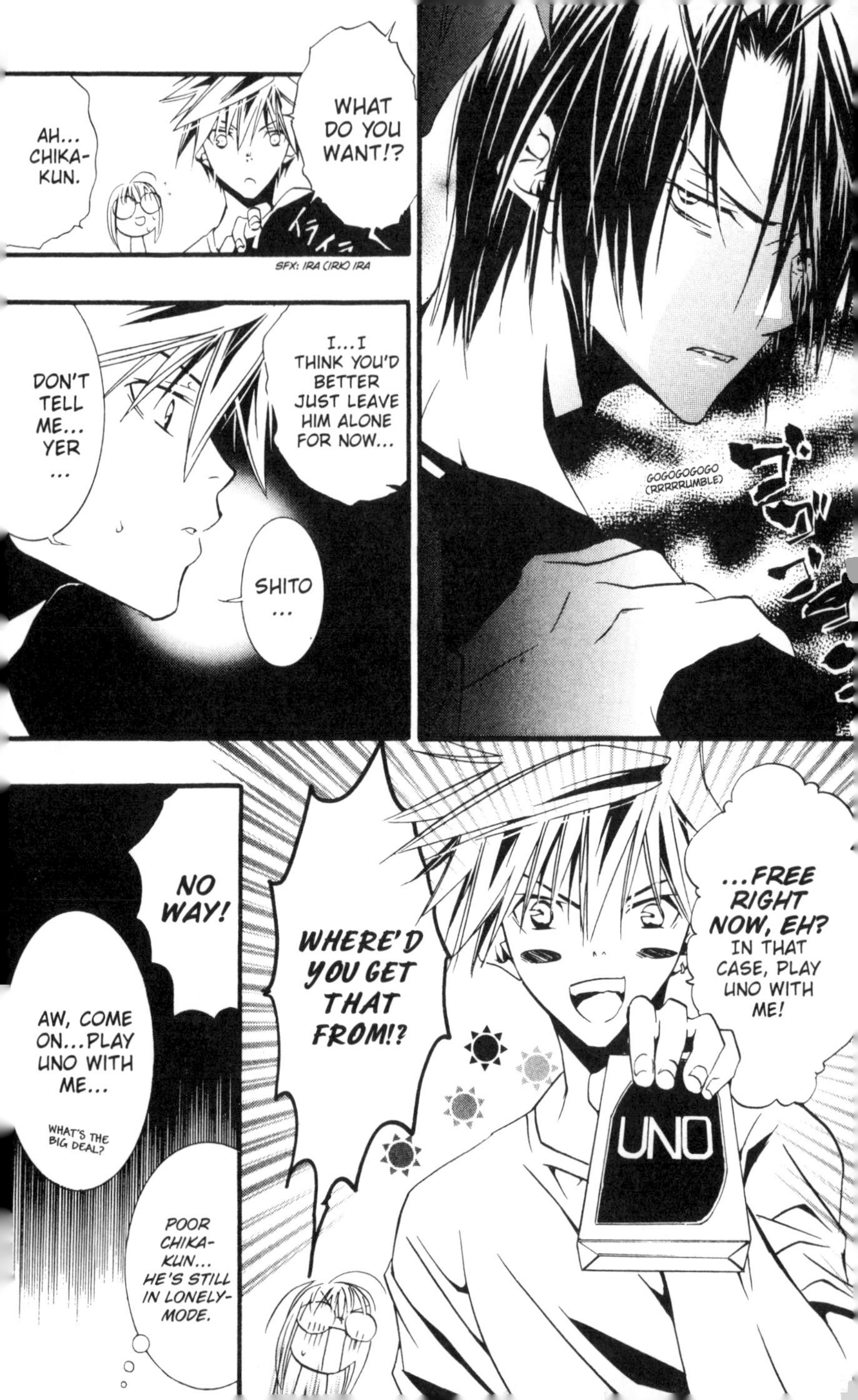
GOGOGOGOGO (RRRRRUMBLE)
WHAT DO YOU WANT!?
AH... CHIKA-KUN.
SFX: IRA (IRK) IRA
I...I THINK YOU'D BETTER JUST LEAVE HIM ALONE FOR NOW...
DON'T TELL ME... YER ...
SHITO ...
...FREE RIGHT NOW, EH? IN THAT CASE, PLAY UNO WITH ME!
WHERE'D YOU GET THAT FROM!?
UNO
NO WAY!
AW, COME ON...PLAY UNO WITH ME...
WHAT'S THE BIG DEAL?
POOR CHIKA-KUN... HE'S STILL IN LONELY-MODE.

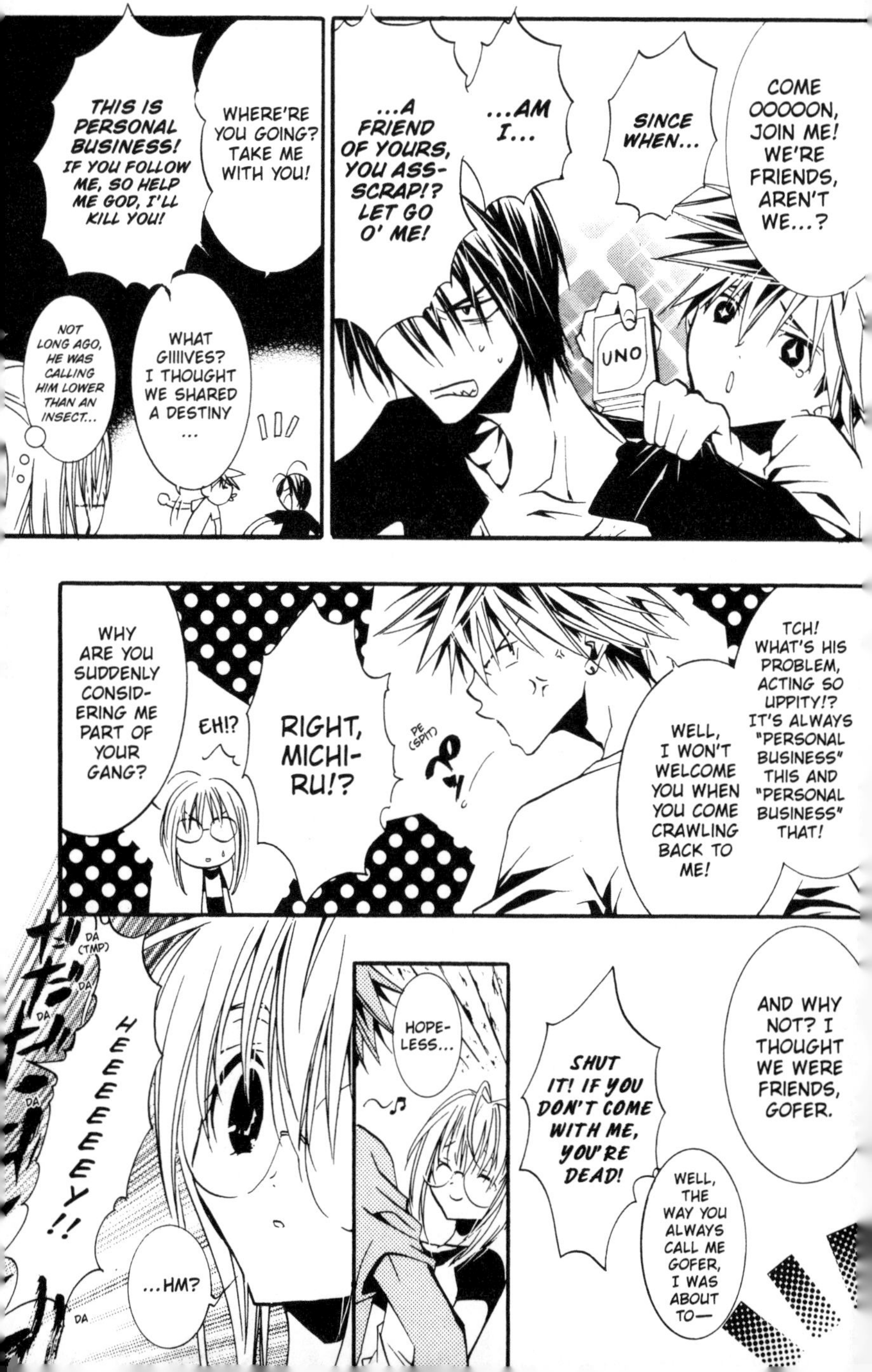
COME OOOOON, JOIN ME! WE'RE FRIENDS, AREN'T WE...?
SINCE WHEN...
...AM I...
...A FRIEND OF YOURS, YOU ASS-SCRAP!? LET GO O' ME!
UNO
WHERE'RE YOU GOING? TAKE ME WITH YOU!
THIS IS PERSONAL BUSINESS! IF YOU FOLLOW ME, SO HELP ME GOD, I'LL KILL YOU!
WHAT GIIIIVES? I THOUGHT WE SHARED A DESTINY...
NOT LONG AGO, HE WAS CALLING HIM LOWER THAN AN INSECT...
TCH! WHAT'S HIS PROBLEM, ACTING SO UPPITY!? IT'S ALWAYS "PERSONAL BUSINESS" THIS AND "PERSONAL BUSINESS" THAT!
WELL, I WON'T WELCOME YOU WHEN YOU COME CRAWLING BACK TO ME!
PE (SPIT)
RIGHT, MICHI-RU!?
EH!?
WHY ARE YOU SUDDENLY CONSID-ERING ME PART OF YOUR GANG?
AND WHY NOT? I THOUGHT WE WERE FRIENDS, GOFER.
SHUT IT! IF YOU DON'T COME WITH ME, YOU'RE DEAD!
WELL, THE WAY YOU ALWAYS CALL ME GOFER, I WAS ABOUT TO—
HOPE-LESS...
~♪
DA (TMP) DA DA DA DA
HEEEEEEEEY!!
...HM?

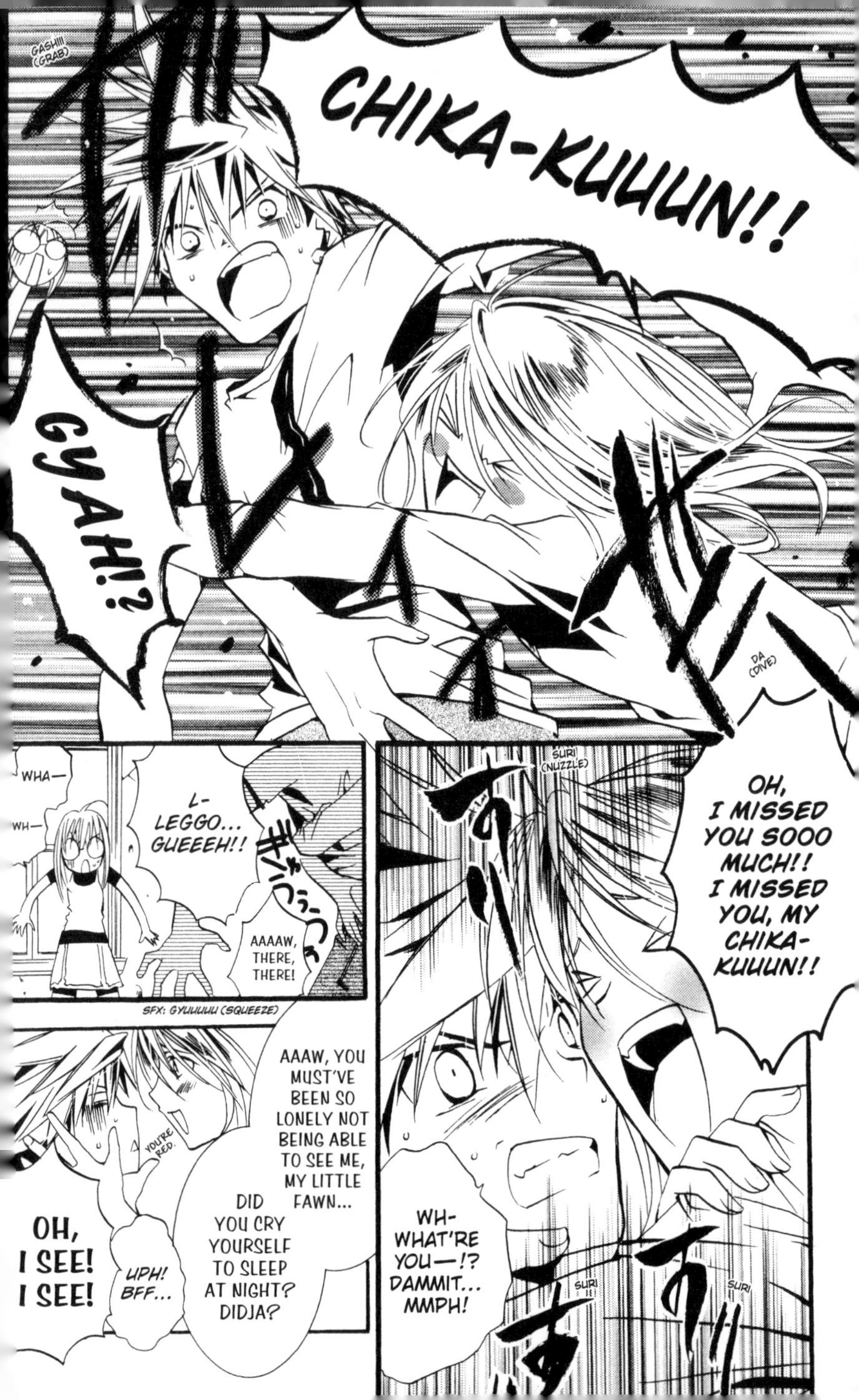
CHIKA-KUUUN!!
GASHIII (GRAB)
GYAH!?
DA (DIVE)
SURI (NUZZLE)
OH, I MISSED YOU SOOO MUCH!! I MISSED YOU, MY CHIKA-KUUUN!!
WH- WHAT'RE YOU—!? DAMMIT... MMPH!
SURI
SURI
L- LEGGO... GUEEEH!!
AAAAW, THERE, THERE!
WHA—
WH—
SFX: GYUUUUU (SQUEEZE)
AAAW, YOU MUST'VE BEEN SO LONELY NOT BEING ABLE TO SEE ME, MY LITTLE FAWN...
YOU'RE RED.
DID YOU CRY YOURSELF TO SLEEP AT NIGHT? DIDJA?
UPH! BFF...
OH, I SEE! I SEE!

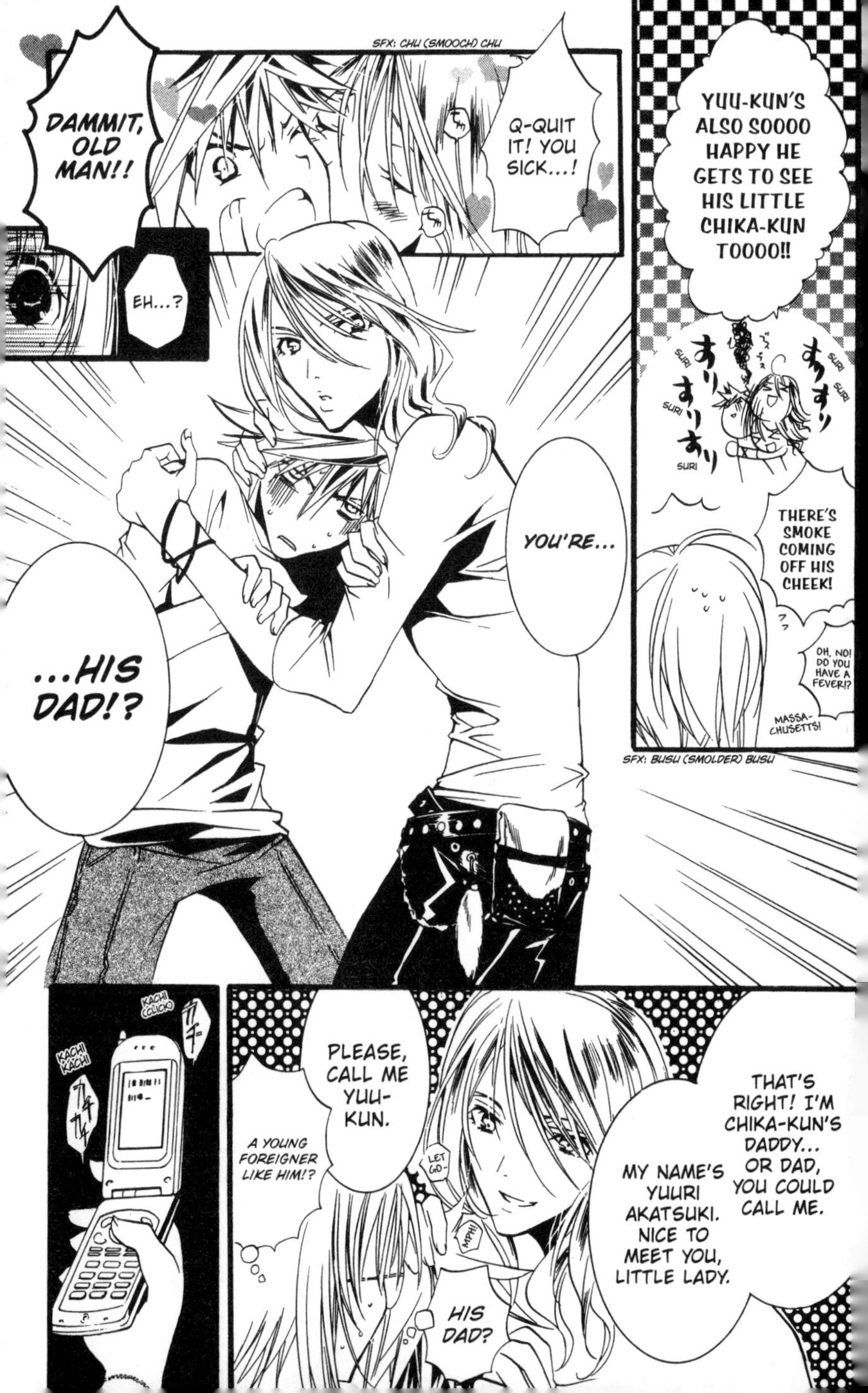
YUU-KUN'S ALSO SOOOO HAPPY HE GETS TO SEE HIS LITTLE CHIKA-KUN TOOOO!!
SURI
SURI
SURI
SURI
THERE'S SMOKE COMING OFF HIS CHEEK!
OH, NO! DO YOU HAVE A FEVER!?
MASSA-CHUSETTS!
SFX: BUSU (SMOLDER) BUSU
SFX: CHU (SMOOCH) CHU
Q-QUIT IT! YOU SICK...!
DAMMIT, OLD MAN!!
EH...?
YOU'RE...
...HIS DAD!?
THAT'S RIGHT! I'M CHIKA-KUN'S DADDY... OR DAD, YOU COULD CALL ME.
MY NAME'S YUURI AKATSUKI. NICE TO MEET YOU, LITTLE LADY.
PLEASE, CALL ME YUU-KUN.
LET GO-
MPH!
A YOUNG FOREIGNER LIKE HIM!?
HIS DAD?
KACHI (CLICK)
KACHI KACHI

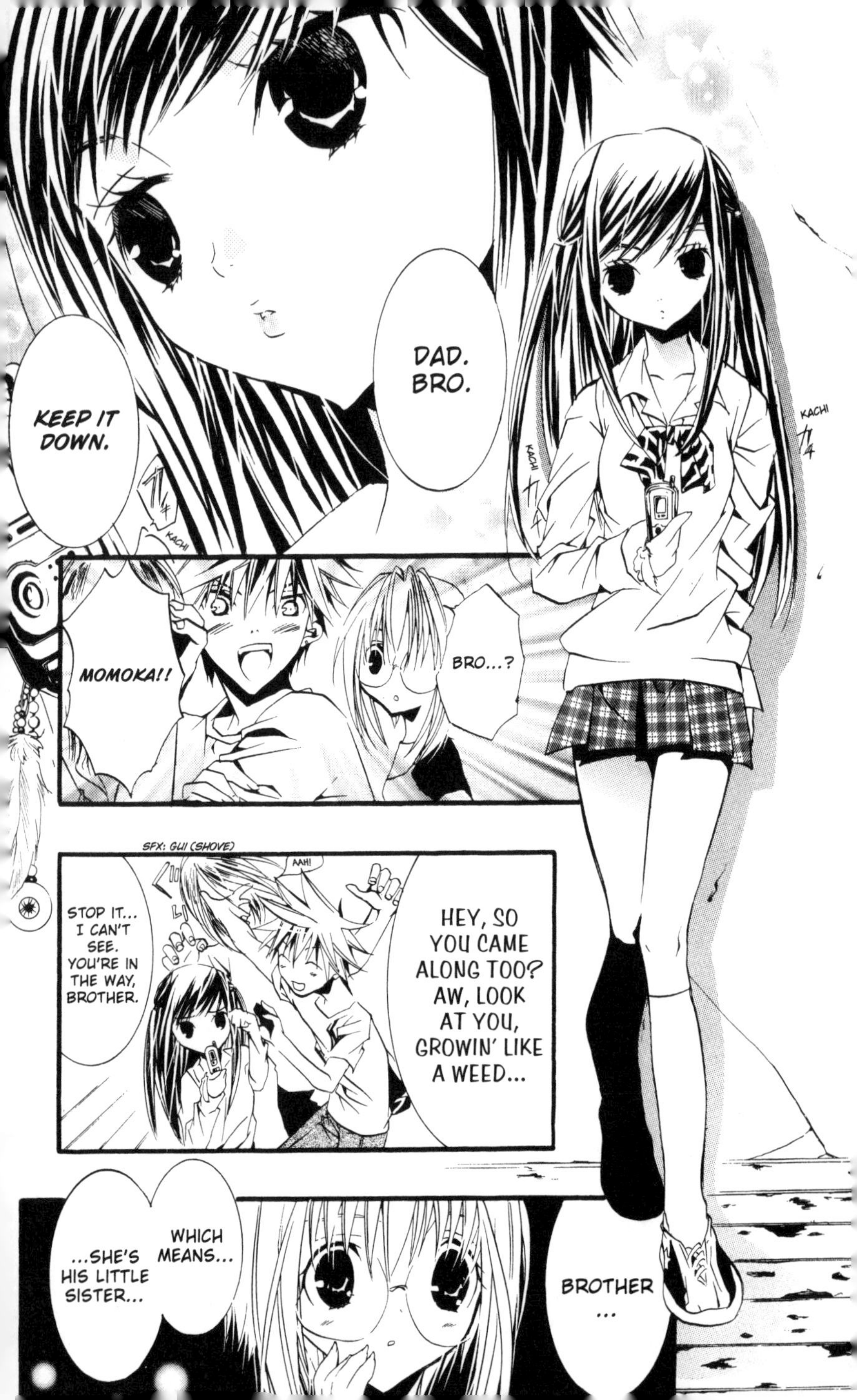
KACHI
KACHI
DAD. BRO.
KEEP IT DOWN.
KACHI
BRO...?
MOMOKA!!
SFX: GUI (SHOVE)
HEY, SO YOU CAME ALONG TOO? AW, LOOK AT YOU, GROWIN' LIKE A WEED...
AAH!
STOP IT... I CAN'T SEE. YOU'RE IN THE WAY, BROTHER.
BROTHER ...
WHICH MEANS...
...SHE'S HIS LITTLE SISTER...

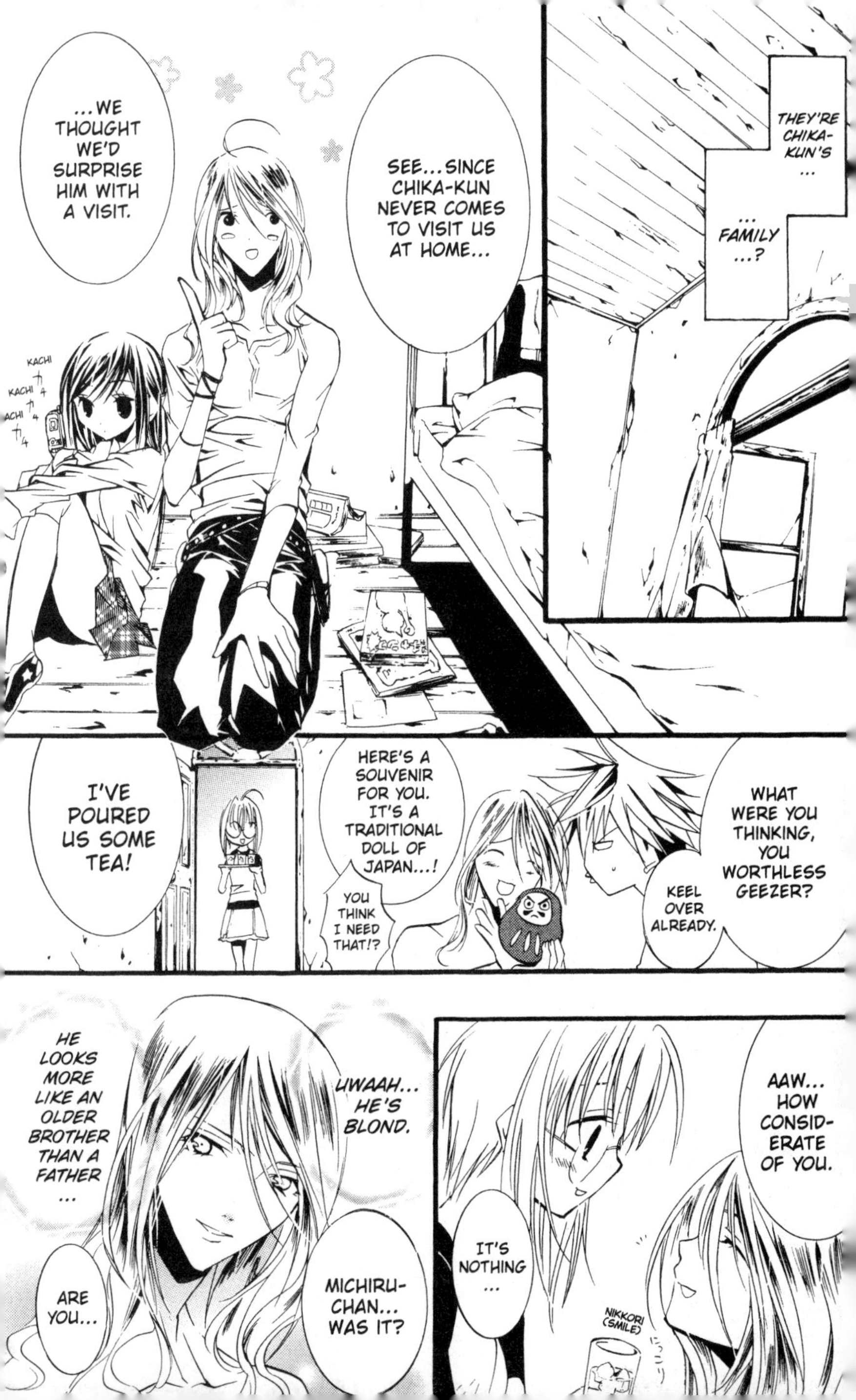
THEY'RE CHIKA-KUN'S ...
... FAMILY ...?
SEE... SINCE CHIKA-KUN NEVER COMES TO VISIT US AT HOME...
...WE THOUGHT WE'D SURPRISE HIM WITH A VISIT.
KACHI KACHI KACHI
WHAT WERE YOU THINKING, YOU WORTHLESS GEEZER?
KEEL OVER ALREADY.
HERE'S A SOUVENIR FOR YOU. IT'S A TRADITIONAL DOLL OF JAPAN...!
YOU THINK I NEED THAT!?
I'VE POURED US SOME TEA!
AAW... HOW CONSIDERATE OF YOU.
IT'S NOTHING ...
NIKKORI (SMILE)
UWAAH... HE'S BLOND.
HE LOOKS MORE LIKE AN OLDER BROTHER THAN A FATHER ...
MICHIRU-CHAN... WAS IT?
ARE YOU...

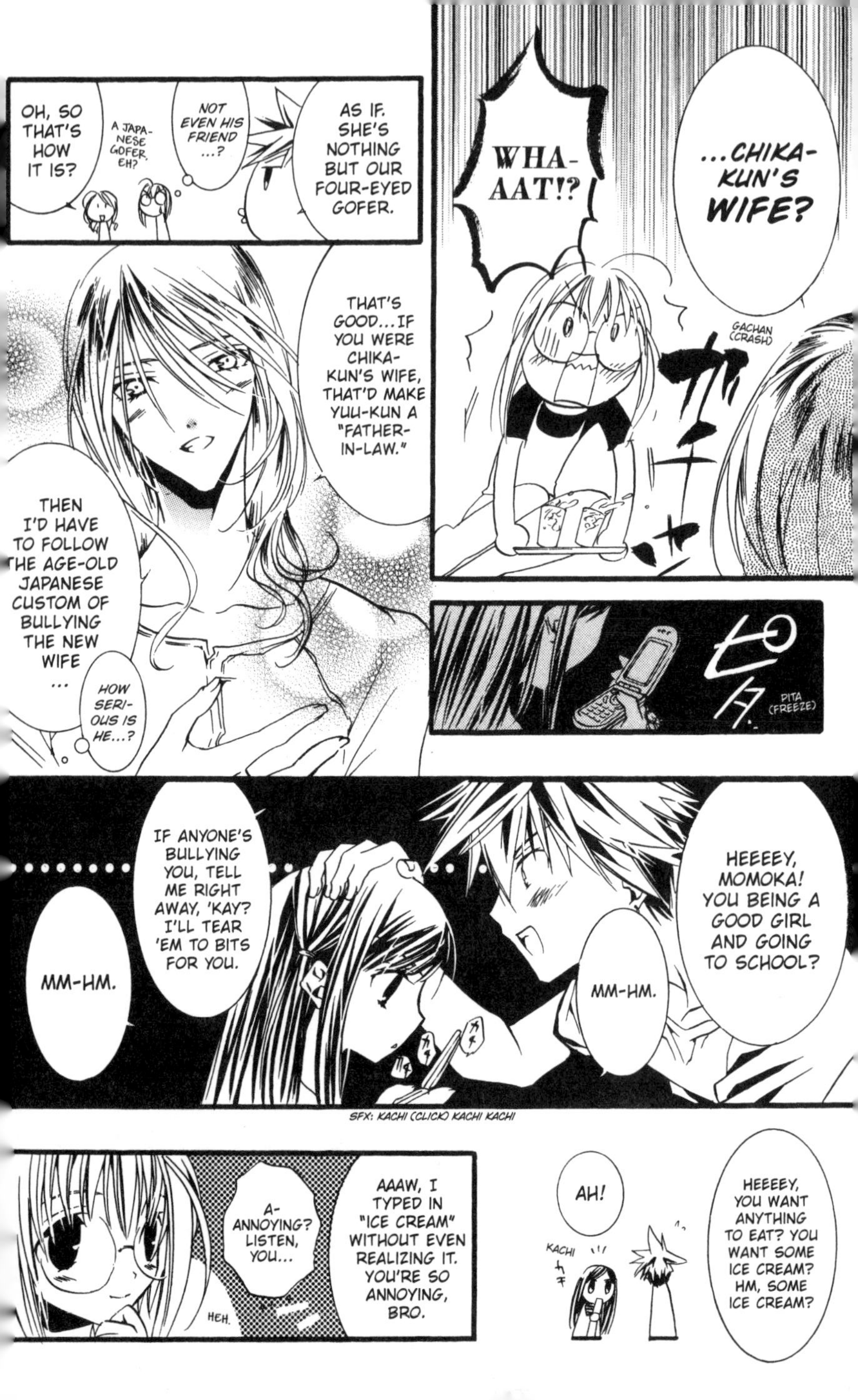
...CHIKA-KUN'S WIFE?
WHA-AAT!?
GACHAN (CRASH)
AS IF. SHE'S NOTHING BUT OUR FOUR-EYED GOFER.
NOT EVEN HIS FRIEND ...?
A JAPANESE GOFER, EH?
OH, SO THAT'S HOW IT IS?
THAT'S GOOD...IF YOU WERE CHIKA-KUN'S WIFE, THAT'D MAKE YUU-KUN A "FATHER-IN-LAW."
THEN I'D HAVE TO FOLLOW THE AGE-OLD JAPANESE CUSTOM OF BULLYING THE NEW WIFE ...
HOW SERIOUS IS HE...?
PITA (FREEZE)
HEEEEY, MOMOKA! YOU BEING A GOOD GIRL AND GOING TO SCHOOL?
MM-HM.
IF ANYONE'S BULLYING YOU, TELL ME RIGHT AWAY, 'KAY? I'LL TEAR 'EM TO BITS FOR YOU.
MM-HM.
SFX: KACHI (CLICK) KACHI KACHI
HEEEEY, YOU WANT ANYTHING TO EAT? YOU WANT SOME ICE CREAM? HM, SOME ICE CREAM?
AH!
KACHI
AAAW, I TYPED IN "ICE CREAM" WITHOUT EVEN REALIZING IT. YOU'RE SO ANNOYING, BRO.
A-ANNOYING? LISTEN, YOU...
HEH.

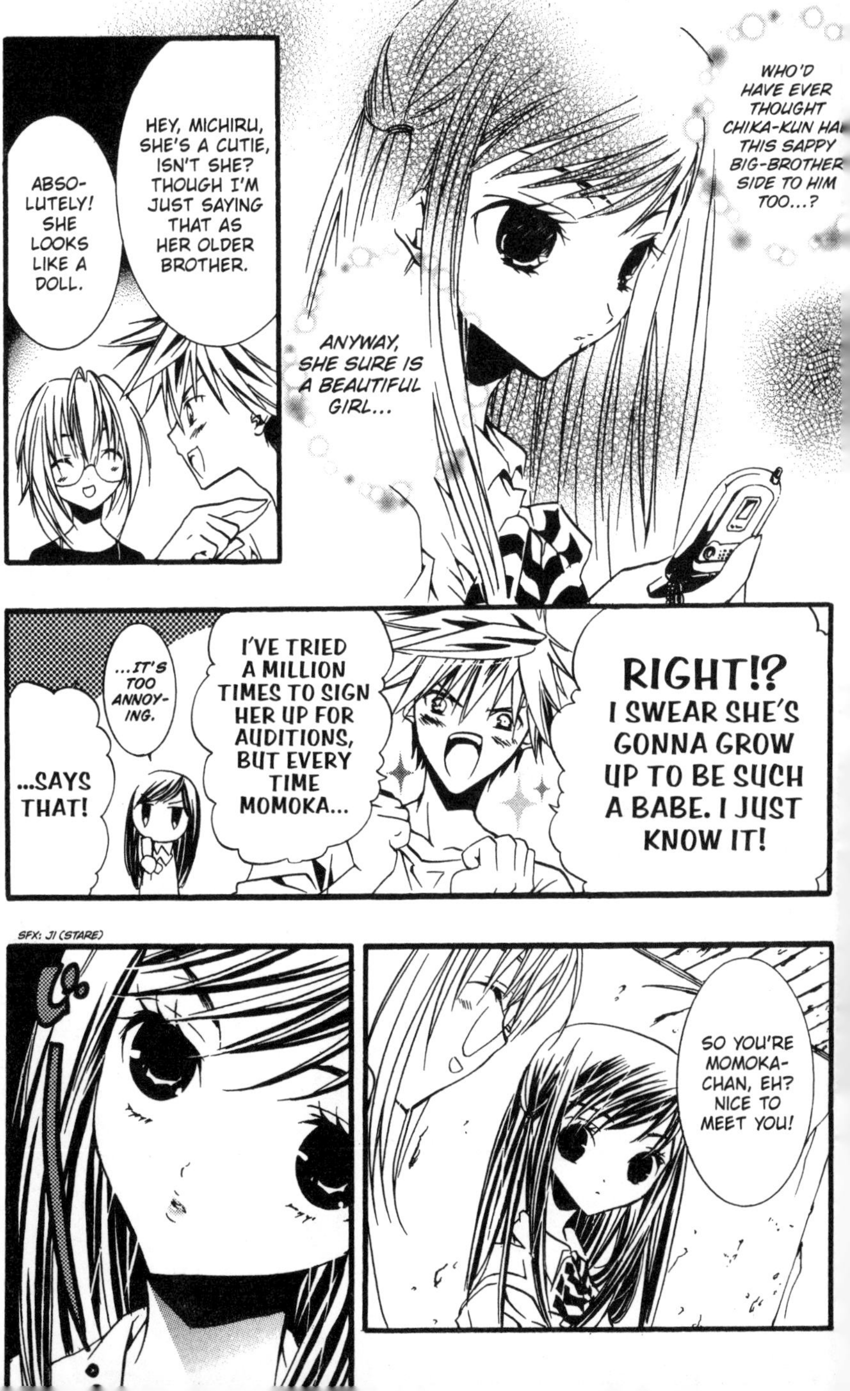
WHO'D HAVE EVER THOUGHT CHIKA-KUN HA THIS SAPPY BIG-BROTHER SIDE TO HIM TOO...?
ANYWAY, SHE SURE IS A BEAUTIFUL GIRL...
HEY, MICHIRU, SHE'S A CUTIE, ISN'T SHE? THOUGH I'M JUST SAYING THAT AS HER OLDER BROTHER.
ABSO-LUTELY! SHE LOOKS LIKE A DOLL.
RIGHT!? I SWEAR SHE'S GONNA GROW UP TO BE SUCH A BABE. I JUST KNOW IT!
I'VE TRIED A MILLION TIMES TO SIGN HER UP FOR AUDITIONS, BUT EVERY TIME MOMOKA...
...IT'S TOO ANNOY-ING.
...SAYS THAT!
SO YOU'RE MOMOKA-CHAN, EH? NICE TO MEET YOU!
SFX: JI (STARE)

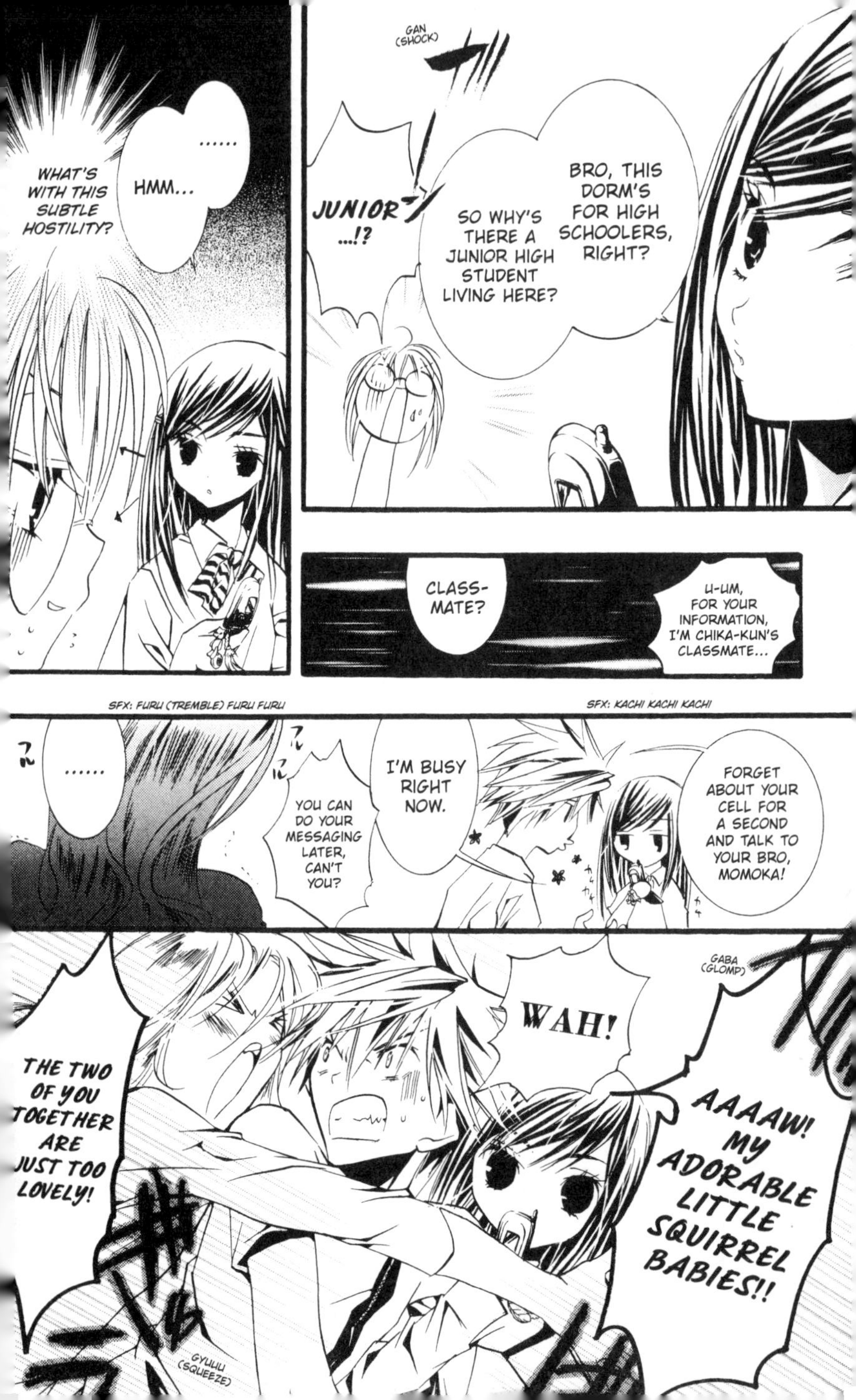
GAN (SHOCK)
BRO, THIS DORM'S FOR HIGH SCHOOLERS, RIGHT?
SO WHY'S THERE A JUNIOR HIGH STUDENT LIVING HERE?
JUNIOR ...!?
U-UM, FOR YOUR INFORMATION, I'M CHIKA-KUN'S CLASSMATE...
CLASS-MATE?
SFX: KACHI KACHI KACHI
......
HMM...
WHAT'S WITH THIS SUBTLE HOSTILITY?
SFX: FURU (TREMBLE) FURU FURU
FORGET ABOUT YOUR CELL FOR A SECOND AND TALK TO YOUR BRO, MOMOKA!
I'M BUSY RIGHT NOW.
YOU CAN DO YOUR MESSAGING LATER, CAN'T YOU?
......
GABA (GLOMP)
WAH!
AAAAW! MY ADORABLE LITTLE SQUIRREL BABIES!!
THE TWO OF YOU TOGETHER ARE JUST TOO LOVELY!
GYUUU (SQUEEZE)

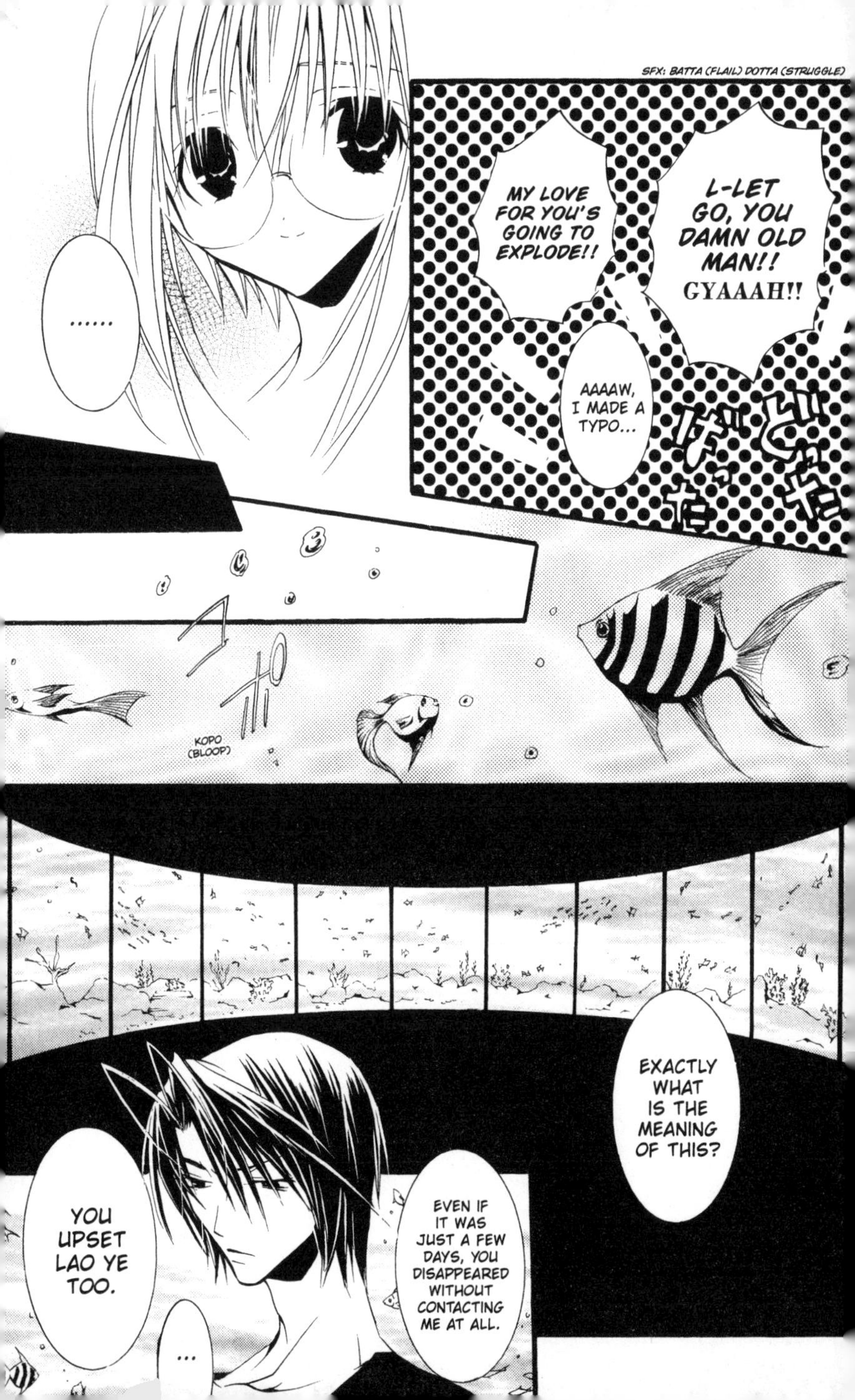
SFX: BATTA (FLAIL) DOTTA (STRUGGLE)
L-LET GO, YOU DAMN OLD MAN!! GYAAAH!!
MY LOVE FOR YOU'S GOING TO EXPLODE!!
AAAAW, I MADE A TYPO...
......
KOPO (BLOOP)
EXACTLY WHAT IS THE MEANING OF THIS?
EVEN IF IT WAS JUST A FEW DAYS, YOU DISAPPEARED WITHOUT CONTACTING ME AT ALL.
YOU UPSET LAO YE TOO.
...

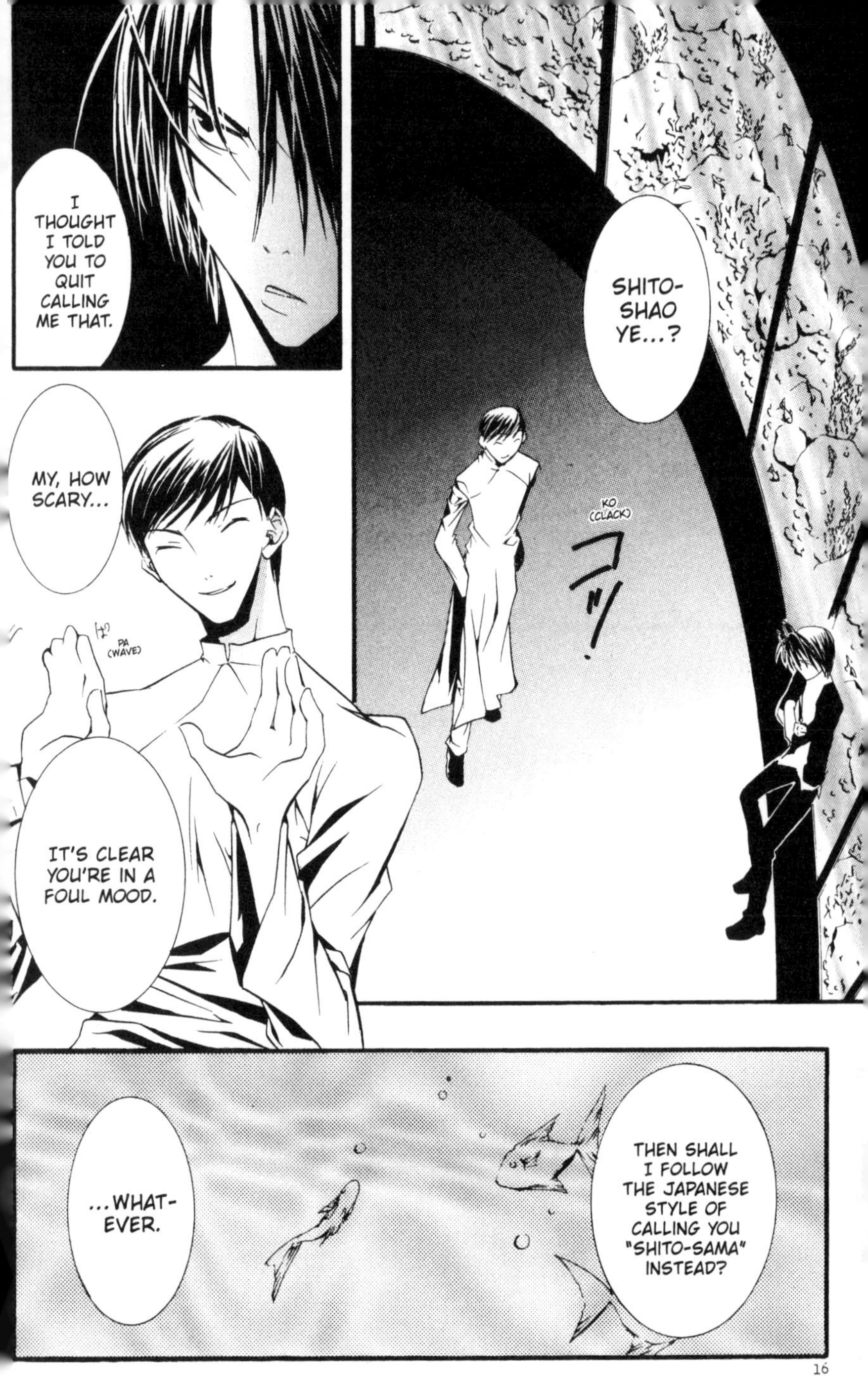
SHITO-SHAO YE...?
KO (CLACK)
I THOUGHT I TOLD YOU TO QUIT CALLING ME THAT.
MY, HOW SCARY...
PA (WAVE)
IT'S CLEAR YOU'RE IN A FOUL MOOD.
THEN SHALL I FOLLOW THE JAPANESE STYLE OF CALLING YOU "SHITO-SAMA" INSTEAD?
...WHAT-EVER.

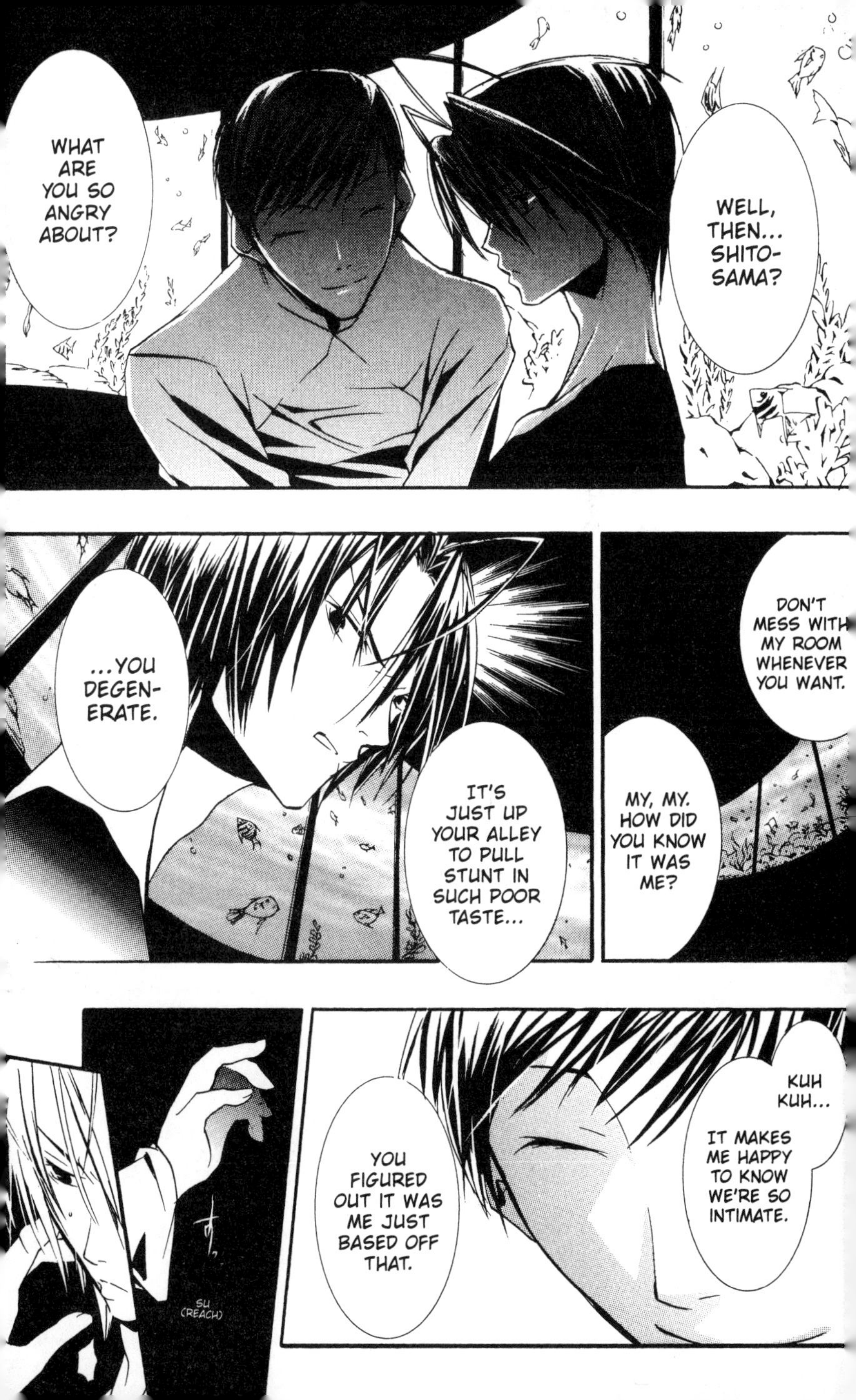
WELL, THEN... SHITO-SAMA?
WHAT ARE YOU SO ANGRY ABOUT?
DON'T MESS WITH MY ROOM WHENEVER YOU WANT.
MY, MY. HOW DID YOU KNOW IT WAS ME?
IT'S JUST UP YOUR ALLEY TO PULL STUNT IN SUCH POOR TASTE...
...YOU DEGENERATE.
KUH KUH...
IT MAKES ME HAPPY TO KNOW WE'RE SO INTIMATE.
YOU FIGURED OUT IT WAS ME JUST BASED OFF THAT.
SU (REACH)

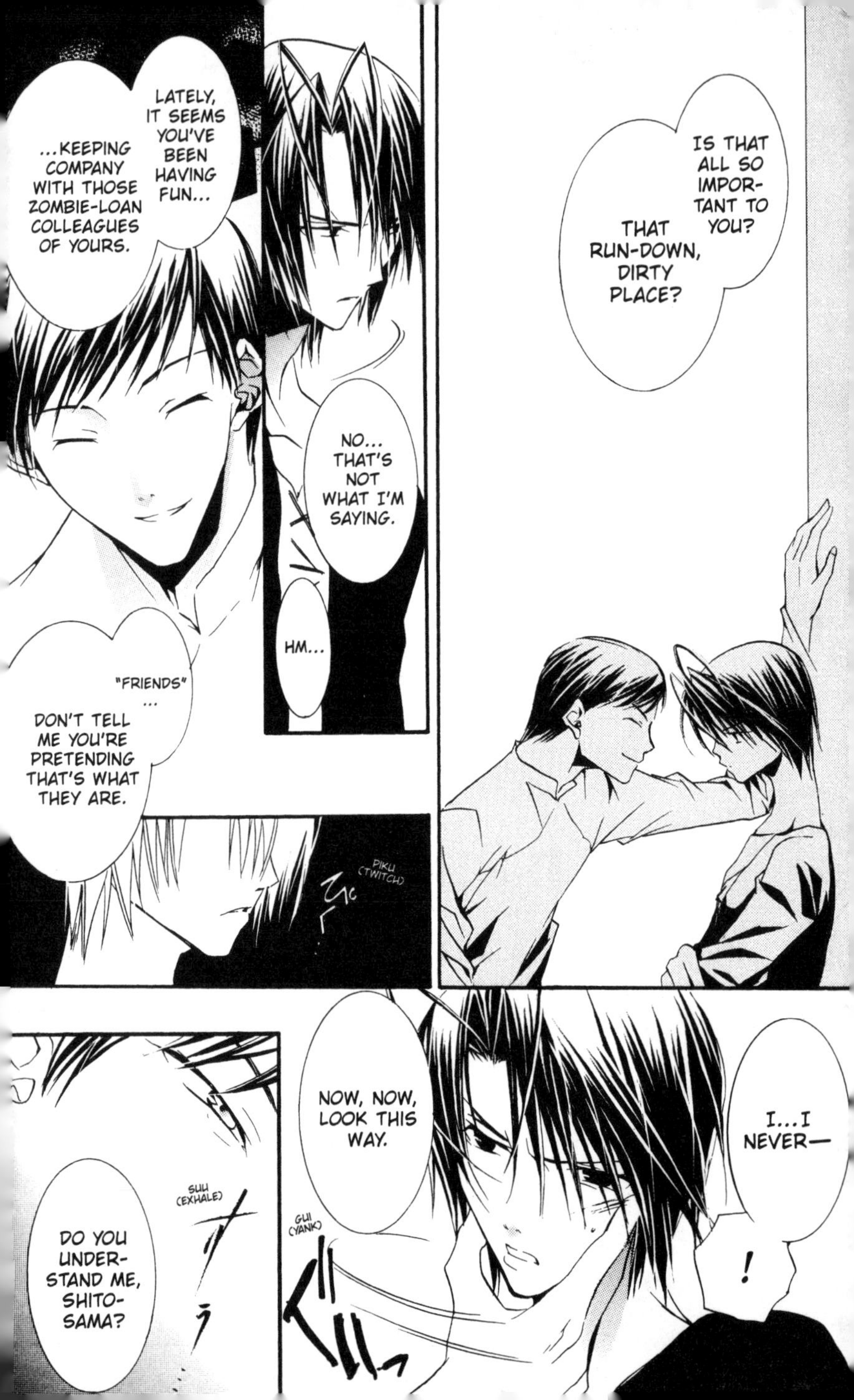
IS THAT ALL SO IMPORTANT TO YOU?
THAT RUN-DOWN, DIRTY PLACE?
NO... THAT'S NOT WHAT I'M SAYING.
HM...
LATELY, IT SEEMS YOU'VE BEEN HAVING FUN...
...KEEPING COMPANY WITH THOSE ZOMBIE-LOAN COLLEAGUES OF YOURS.
"FRIENDS"...
DON'T TELL ME YOU'RE PRETENDING THAT'S WHAT THEY ARE.
PIKU (TWITCH)
I...I NEVER—
!
NOW, NOW, LOOK THIS WAY.
GUI (YANK)
SUU (EXHALE)
DO YOU UNDERSTAND ME, SHITO-SAMA?

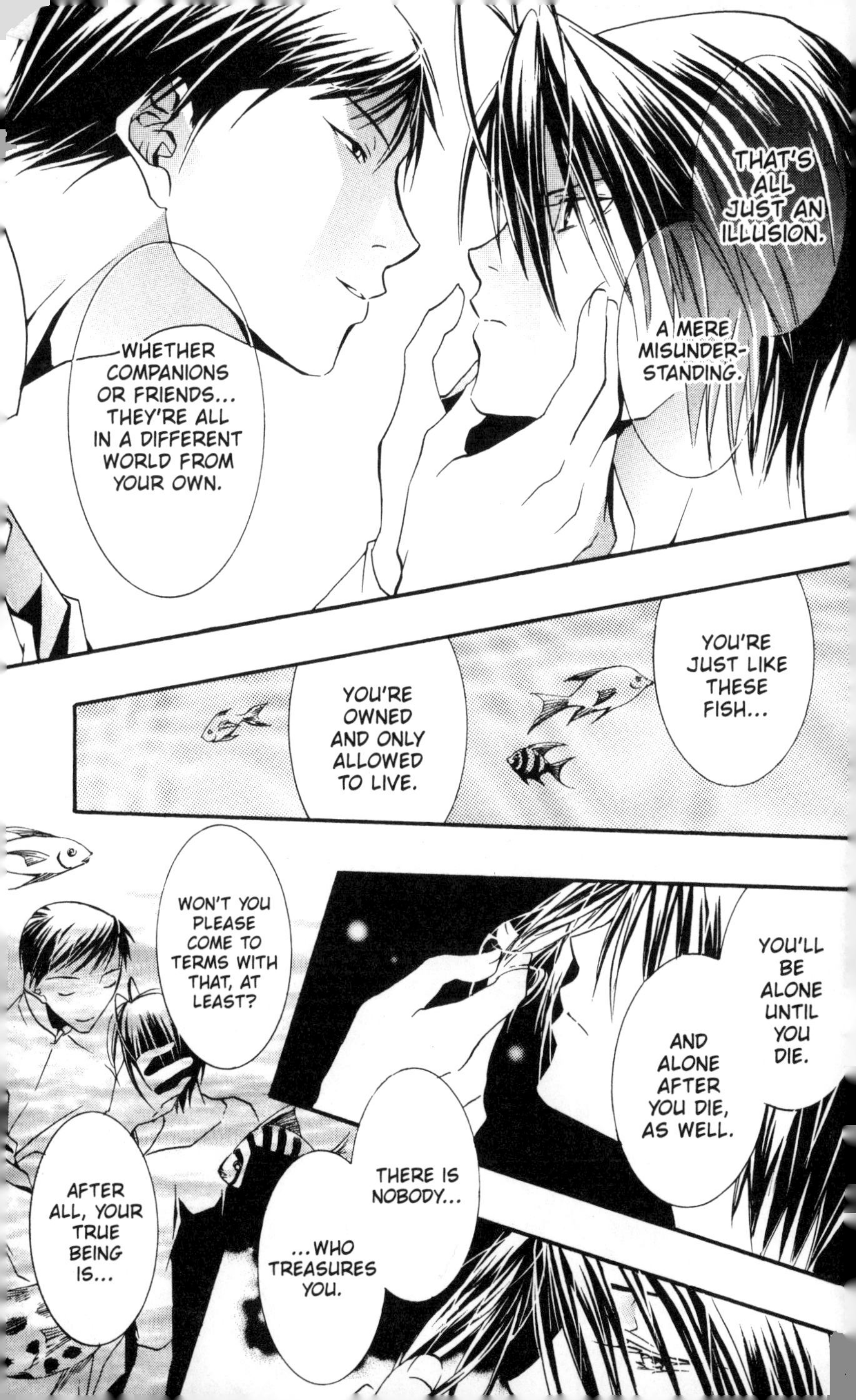
THAT'S ALL JUST AN ILLUSION.
A MERE MISUNDER-STANDING.
WHETHER COMPANIONS OR FRIENDS... THEY'RE ALL IN A DIFFERENT WORLD FROM YOUR OWN.
YOU'RE JUST LIKE THESE FISH...
YOU'RE OWNED AND ONLY ALLOWED TO LIVE.
YOU'LL BE ALONE UNTIL YOU DIE.
AND ALONE AFTER YOU DIE, AS WELL.
THERE IS NOBODY...
...WHO TREASURES YOU.
WON'T YOU PLEASE COME TO TERMS WITH THAT, AT LEAST?
AFTER ALL, YOUR TRUE BEING IS...

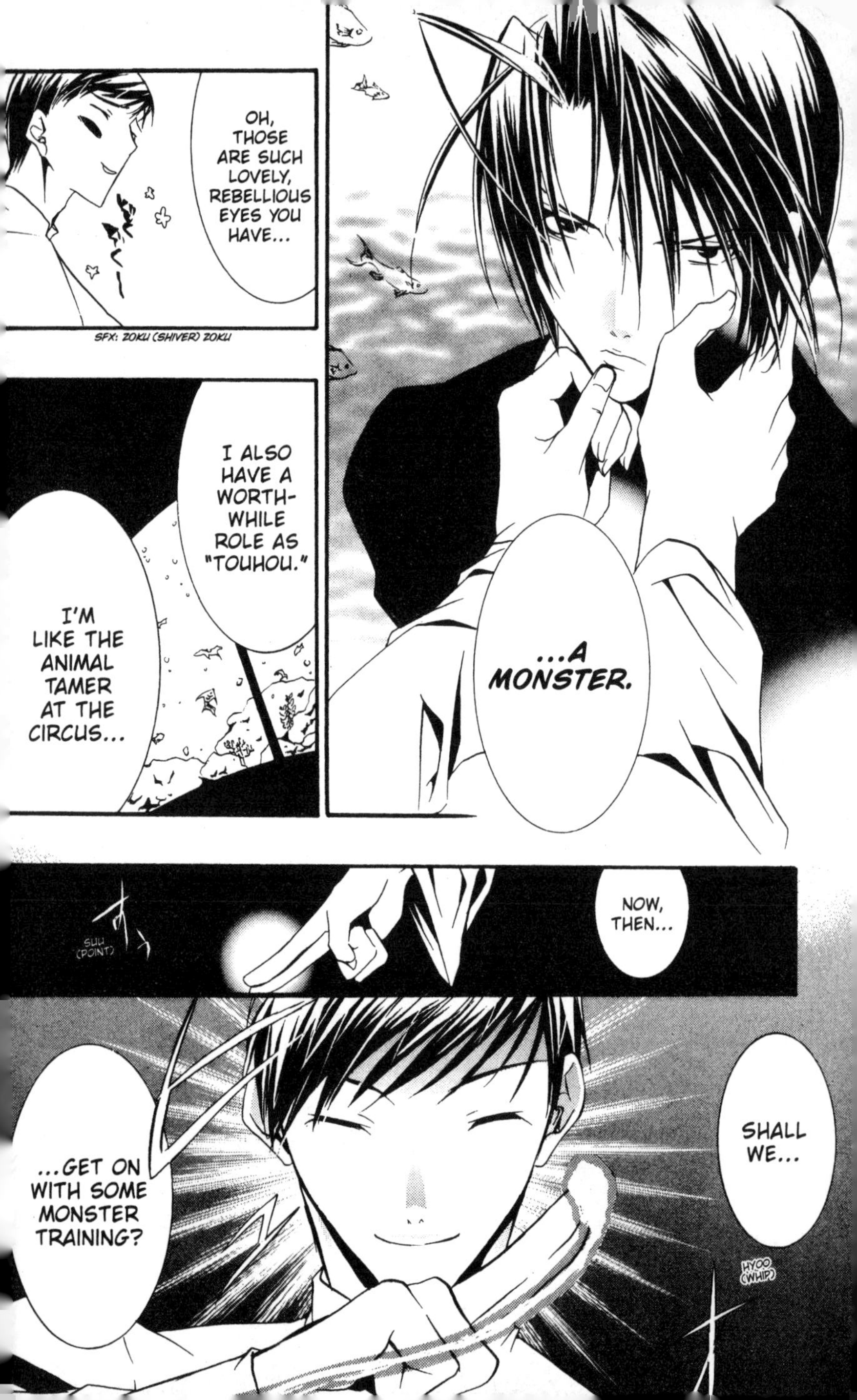
...A MONSTER.
OH, THOSE ARE SUCH LOVELY, REBELLIOUS EYES YOU HAVE...
SFX: ZOKU (SHIVER) ZOKU
I ALSO HAVE A WORTH-WHILE ROLE AS "TOUHOU."
I'M LIKE THE ANIMAL TAMER AT THE CIRCUS...
NOW, THEN...
SUU (POINT)
SHALL WE...
HYOO (WHIP)
...GET ON WITH SOME MONSTER TRAINING?

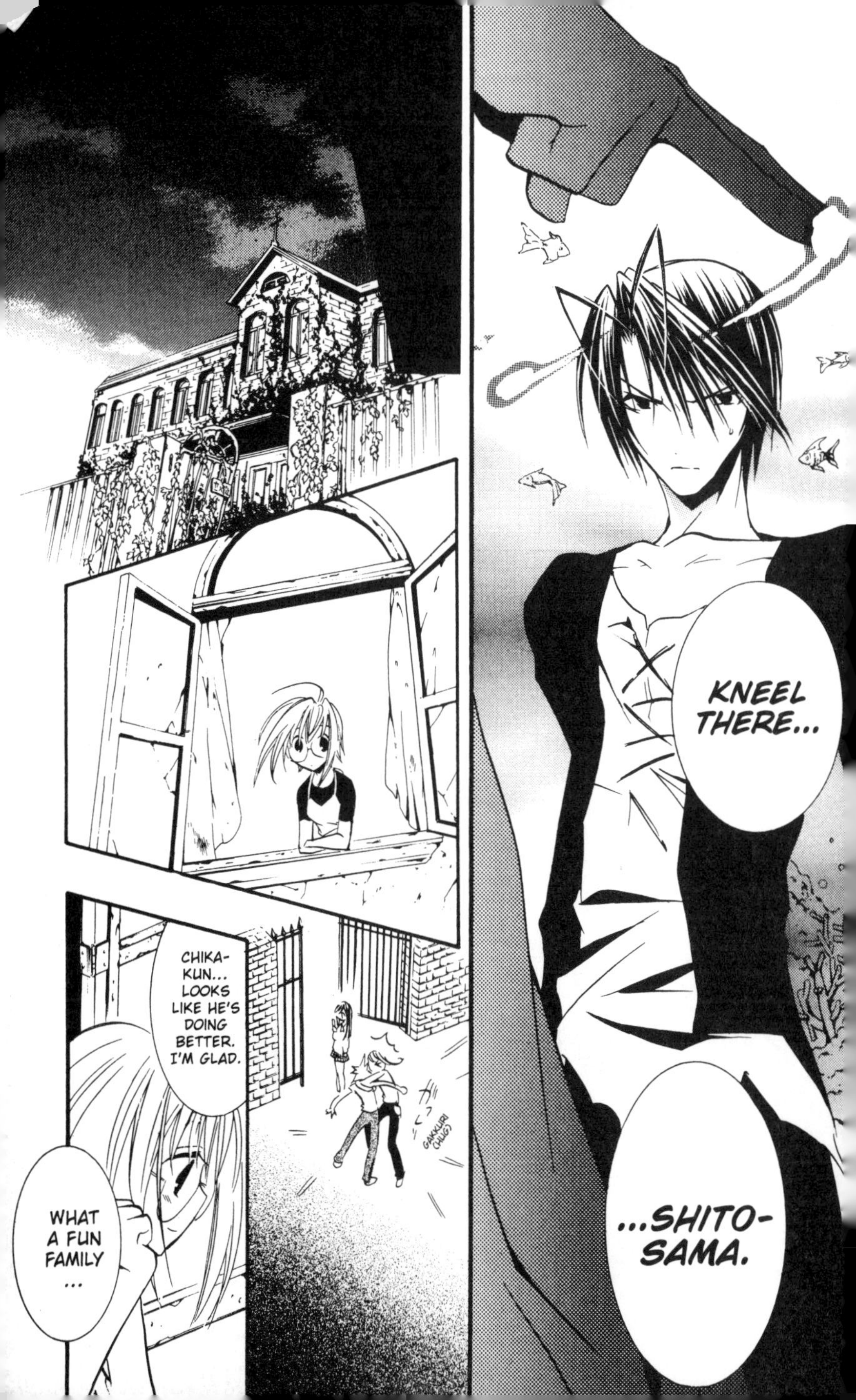
KNEEL THERE...
...SHITO-SAMA.
CHIKA-KUN... LOOKS LIKE HE'S DOING BETTER. I'M GLAD.
GAKKURI (HUG)
WHAT A FUN FAMILY ...

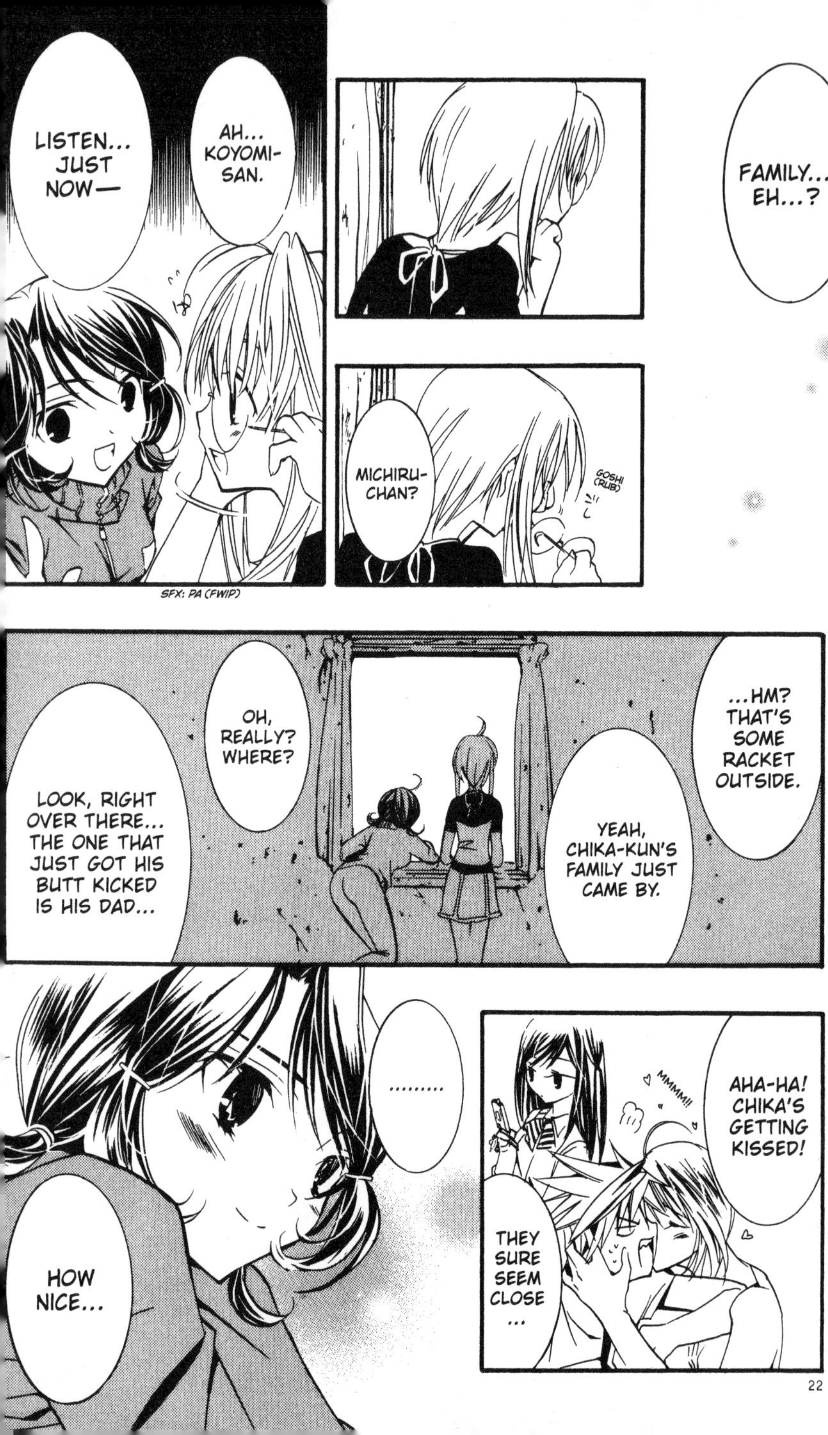
FAMILY... EH...?
MICHIRU-CHAN?
GOSHI (RUB)
AH... KOYOMI-SAN.
LISTEN... JUST NOW—
SFX: PA (FWIP)
...HM? THAT'S SOME RACKET OUTSIDE.
YEAH, CHIKA-KUN'S FAMILY JUST CAME BY.
OH, REALLY? WHERE?
LOOK, RIGHT OVER THERE... THE ONE THAT JUST GOT HIS BUTT KICKED IS HIS DAD...
AHA-HA! CHIKA'S GETTING KISSED!
MMMM!!
THEY SURE SEEM CLOSE...
....
HOW NICE...

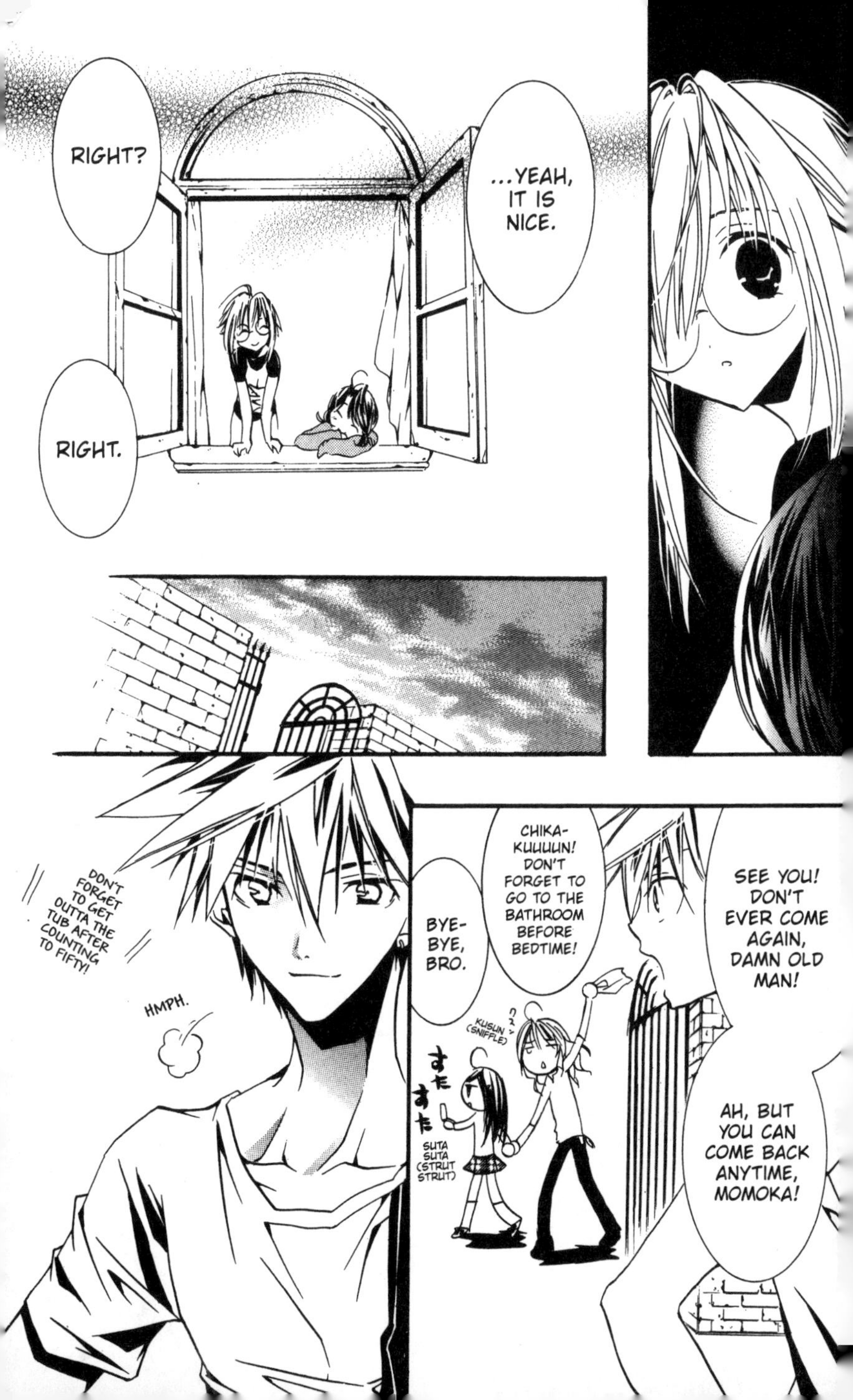
RIGHT?
...YEAH, IT IS NICE.
RIGHT.
SEE YOU! DON'T EVER COME AGAIN, DAMN OLD MAN!
CHIKA-KUUUUN! DON'T FORGET TO GO TO THE BATHROOM BEFORE BEDTIME!
BYE-BYE, BRO.
AH, BUT YOU CAN COME BACK ANYTIME, MOMOKA!
KUSUN (SNIFFLE)
すた すた
SUTA SUTA (STRUT STRUT)
DON'T FORGET TO GET OUTTA THE TUB AFTER COUNTING TO FIFTY!
HMPH.

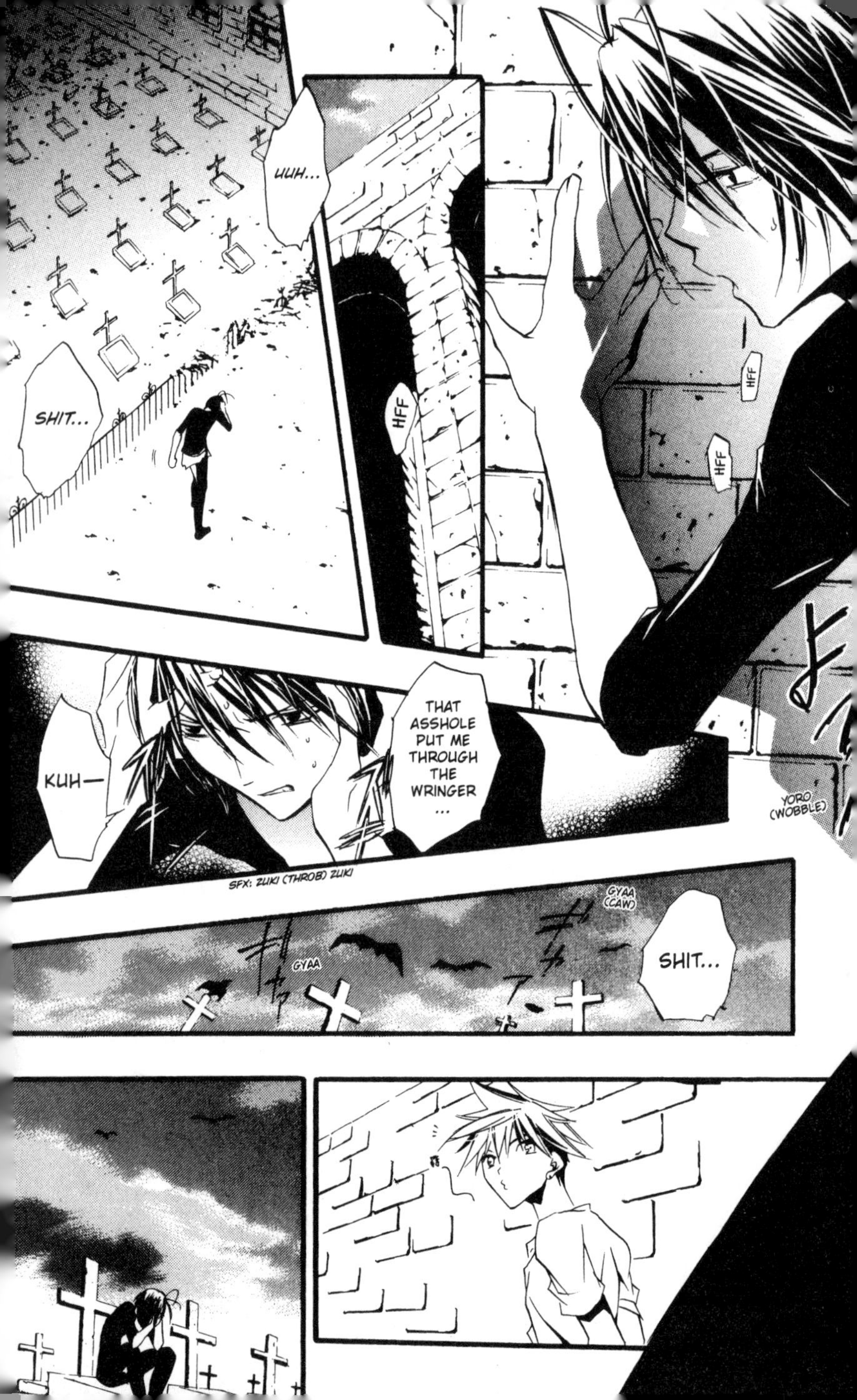
HFF
HFF
YORO (WOBBLE)
HFF
UUH...
SHIT...
THAT ASSHOLE PUT ME THROUGH THE WRINGER ...
KUH—
SFX: ZUKI (THROB) ZUKI
GYAA (CAW)
SHIT...
GYAA

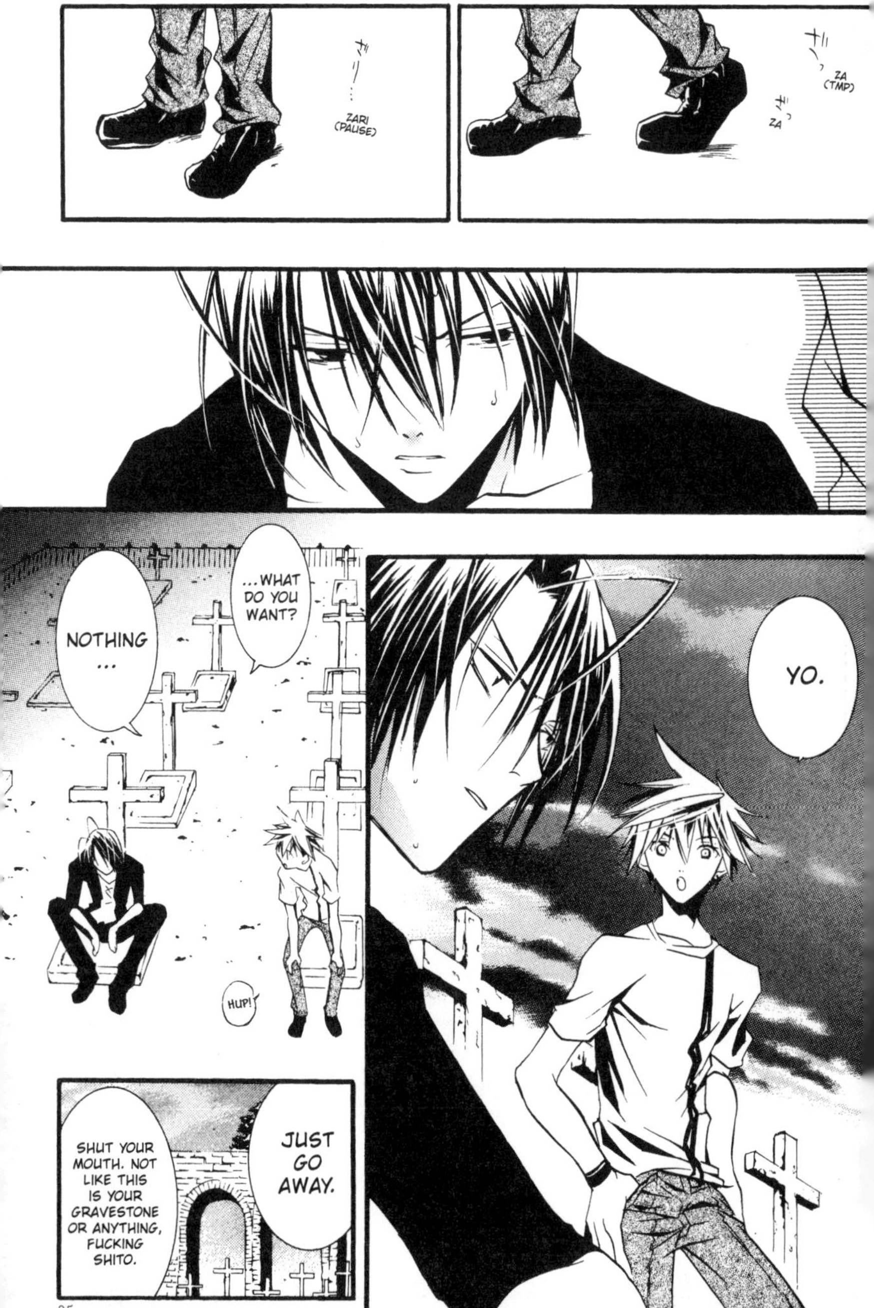
ZA (TMP)
ZA
ZARI (PAUSE)
YO.
...WHAT DO YOU WANT?
NOTHING ...
HUP!
JUST GO AWAY.
SHUT YOUR MOUTH. NOT LIKE THIS IS YOUR GRAVESTONE OR ANYTHING, FUCKING SHITO.

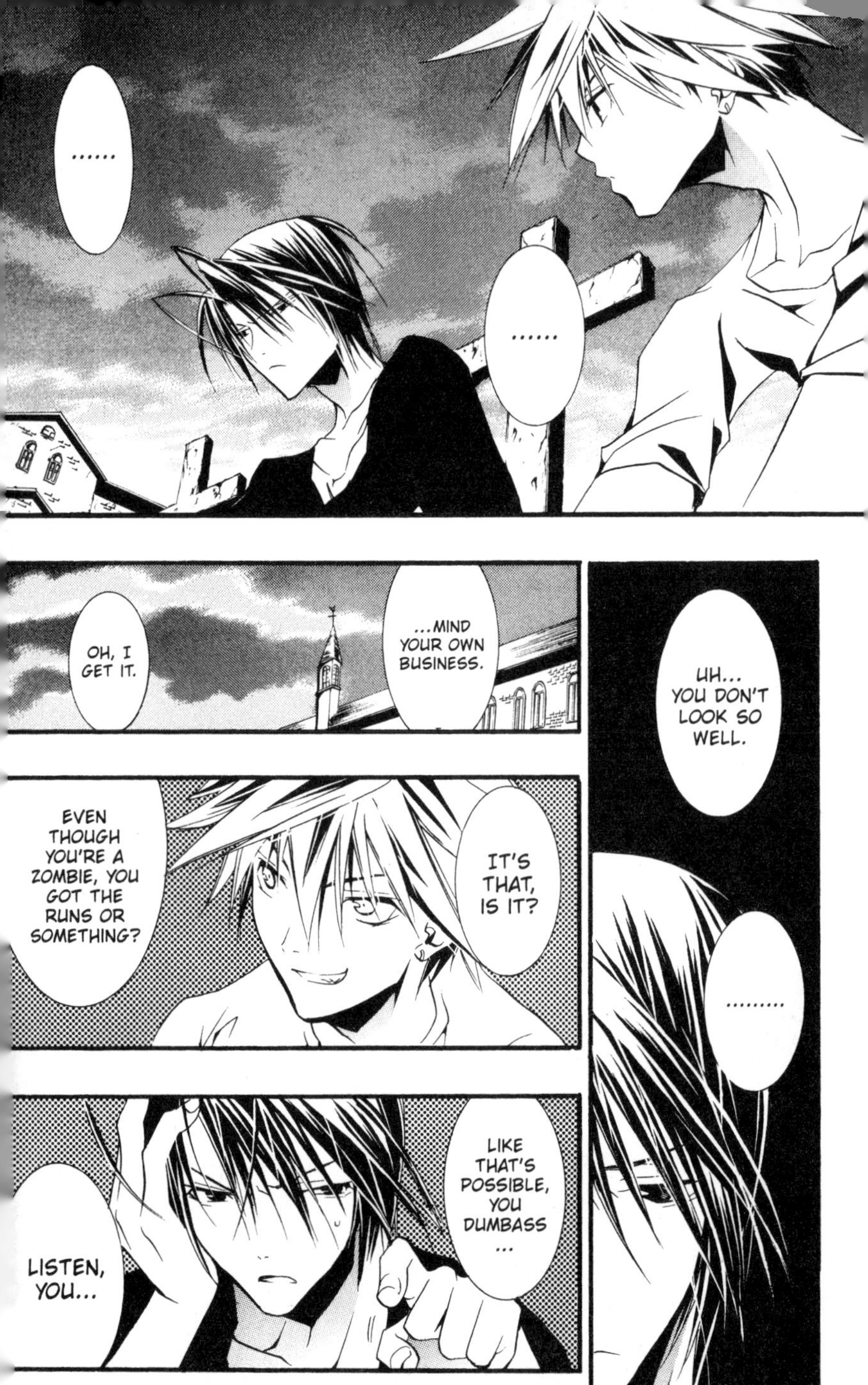
......
......
UH... YOU DON'T LOOK SO WELL.
....
...MIND YOUR OWN BUSINESS.
OH, I GET IT.
IT'S THAT, IS IT?
EVEN THOUGH YOU'RE A ZOMBIE, YOU GOT THE RUNS OR SOMETHING?
LIKE THAT'S POSSIBLE, YOU DUMBASS ...
LISTEN, YOU...

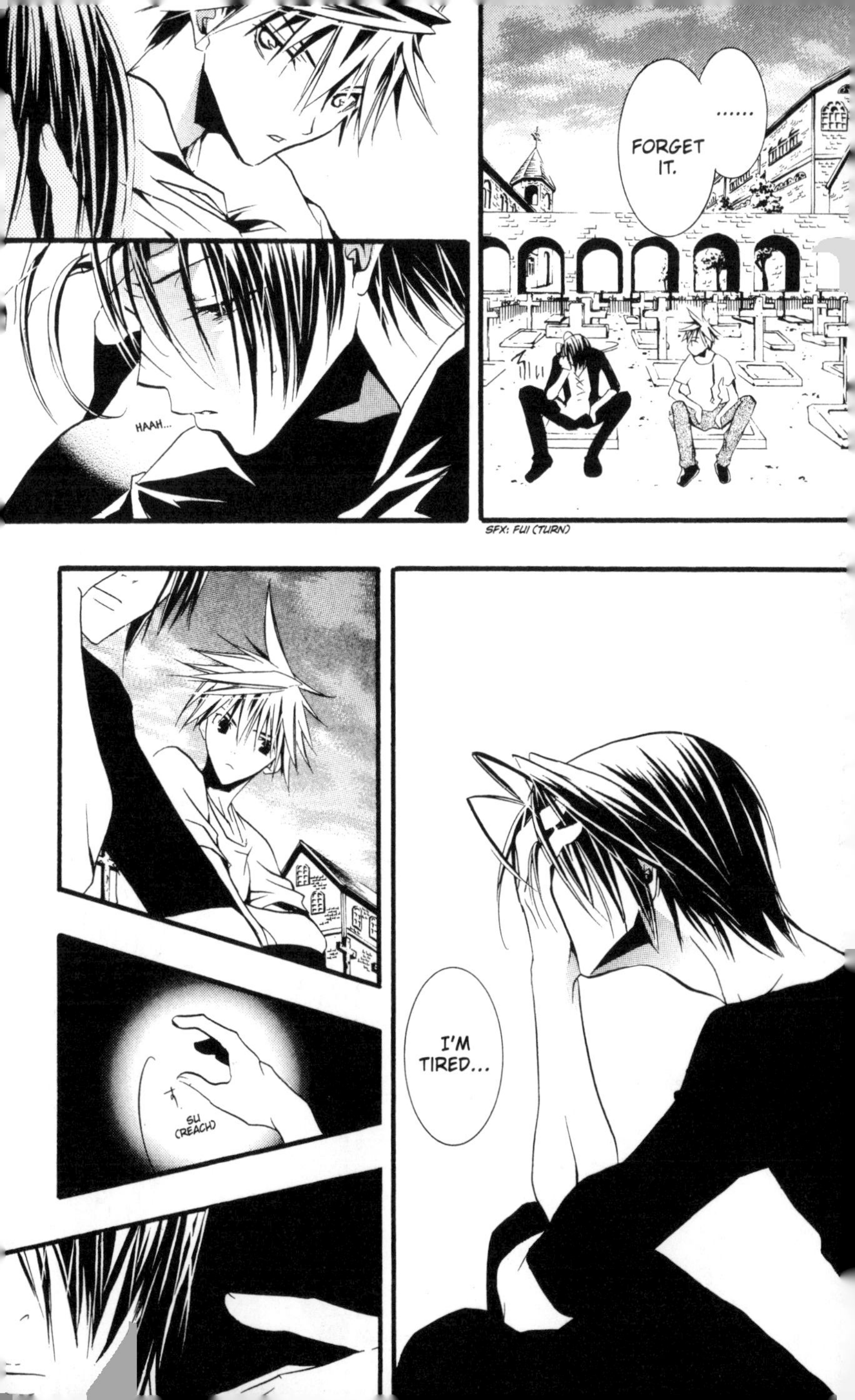
......
FORGET IT.
SFX: FUI (TURN)
HAAH...
I'M TIRED...
SU (REACH)

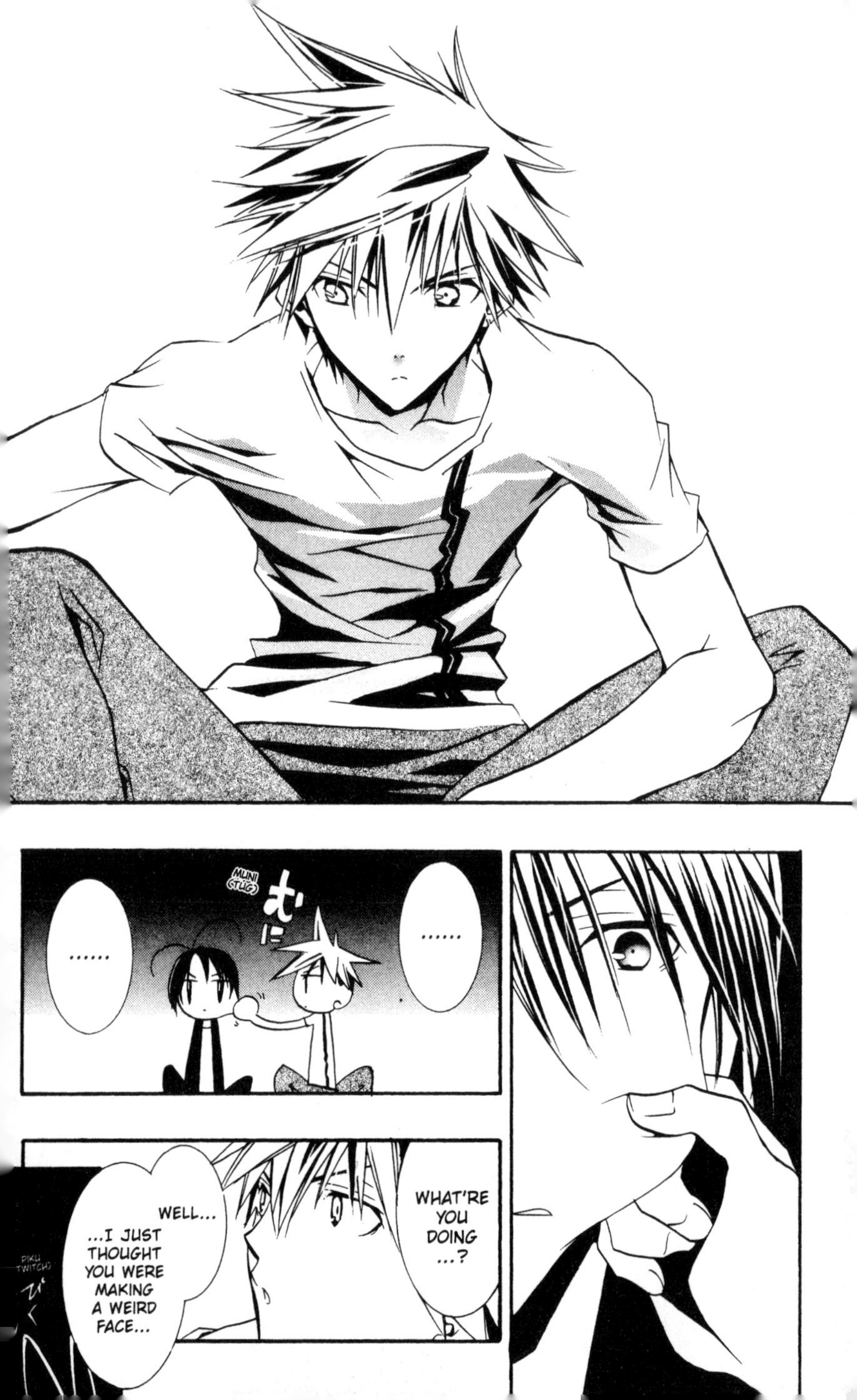
......
MUNI (TUG)
......
WHAT'RE YOU DOING ...?
WELL... ...I JUST THOUGHT YOU WERE MAKING A WEIRD FACE...
PIKU TWITCH

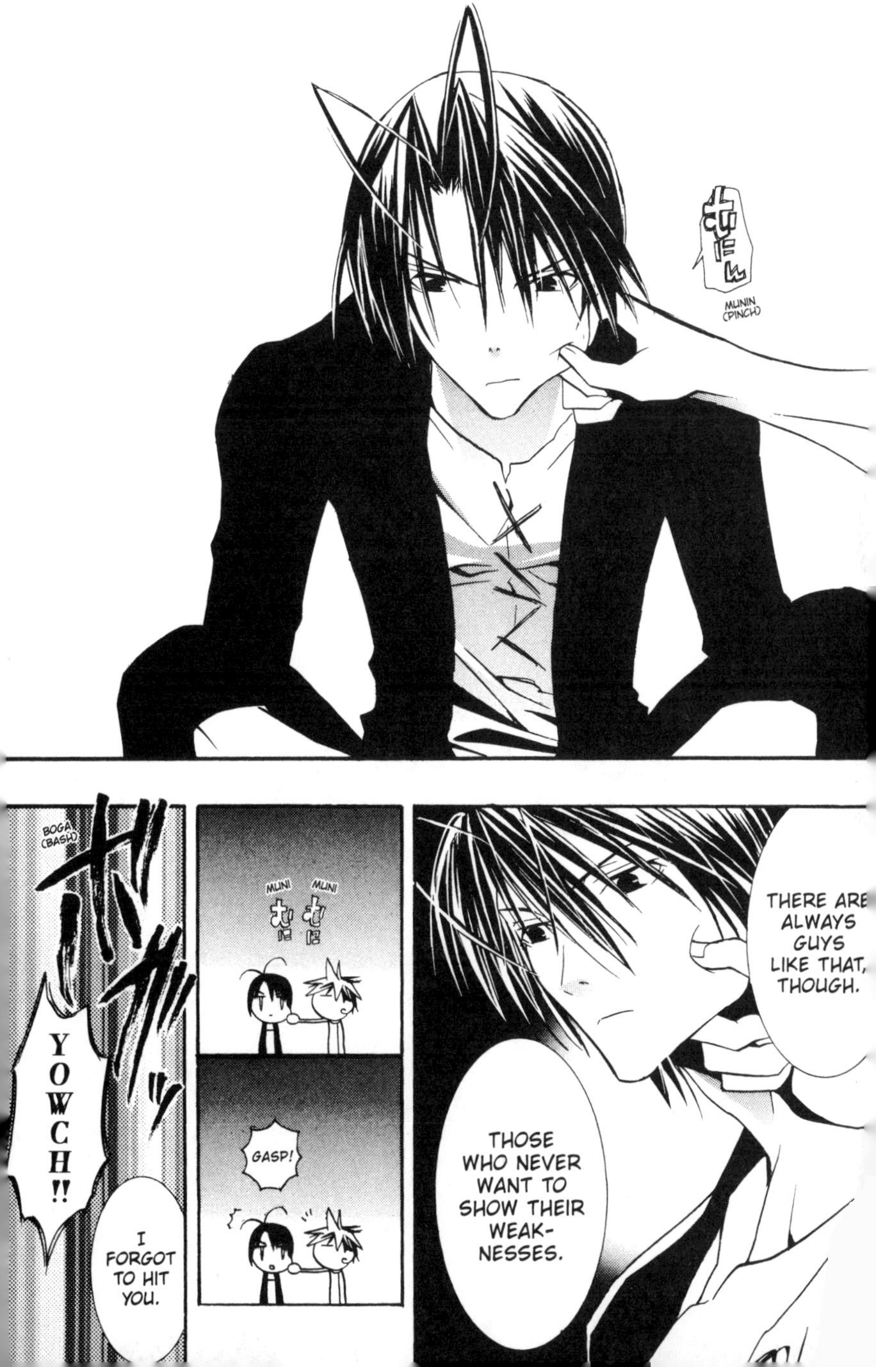
MUNIN
(PINCH)
THERE ARE ALWAYS GUYS LIKE THAT, THOUGH.
THOSE WHO NEVER WANT TO SHOW THEIR WEAK-NESSES.
MUNI
MUNI
GASP!
BOGA
(BASH)
YOWCH!!
I FORGOT TO HIT YOU.

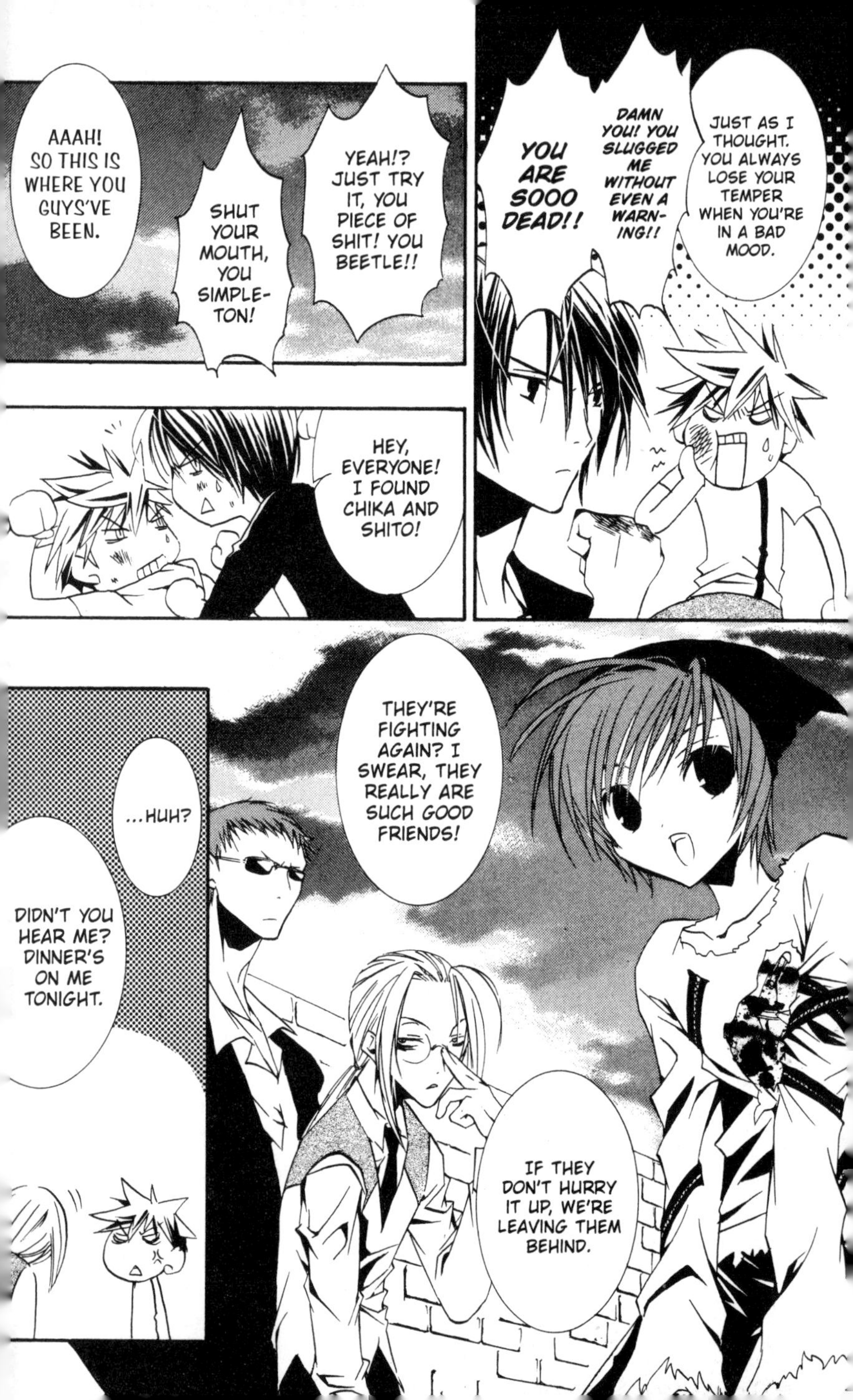
JUST AS I THOUGHT. YOU ALWAYS LOSE YOUR TEMPER WHEN YOU'RE IN A BAD MOOD.
DAMN YOU! YOU SLUGGED ME WITHOUT EVEN A WARN-ING!!
YOU ARE SOOO DEAD!!
YEAH!? JUST TRY IT, YOU PIECE OF SHIT! YOU BEETLE!!
SHUT YOUR MOUTH, YOU SIMPLE-TON!
AAAH! SO THIS IS WHERE YOU GUYS'VE BEEN.
HEY, EVERYONE! I FOUND CHIKA AND SHITO!
THEY'RE FIGHTING AGAIN? I SWEAR, THEY REALLY ARE SUCH GOOD FRIENDS!
IF THEY DON'T HURRY IT UP, WE'RE LEAVING THEM BEHIND.
...HUH?
DIDN'T YOU HEAR ME? DINNER'S ON ME TONIGHT.

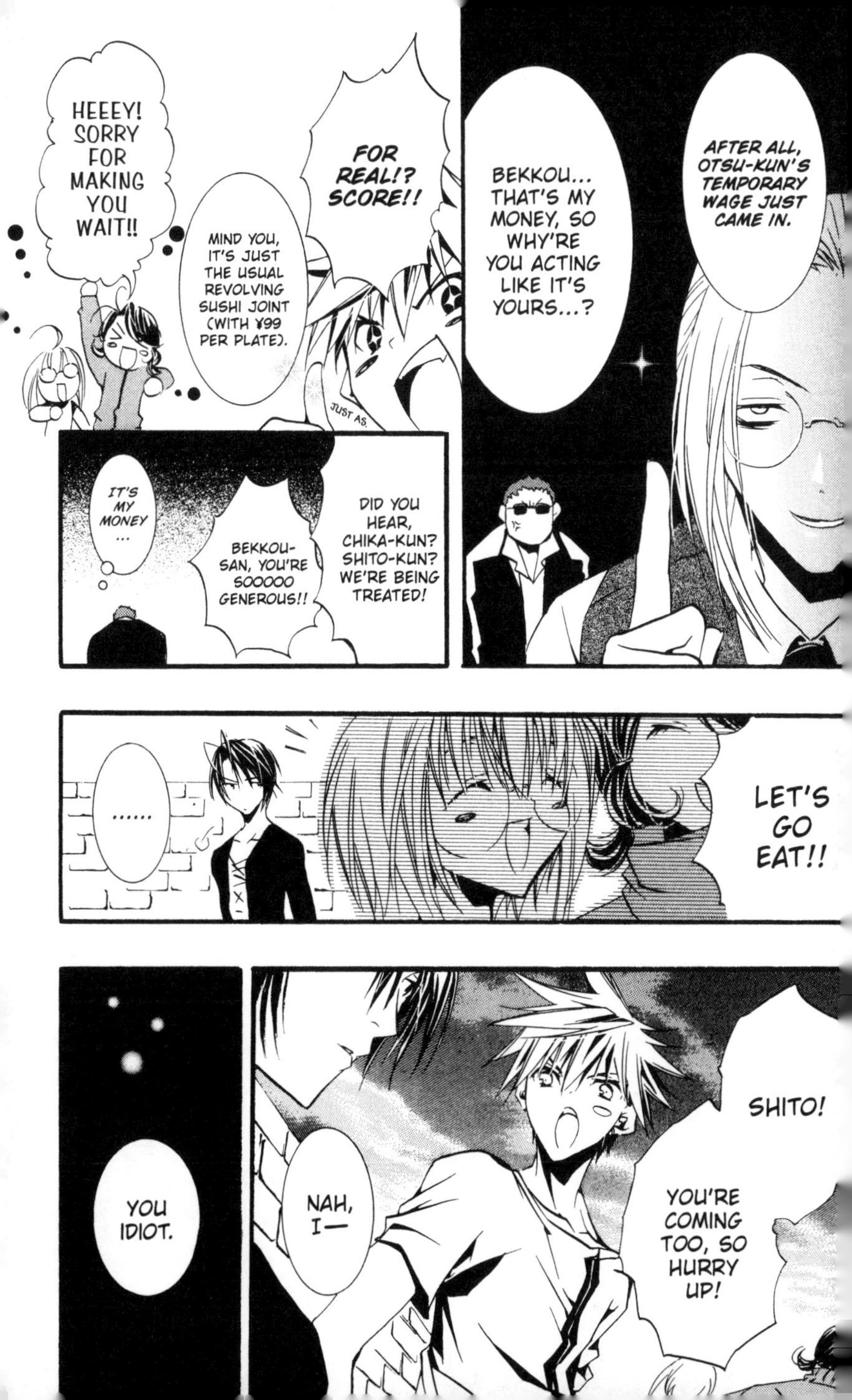
AFTER ALL, OTSU-KUN'S TEMPORARY WAGE JUST CAME IN.
BEKKOU... THAT'S MY MONEY, SO WHY'RE YOU ACTING LIKE IT'S YOURS...?
FOR REAL!? SCORE!!
MIND YOU, IT'S JUST THE USUAL REVOLVING SUSHI JOINT (WITH ¥99 PER PLATE).
JUST AS.
HEEEY! SORRY FOR MAKING YOU WAIT!!
DID YOU HEAR, CHIKA-KUN? SHITO-KUN? WE'RE BEING TREATED!
BEKKOU-SAN, YOU'RE SOOOOO GENEROUS!!
IT'S MY MONEY...
LET'S GO EAT!!
......
SHITO!
YOU'RE COMING TOO, SO HURRY UP!
NAH, I—
YOU IDIOT.

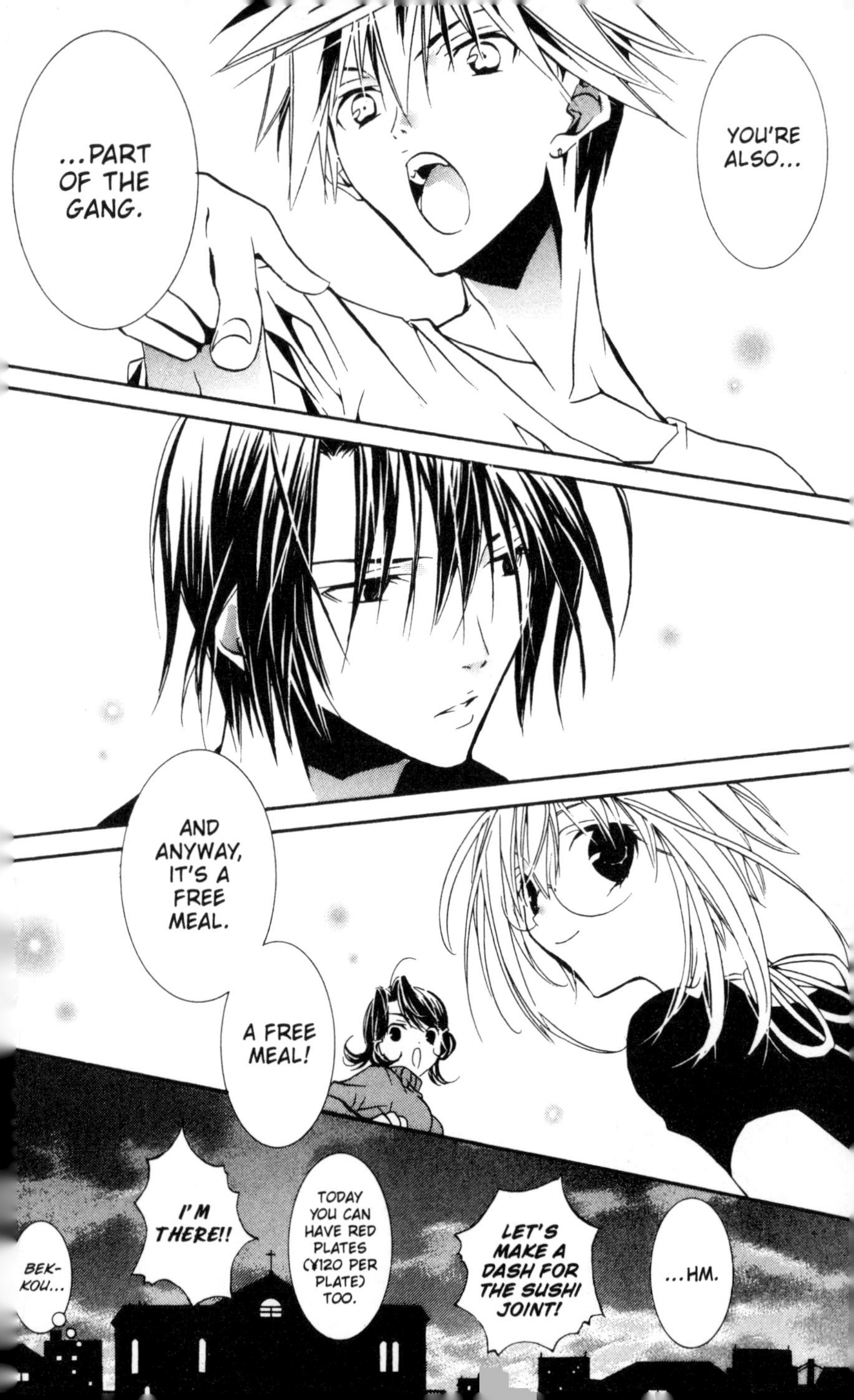
YOU'RE ALSO...
...PART OF THE GANG.
AND ANYWAY, IT'S A FREE MEAL.
A FREE MEAL!
...HM.
LET'S MAKE A DASH FOR THE SUSHI JOINT!
TODAY YOU CAN HAVE RED PLATES (¥120 PER PLATE) TOO.
I'M THERE!!
BEK-KOU...

PAYMENT:21

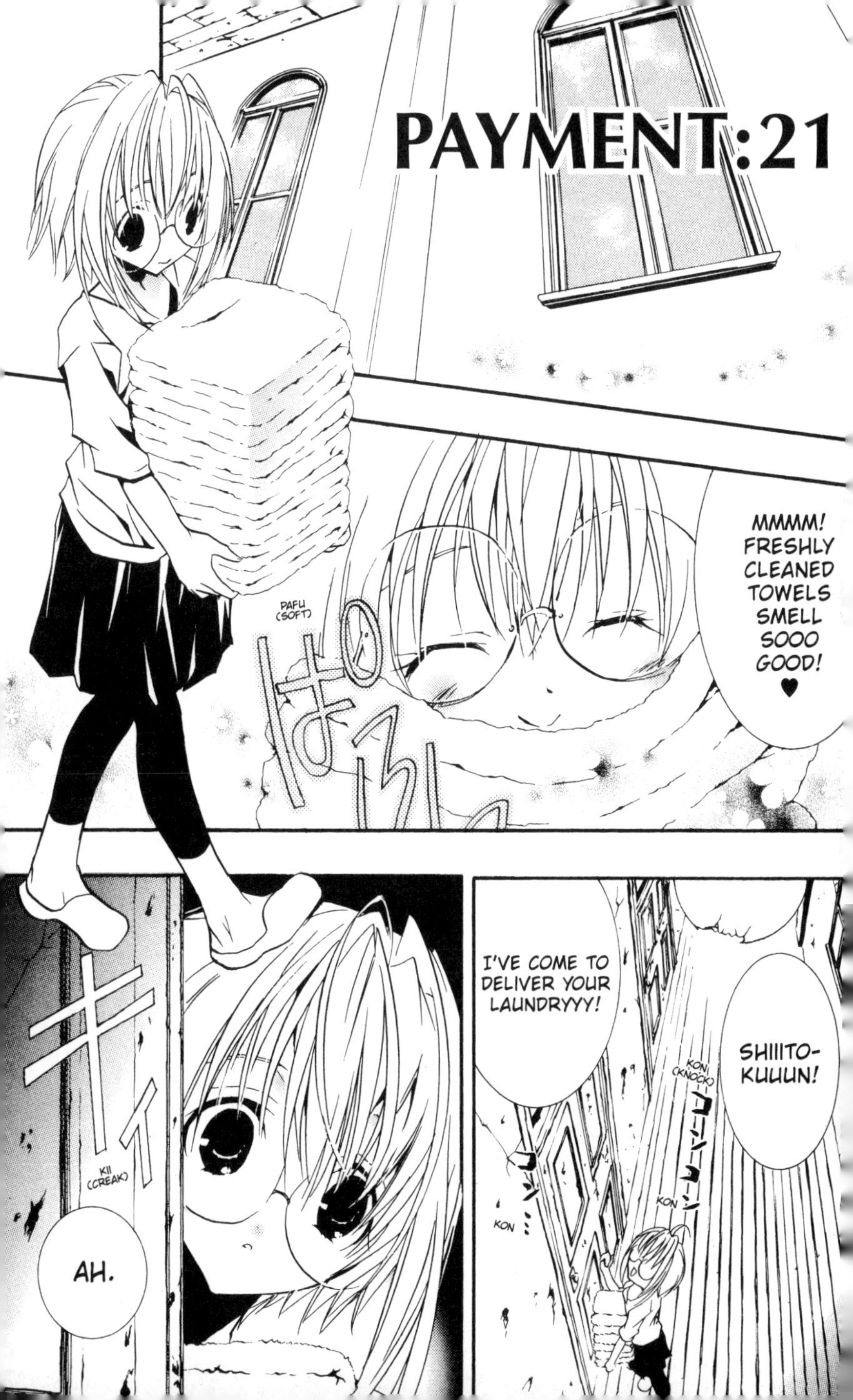

MMMM! FRESHLY CLEANED TOWELS SMELL SOOO GOOD! ♥
PAFU (SOFT)
SHIIITO-KUUUN!
I'VE COME TO DELIVER YOUR LAUNDRYYY!
KON (KNOCK)
KON
KON
KII (CREAK)
AH.

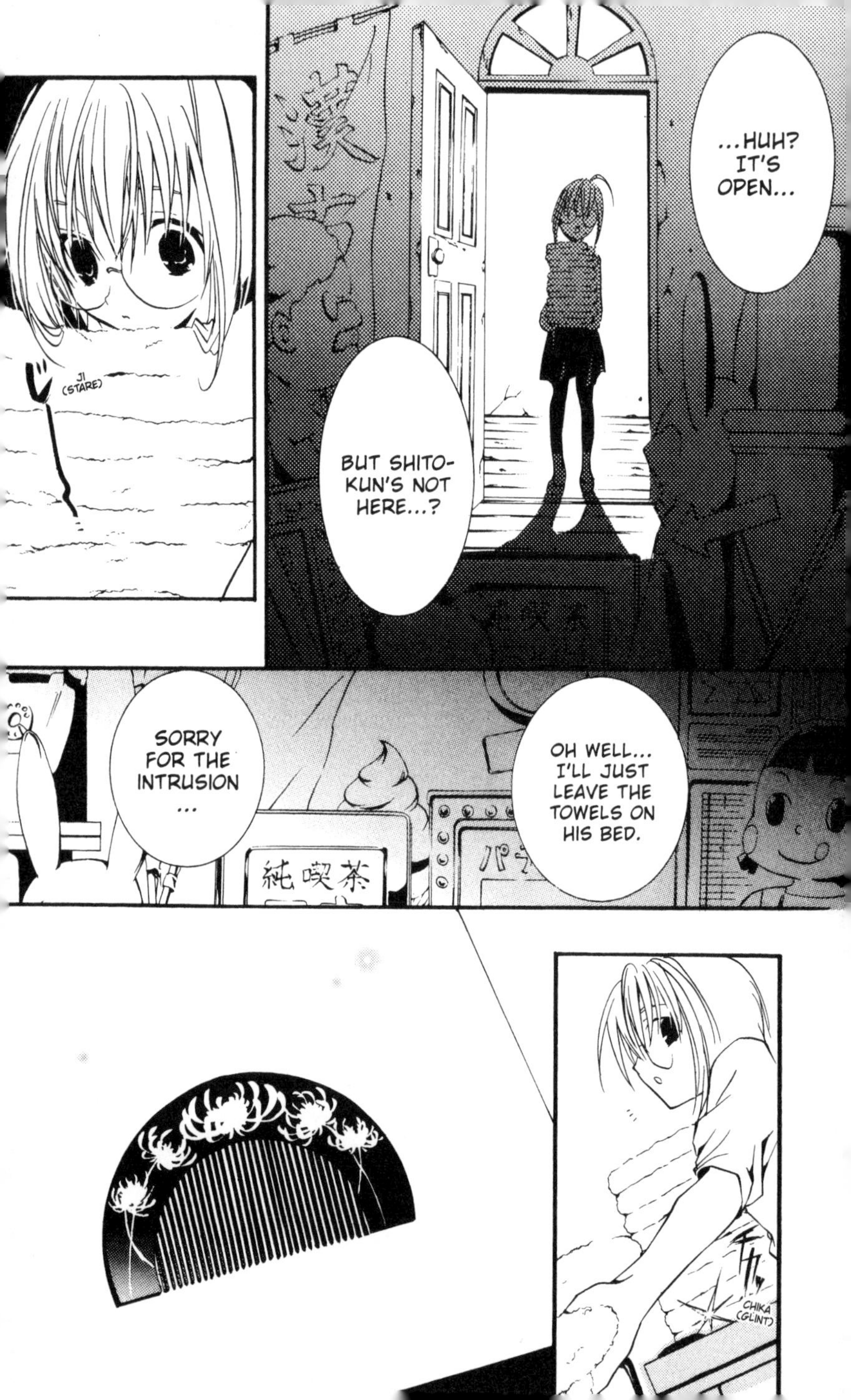
...HUH? IT'S OPEN...
BUT SHITO-KUN'S NOT HERE...?
JI (STARE)
OH WELL... I'LL JUST LEAVE THE TOWELS ON HIS BED.
SORRY FOR THE INTRUSION ...
純喫茶
...
CHIKA (GLINT)

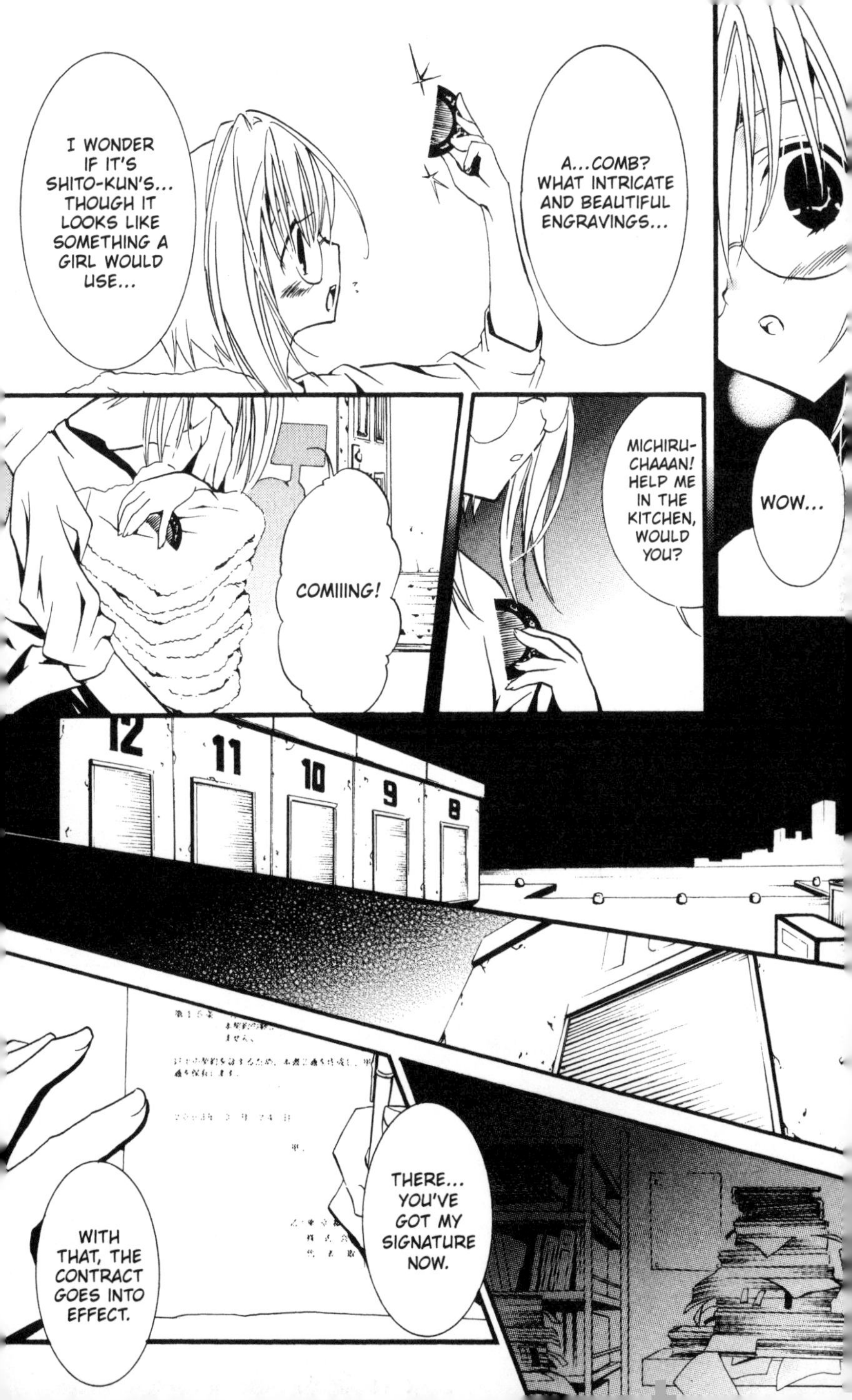
WOW...
A...COMB? WHAT INTRICATE AND BEAUTIFUL ENGRAVINGS...
I WONDER IF IT'S SHITO-KUN'S... THOUGH IT LOOKS LIKE SOMETHING A GIRL WOULD USE...
MICHIRU-CHAAAN! HELP ME IN THE KITCHEN, WOULD YOU?
COMIIING!
12
11
10
9
8
THERE... YOU'VE GOT MY SIGNATURE NOW.
WITH THAT, THE CONTRACT GOES INTO EFFECT.

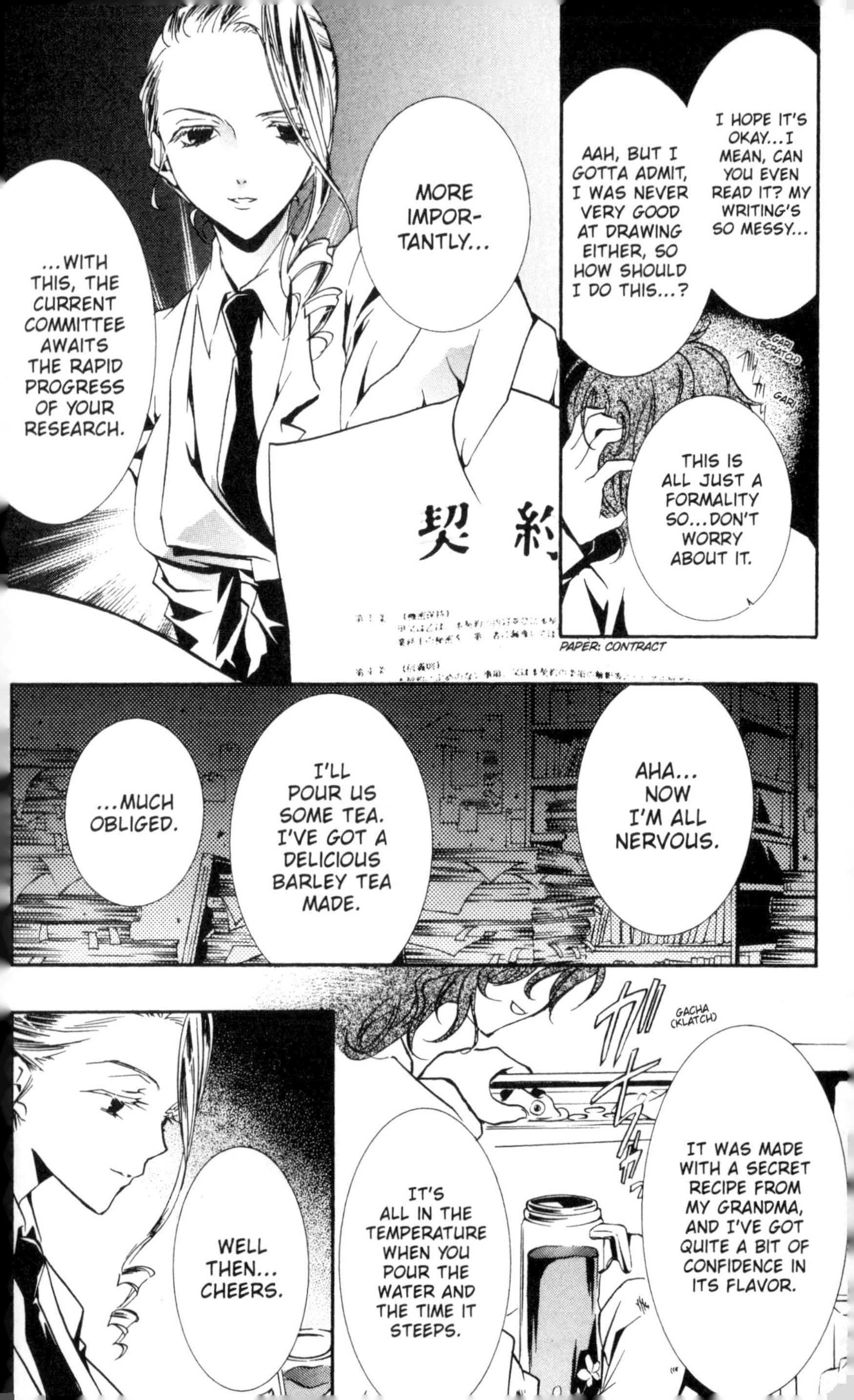
I HOPE IT'S OKAY...I MEAN, CAN YOU EVEN READ IT? MY WRITING'S SO MESSY...
AAH, BUT I GOTTA ADMIT, I WAS NEVER VERY GOOD AT DRAWING EITHER, SO HOW SHOULD I DO THIS...?
GARI (SCRATCH)
GARI
THIS IS ALL JUST A FORMALITY SO...DON'T WORRY ABOUT IT.
MORE IMPOR-TANTLY...
...WITH THIS, THE CURRENT COMMITTEE AWAITS THE RAPID PROGRESS OF YOUR RESEARCH.
契約
PAPER: CONTRACT
AHA... NOW I'M ALL NERVOUS.
I'LL POUR US SOME TEA. I'VE GOT A DELICIOUS BARLEY TEA MADE.
...MUCH OBLIGED.
GACHA (KLATCH)
IT WAS MADE WITH A SECRET RECIPE FROM MY GRANDMA, AND I'VE GOT QUITE A BIT OF CONFIDENCE IN ITS FLAVOR.
IT'S ALL IN THE TEMPERATURE WHEN YOU POUR THE WATER AND THE TIME IT STEEPS.
WELL THEN... CHEERS.

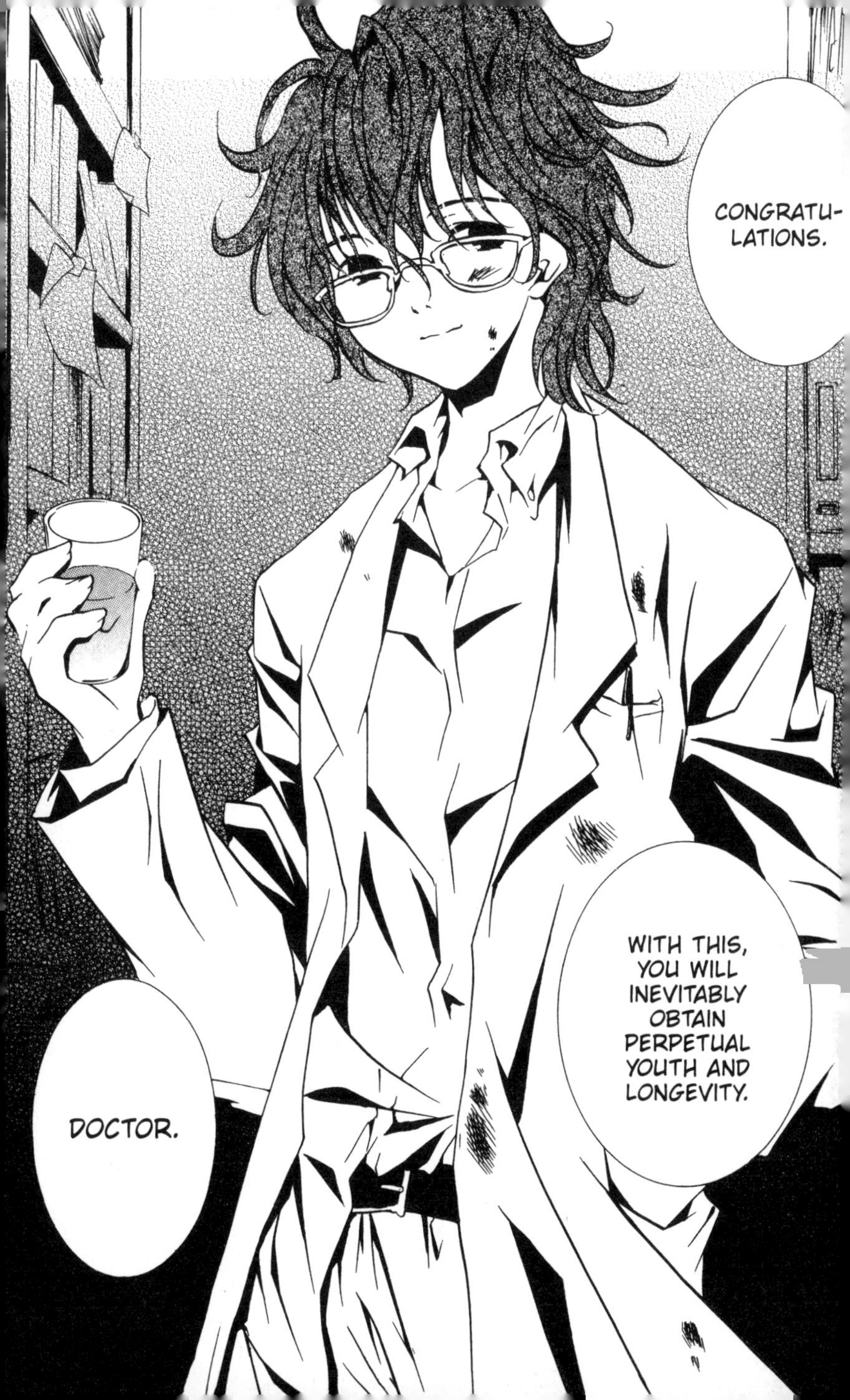
CONGRATU-LATIONS.
WITH THIS, YOU WILL INEVITABLY OBTAIN PERPETUAL YOUTH AND LONGEVITY.
DOCTOR.

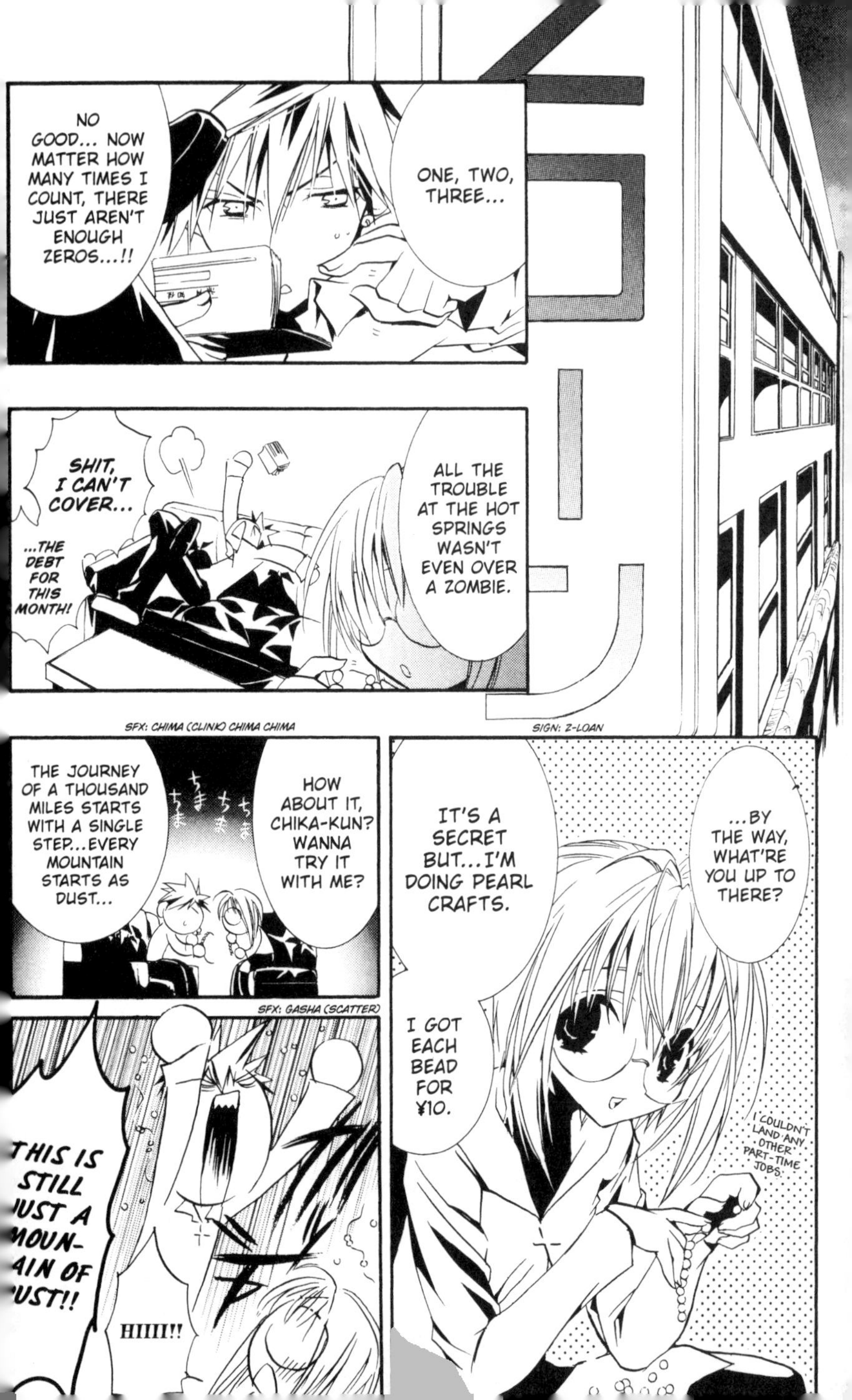
SIGN: Z-LOAN
ONE, TWO, THREE...
NO GOOD... NOW MATTER HOW MANY TIMES I COUNT, THERE JUST AREN'T ENOUGH ZEROS...!!
ALL THE TROUBLE AT THE HOT SPRINGS WASN'T EVEN OVER A ZOMBIE.
SHIT, I CAN'T COVER...
...THE DEBT FOR THIS MONTH!
SFX: CHIMA (CLINK) CHIMA CHIMA
...BY THE WAY, WHAT'RE YOU UP TO THERE?
IT'S A SECRET BUT... I'M DOING PEARL CRAFTS.
I COULDN'T LAND ANY OTHER PART-TIME JOBS.
I GOT EACH BEAD FOR ¥10.
HOW ABOUT IT, CHIKA-KUN? WANNA TRY IT WITH ME?
ちま ちま ちま ちま
THE JOURNEY OF A THOUSAND MILES STARTS WITH A SINGLE STEP...EVERY MOUNTAIN STARTS AS DUST...
SFX: GASHA (SCATTER)
THIS IS STILL UST A MOUN- AIN OF UST!!
HIIII!!

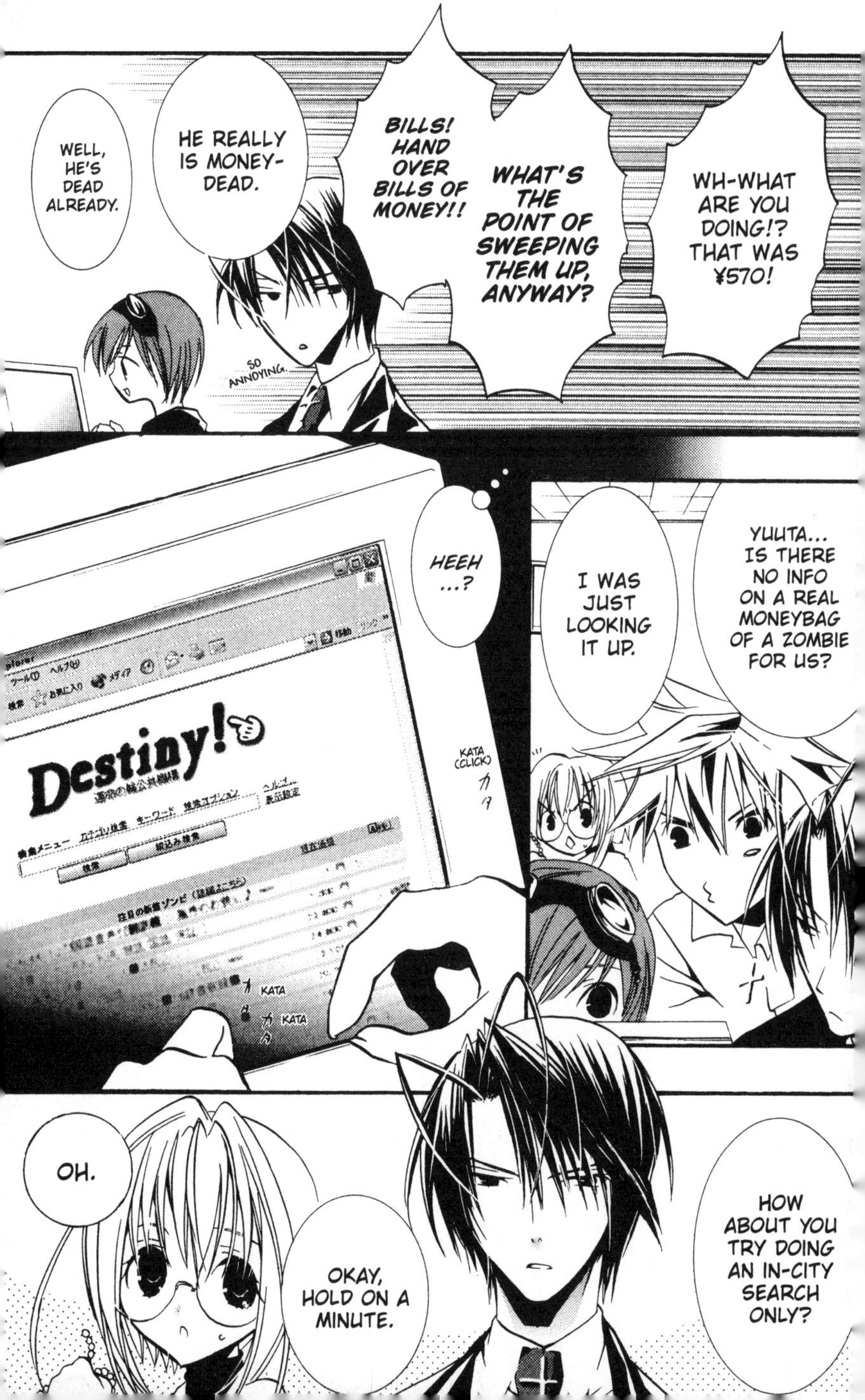
WH-WHAT ARE YOU DOING!? THAT WAS ¥570!
WHAT'S THE POINT OF SWEEPING THEM UP, ANYWAY?
BILLS! HAND OVER BILLS OF MONEY!!
HE REALLY IS MONEY-DEAD.
WELL, HE'S DEAD ALREADY.
SO ANNOYING.
YUUTA... IS THERE NO INFO ON A REAL MONEYBAG OF A ZOMBIE FOR US?
I WAS JUST LOOKING IT UP.
KATA (CLICK)
HEEH ...?
Destiny!
KATA
KATA
HOW ABOUT YOU TRY DOING AN IN-CITY SEARCH ONLY?
OKAY, HOLD ON A MINUTE.
OH.

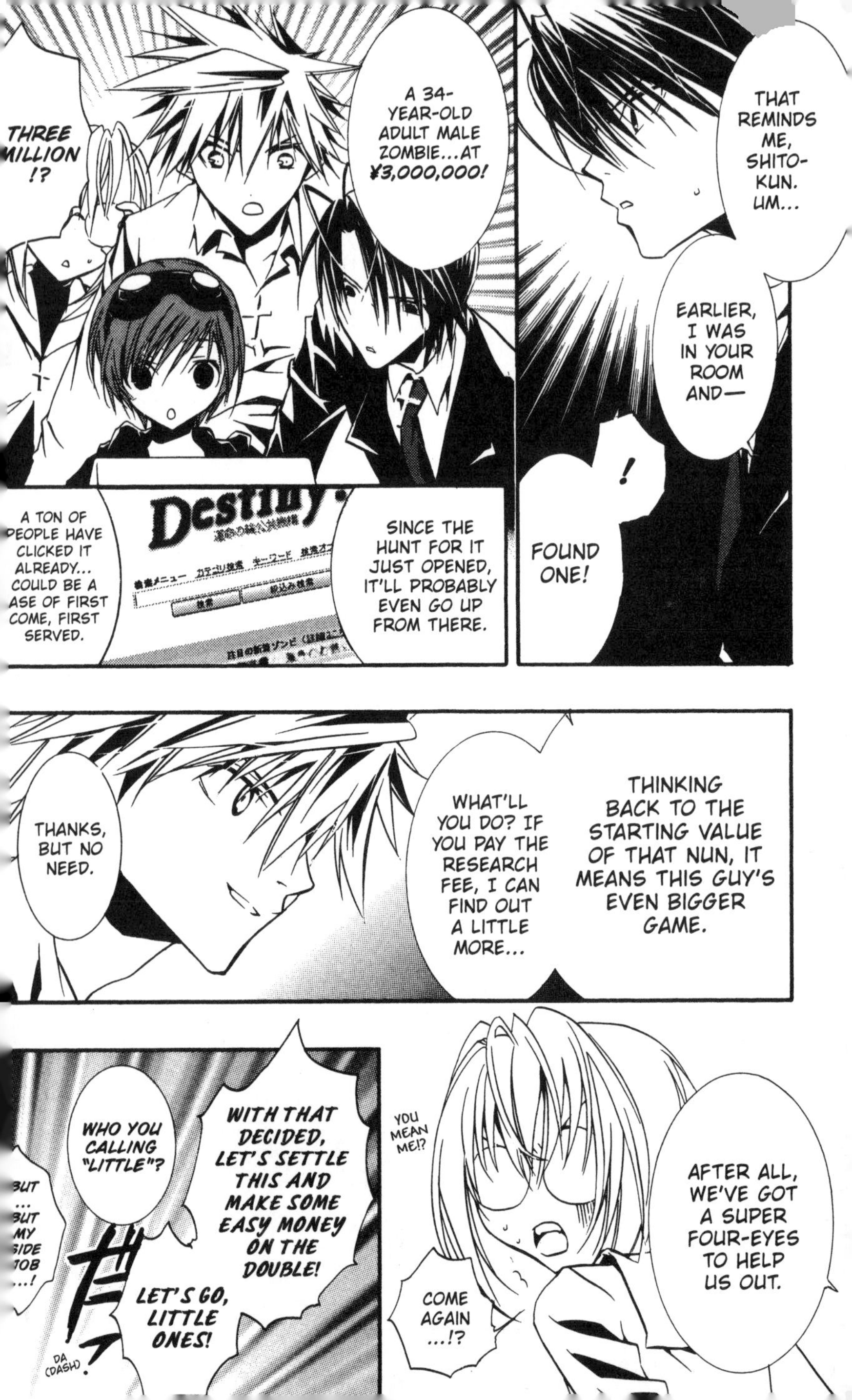
THAT REMINDS ME, SHITO-KUN. UM...
EARLIER, I WAS IN YOUR ROOM AND—
!
FOUND ONE!
A 34-YEAR-OLD ADULT MALE ZOMBIE...AT ¥3,000,000!
THREE MILLION !?
Destiny
SINCE THE HUNT FOR IT JUST OPENED, IT'LL PROBABLY EVEN GO UP FROM THERE.
A TON OF PEOPLE HAVE CLICKED IT ALREADY... COULD BE A ASE OF FIRST COME, FIRST SERVED.
THINKING BACK TO THE STARTING VALUE OF THAT NUN, IT MEANS THIS GUY'S EVEN BIGGER GAME.
WHAT'LL YOU DO? IF YOU PAY THE RESEARCH FEE, I CAN FIND OUT A LITTLE MORE...
THANKS, BUT NO NEED.
AFTER ALL, WE'VE GOT A SUPER FOUR-EYES TO HELP US OUT.
YOU MEAN ME!?
COME AGAIN ...!?
WITH THAT DECIDED, LET'S SETTLE THIS AND MAKE SOME EASY MONEY ON THE DOUBLE!
WHO YOU CALLING "LITTLE"?
LET'S GO, LITTLE ONES!
BUT ... BUT MY IDE JOB ...!
DA (DASH)

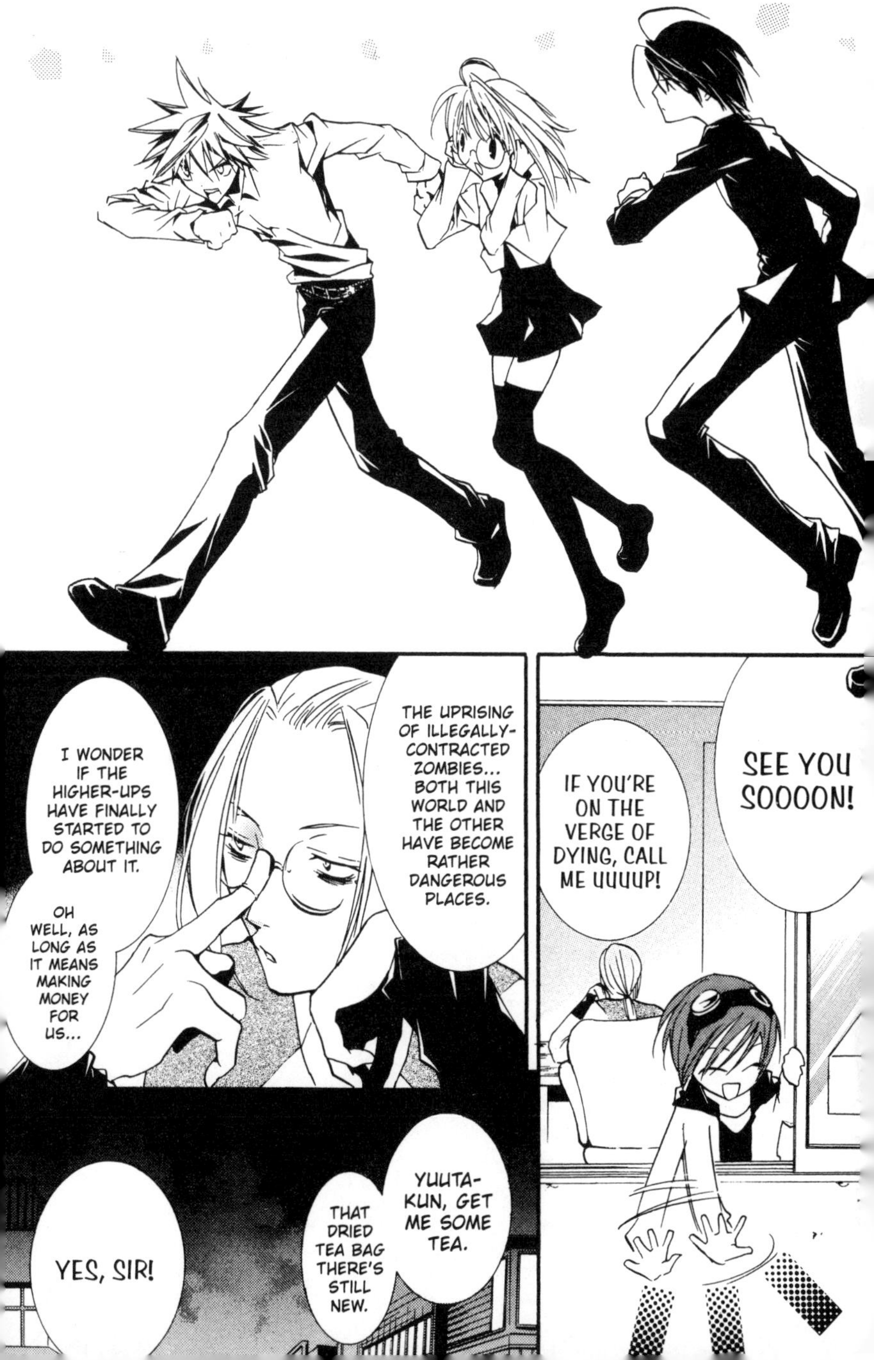
SEE YOU SOOOON!
IF YOU'RE ON THE VERGE OF DYING, CALL ME UUUUP!
THE UPRISING OF ILLEGALLY-CONTRACTED ZOMBIES... BOTH THIS WORLD AND THE OTHER HAVE BECOME RATHER DANGEROUS PLACES.
I WONDER IF THE HIGHER-UPS HAVE FINALLY STARTED TO DO SOMETHING ABOUT IT.
OH WELL, AS LONG AS IT MEANS MAKING MONEY FOR US...
YUUTA-KUN, GET ME SOME TEA.
THAT DRIED TEA BAG THERE'S STILL NEW.
YES, SIR!

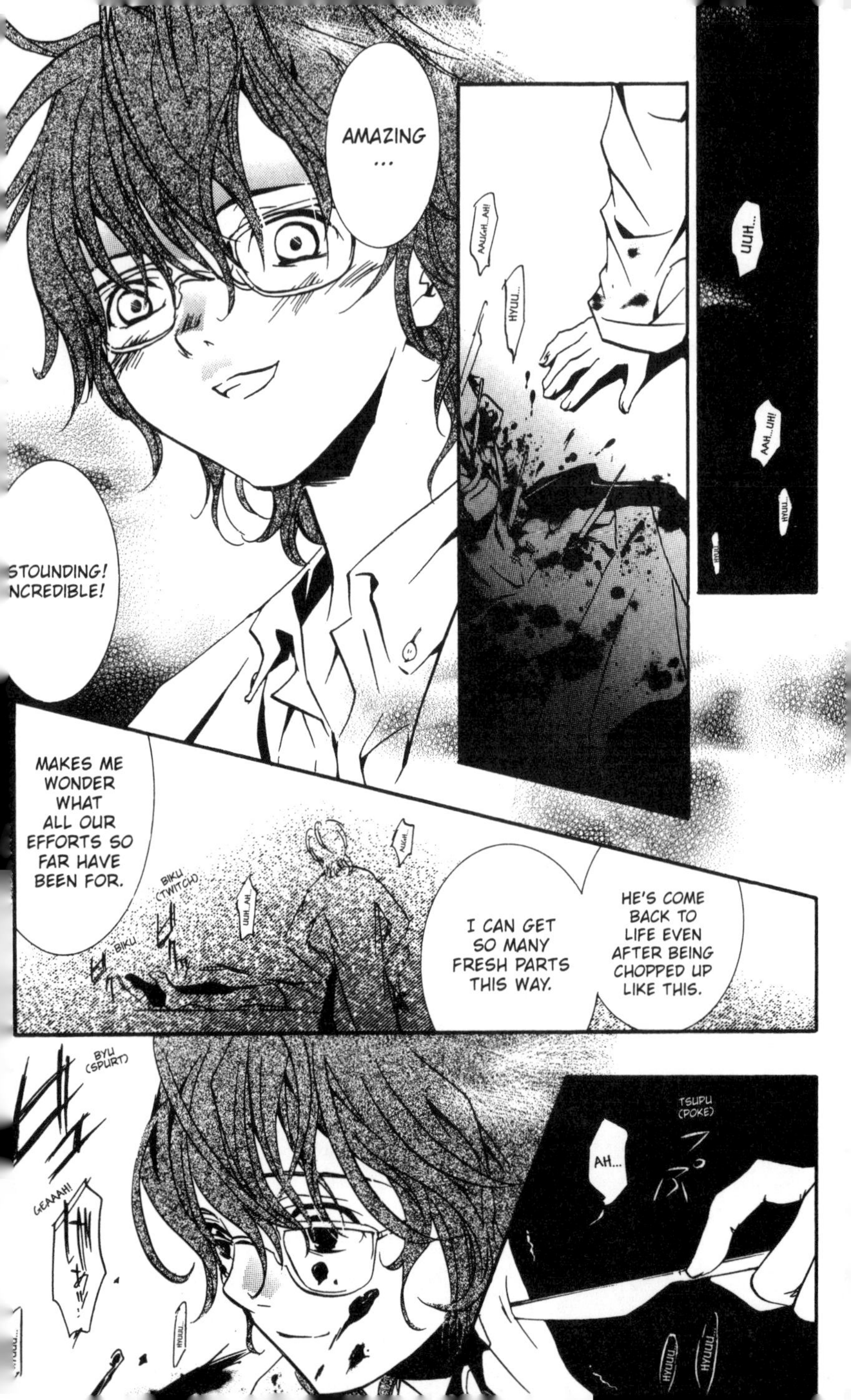
UUH...
AAH...UH!
HYUU...
HYUU...
AAUGH...AH!
HYUU...
AMAZING ...
...STOUNDING! ...NCREDIBLE!
HE'S COME BACK TO LIFE EVEN AFTER BEING CHOPPED UP LIKE THIS.
I CAN GET SO MANY FRESH PARTS THIS WAY.
AUGH...
UUH...AH
BIKU (TWITCH)
BIKU
MAKES ME WONDER WHAT ALL OUR EFFORTS SO FAR HAVE BEEN FOR.
TSUPU (POKE)
AH...
HYUUU...
HYUUU...
BYU (SPURT)
GEAAAH!
HYUUU...

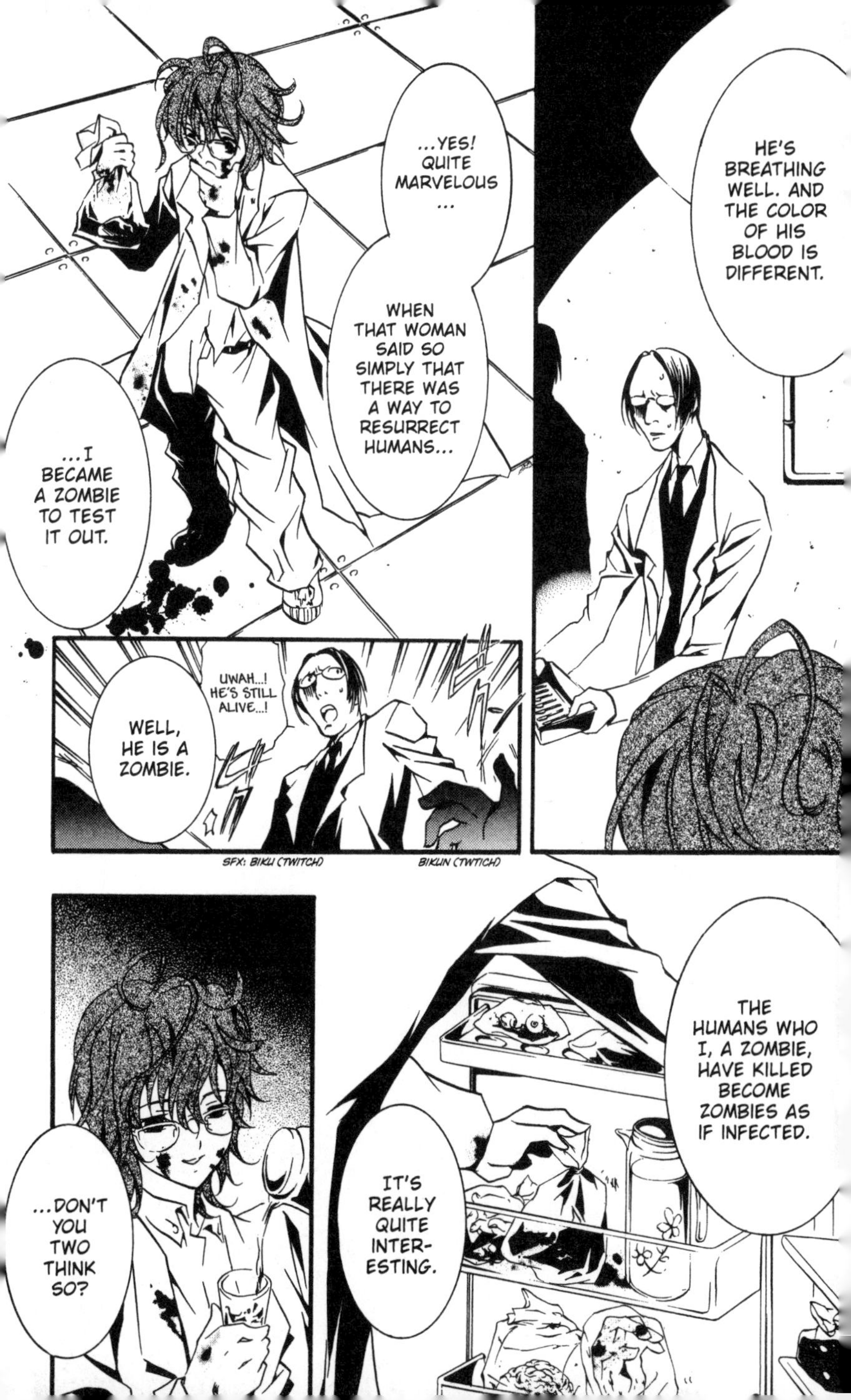
HE'S BREATHING WELL. AND THE COLOR OF HIS BLOOD IS DIFFERENT.
...YES! QUITE MARVELOUS ...
WHEN THAT WOMAN SAID SO SIMPLY THAT THERE WAS A WAY TO RESURRECT HUMANS...
...I BECAME A ZOMBIE TO TEST IT OUT.
UWAH...! HE'S STILL ALIVE...!
WELL, HE IS A ZOMBIE.
SFX: BIKU (TWITCH)
BIKUN (TWITCH)
THE HUMANS WHO I, A ZOMBIE, HAVE KILLED BECOME ZOMBIES AS IF INFECTED.
IT'S REALLY QUITE INTER-ESTING.
...DON'T YOU TWO THINK SO?

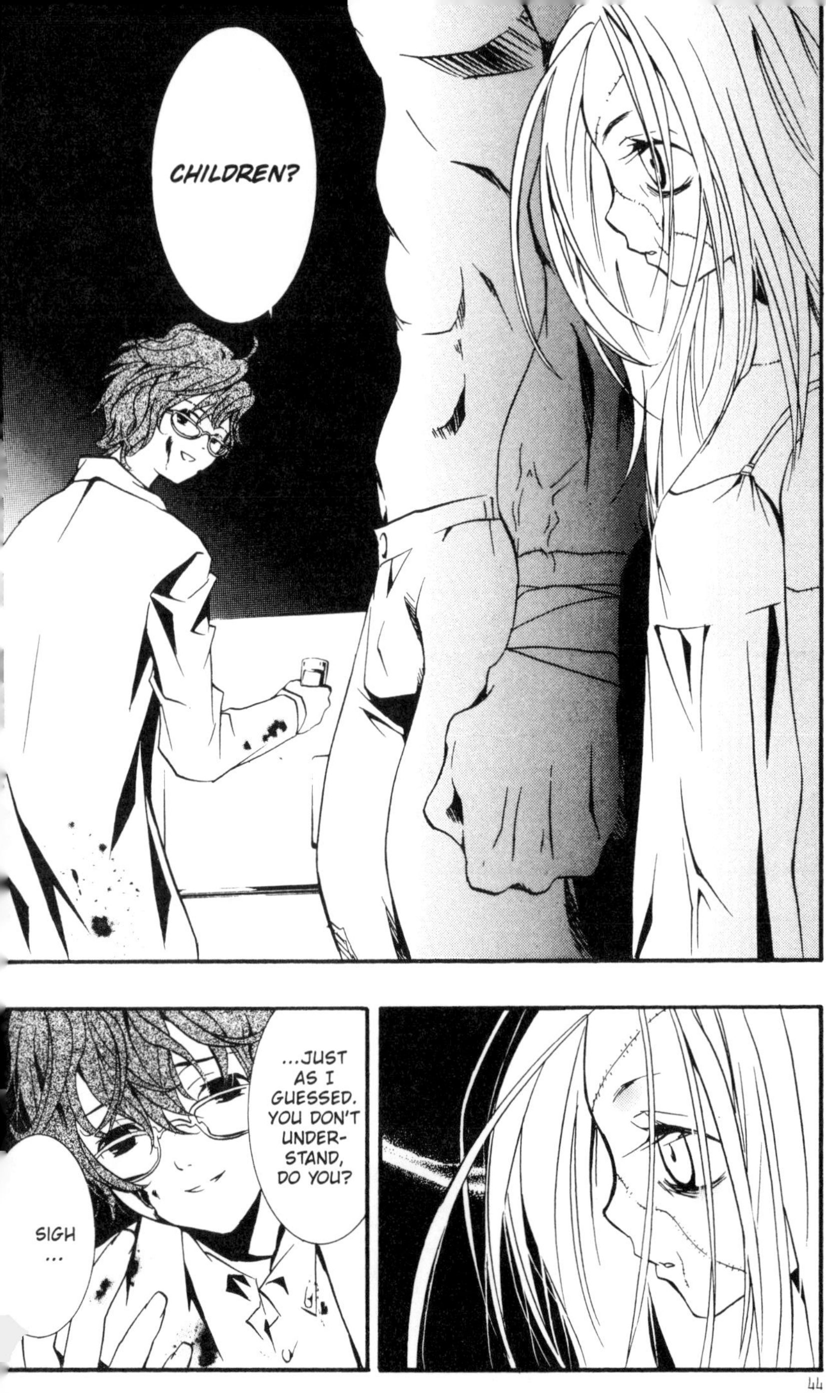
CHILDREN?
...JUST AS I GUESSED. YOU DON'T UNDER-STAND, DO YOU?
SIGH ...

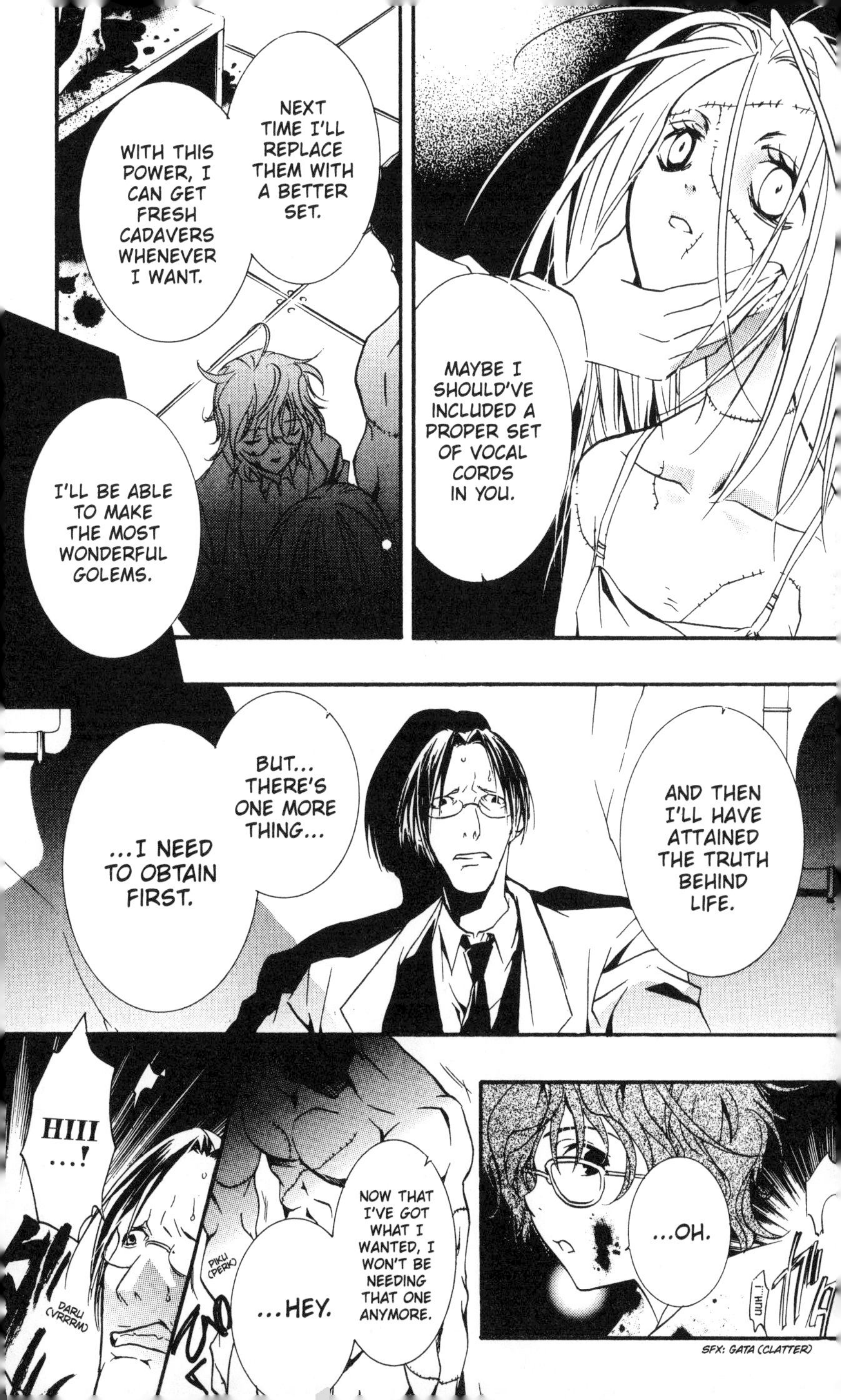
MAYBE I SHOULD'VE INCLUDED A PROPER SET OF VOCAL CORDS IN YOU.
NEXT TIME I'LL REPLACE THEM WITH A BETTER SET.
WITH THIS POWER, I CAN GET FRESH CADAVERS WHENEVER I WANT.
I'LL BE ABLE TO MAKE THE MOST WONDERFUL GOLEMS.
AND THEN I'LL HAVE ATTAINED THE TRUTH BEHIND LIFE.
BUT... THERE'S ONE MORE THING...
...I NEED TO OBTAIN FIRST.
...OH.
HUH...!
SFX: GATA (CLATTER)
NOW THAT I'VE GOT WHAT I WANTED, I WON'T BE NEEDING THAT ONE ANYMORE.
...HEY.
PIKU (PERK)
HIII...!
DARU (VRRRM)

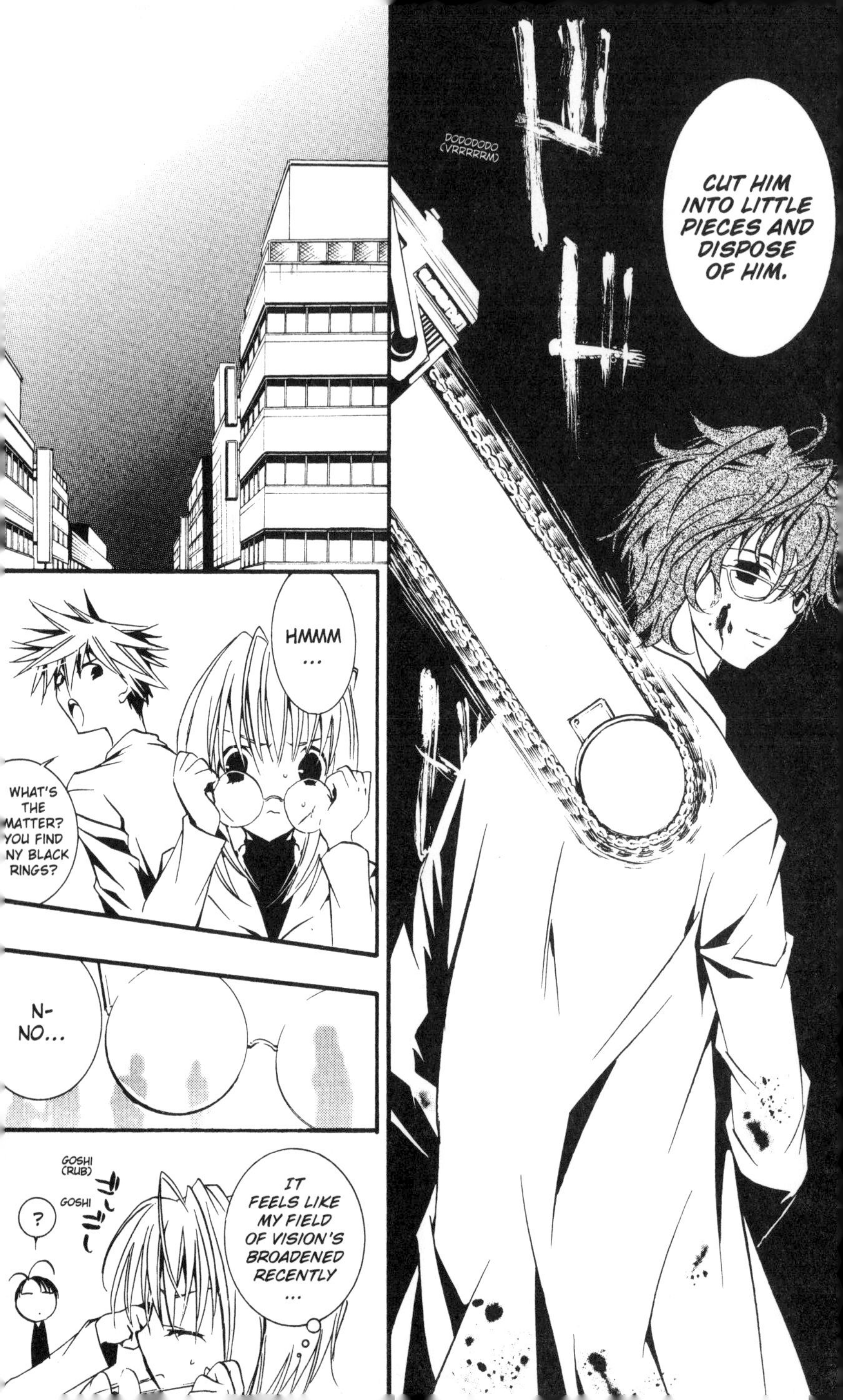
DODODODO (VRRRRRM)
CUT HIM INTO LITTLE PIECES AND DISPOSE OF HIM.
HMMM ...
WHAT'S THE MATTER? YOU FIND NY BLACK RINGS?
N- NO...
IT FEELS LIKE MY FIELD OF VISION'S BROADENED RECENTLY ...
GOSHI (RUB)
GOSHI
?

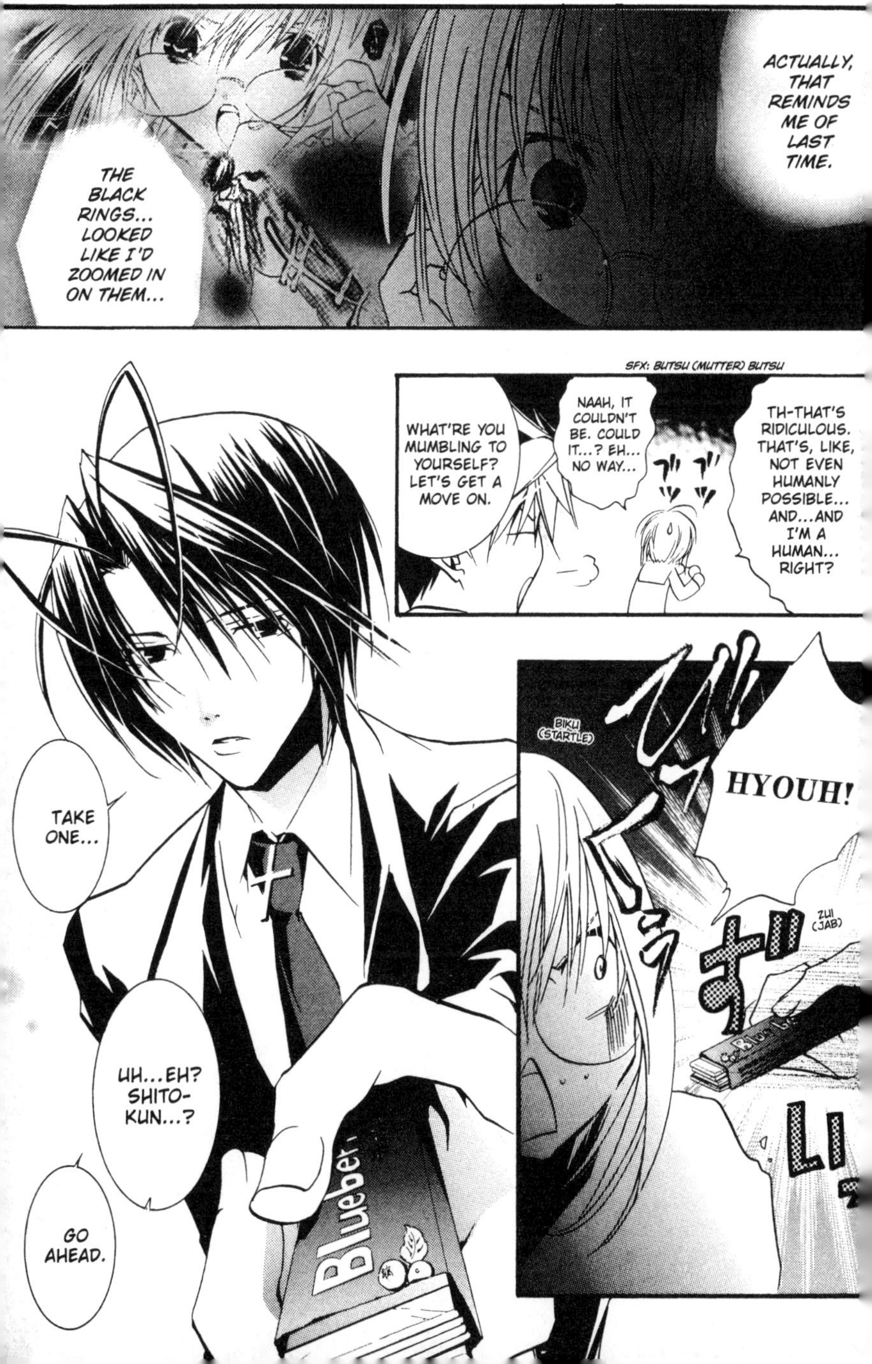
ACTUALLY, THAT REMINDS ME OF LAST TIME.
THE BLACK RINGS... LOOKED LIKE I'D ZOOMED IN ON THEM...
SFX: BUTSU (MUTTER) BUTSU
TH-THAT'S RIDICULOUS. THAT'S, LIKE, NOT EVEN HUMANLY POSSIBLE... AND...AND I'M A HUMAN... RIGHT?
NAAH, IT COULDN'T BE. COULD IT...? EH... NO WAY...
WHAT'RE YOU MUMBLING TO YOURSELF? LET'S GET A MOVE ON.
BIKU (STARTLE)
HYOUH!
ZUI (JAB)
TAKE ONE...
UH...EH? SHITO-KUN...?
GO AHEAD.

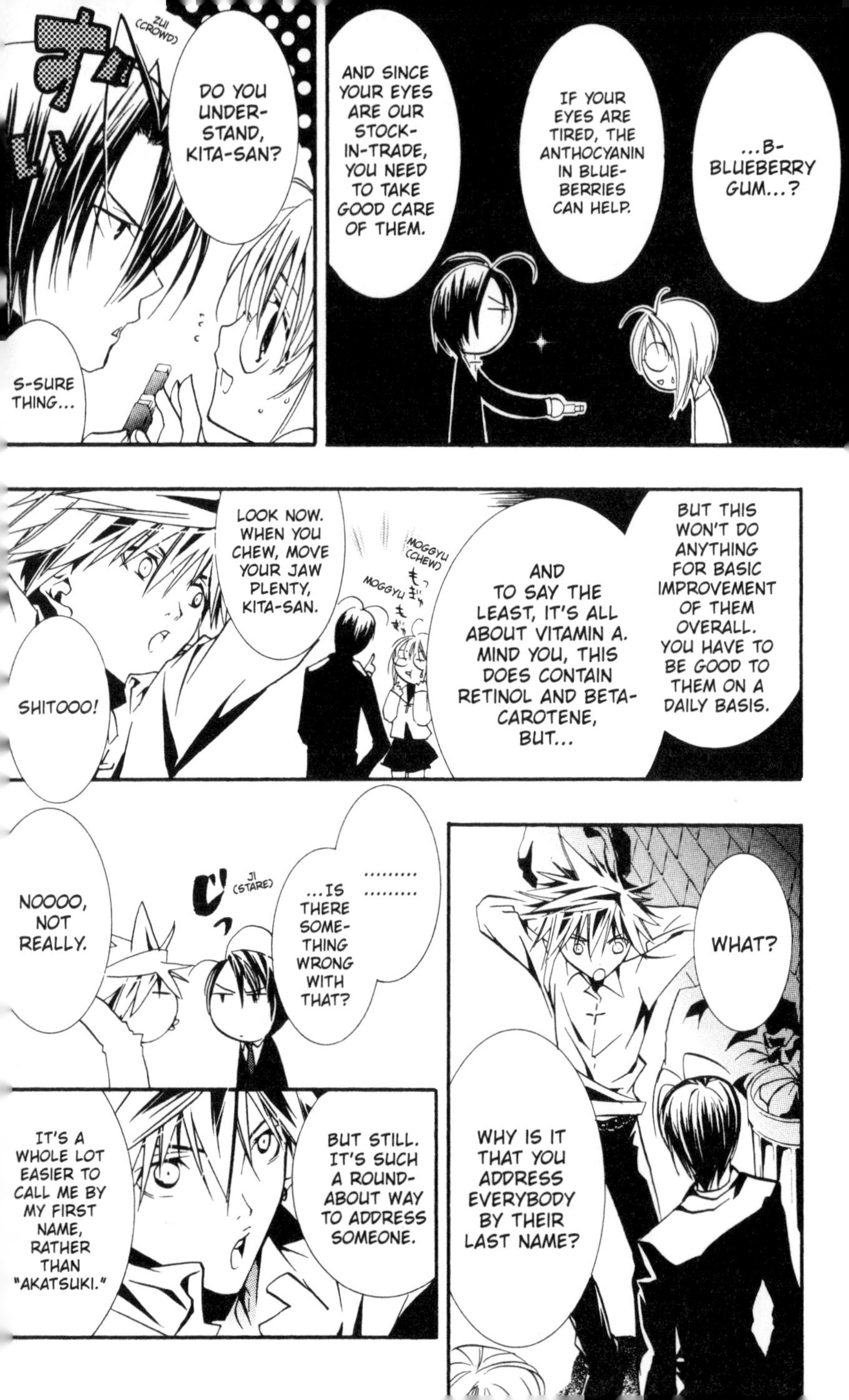
...B-BLUEBERRY GUM...?
IF YOUR EYES ARE TIRED, THE ANTHOCYANIN IN BLUEBERRIES CAN HELP.
AND SINCE YOUR EYES ARE OUR STOCK-IN-TRADE, YOU NEED TO TAKE GOOD CARE OF THEM.
ZUI (CROWD)
DO YOU UNDERSTAND, KITA-SAN?
S-SURE THING...
BUT THIS WON'T DO ANYTHING FOR BASIC IMPROVEMENT OF THEM OVERALL. YOU HAVE TO BE GOOD TO THEM ON A DAILY BASIS.
AND TO SAY THE LEAST, IT'S ALL ABOUT VITAMIN A. MIND YOU, THIS DOES CONTAIN RETINOL AND BETA-CAROTENE, BUT...
MOGGYU (CHEW)
MOGGYU
LOOK NOW. WHEN YOU CHEW, MOVE YOUR JAW PLENTY, KITA-SAN.
SHITOOO!
WHAT?
WHY IS IT THAT YOU ADDRESS EVERYBODY BY THEIR LAST NAME?
....
....
...IS THERE SOMETHING WRONG WITH THAT?
JI (STARE)
NOOOO, NOT REALLY.
BUT STILL. IT'S SUCH A ROUND-ABOUT WAY TO ADDRESS SOMEONE.
IT'S A WHOLE LOT EASIER TO CALL ME BY MY FIRST NAME, RATHER THAN "AKATSUKI."

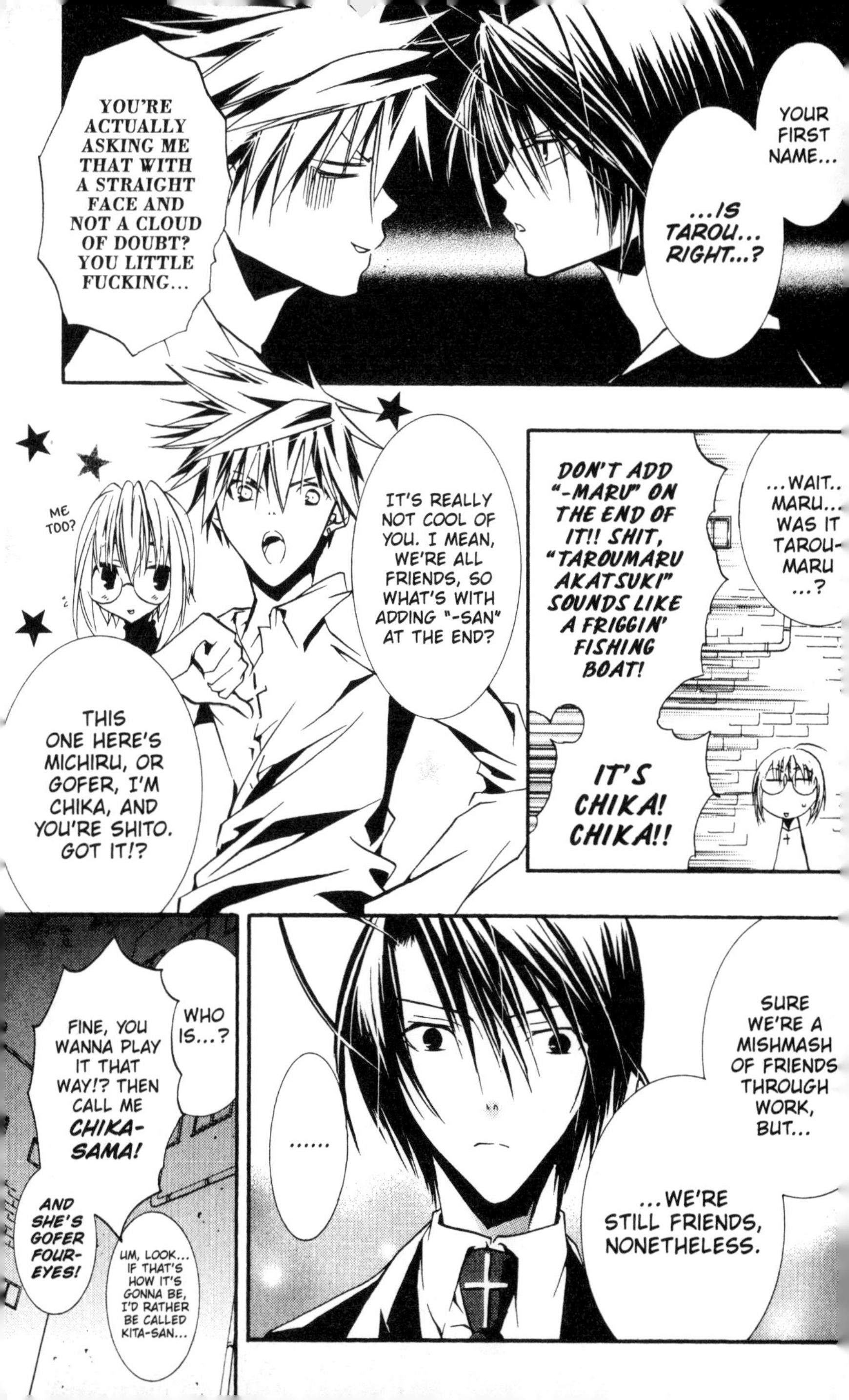
YOUR FIRST NAME...
...IS TAROU... RIGHT...?
YOU'RE ACTUALLY ASKING ME THAT WITH A STRAIGHT FACE AND NOT A CLOUD OF DOUBT? YOU LITTLE FUCKING...
...WAIT.. MARU... WAS IT TAROU-MARU ...?
DON'T ADD "-MARU" ON THE END OF IT!! SHIT, "TAROUMARU AKATSUKI" SOUNDS LIKE A FRIGGIN' FISHING BOAT!
IT'S CHIKA! CHIKA!!
IT'S REALLY NOT COOL OF YOU. I MEAN, WE'RE ALL FRIENDS, SO WHAT'S WITH ADDING "-SAN" AT THE END?
ME TOO?
THIS ONE HERE'S MICHIRU, OR GOFER, I'M CHIKA, AND YOU'RE SHITO. GOT IT!?
SURE WE'RE A MISHMASH OF FRIENDS THROUGH WORK, BUT...
...WE'RE STILL FRIENDS, NONETHELESS.
......
WHO IS...?
FINE, YOU WANNA PLAY IT THAT WAY!? THEN CALL ME CHIKA-SAMA!
AND SHE'S GOFER FOUR-EYES!
UM, LOOK... IF THAT'S HOW IT'S GONNA BE, I'D RATHER BE CALLED KITA-SAN...

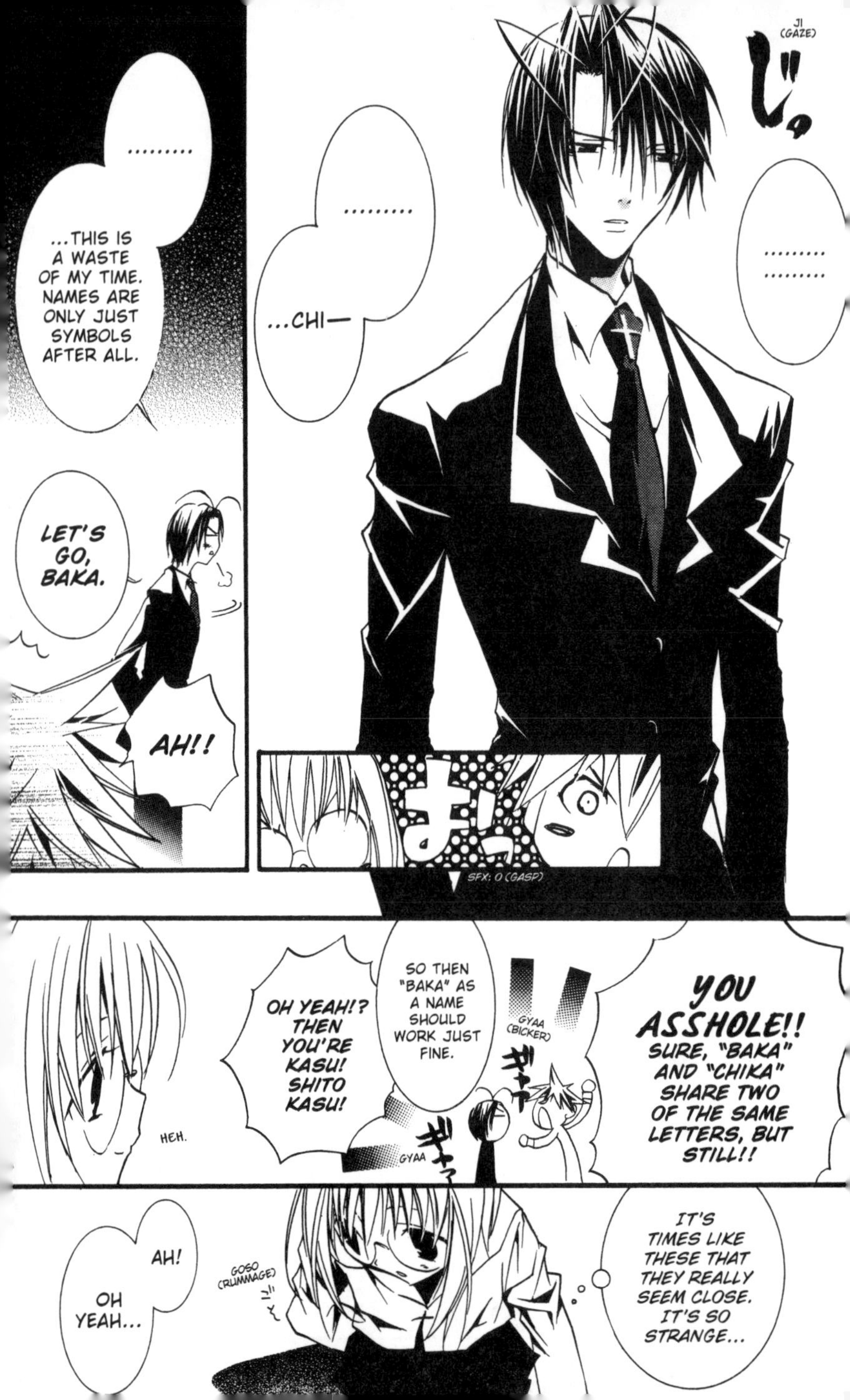

JI (GAZE)
....
....
....
...CHI—
....
...THIS IS A WASTE OF MY TIME. NAMES ARE ONLY JUST SYMBOLS AFTER ALL.
LET'S GO, BAKA.
AH!!
SFX: O (GASP)
YOU ASSHOLE!! SURE, "BAKA" AND "CHIKA" SHARE TWO OF THE SAME LETTERS, BUT STILL!!
GYAA (BICKER)
SO THEN "BAKA" AS A NAME SHOULD WORK JUST FINE.
OH YEAH!? THEN YOU'RE KASU! SHITO KASU!
GYAA
HEH.
IT'S TIMES LIKE THESE THAT THEY REALLY SEEM CLOSE. IT'S SO STRANGE...
GOSO (RUMMAGE)
AH!
OH YEAH...

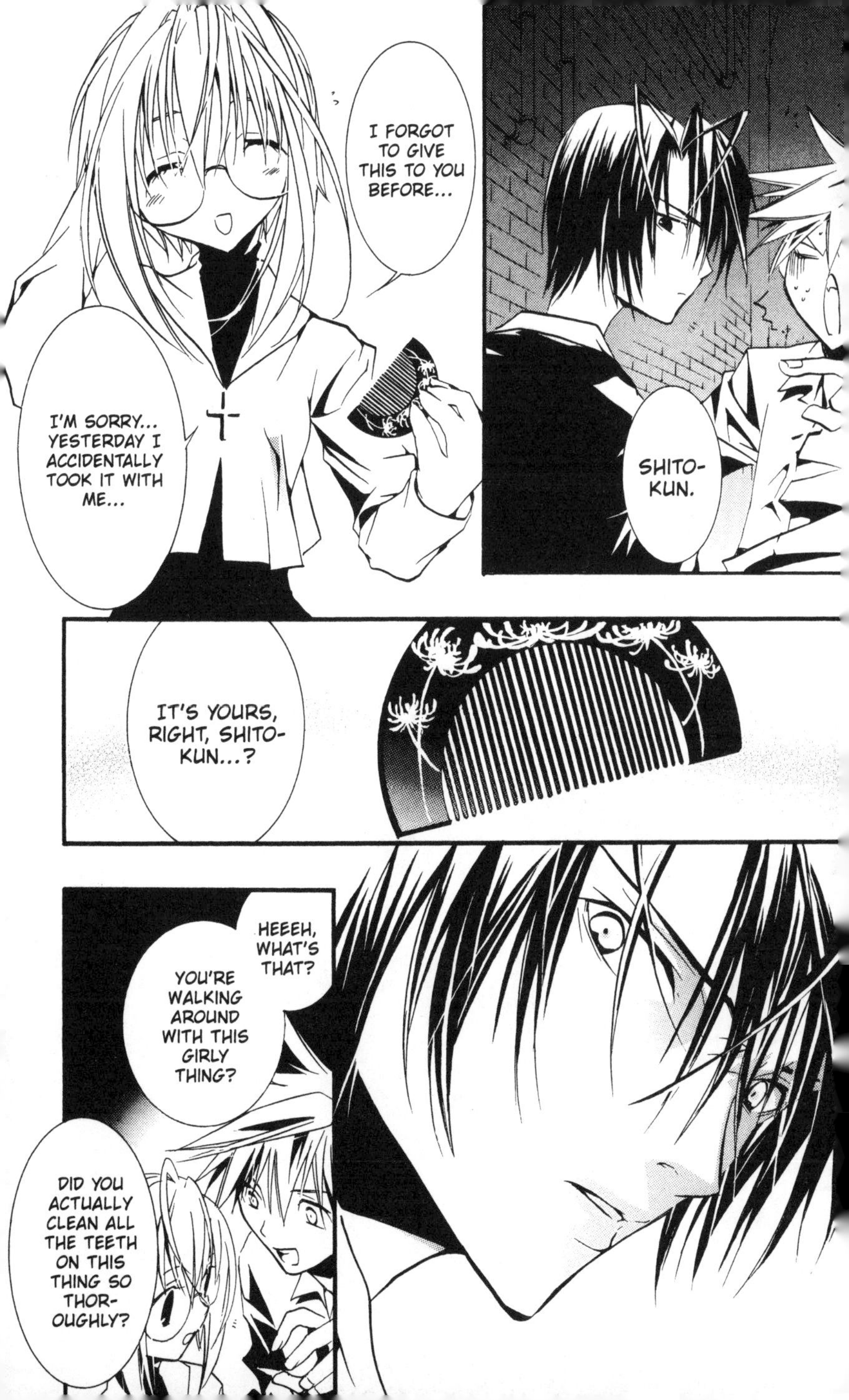
SHITO-KUN.
I FORGOT TO GIVE THIS TO YOU BEFORE...
I'M SORRY... YESTERDAY I ACCIDENTALLY TOOK IT WITH ME...
IT'S YOURS, RIGHT, SHITO-KUN...?
HEEEH, WHAT'S THAT?
YOU'RE WALKING AROUND WITH THIS GIRLY THING?
DID YOU ACTUALLY CLEAN ALL THE TEETH ON THIS THING SO THOR-OUGHLY?

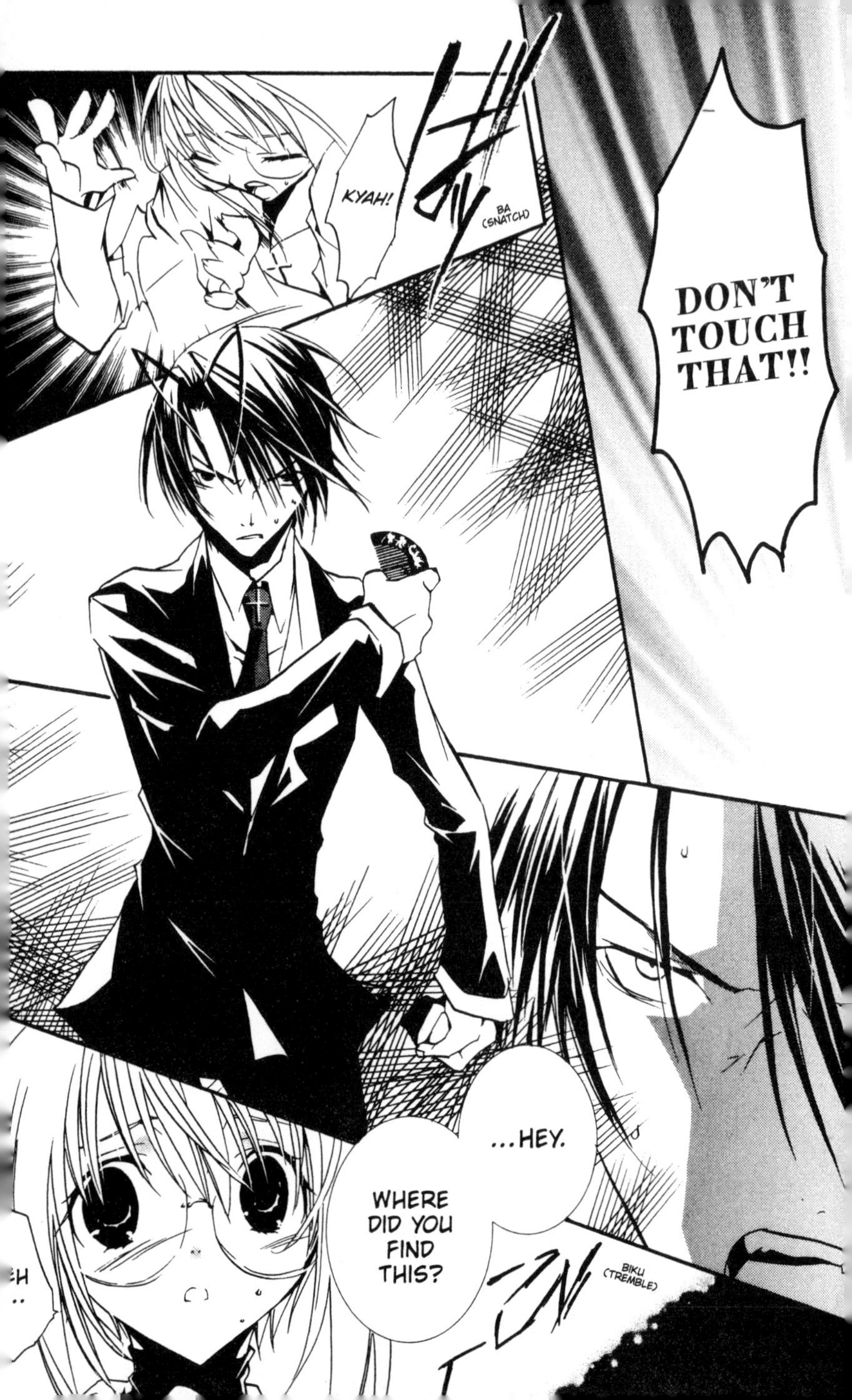
DON'T TOUCH THAT!!
BA (SNATCH)
KYAH!
...HEY.
WHERE DID YOU FIND THIS?
BIKU (TREMBLE)

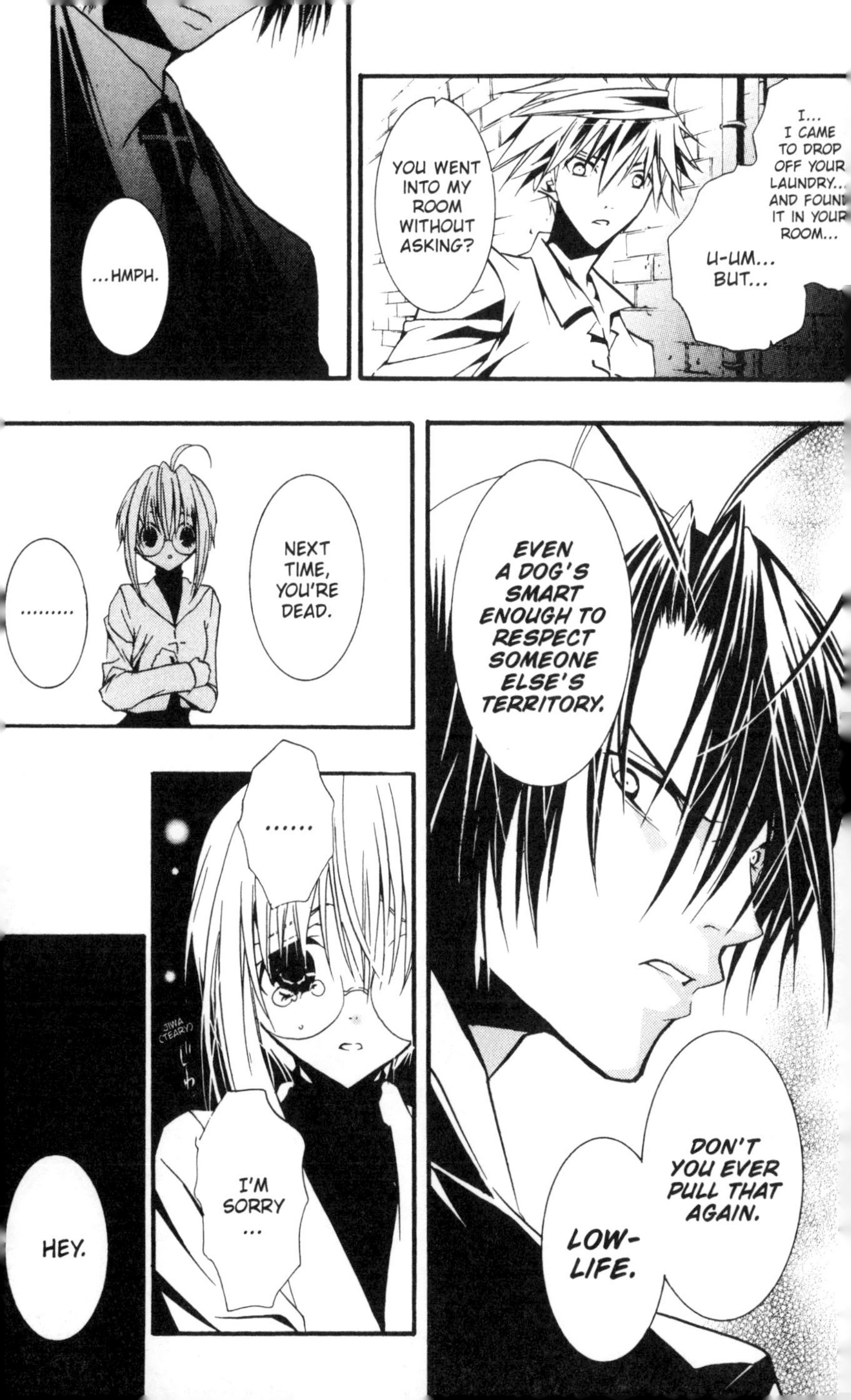
YOU WENT INTO MY ROOM WITHOUT ASKING?
U-UM... BUT...
I... I CAME TO DROP OFF YOUR LAUNDRY... AND FOUND IT IN YOUR ROOM...
...HMPH.
EVEN A DOG'S SMART ENOUGH TO RESPECT SOMEONE ELSE'S TERRITORY.
DON'T YOU EVER PULL THAT AGAIN.
LOW-LIFE.
NEXT TIME, YOU'RE DEAD.
....
......
JIWA (TEARY)
I'M SORRY ...
HEY.

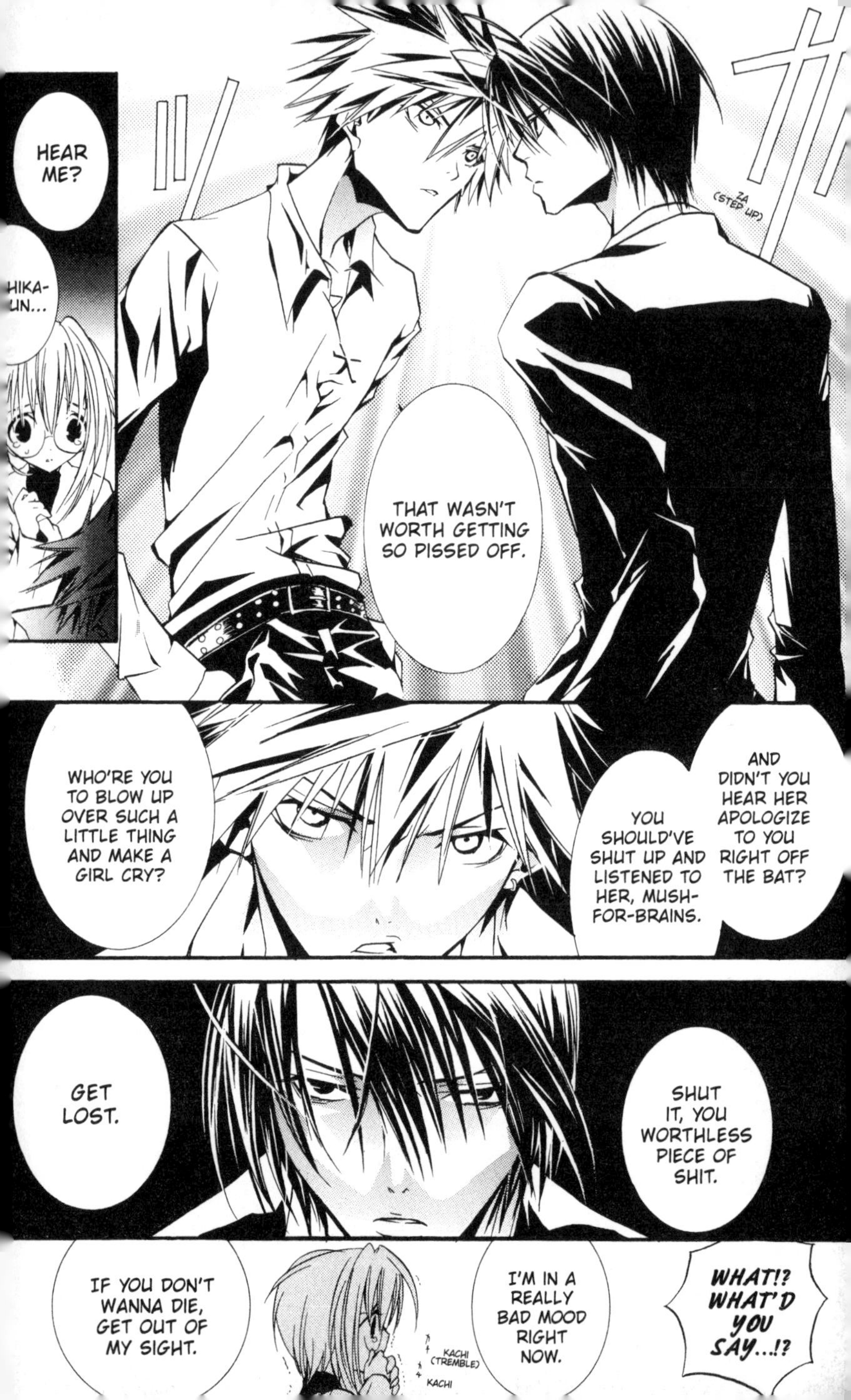
ZA (STEP UP)
THAT WASN'T WORTH GETTING SO PISSED OFF.
HEAR ME?
HIKA-UN...
AND DIDN'T YOU HEAR HER APOLOGIZE TO YOU RIGHT OFF THE BAT?
YOU SHOULD'VE SHUT UP AND LISTENED TO HER, MUSH-FOR-BRAINS.
WHO'RE YOU TO BLOW UP OVER SUCH A LITTLE THING AND MAKE A GIRL CRY?
SHUT IT, YOU WORTHLESS PIECE OF SHIT.
GET LOST.
WHAT!? WHAT'D YOU SAY...!?
I'M IN A REALLY BAD MOOD RIGHT NOW.
KACHI (TREMBLE)
KACHI
IF YOU DON'T WANNA DIE, GET OUT OF MY SIGHT.

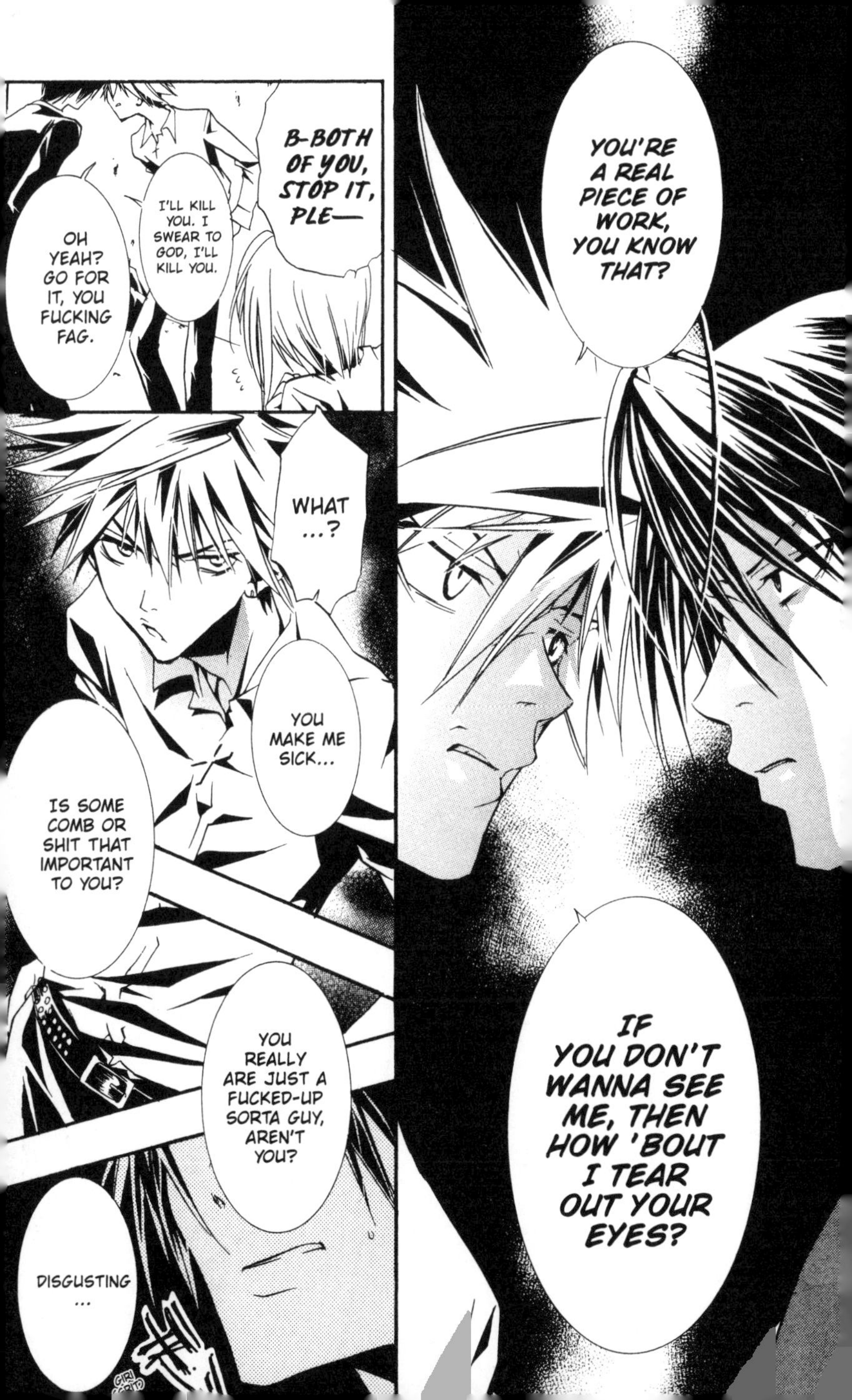
YOU'RE A REAL PIECE OF WORK, YOU KNOW THAT?
IF YOU DON'T WANNA SEE ME, THEN HOW 'BOUT I TEAR OUT YOUR EYES?
B-BOTH OF YOU, STOP IT, PLE—
I'LL KILL YOU. I SWEAR TO GOD, I'LL KILL YOU.
OH YEAH? GO FOR IT, YOU FUCKING FAG.
WHAT ...?
YOU MAKE ME SICK...
IS SOME COMB OR SHIT THAT IMPORTANT TO YOU?
YOU REALLY ARE JUST A FUCKED-UP SORTA GUY, AREN'T YOU?
DISGUSTING ...

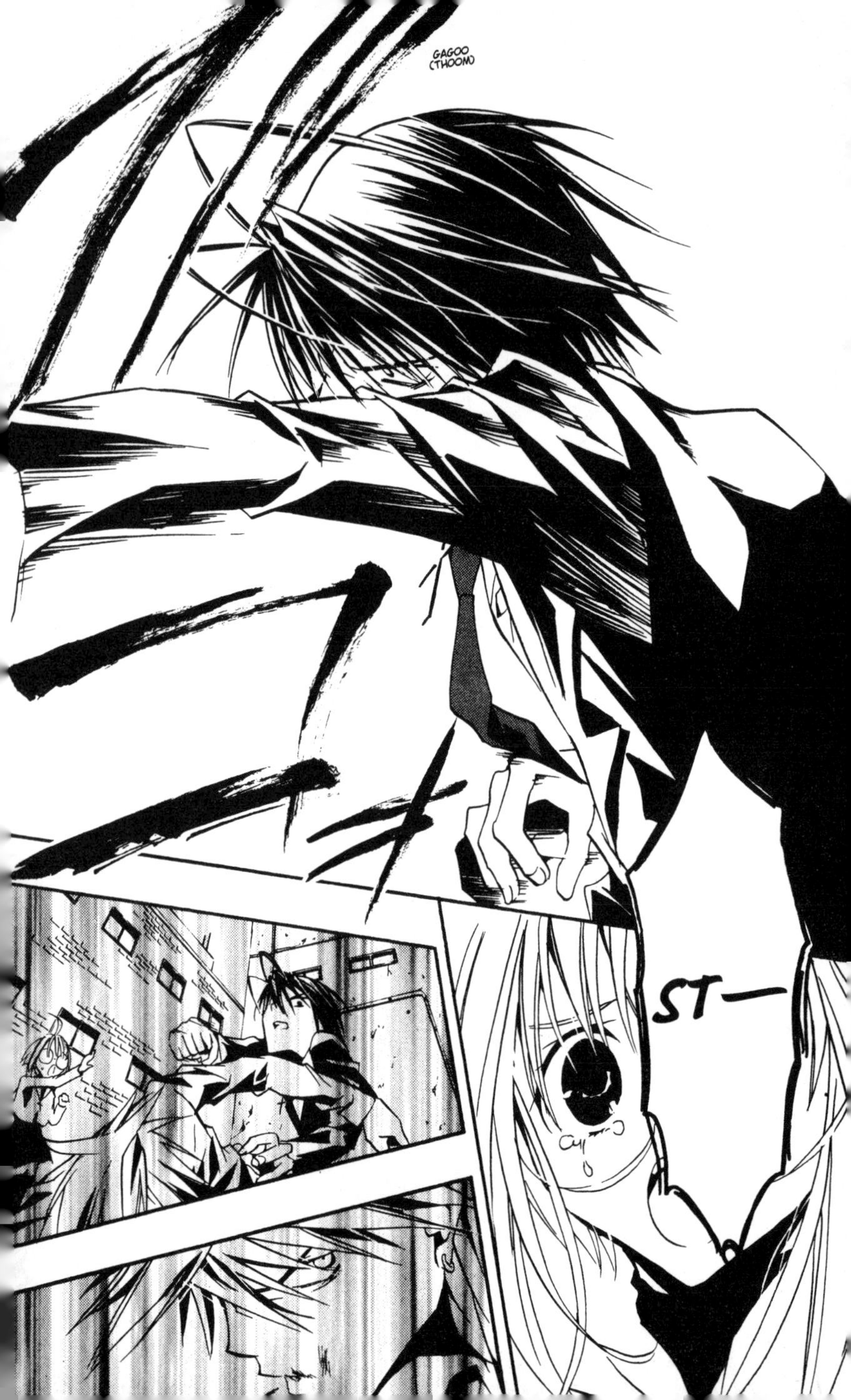
GAGOO (THOOM)
ST—

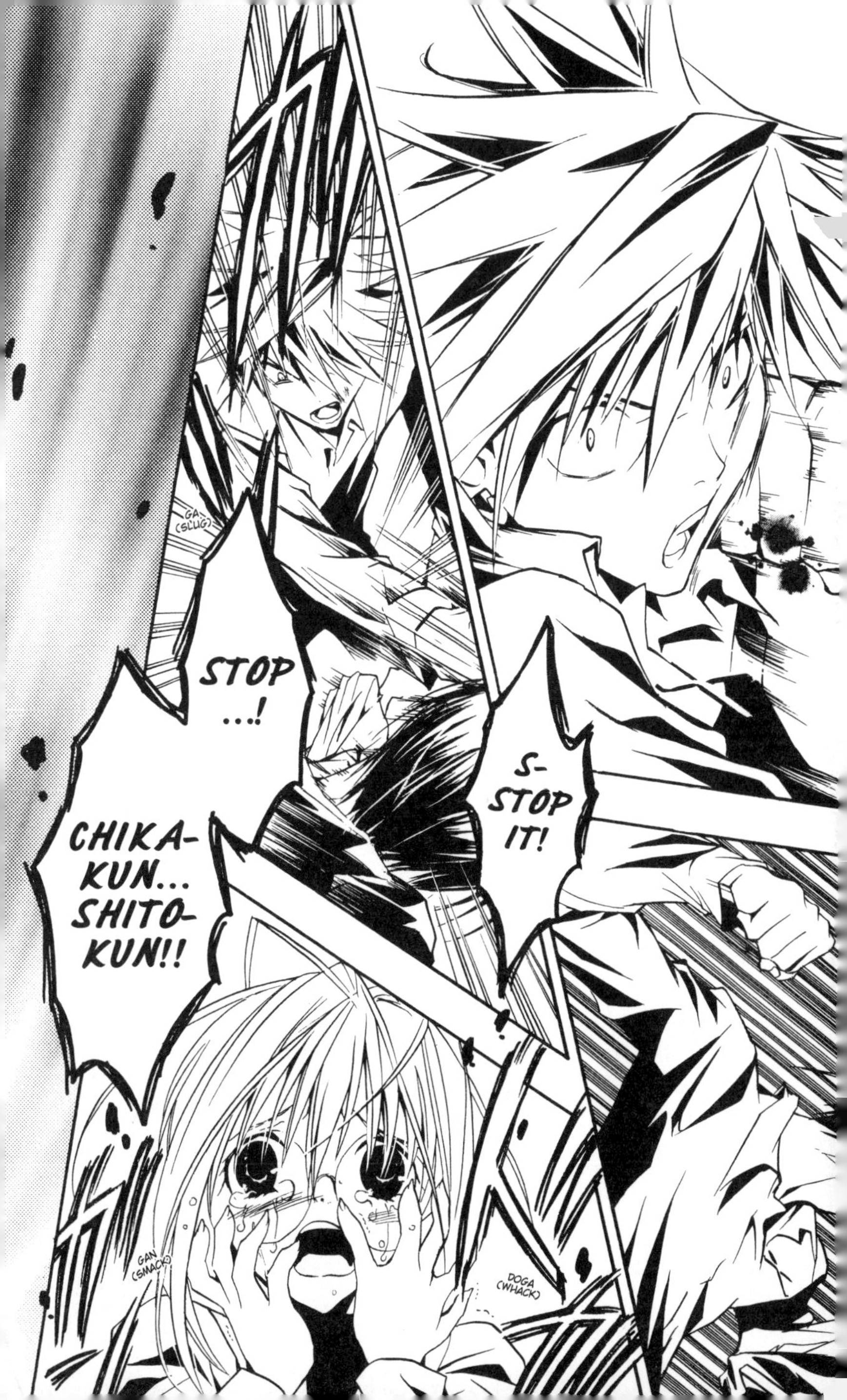
GA (SLUG)
S-STOP IT!
STOP ...!
CHIKA-KUN... SHITO-KUN!!
DOGA (WHACK)
GAN (SMACK)

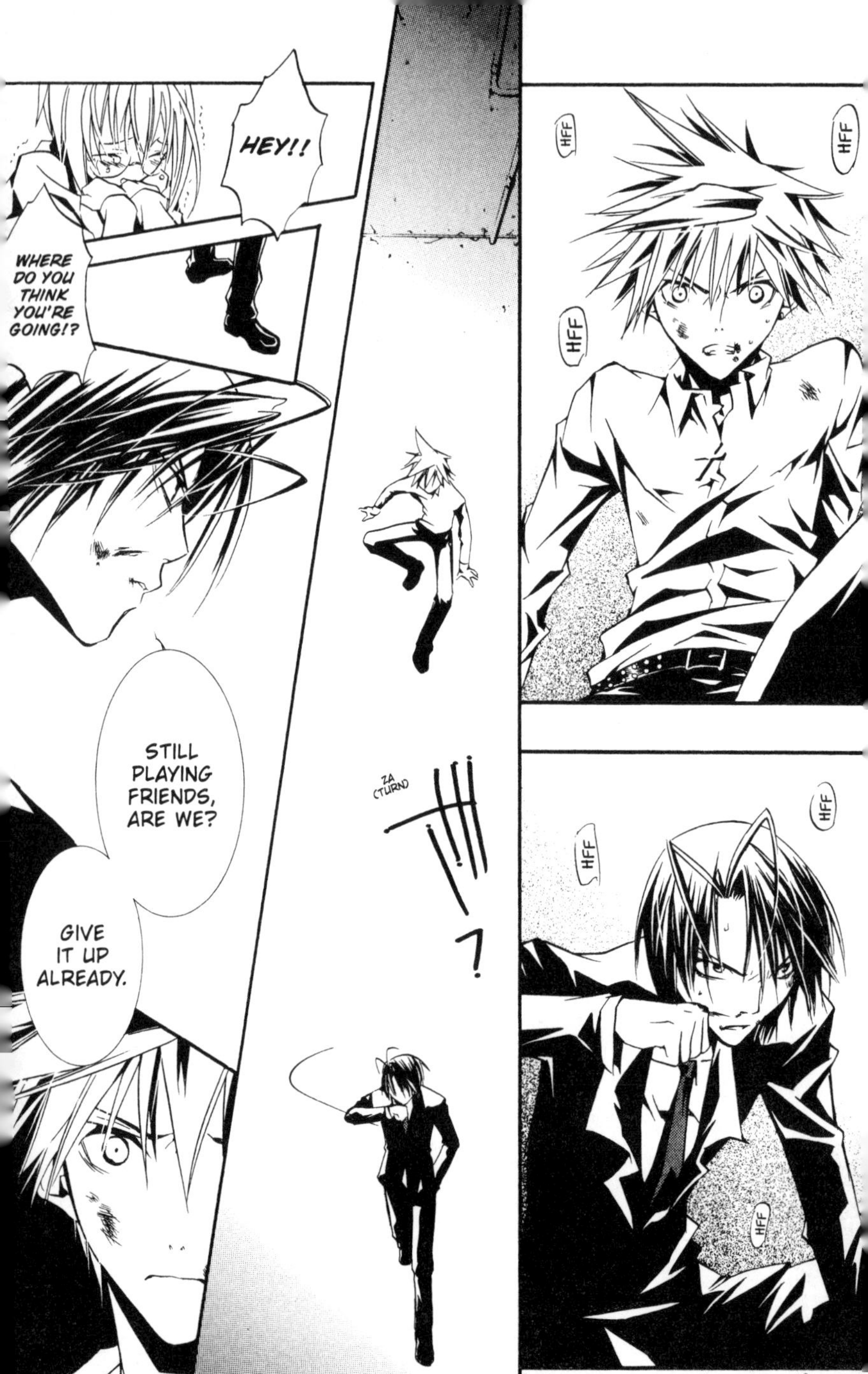
HFF
HFF
HFF
HFF
HFF
HFF
ZA (TURN)
HEY!!
WHERE DO YOU THINK YOU'RE GOING!?
STILL PLAYING FRIENDS, ARE WE?
GIVE IT UP ALREADY.

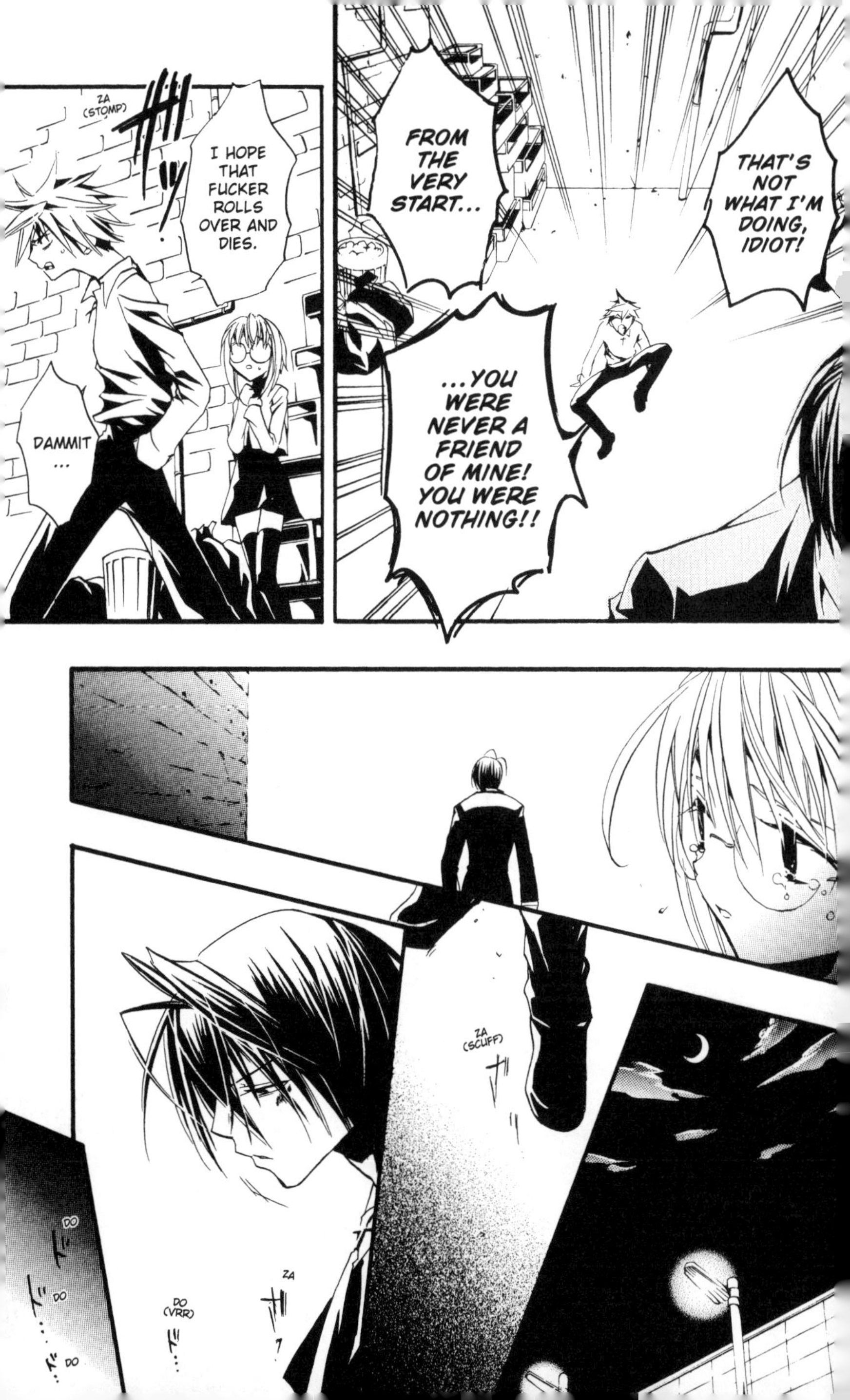
THAT'S NOT WHAT I'M DOING, IDIOT!
FROM THE VERY START...
...YOU WERE NEVER A FRIEND OF MINE! YOU WERE NOTHING!!
ZA (STOMP)
I HOPE THAT FUCKER ROLLS OVER AND DIES.
DAMMIT ...
ZA (SCUFF)
ZA
DO (VRR)
DO
DO
DO

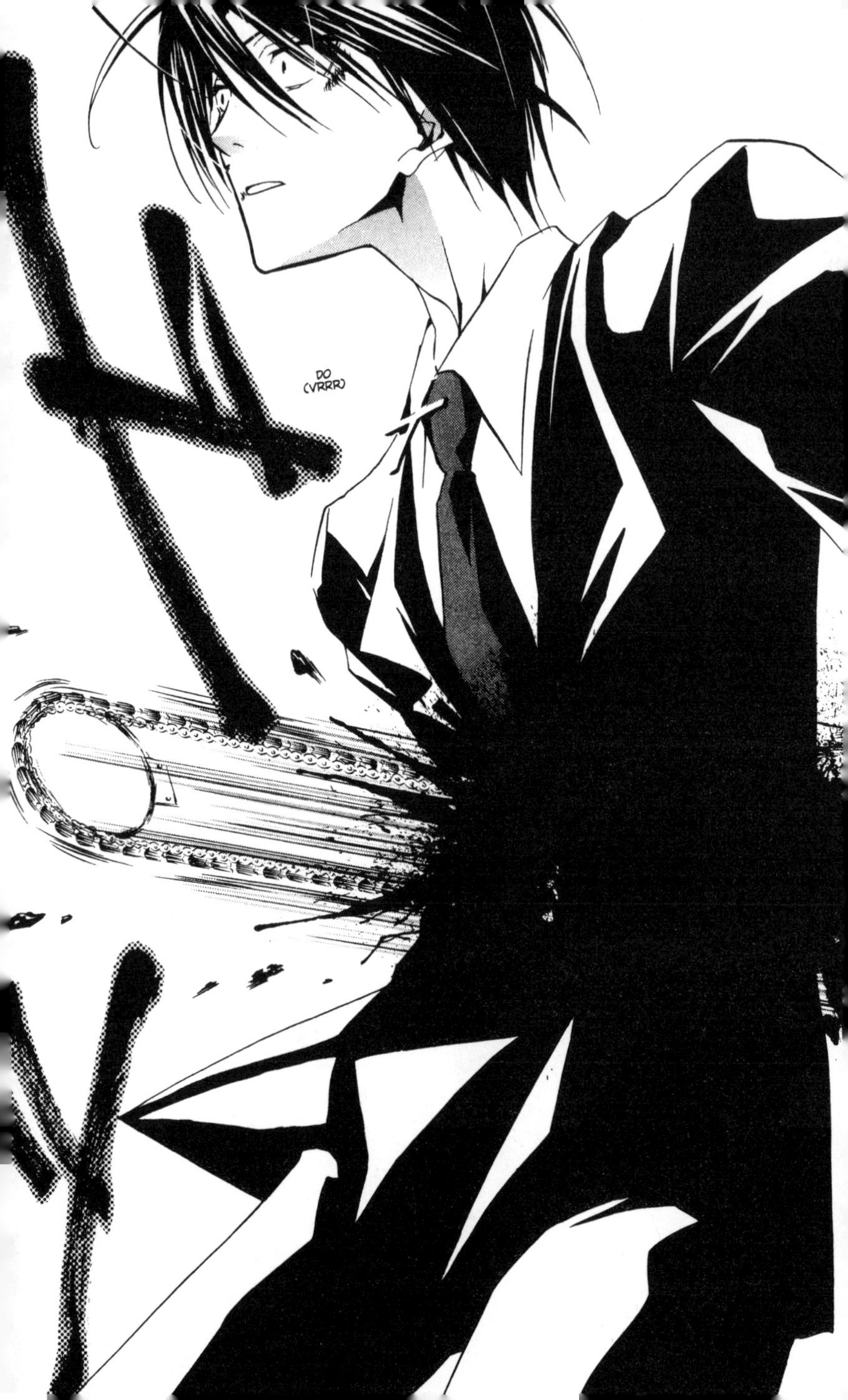
DO
(VRRR)

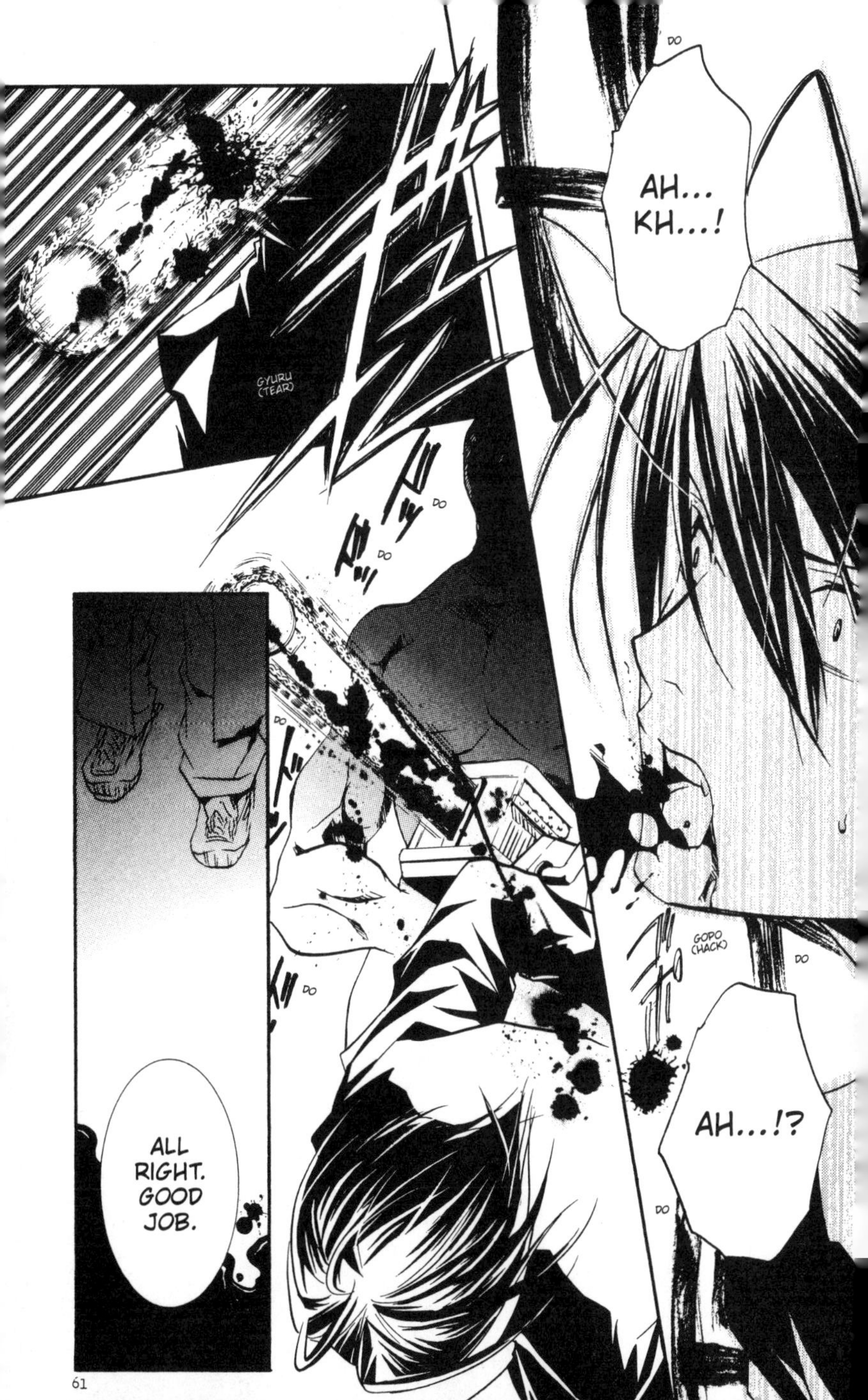
DO
AH... KH...!
GYURU (TEAR)
DO
DO
GOPO (HACK)
DO
AH...!?
DO
DO
DO
ALL RIGHT. GOOD JOB.

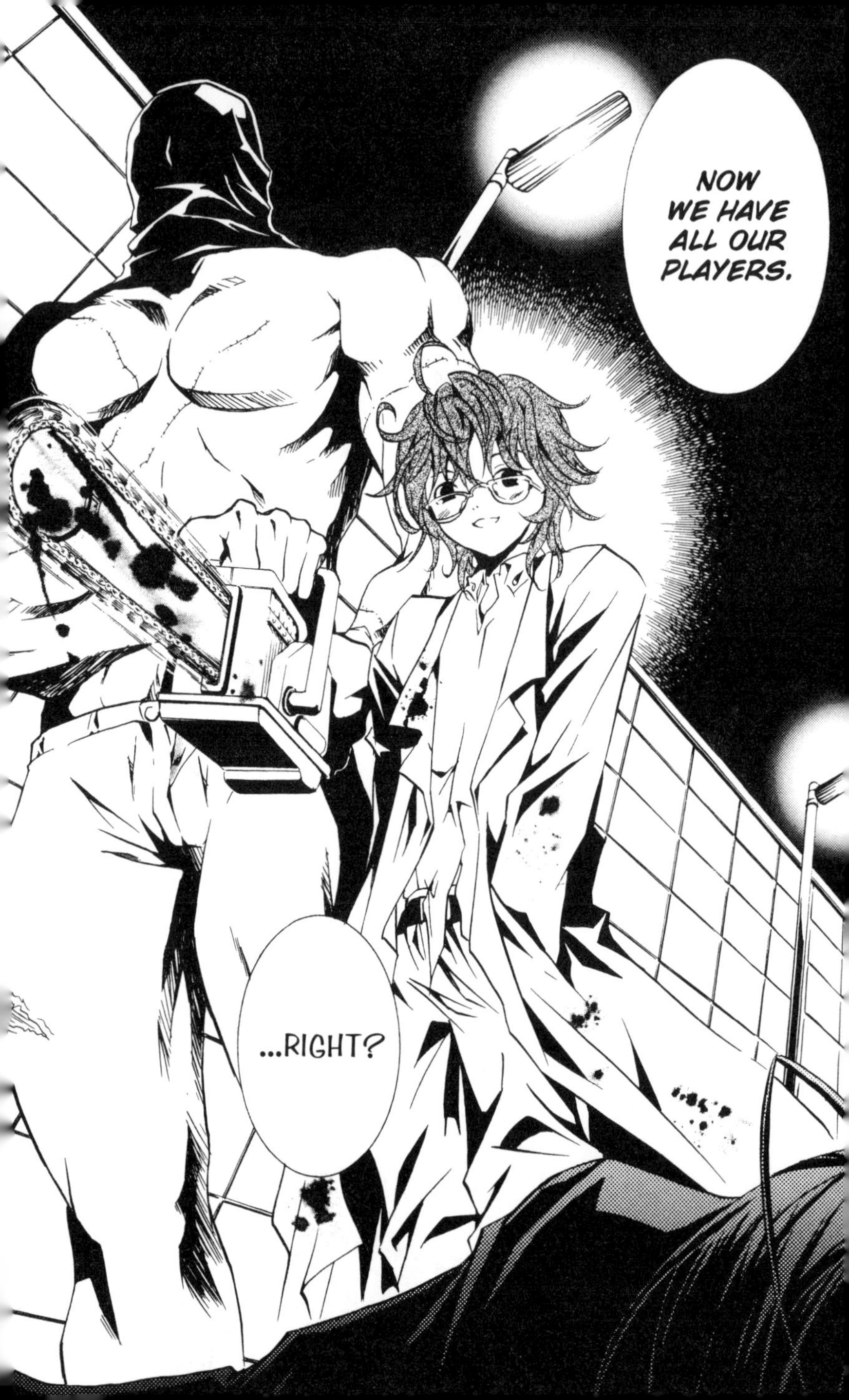
NOW WE HAVE ALL OUR PLAYERS.
...RIGHT?

PAYMENT:22

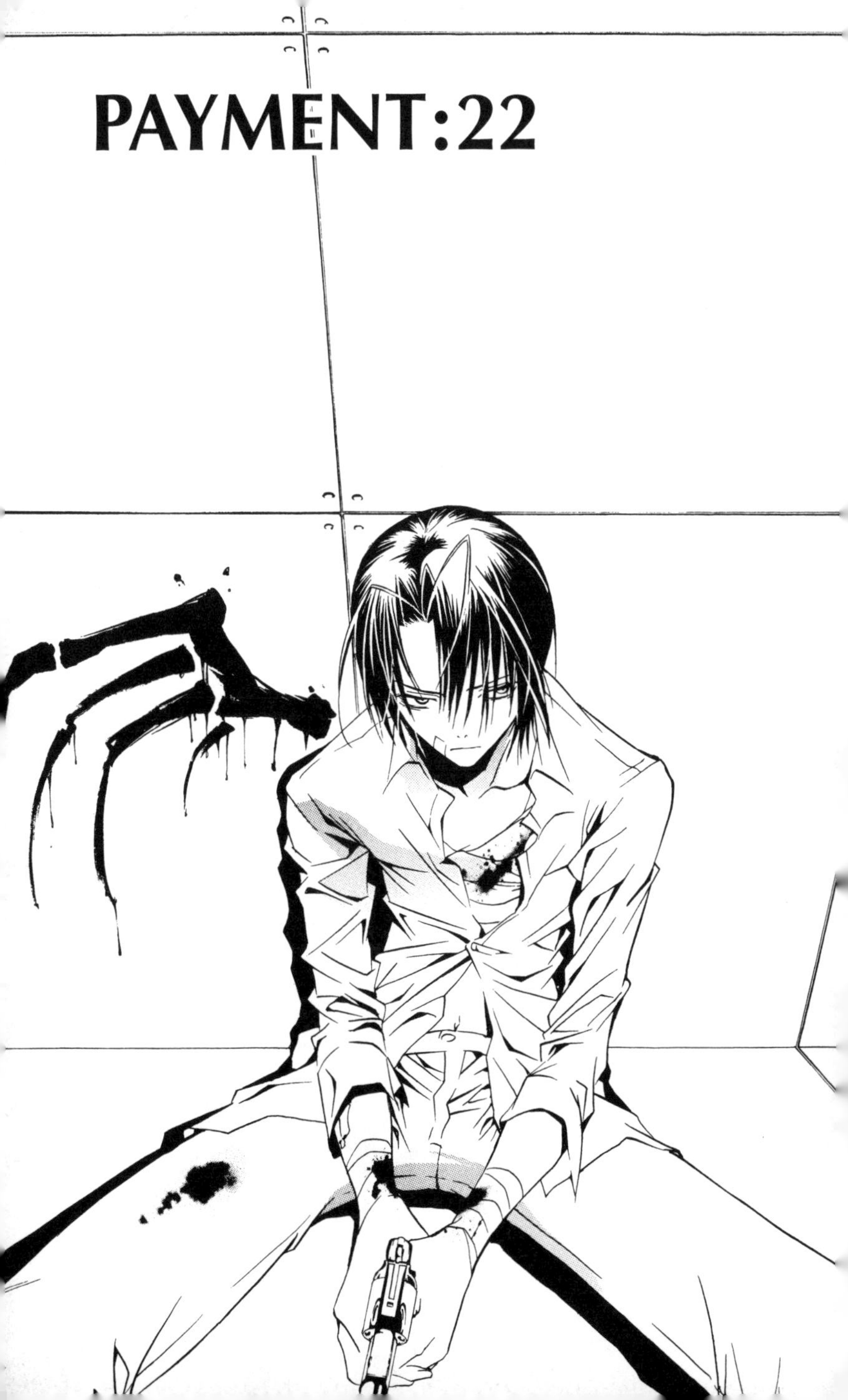

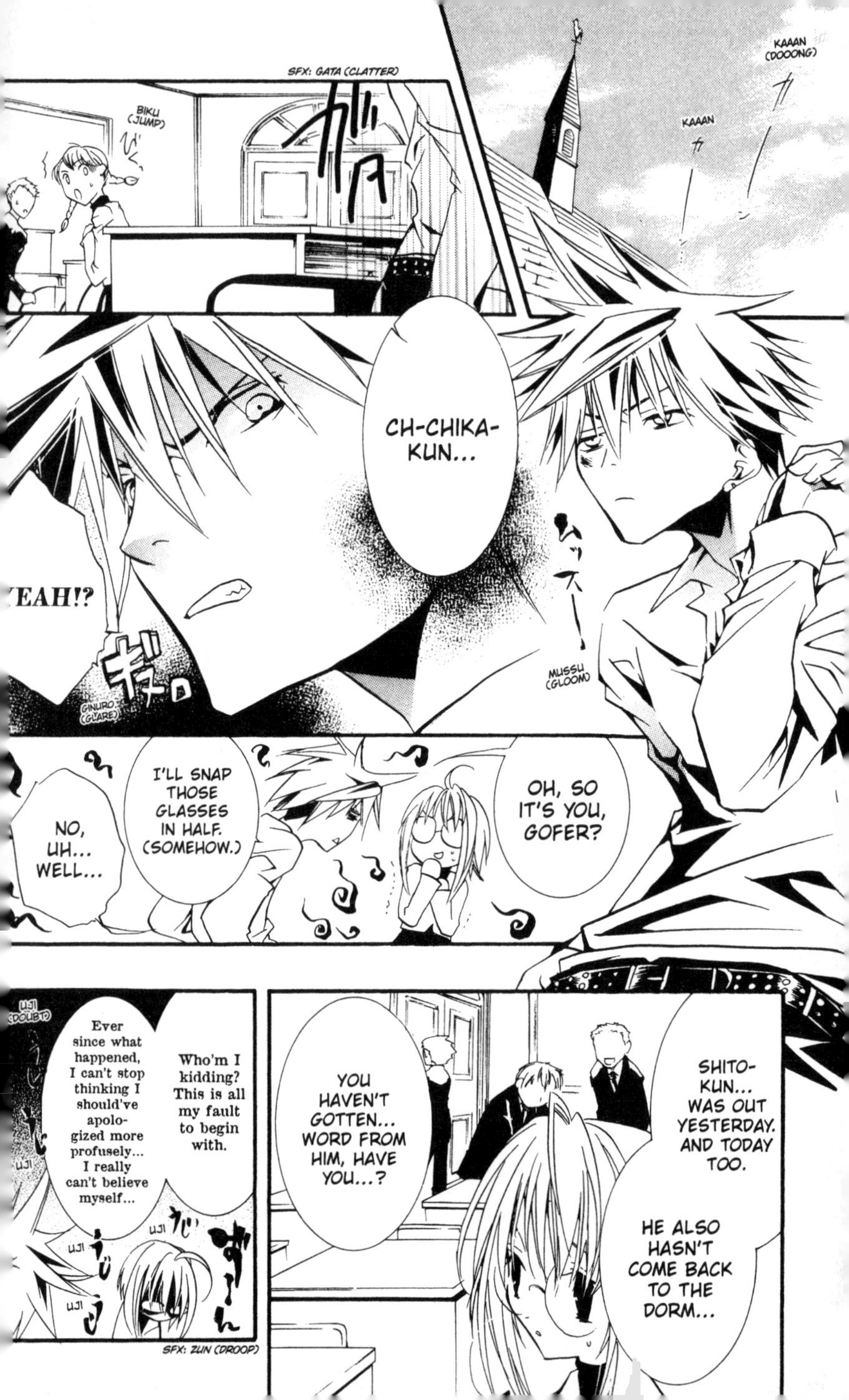
KAAAN (DOOONG)
KAAAN
SFX: GATA (CLATTER)
BIKU (JUMP)
MUSSU (GLOOM)
CH-CHIKA-KUN...
YEAH!?
GINURO (GLARE)
OH, SO IT'S YOU, GOFER?
I'LL SNAP THOSE GLASSES IN HALF. (SOMEHOW.)
NO, UH... WELL...
SHITO-KUN... WAS OUT YESTERDAY. AND TODAY TOO.
HE ALSO HASN'T COME BACK TO THE DORM...
YOU HAVEN'T GOTTEN... WORD FROM HIM, HAVE YOU...?
UJI (DOUBT)
Who'm I kidding? This is all my fault to begin with.
Ever since what happened, I can't stop thinking I should've apologized more profusely... I really can't believe myself...
UJI
UJI
UJI
UJI
SFX: ZUN (DROOP)

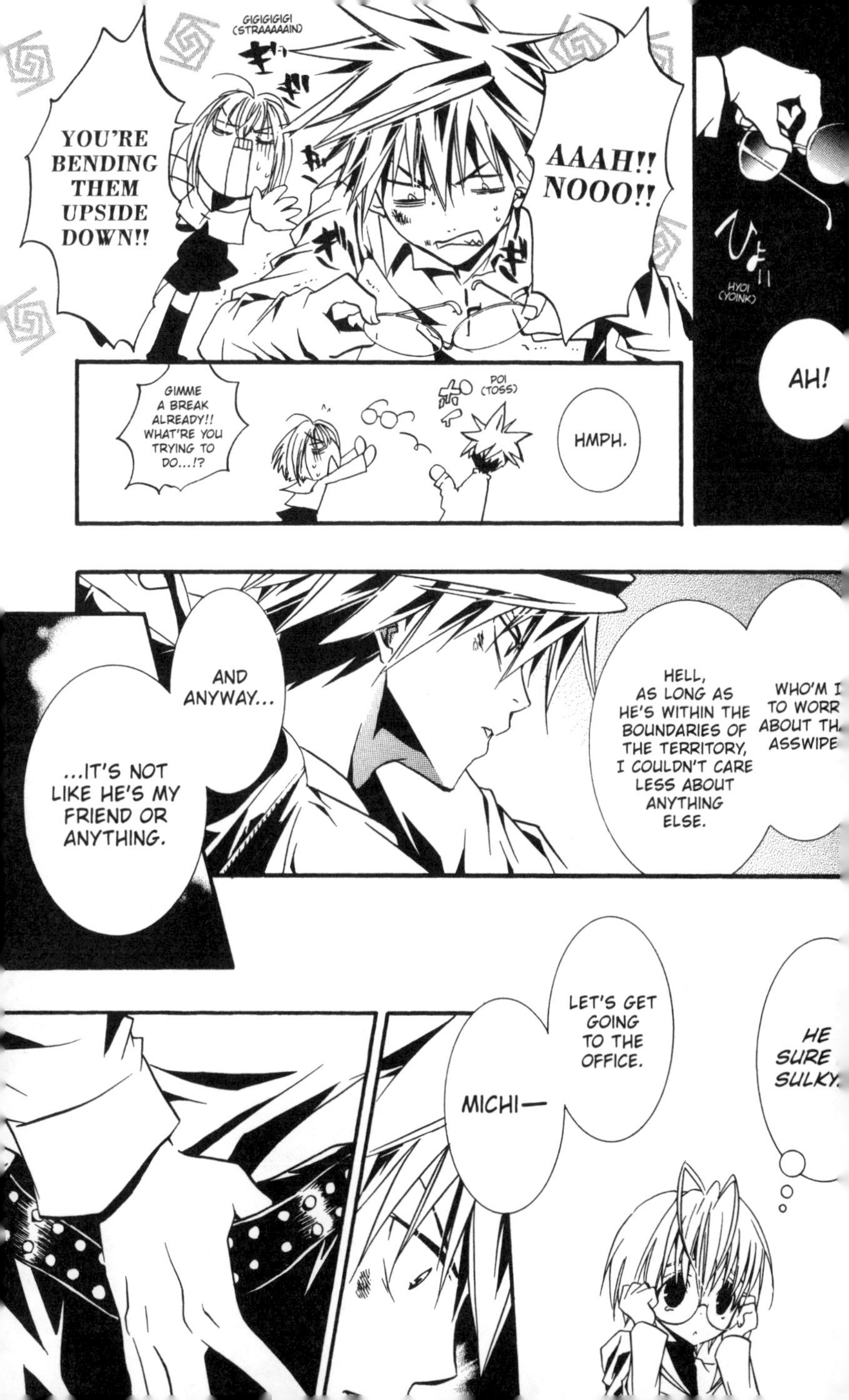
HYOI (YOINK)
AH!
GIGIGIGIGI (STRAAAAAIN)
AAAH!! NOOO!!
YOU'RE BENDING THEM UPSIDE DOWN!!
HMPH.
POI (TOSS)
GIMME A BREAK ALREADY!! WHAT'RE YOU TRYING TO DO...!?
WHO'M I TO WORR ABOUT TH ASSWIPE
HELL, AS LONG AS HE'S WITHIN THE BOUNDARIES OF THE TERRITORY, I COULDN'T CARE LESS ABOUT ANYTHING ELSE.
AND ANYWAY...
...IT'S NOT LIKE HE'S MY FRIEND OR ANYTHING.
HE SURE SULKY.
LET'S GET GOING TO THE OFFICE.
MICHI—

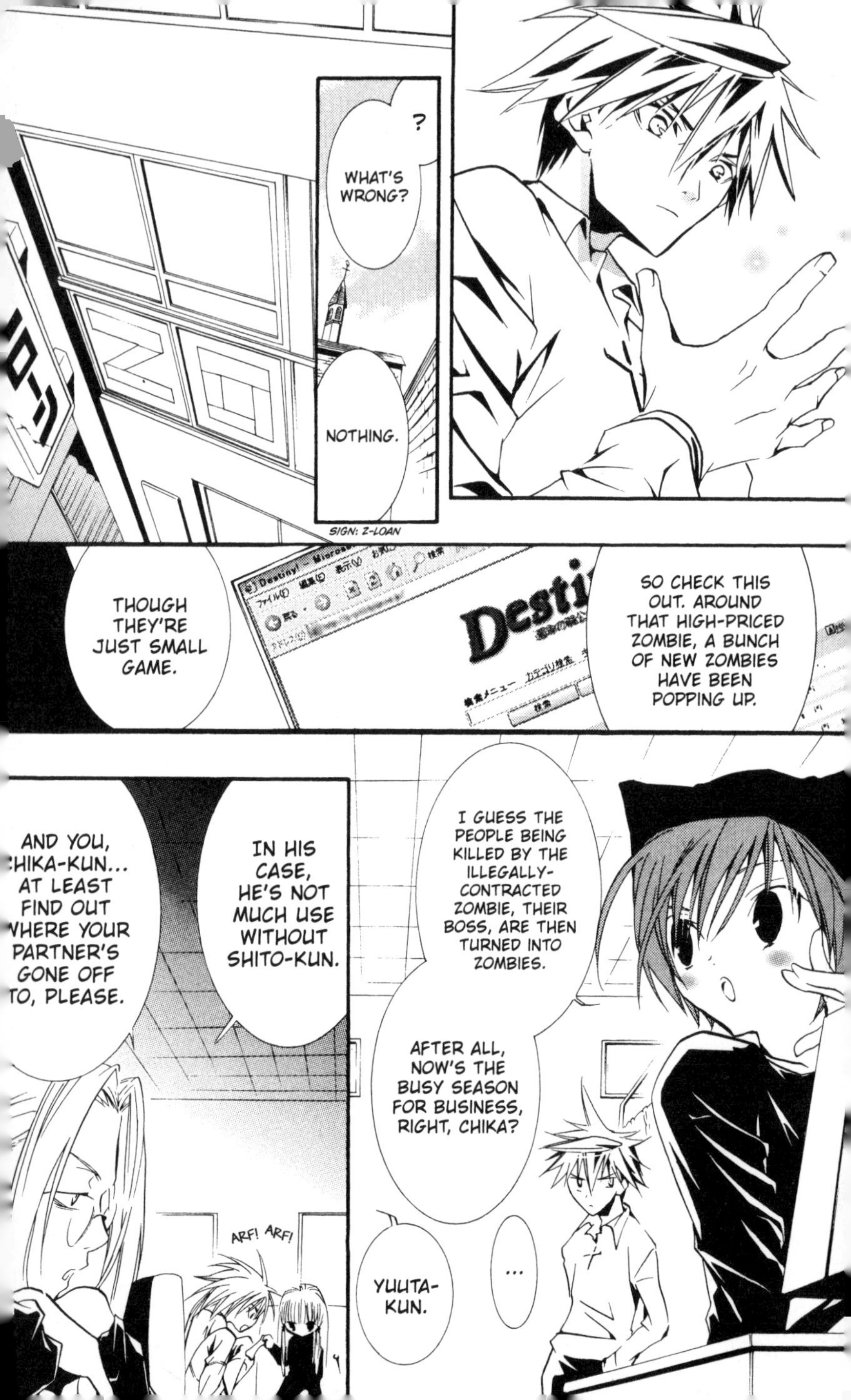
?
WHAT'S WRONG?
NOTHING.
SIGN: Z-LOAN
SO CHECK THIS OUT. AROUND THAT HIGH-PRICED ZOMBIE, A BUNCH OF NEW ZOMBIES HAVE BEEN POPPING UP.
THOUGH THEY'RE JUST SMALL GAME.
I GUESS THE PEOPLE BEING KILLED BY THE ILLEGALLY-CONTRACTED ZOMBIE, THEIR BOSS, ARE THEN TURNED INTO ZOMBIES.
AFTER ALL, NOW'S THE BUSY SEASON FOR BUSINESS, RIGHT, CHIKA?
...
YUUTA-KUN.
IN HIS CASE, HE'S NOT MUCH USE WITHOUT SHITO-KUN.
AND YOU, HIKA-KUN... AT LEAST FIND OUT HERE YOUR PARTNER'S GONE OFF O, PLEASE.
ARF! ARF!

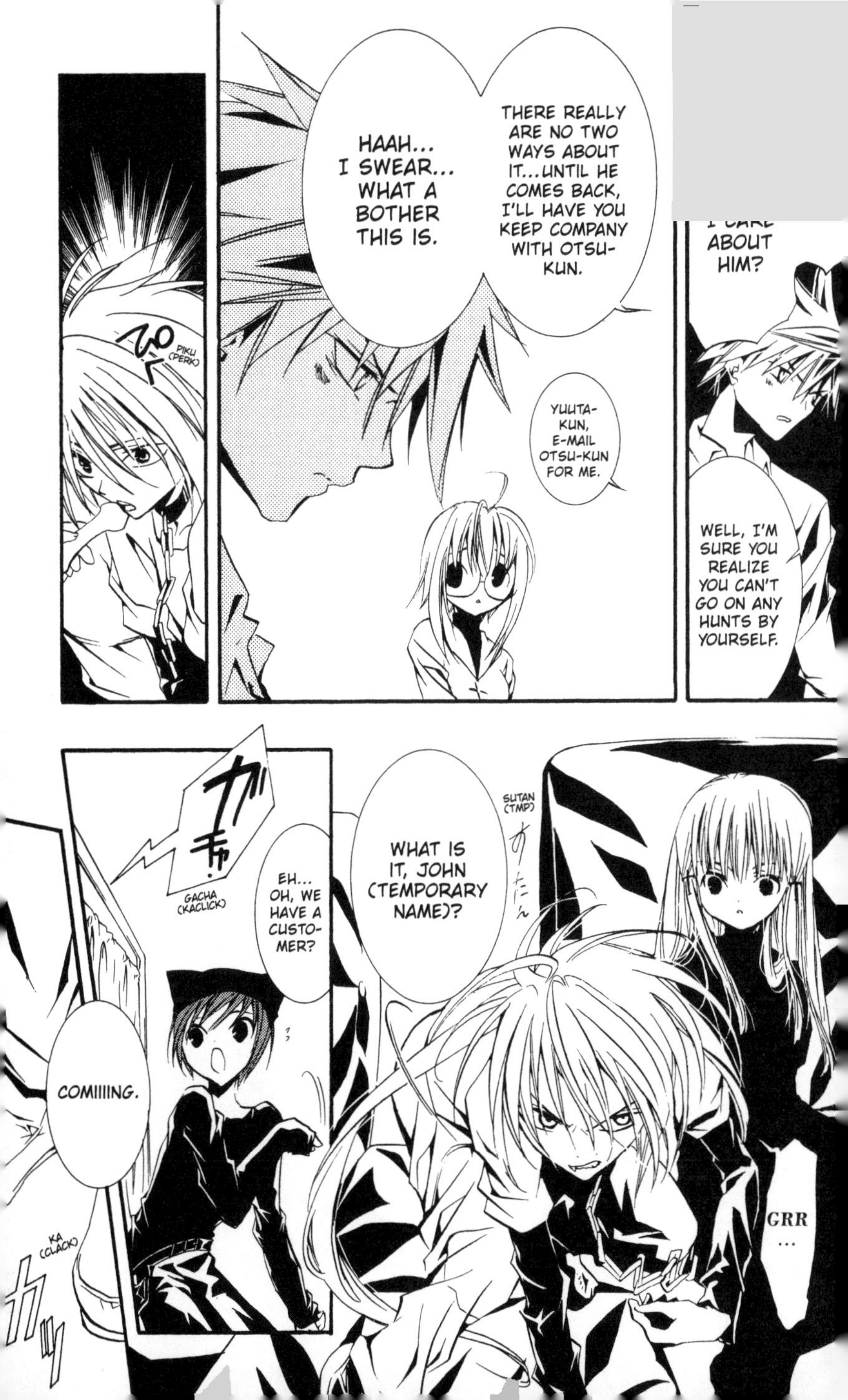
ABOUT HIM?
WELL, I'M SURE YOU REALIZE YOU CAN'T GO ON ANY HUNTS BY YOURSELF.
THERE REALLY ARE NO TWO WAYS ABOUT IT...UNTIL HE COMES BACK, I'LL HAVE YOU KEEP COMPANY WITH OTSU-KUN.
HAAH... I SWEAR... WHAT A BOTHER THIS IS.
YUUTA-KUN, E-MAIL OTSU-KUN FOR ME.
PIKU (PERK)
SUTAN (TMP)
WHAT IS IT, JOHN (TEMPORARY NAME)?
GRR...
GACHA (KACLICK)
EH... OH, WE HAVE A CUSTOMER?
COMIIIING.
KA (CLACK)

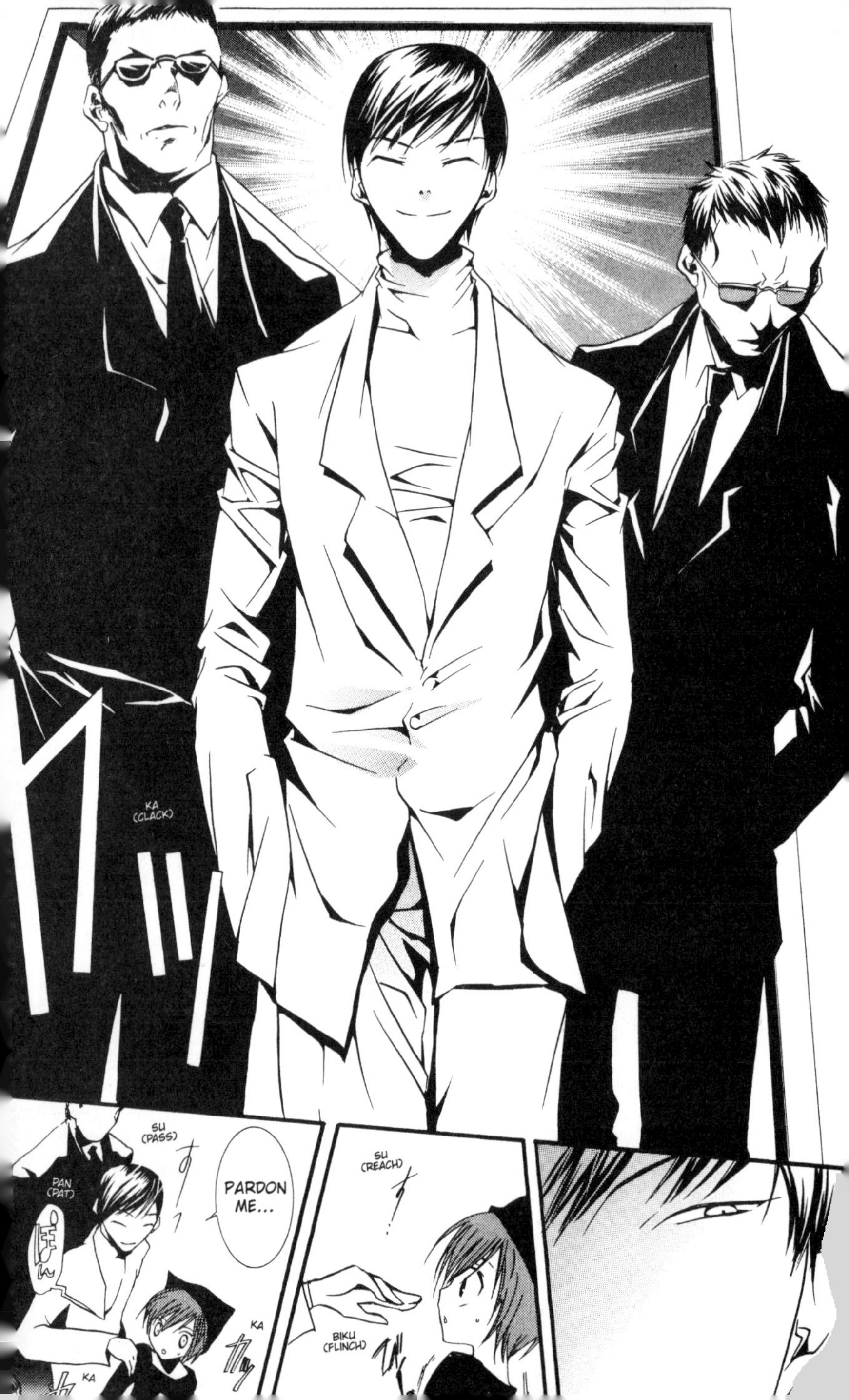
KA
(CLACK)
SU
(REACH)
BIKU
(FLINCH)
SU
(PASS)
PARDON ME...
PAN
(PAT)
KA
KA

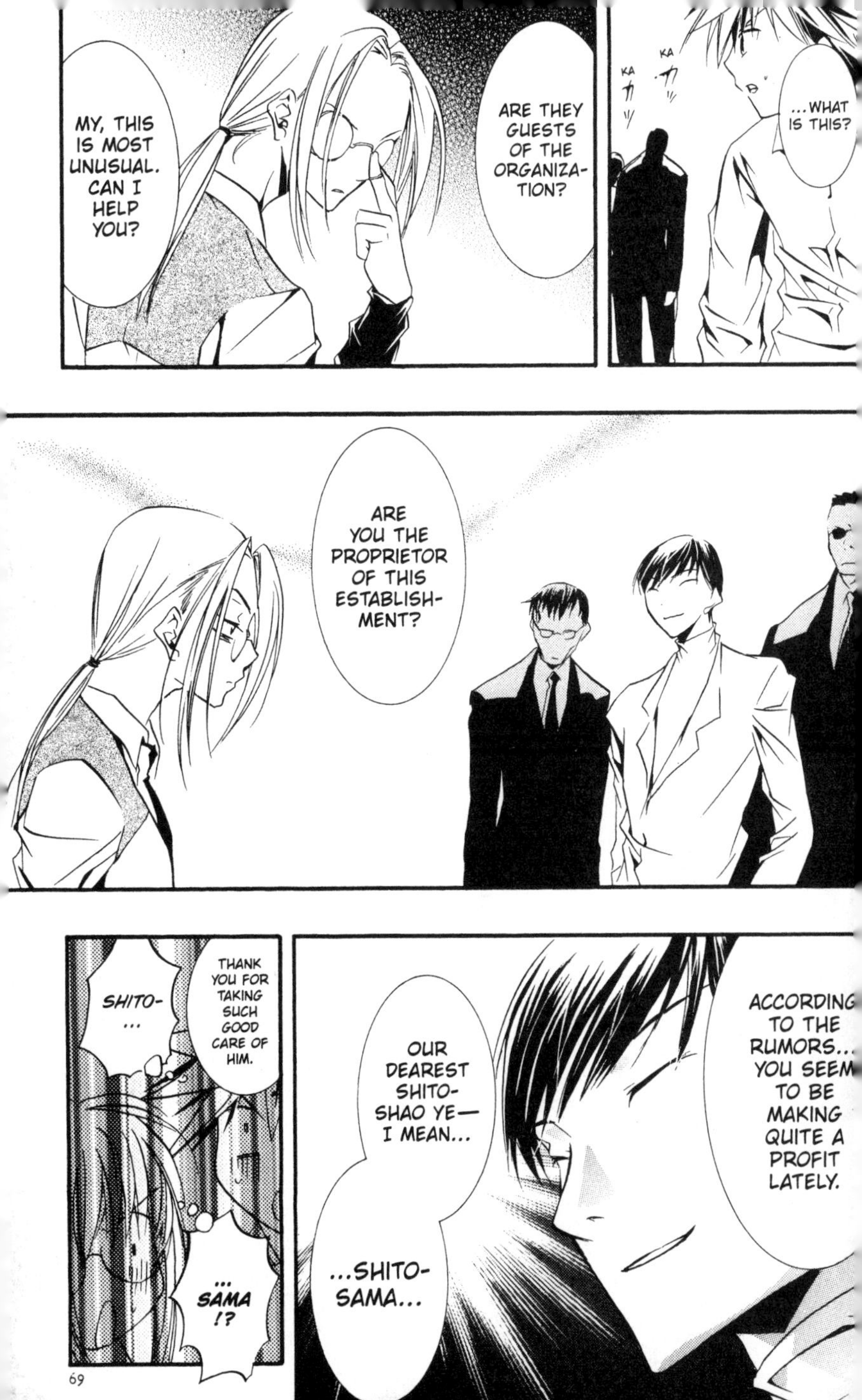
KA KA
...WHAT IS THIS?
ARE THEY GUESTS OF THE ORGANIZATION?
MY, THIS IS MOST UNUSUAL. CAN I HELP YOU?
ARE YOU THE PROPRIETOR OF THIS ESTABLISHMENT?
ACCORDING TO THE RUMORS... YOU SEEM TO BE MAKING QUITE A PROFIT LATELY.
OUR DEAREST SHITO-SHAO YE— I MEAN...
...SHITO-SAMA...
THANK YOU FOR TAKING SUCH GOOD CARE OF HIM.
SHITO-...
...SAMA!?

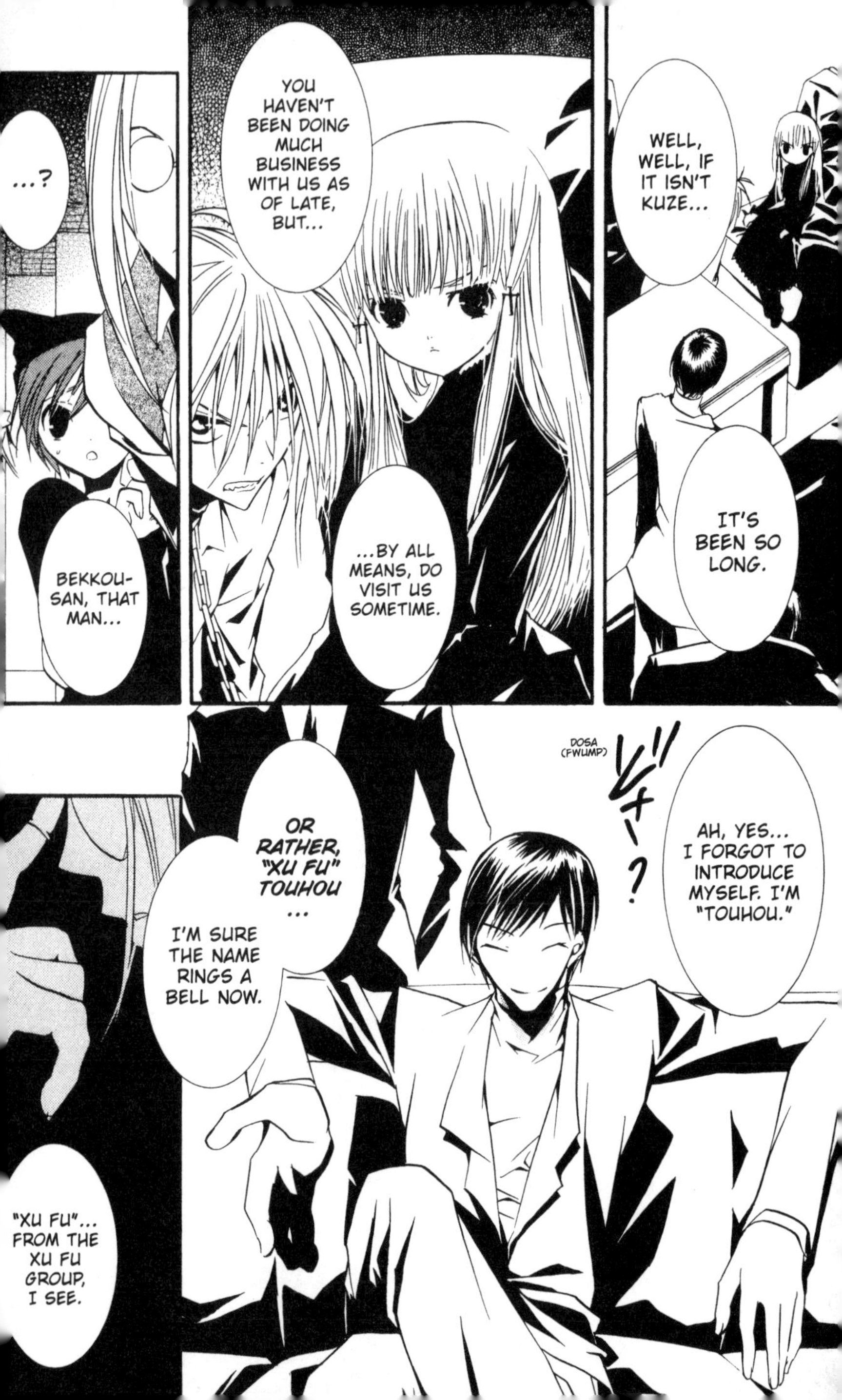
WELL, WELL, IF IT ISN'T KUZE...
IT'S BEEN SO LONG.
YOU HAVEN'T BEEN DOING MUCH BUSINESS WITH US AS OF LATE, BUT...
...BY ALL MEANS, DO VISIT US SOMETIME.
...?
BEKKOU-SAN, THAT MAN...
DOSA (FWUMP)
?
AH, YES... I FORGOT TO INTRODUCE MYSELF. I'M "TOUHOU."
OR RATHER, "XU FU" TOUHOU ...
I'M SURE THE NAME RINGS A BELL NOW.
"XU FU"... FROM THE XU FU GROUP, I SEE.

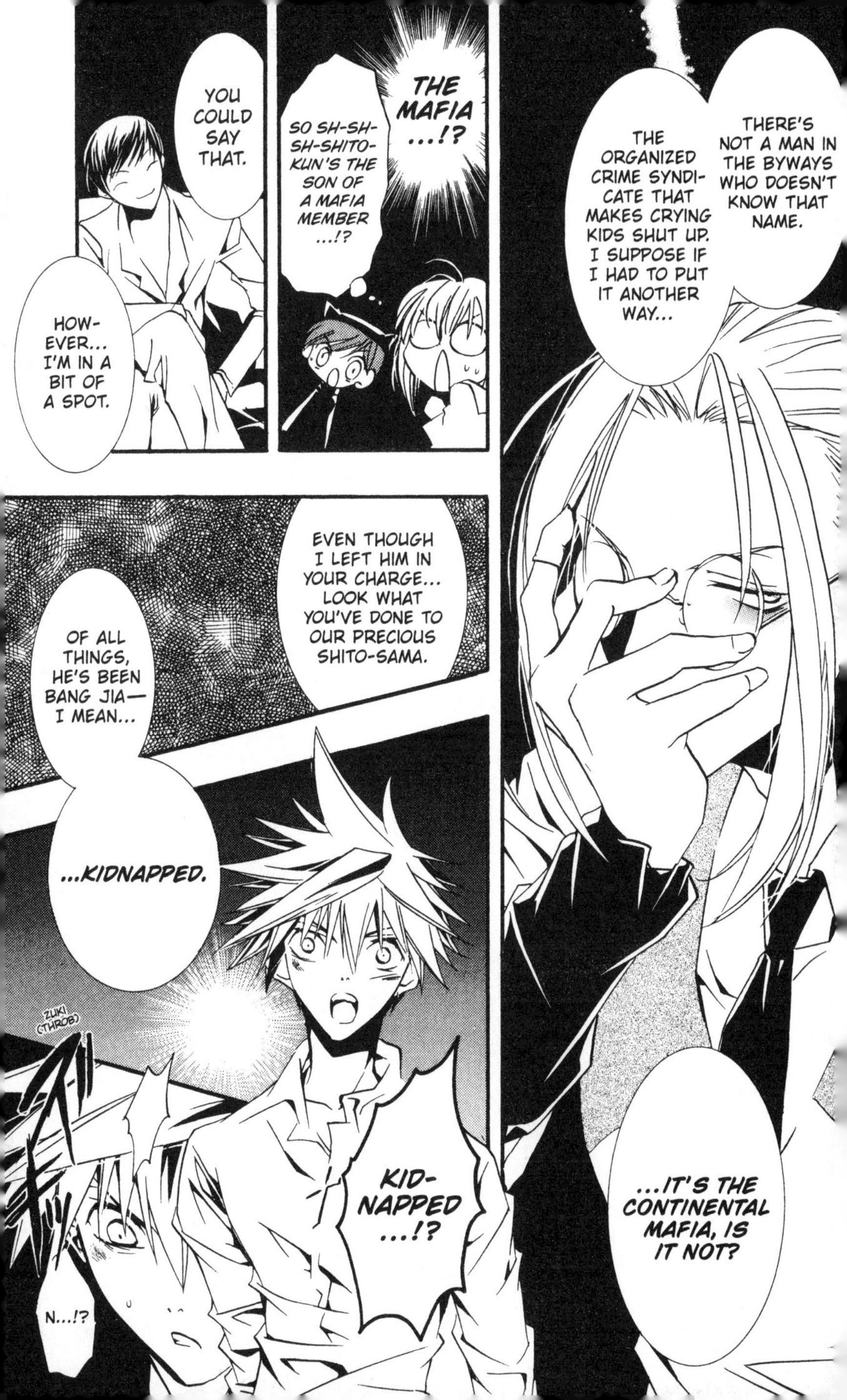
THERE'S NOT A MAN IN THE BYWAYS WHO DOESN'T KNOW THAT NAME.
THE ORGANIZED CRIME SYNDICATE THAT MAKES CRYING KIDS SHUT UP. I SUPPOSE IF I HAD TO PUT IT ANOTHER WAY...
...IT'S THE CONTINENTAL MAFIA, IS IT NOT?
THE MAFIA ...!?
SO SH-SH-SH-SHITO-KUN'S THE SON OF A MAFIA MEMBER ...!?
YOU COULD SAY THAT.
HOW-EVER... I'M IN A BIT OF A SPOT.
EVEN THOUGH I LEFT HIM IN YOUR CHARGE... LOOK WHAT YOU'VE DONE TO OUR PRECIOUS SHITO-SAMA.
OF ALL THINGS, HE'S BEEN BANG JIA— I MEAN...
...KIDNAPPED.
KID-NAPPED ...!?
ZUKI (THROB)
N...!?

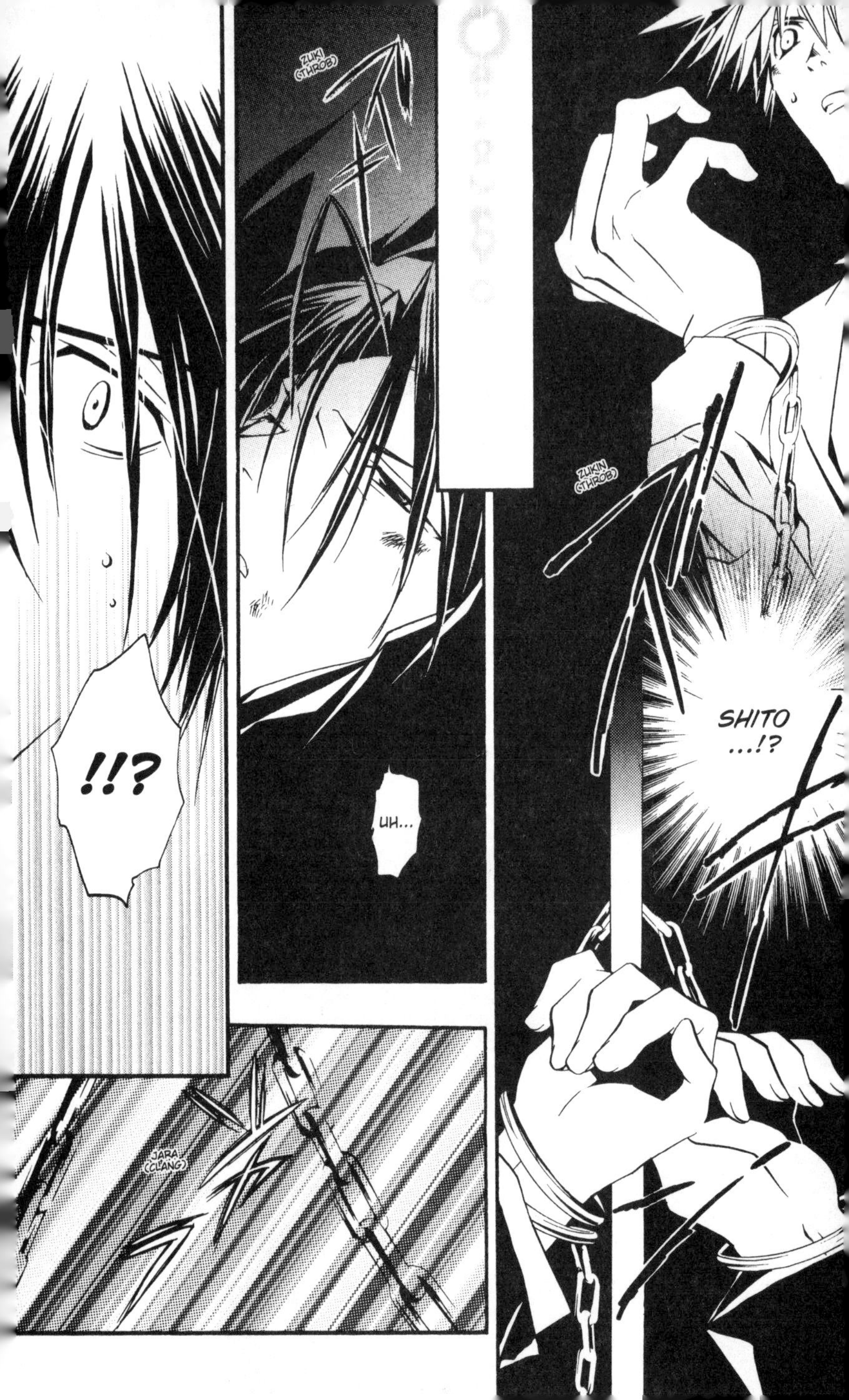
ZUKIN (THROB)
SHITO ...!?
ZUKI (THROB)
UH...
!!?
JARA (CLANG)

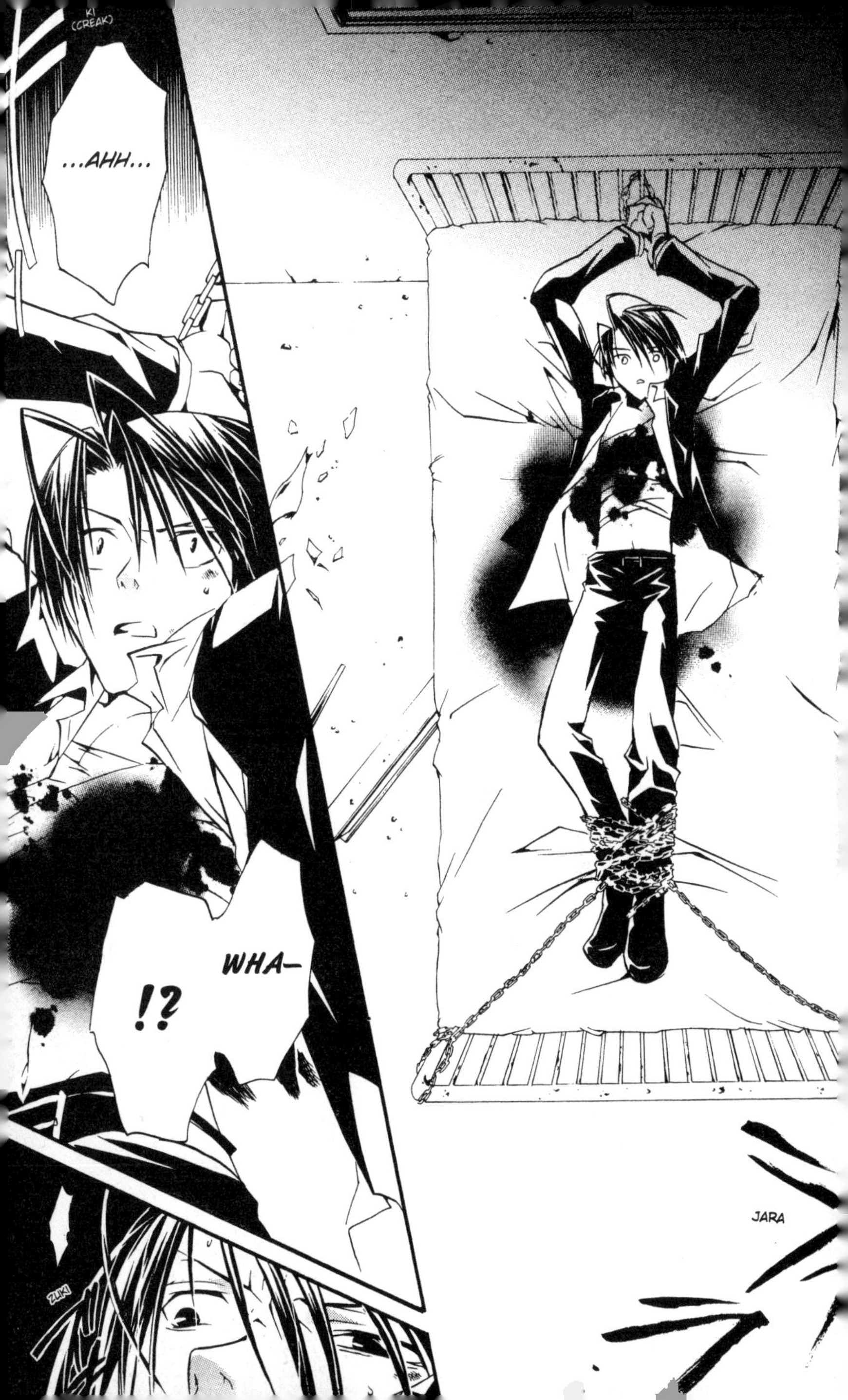
JARA
KI (CREAK)
...AHH...
WHA-
!?
ZUKI

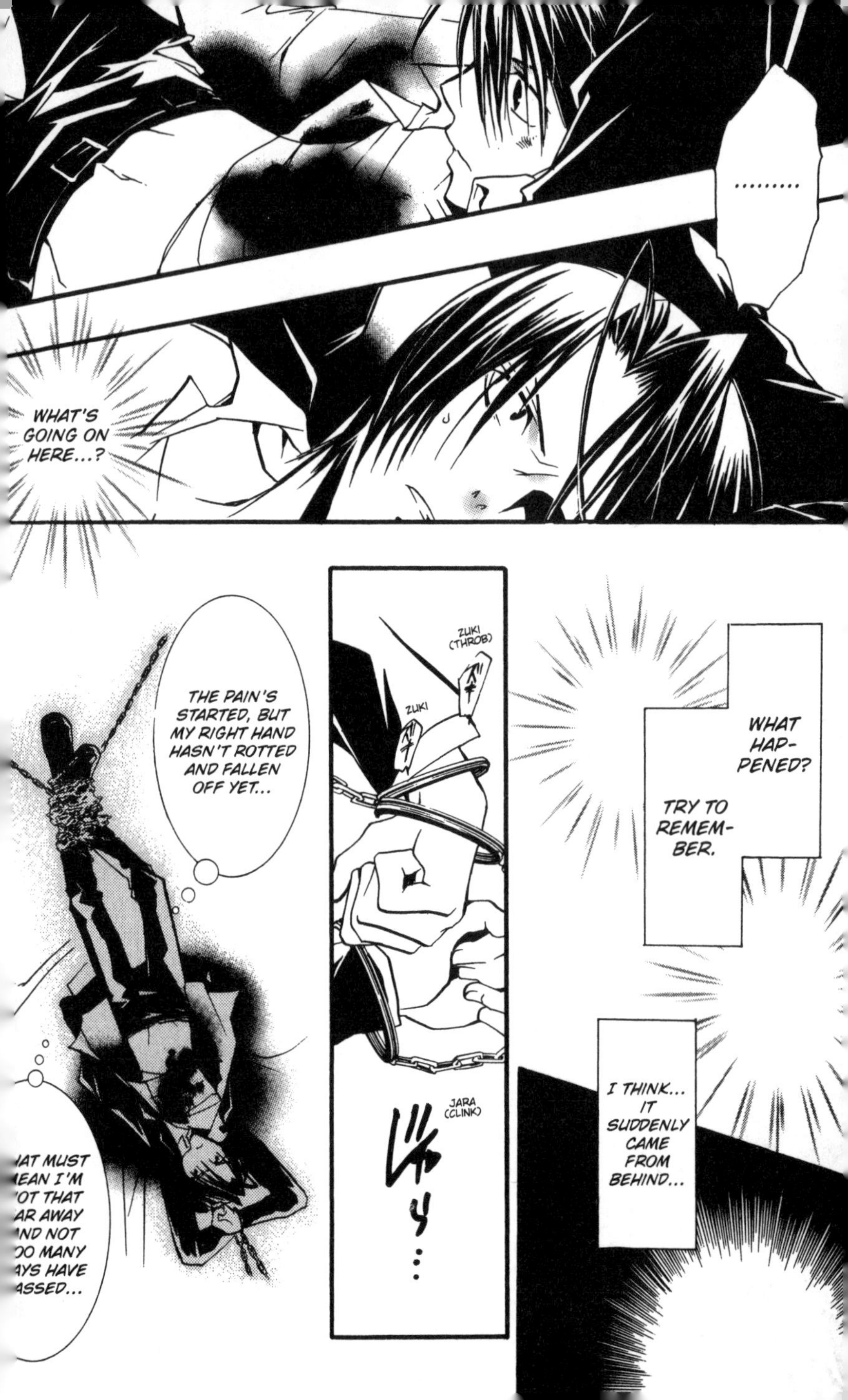
....
WHAT'S GOING ON HERE...?
WHAT HAPPENED?
TRY TO REMEMBER.
I THINK... IT SUDDENLY CAME FROM BEHIND...
ZUKI (THROB)
ZUKI
JARA (CLINK)
THE PAIN'S STARTED, BUT MY RIGHT HAND HASN'T ROTTED AND FALLEN OFF YET...
HAT MUST EAN I'M OT THAT AR AWAY ND NOT OO MANY AYS HAVE ASSED...

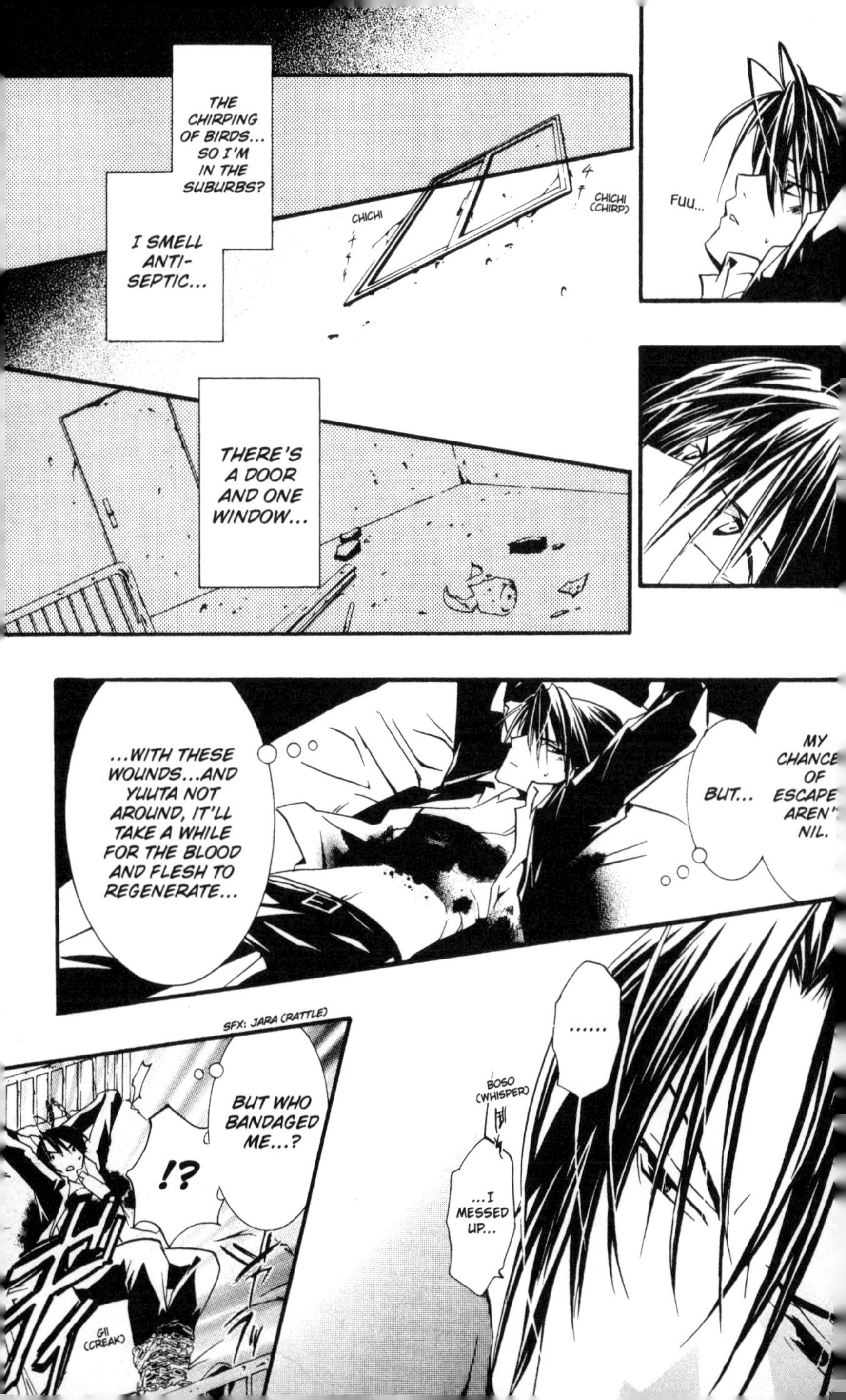
FUU...
THE CHIRPING OF BIRDS... SO I'M IN THE SUBURBS?
CHICHI (CHIRP)
CHICHI
I SMELL ANTI-SEPTIC...
THERE'S A DOOR AND ONE WINDOW...
MY CHANCE OF ESCAPE AREN'T NIL.
BUT...
...WITH THESE WOUNDS...AND YUUTA NOT AROUND, IT'LL TAKE A WHILE FOR THE BLOOD AND FLESH TO REGENERATE...
......
BOSO (WHISPER)
...I MESSED UP...
SFX: JARA (RATTLE)
BUT WHO BANDAGED ME...?
!?
GII (CREAK)

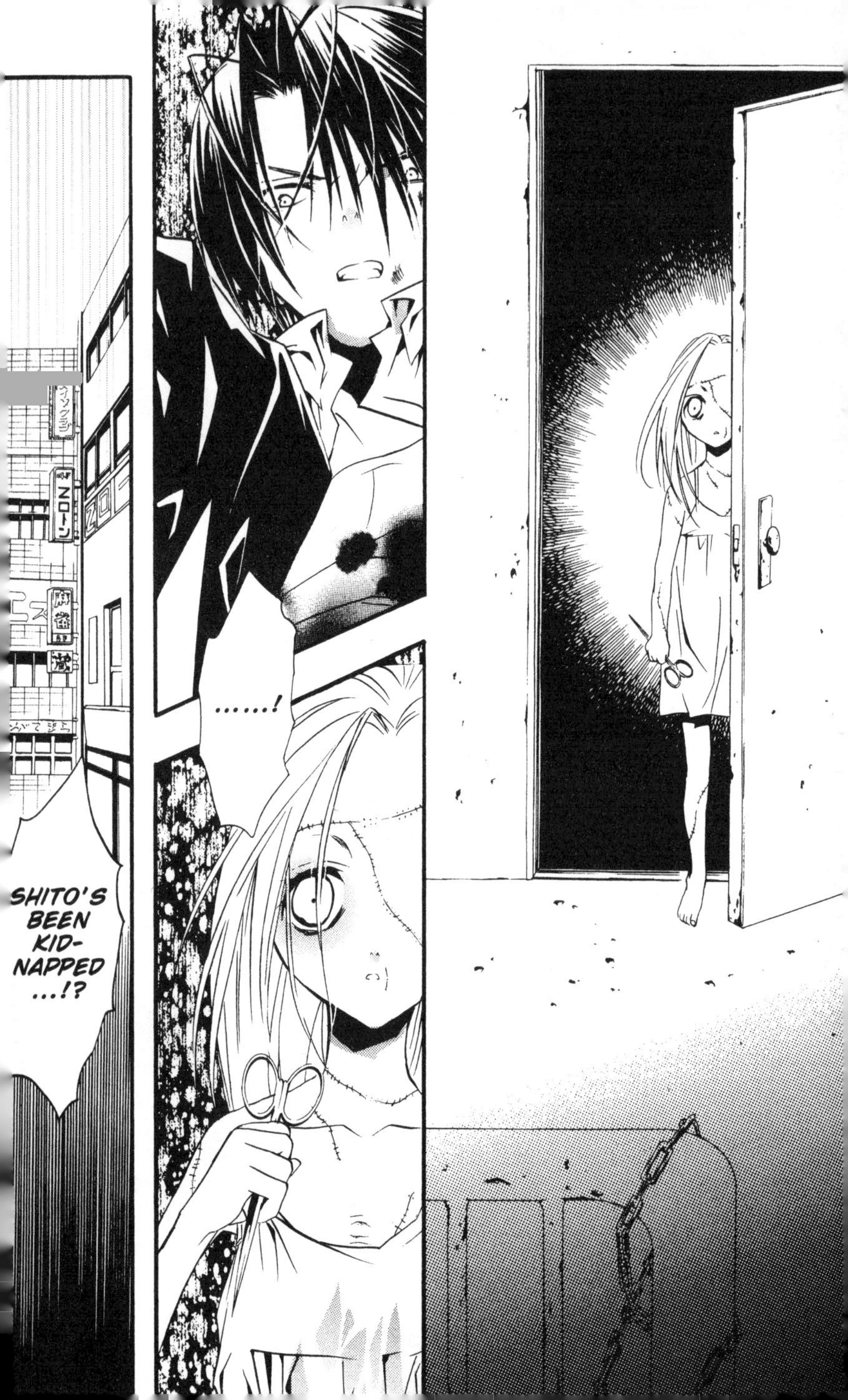
......!
SHITO'S BEEN KID-NAPPED ...!?

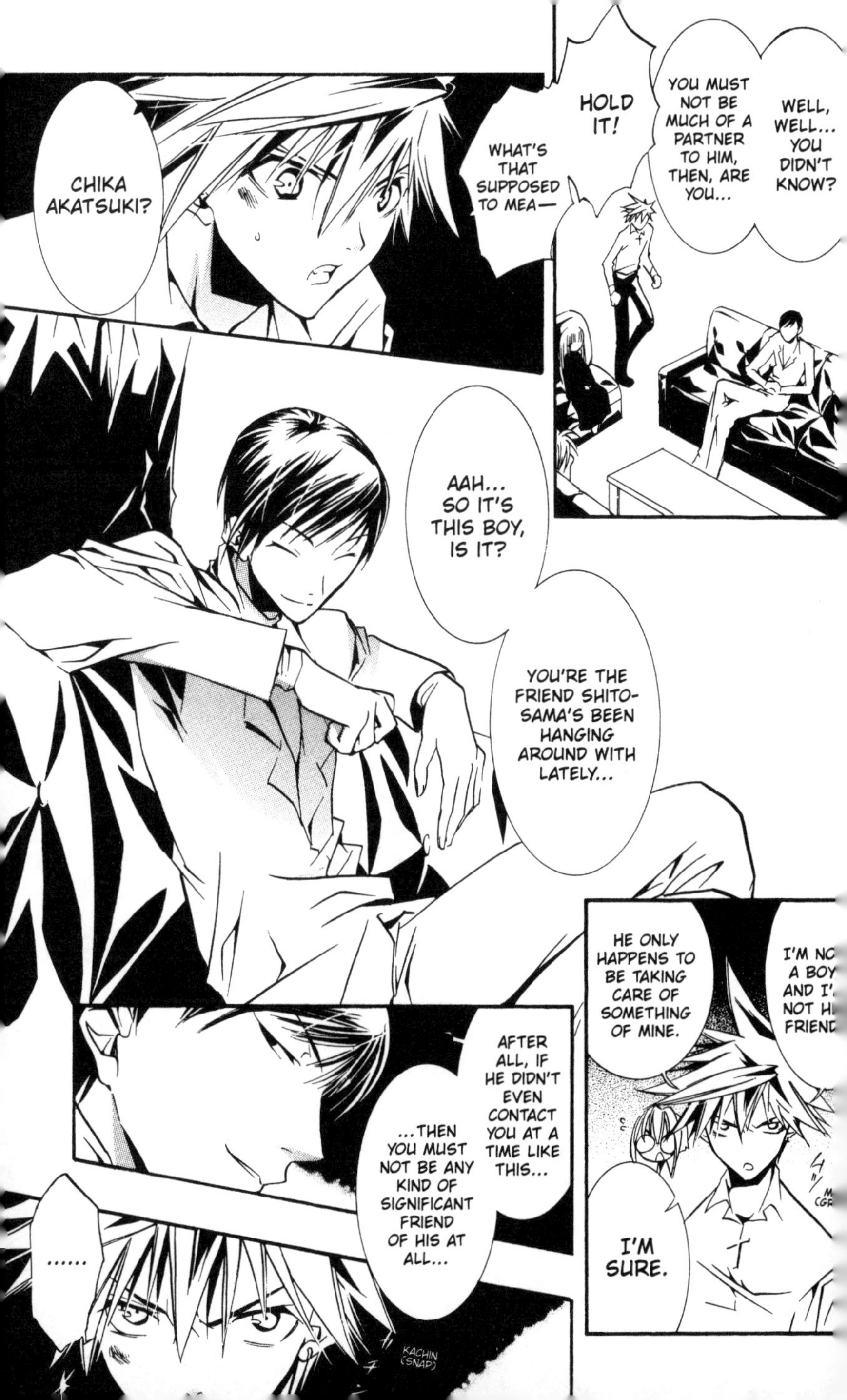
WELL, WELL... YOU DIDN'T KNOW?
YOU MUST NOT BE MUCH OF A PARTNER TO HIM, THEN, ARE YOU...
HOLD IT!
WHAT'S THAT SUPPOSED TO MEA—
CHIKA AKATSUKI?
AAH... SO IT'S THIS BOY, IS IT?
YOU'RE THE FRIEND SHITO-SAMA'S BEEN HANGING AROUND WITH LATELY...
I'M NO
A BOY
AND I'
NOT HI
FRIEND
HE ONLY HAPPENS TO BE TAKING CARE OF SOMETHING OF MINE.
I'M SURE.
AFTER ALL, IF HE DIDN'T EVEN CONTACT YOU AT A TIME LIKE THIS...
...THEN YOU MUST NOT BE ANY KIND OF SIGNIFICANT FRIEND OF HIS AT ALL...
......
KACHIN (SNAP)

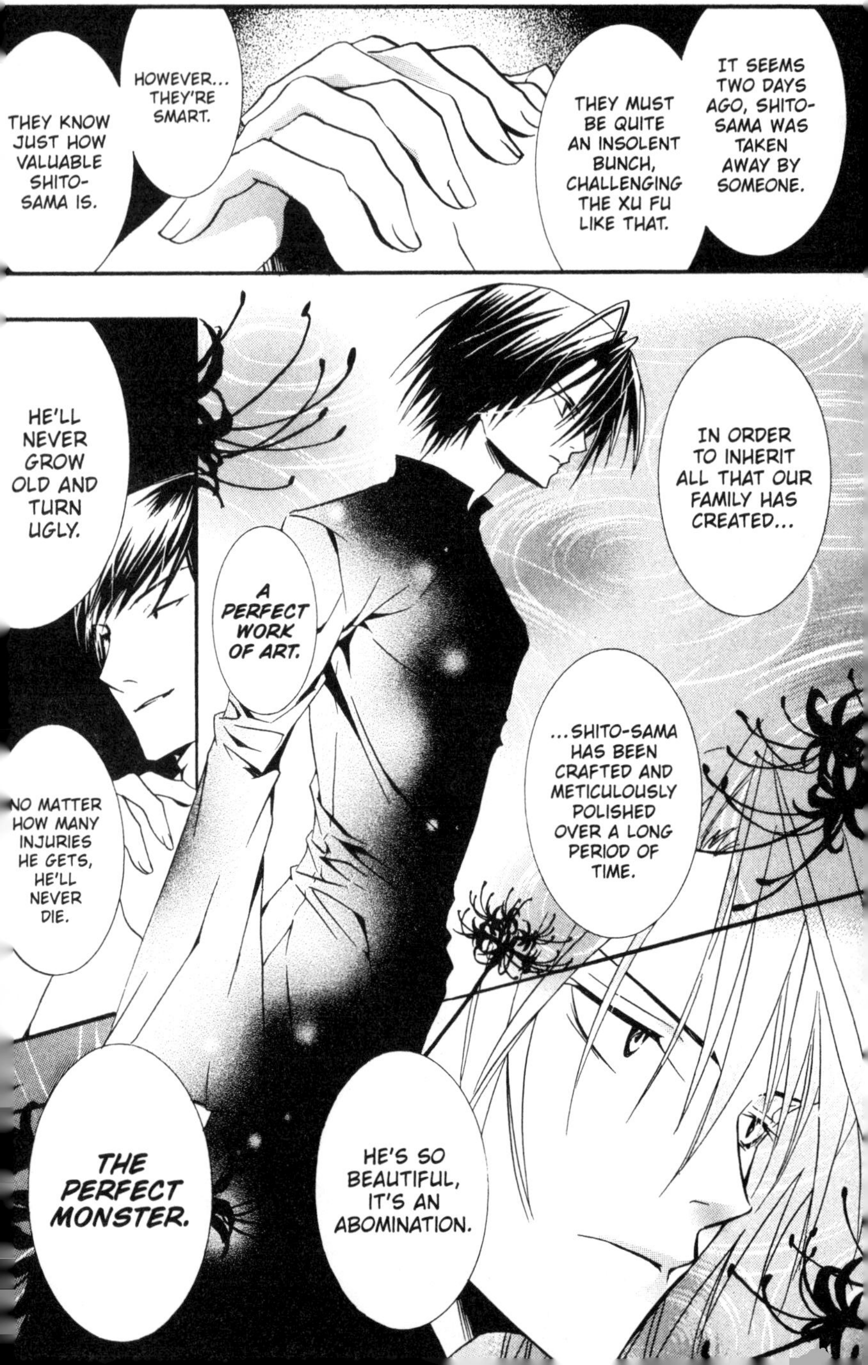
IT SEEMS TWO DAYS AGO, SHITO-SAMA WAS TAKEN AWAY BY SOMEONE.
THEY MUST BE QUITE AN INSOLENT BUNCH, CHALLENGING THE XU FU LIKE THAT.
HOWEVER... THEY'RE SMART.
THEY KNOW JUST HOW VALUABLE SHITO-SAMA IS.
IN ORDER TO INHERIT ALL THAT OUR FAMILY HAS CREATED...
...SHITO-SAMA HAS BEEN CRAFTED AND METICULOUSLY POLISHED OVER A LONG PERIOD OF TIME.
A PERFECT WORK OF ART.
HE'LL NEVER GROW OLD AND TURN UGLY.
NO MATTER HOW MANY INJURIES HE GETS, HE'LL NEVER DIE.
HE'S SO BEAUTIFUL, IT'S AN ABOMINATION.
THE PERFECT MONSTER.

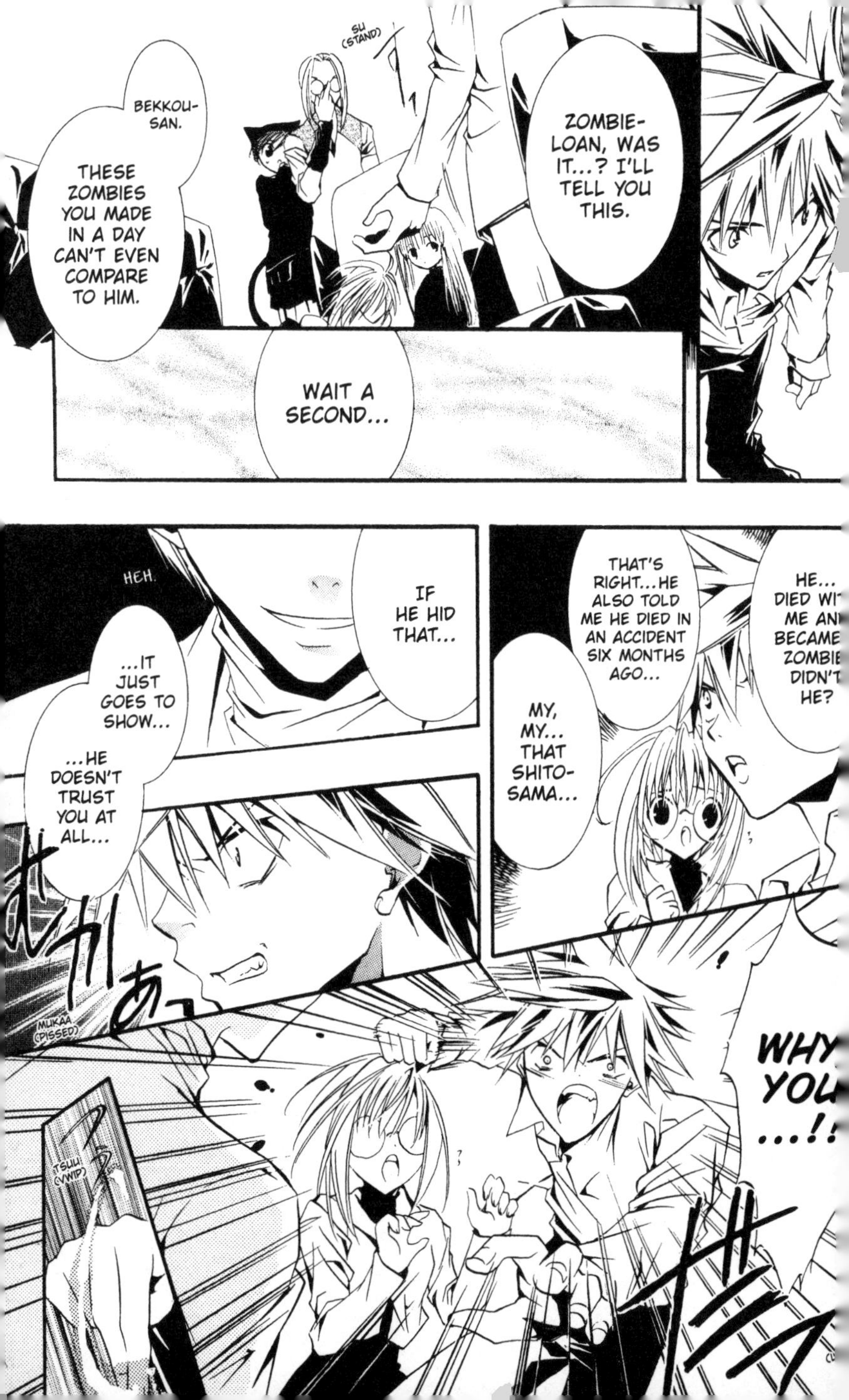
SU (STAND)
ZOMBIE-LOAN, WAS IT...? I'LL TELL YOU THIS.
BEKKOU-SAN.
THESE ZOMBIES YOU MADE IN A DAY CAN'T EVEN COMPARE TO HIM.
WAIT A SECOND...
HE... DIED WIT ME AN BECAME ZOMBIE DIDN'T HE?
THAT'S RIGHT...HE ALSO TOLD ME HE DIED IN AN ACCIDENT SIX MONTHS AGO...
MY, MY... THAT SHITO-SAMA...
HEH.
IF HE HID THAT...
...IT JUST GOES TO SHOW...
...HE DOESN'T TRUST YOU AT ALL...
MUKAA (PISSED)
WHY YOU ...!!
TSUU (VWIP)

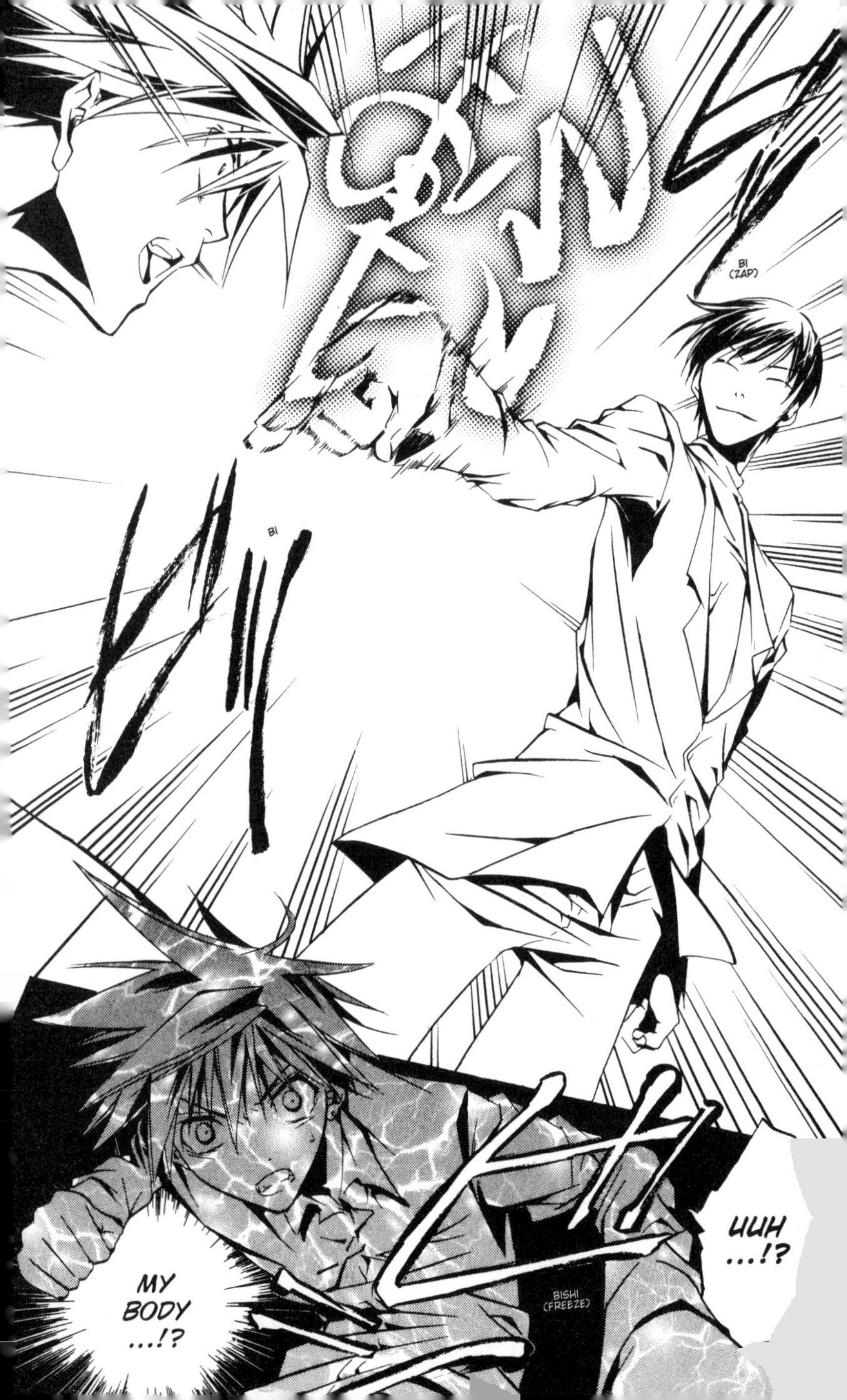
BI
(ZAP)
BI
UUH ...!?
BISHI
(FREEZE)
MY BODY ...!?

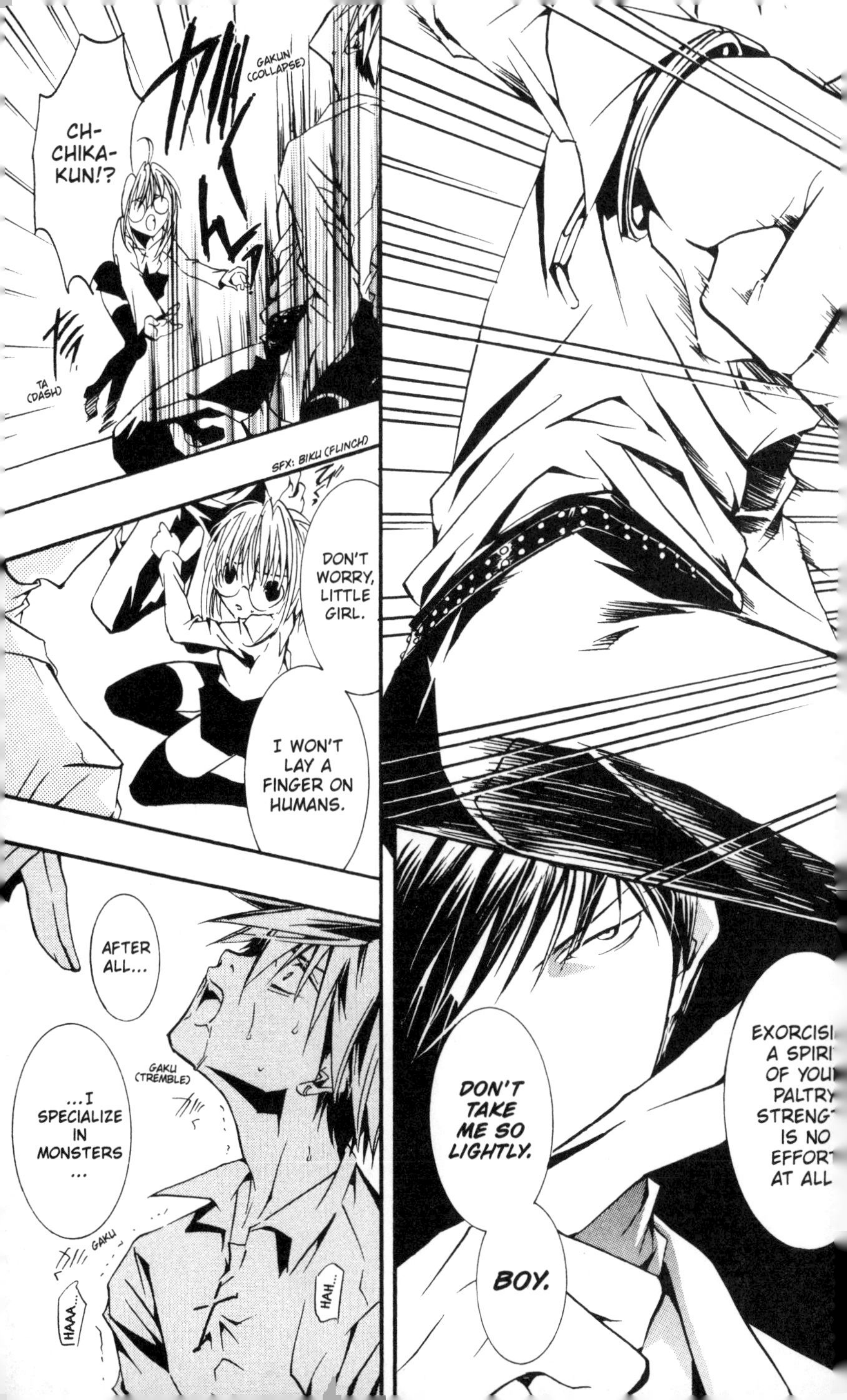
GAKUN (COLLAPSE)
CH-CHIKA-KUN!?
TA (DASH)
SFX: BIKU (FLINCH)
DON'T WORRY, LITTLE GIRL.
I WON'T LAY A FINGER ON HUMANS.
AFTER ALL...
GAKU (TREMBLE)
...I SPECIALIZE IN MONSTERS ...
HAH...
GAKU
HAAA...
EXORCISI A SPIRI OF YOU PALTRY STRENGT IS NO EFFORT AT ALL
DON'T TAKE ME SO LIGHTLY.
BOY.

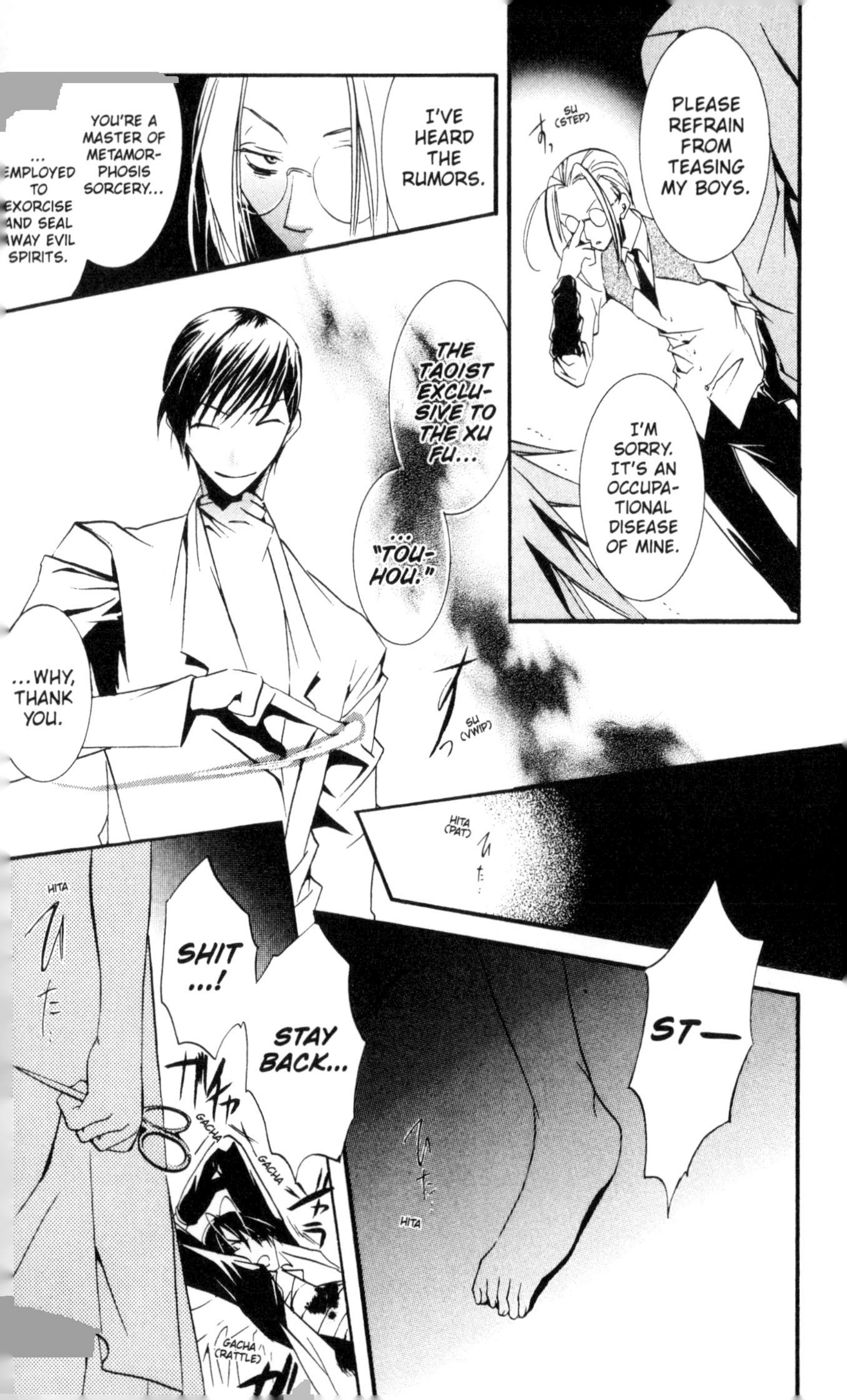
SU (STEP)
PLEASE REFRAIN FROM TEASING MY BOYS.
I'M SORRY. IT'S AN OCCUPATIONAL DISEASE OF MINE.
I'VE HEARD THE RUMORS.
YOU'RE A MASTER OF METAMORPHOSIS SORCERY...
...EMPLOYED TO EXORCISE AND SEAL AWAY EVIL SPIRITS.
THE TAOIST EXCLUSIVE TO THE XU FU...
..."TOU-HOU."
SU (VWIP)
...WHY, THANK YOU.
HITA (PAT)
ST—
HITA
STAY BACK...
SHIT ...!
GACHA
GACHA
GACHA (RATTLE)
HITA

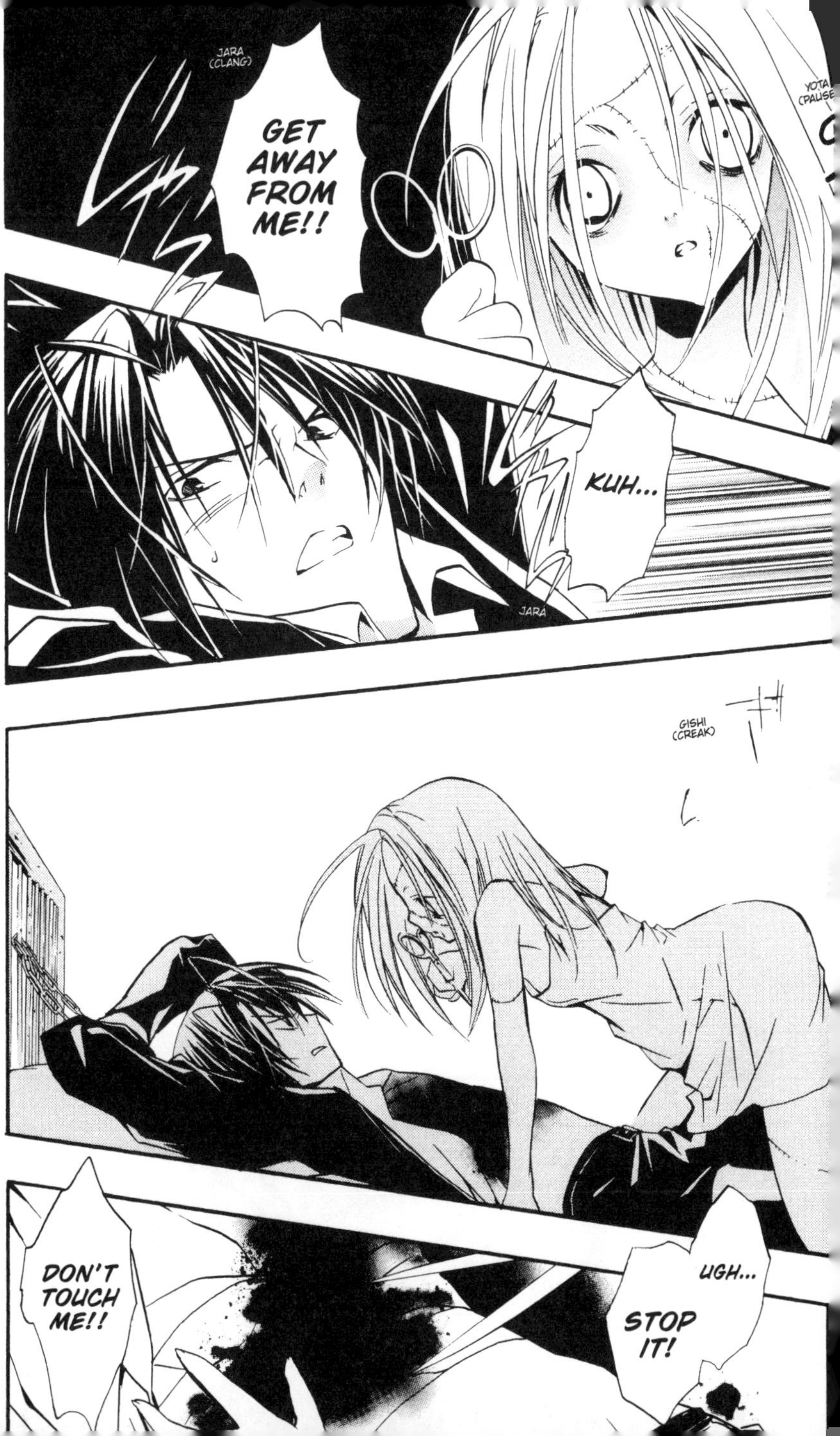
YOTA (PAUSE)
JARA (CLANG)
GET AWAY FROM ME!!
KUH...
JARA
GISHI (CREAK)
UGH...
STOP IT!
DON'T TOUCH ME!!

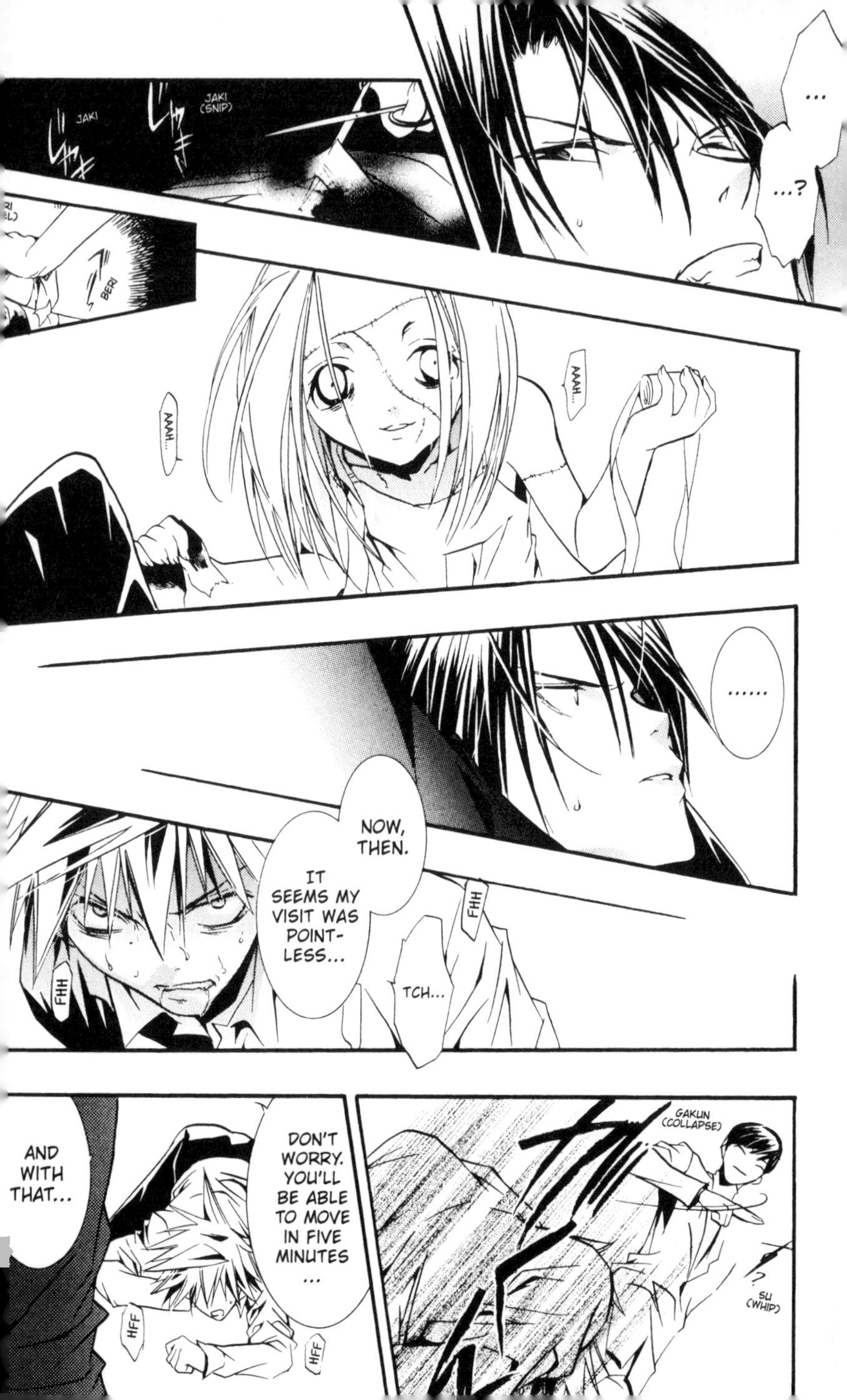
...
...?
JAKI (SNIP)
JAKI
BERI
AAAH...
AAAH...
......
NOW, THEN.
IT SEEMS MY VISIT WAS POINTLESS...
FHH
TCH...
FHH
GAKUN (COLLAPSE)
?
SU (WHIP)
DON'T WORRY. YOU'LL BE ABLE TO MOVE IN FIVE MINUTES ...
AND WITH THAT...
HFF
HFF

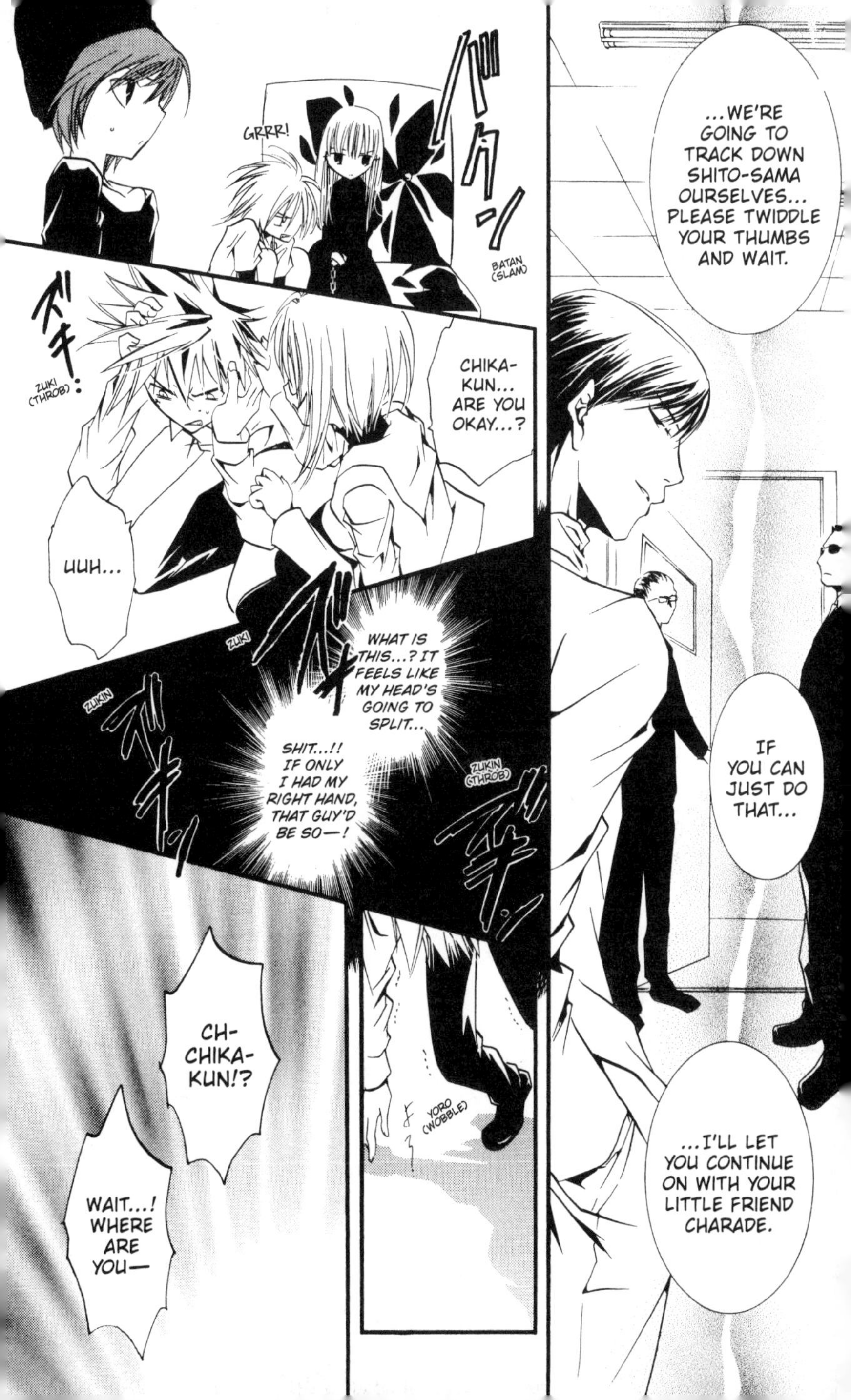
...WE'RE GOING TO TRACK DOWN SHITO-SAMA OURSELVES... PLEASE TWIDDLE YOUR THUMBS AND WAIT.
IF YOU CAN JUST DO THAT...
...I'LL LET YOU CONTINUE ON WITH YOUR LITTLE FRIEND CHARADE.
BATAN (SLAM)
GRRR!
CHIKA-KUN... ARE YOU OKAY...?
ZUKI (THROB)
UUH...
ZUKIN (THROB)
WHAT IS THIS...? IT FEELS LIKE MY HEAD'S GOING TO SPLIT...
ZUKI
SHIT...!! IF ONLY I HAD MY RIGHT HAND, THAT GUY'D BE SO—!
ZUKIN
YORO (WOBBLE)
CH-CHIKA-KUN!?
WAIT...! WHERE ARE YOU—

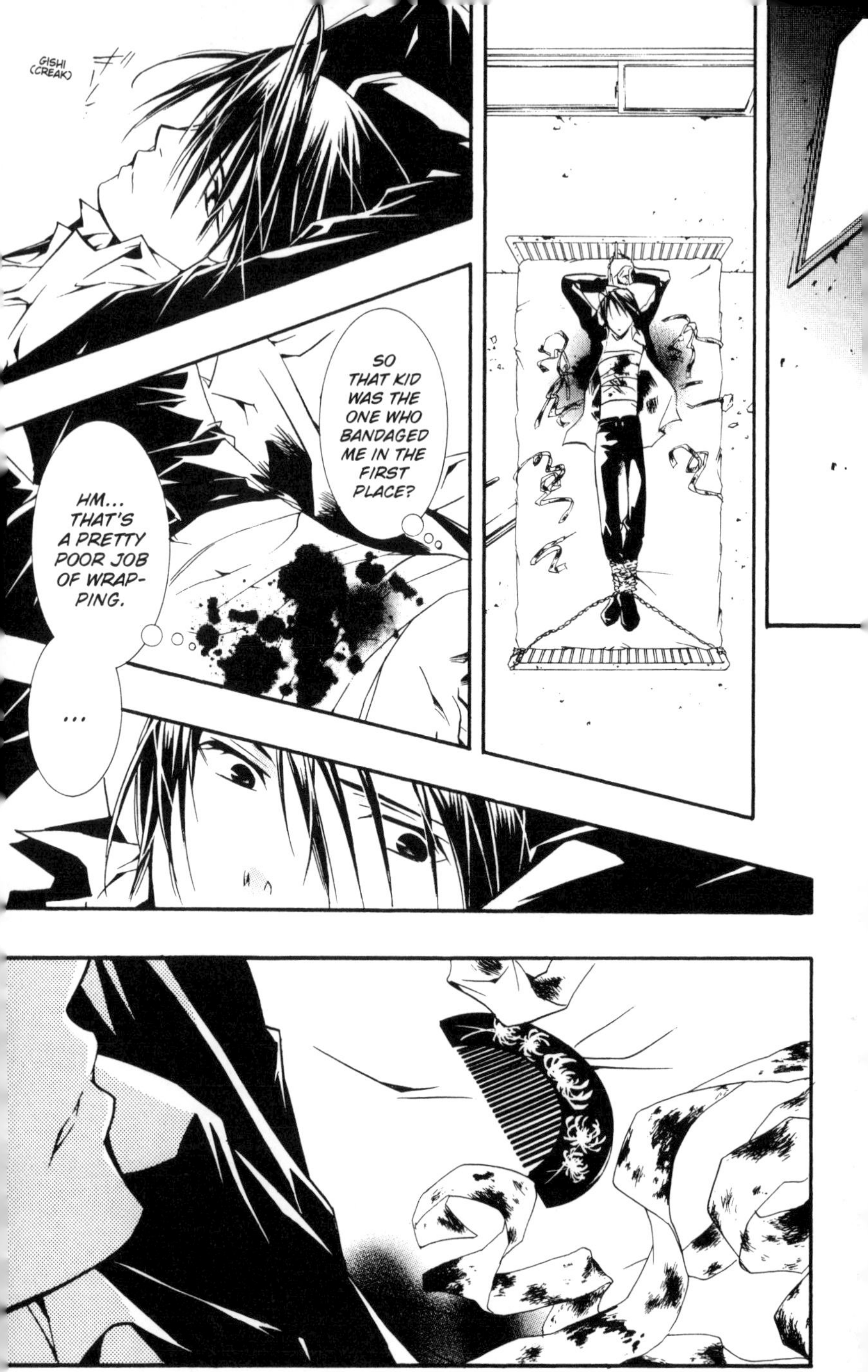
GISHI (CREAK)
SO THAT KID WAS THE ONE WHO BANDAGED ME IN THE FIRST PLACE?
HM... THAT'S A PRETTY POOR JOB OF WRAP-PING.
...

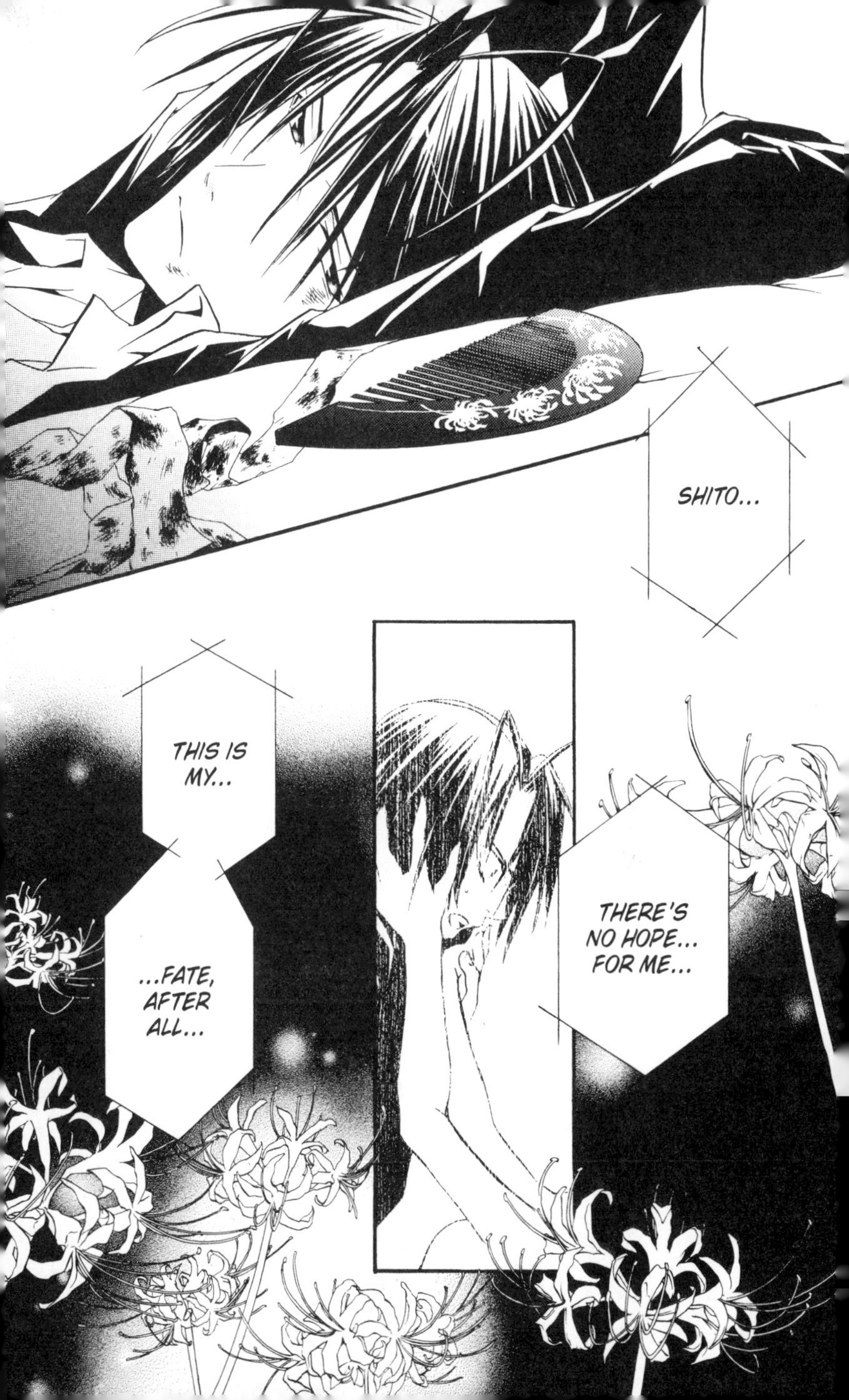
SHITO...
THERE'S NO HOPE... FOR ME...
THIS IS MY...
...FATE, AFTER ALL...

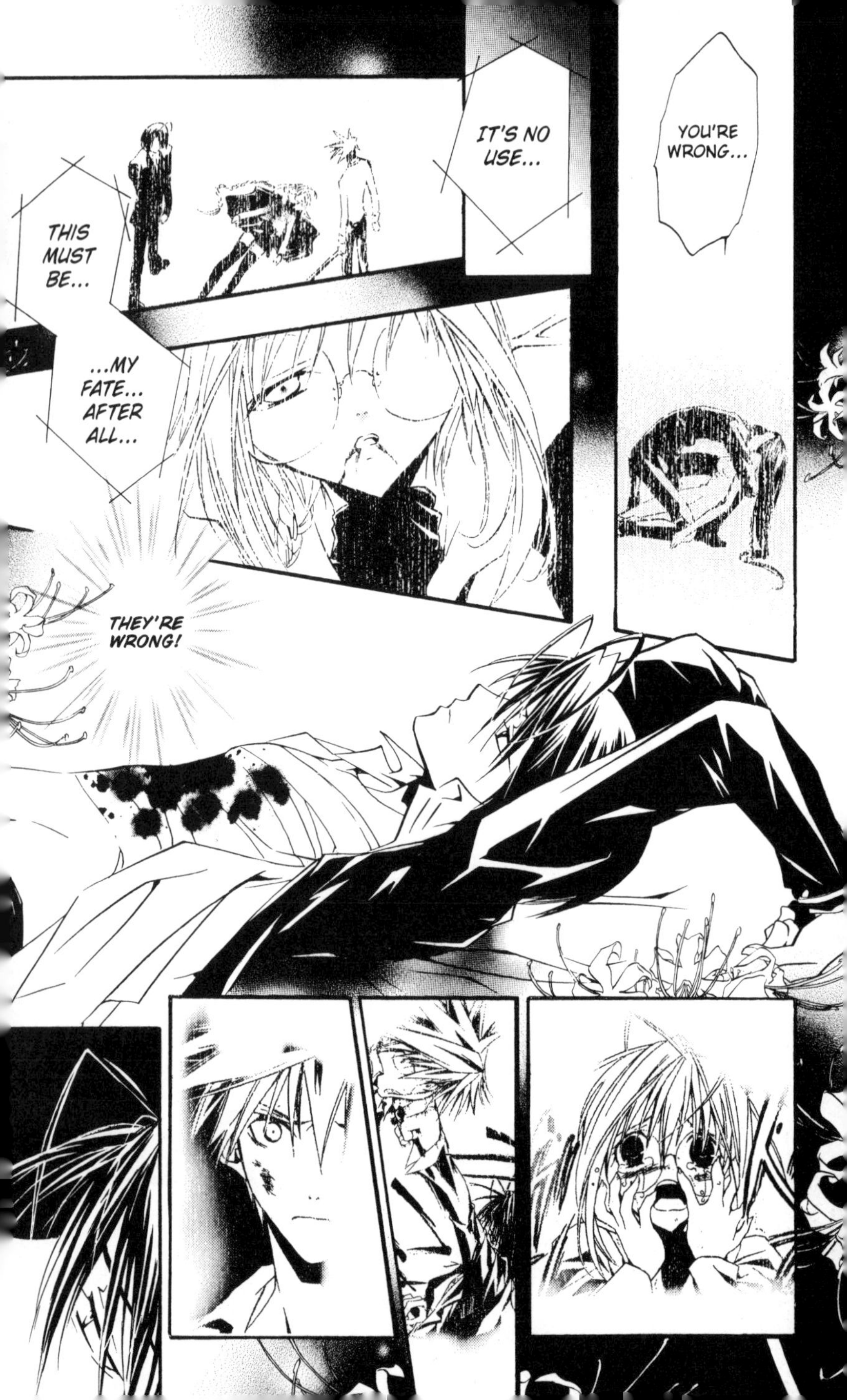
YOU'RE WRONG...
IT'S NO USE...
THIS MUST BE...
...MY FATE... AFTER ALL...
THEY'RE WRONG!

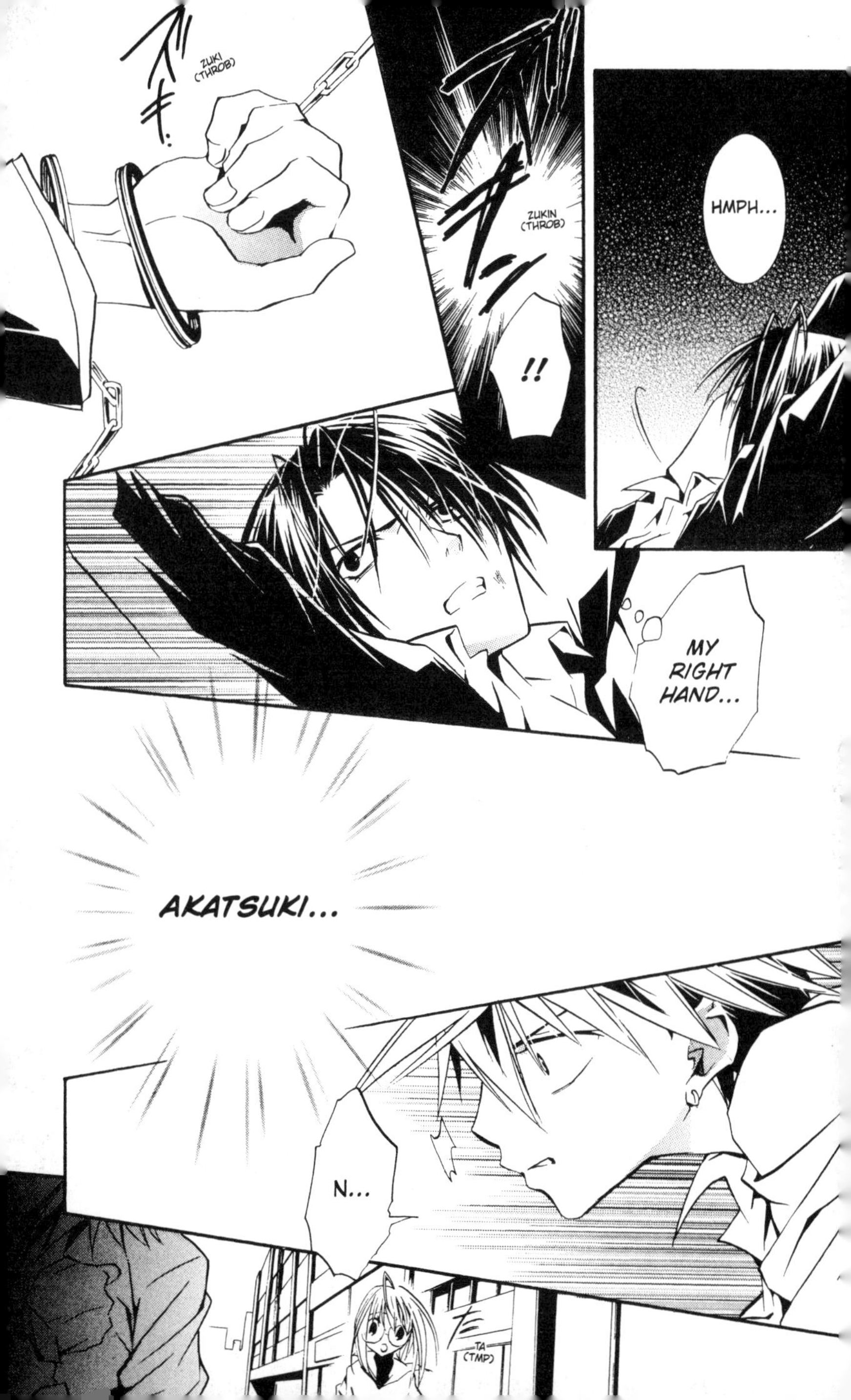
HMPH...
ZUKIN (THROB)
!!
ZUKI (THROB)
MY RIGHT HAND...
AKATSUKI...
N...
TA (TMP)

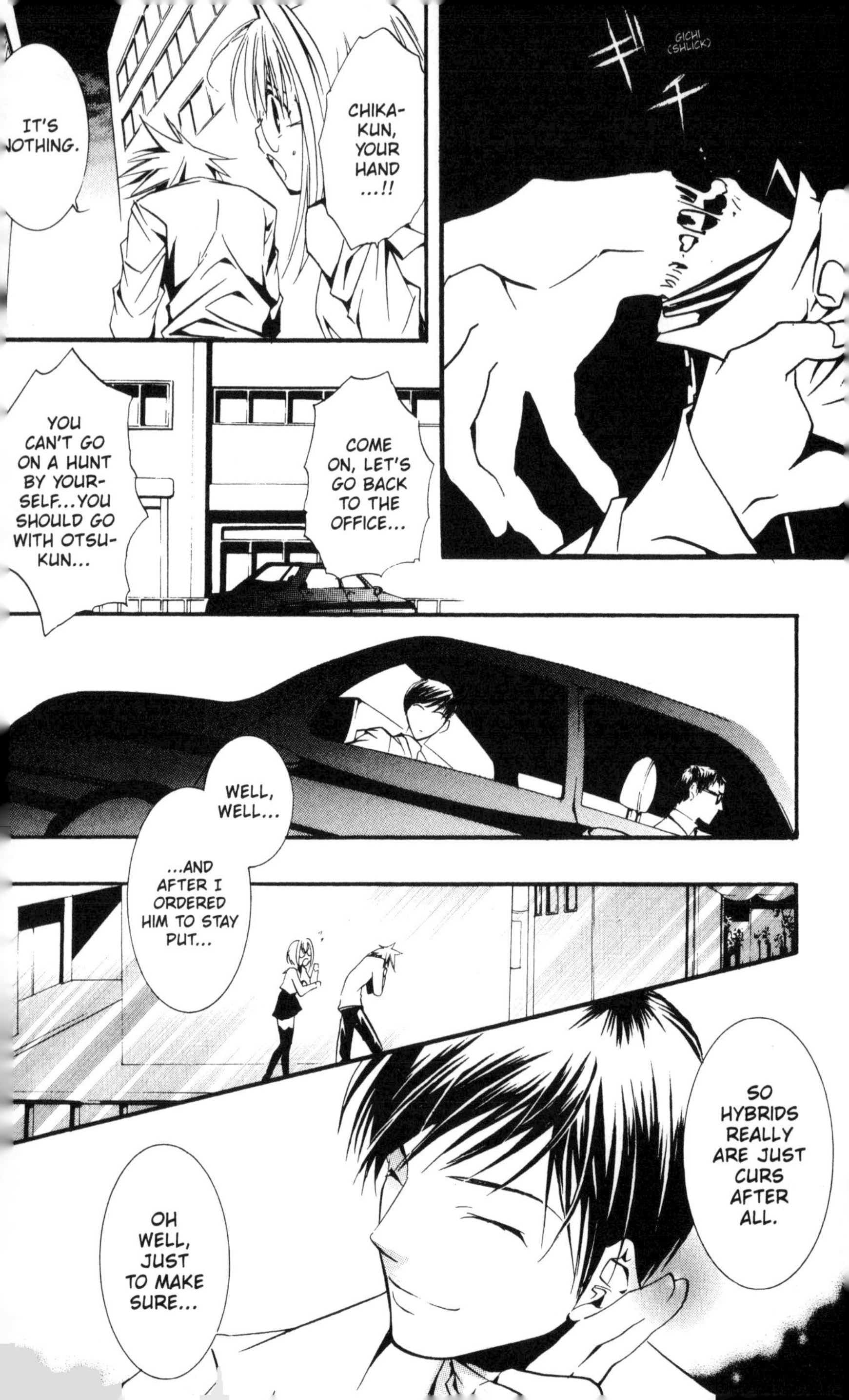
GICHI (SHLICK)
CHIKA-KUN, YOUR HAND ...!!
IT'S NOTHING.
COME ON, LET'S GO BACK TO THE OFFICE...
YOU CAN'T GO ON A HUNT BY YOURSELF...YOU SHOULD GO WITH OTSU-KUN...
WELL, WELL...
...AND AFTER I ORDERED HIM TO STAY PUT...
SO HYBRIDS REALLY ARE JUST CURS AFTER ALL.
OH WELL, JUST TO MAKE SURE...

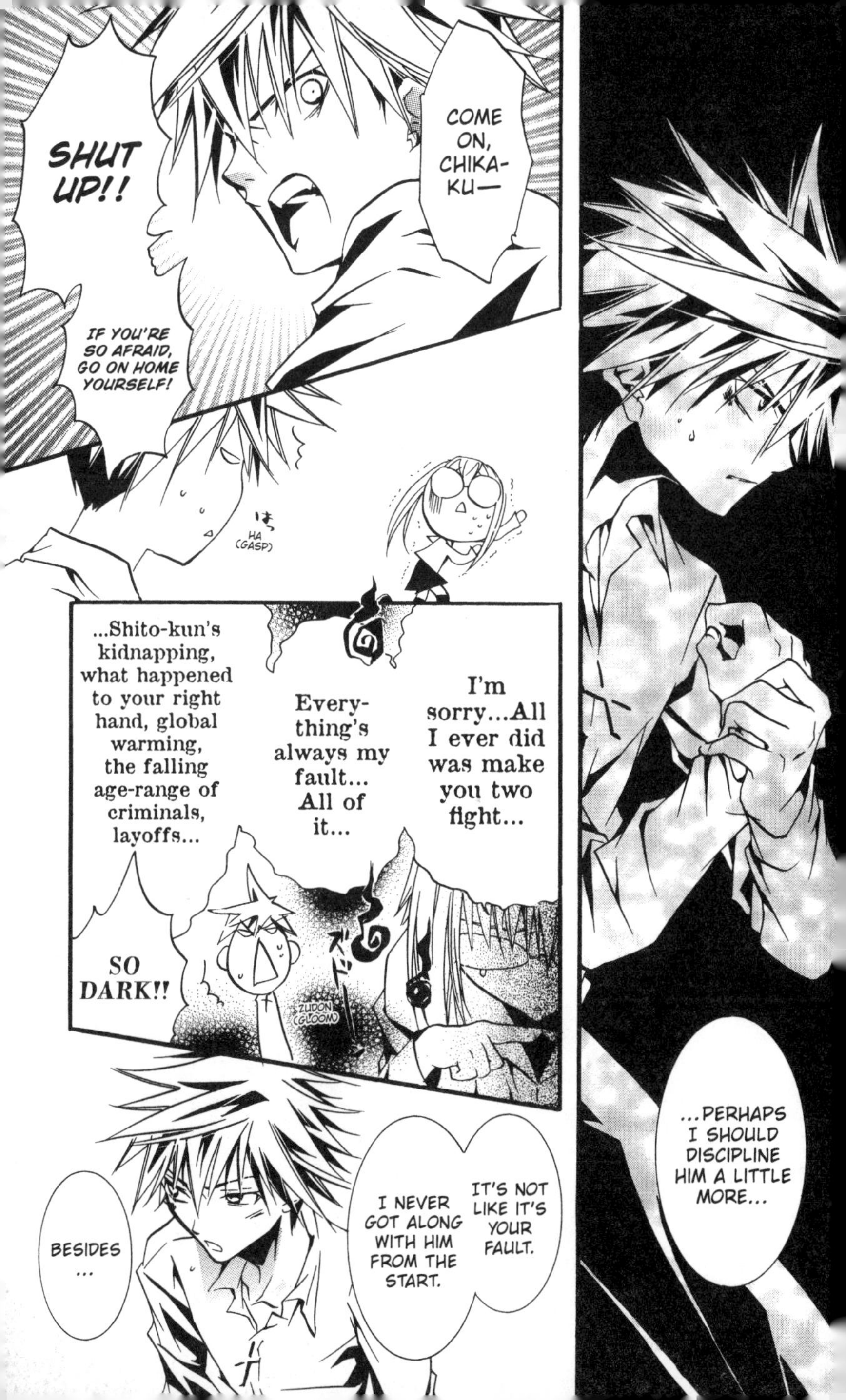
...PERHAPS I SHOULD DISCIPLINE HIM A LITTLE MORE...
COME ON, CHIKAKU—
SHUT UP!!
IF YOU'RE SO AFRAID, GO ON HOME YOURSELF!
はっ
HA (GASP)
I'm sorry...All I ever did was make you two fight...
Every-thing's always my fault... All of it...
...Shito-kun's kidnapping, what happened to your right hand, global warming, the falling age-range of criminals, layoffs...
ズドーン
ZUDON (GLOOM)
SO DARK!!
IT'S NOT LIKE IT'S YOUR FAULT.
I NEVER GOT ALONG WITH HIM FROM THE START.
BESIDES...

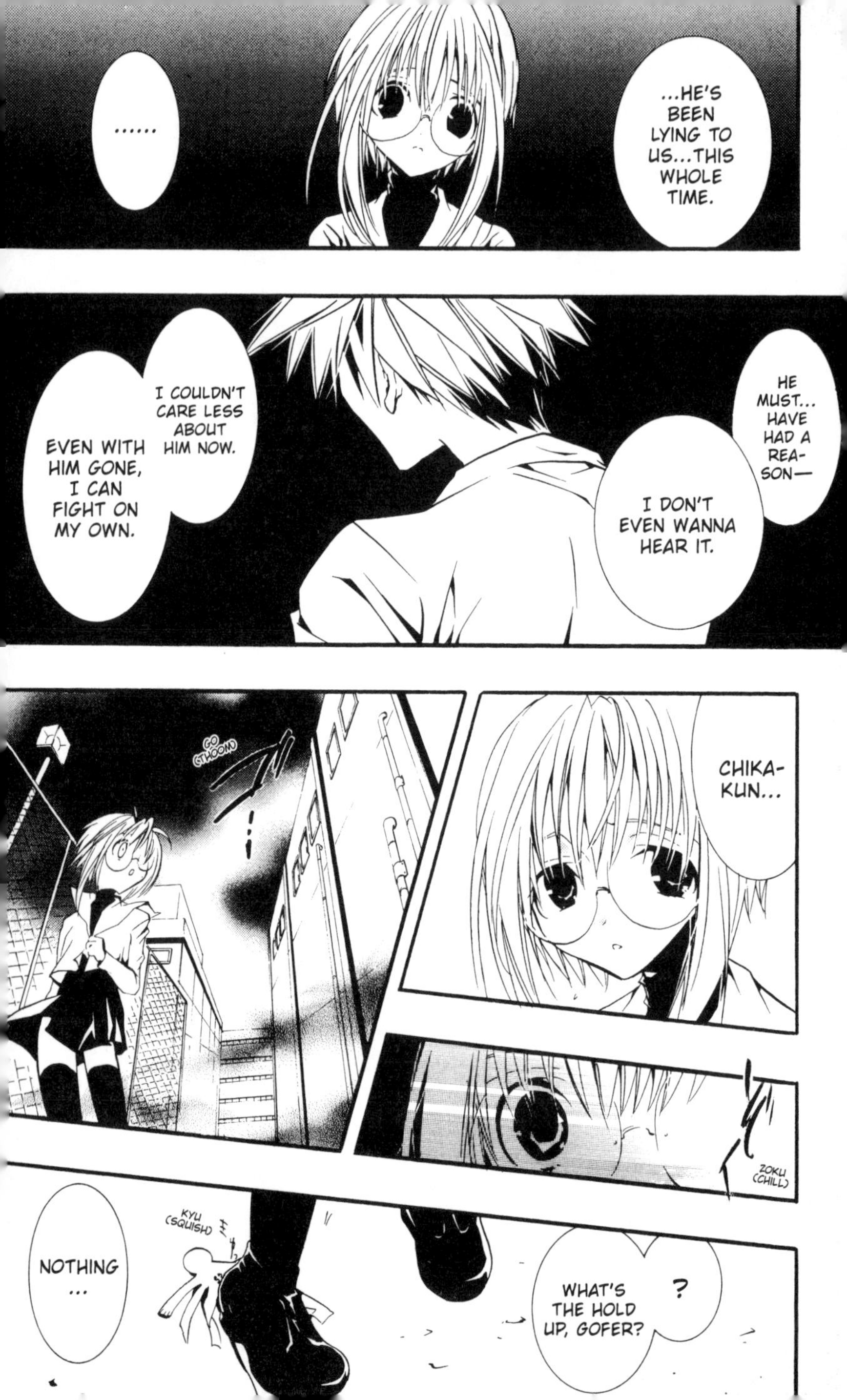
...HE'S BEEN LYING TO US...THIS WHOLE TIME.
......
HE MUST... HAVE HAD A REA-SON—
I DON'T EVEN WANNA HEAR IT.
I COULDN'T CARE LESS ABOUT HIM NOW.
EVEN WITH HIM GONE, I CAN FIGHT ON MY OWN.
CHIKA-KUN...
ZOKU (CHILL)
GO (THOOM)
!
WHAT'S THE HOLD UP, GOFER?
?
KYU (SQUISH)
NOTHING...

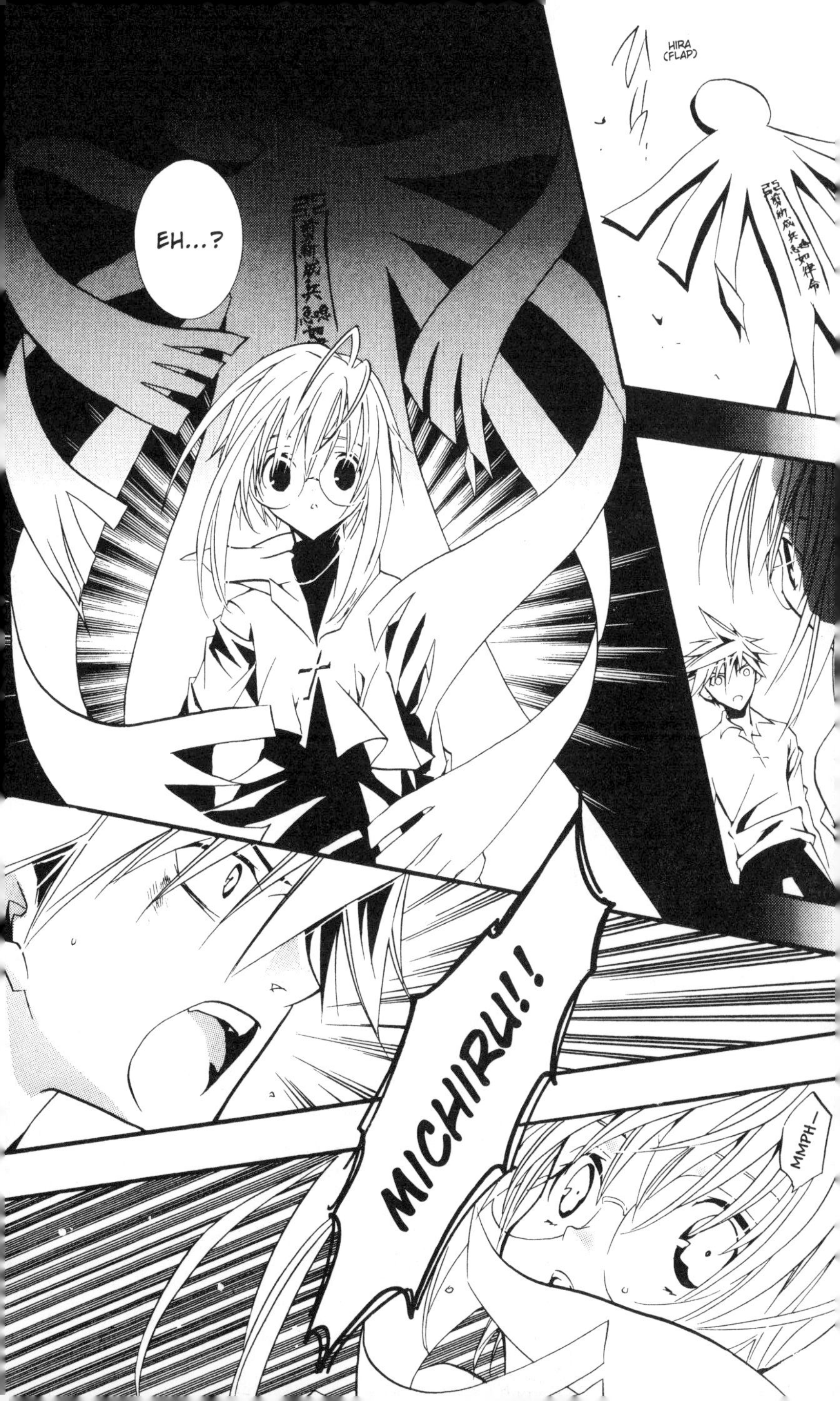
HIRA
(FLAP)
EH...?
MICHIRU!!
MMPH—

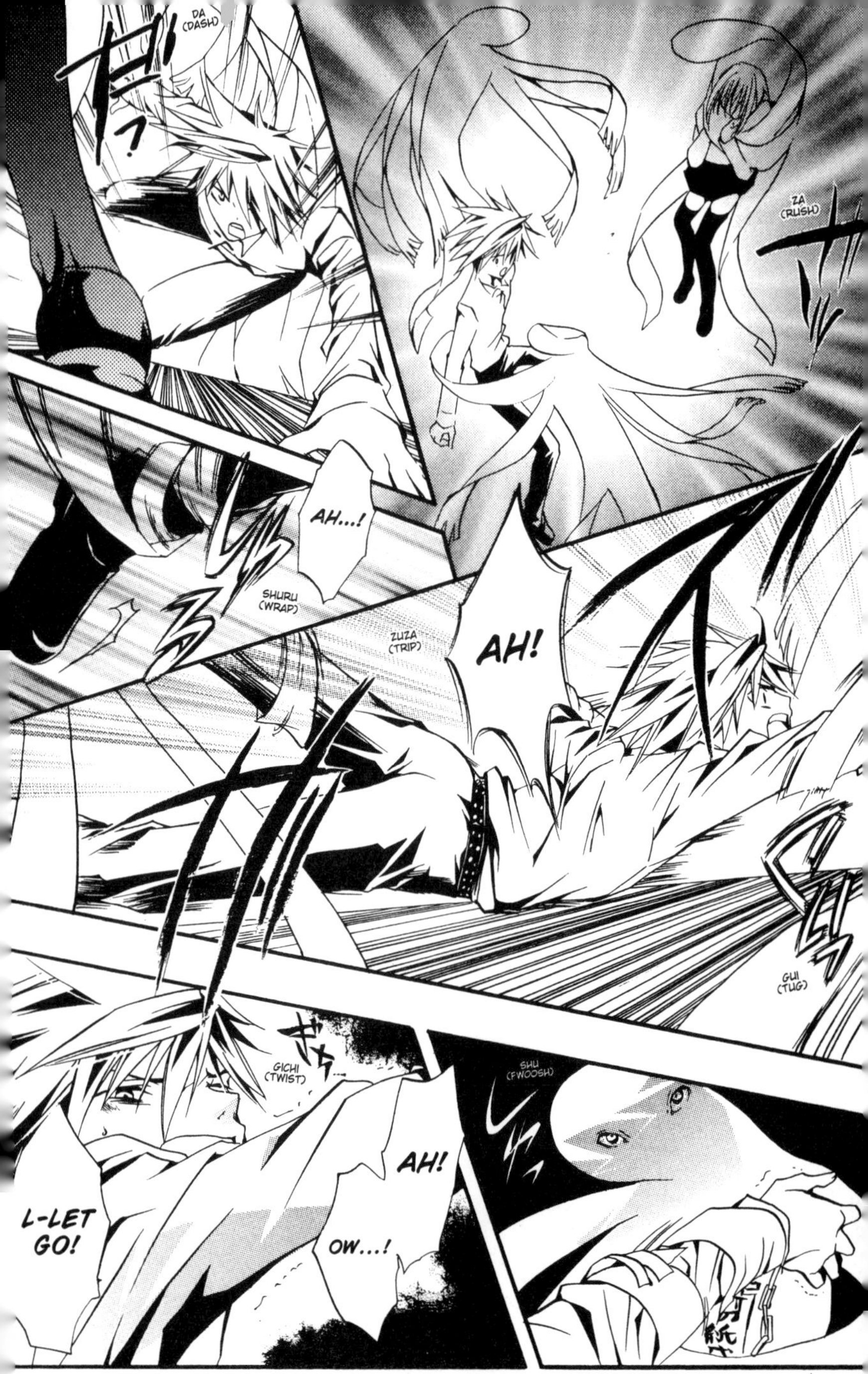
ZA (RUSH)
DA (DASH)
?
AH...!
SHURU (WRAP)
AH!
ZUZA (TRIP)
GUI (TUG)
SHU (FWOOSH)
GICHI (TWIST)
AH!
OW...!
L-LET GO!

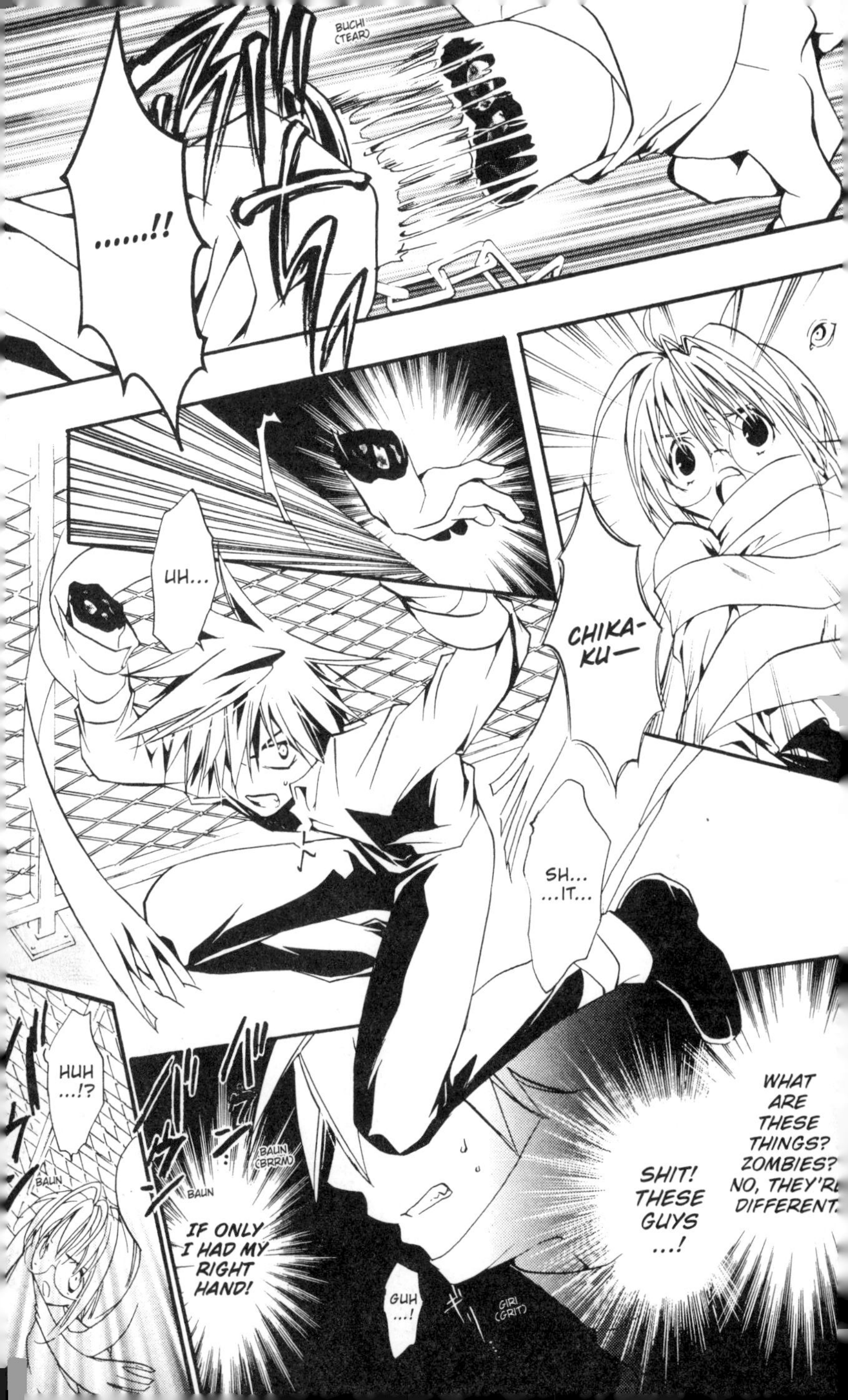
BUCHI (TEAR)
......!!
CHIKA-KU—
UH...
SH... ...IT...
WHAT ARE THESE THINGS? ZOMBIES? NO, THEY'RE DIFFERENT.
SHIT! THESE GUYS ...!
BAUN (BRRM)
BAUN
IF ONLY I HAD MY RIGHT HAND!
GUH ...!
GIRI (GRIT)
HUH ...!?
BAUN

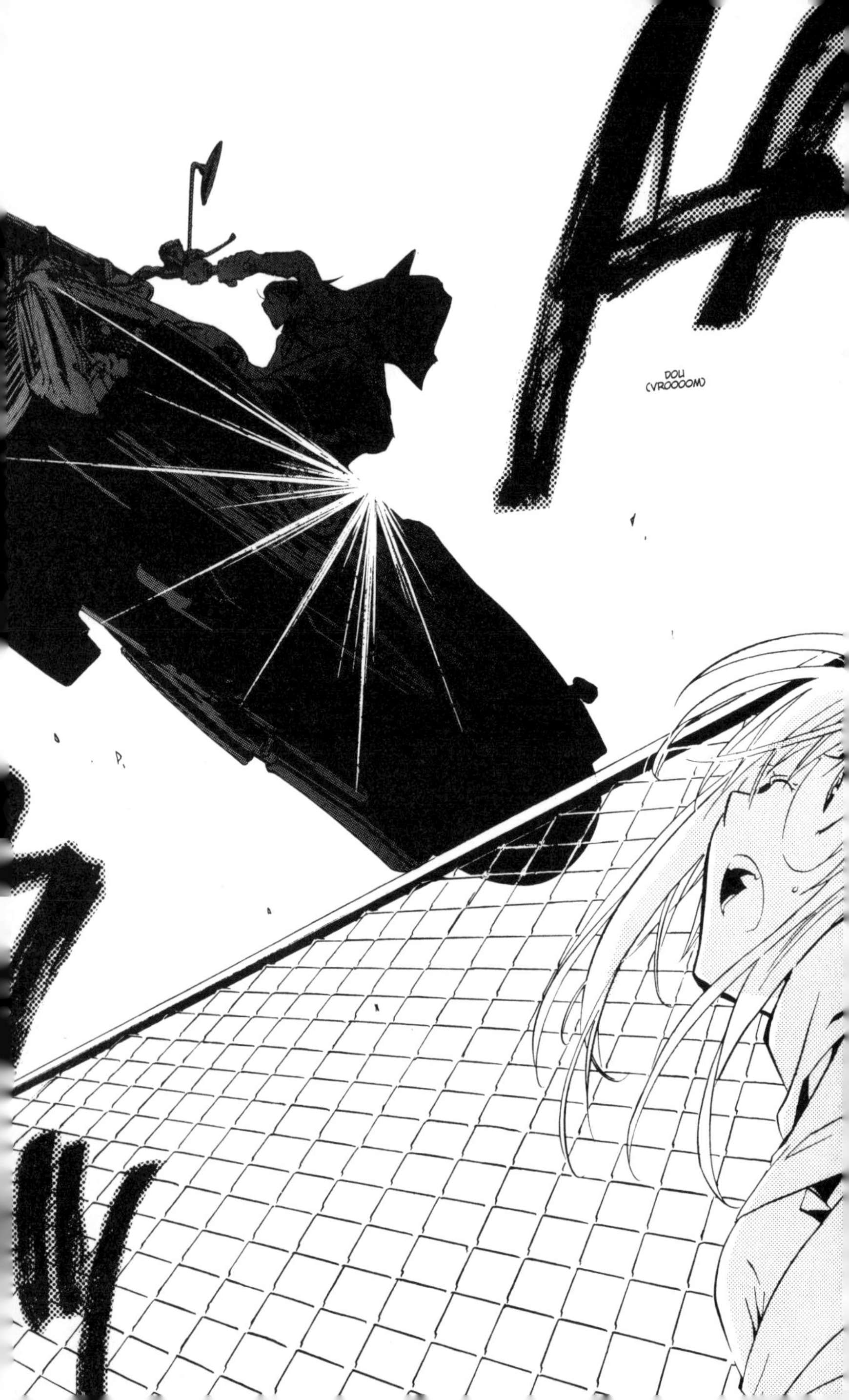
DOU
(VROOOOM)

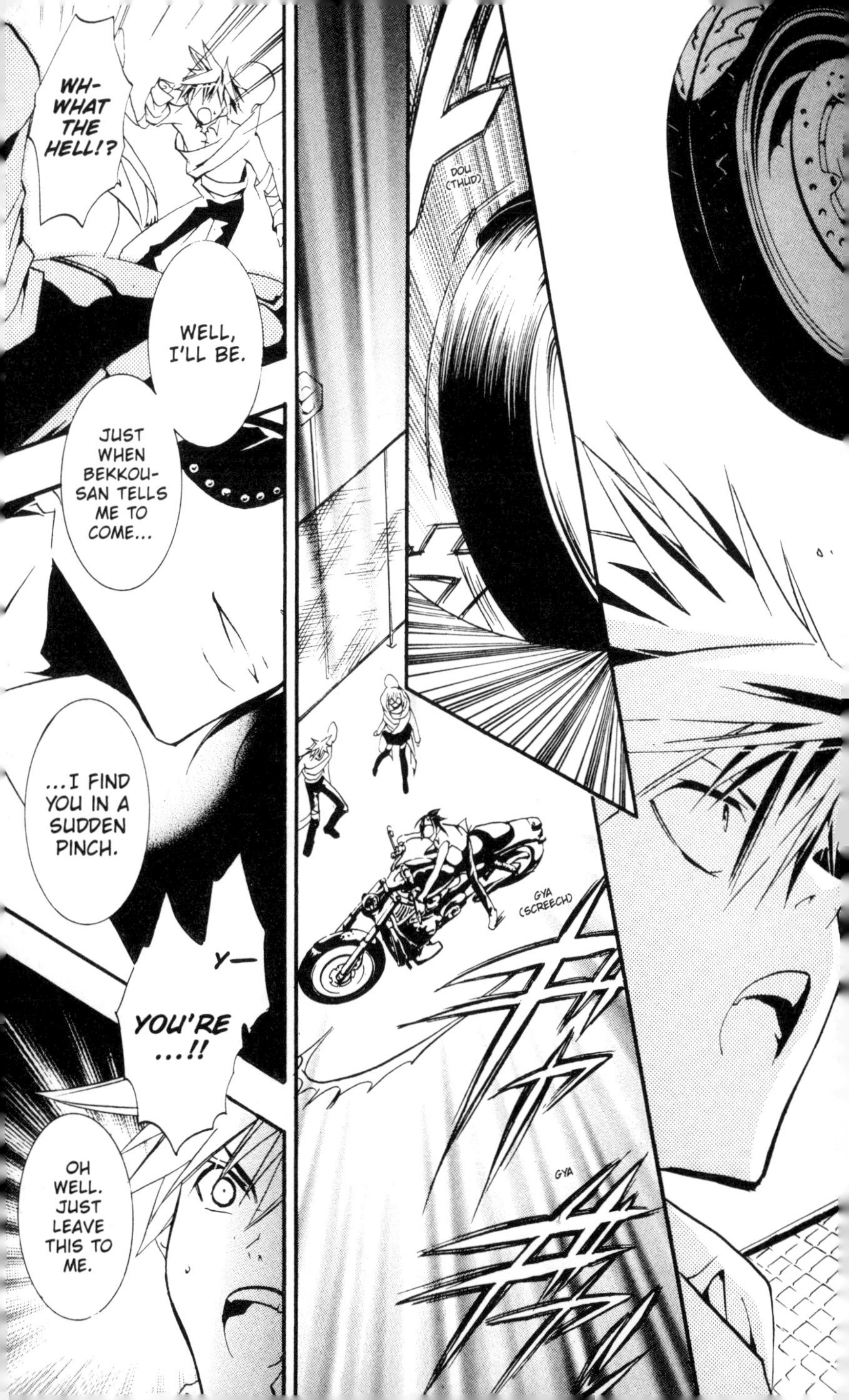
DOU (THUD)
GYA (SCREECH)
GYA
WH-WHAT THE HELL!?
WELL, I'LL BE.
JUST WHEN BEKKOU-SAN TELLS ME TO COME...
...I FIND YOU IN A SUDDEN PINCH.
Y—
YOU'RE ...!!
OH WELL. JUST LEAVE THIS TO ME.

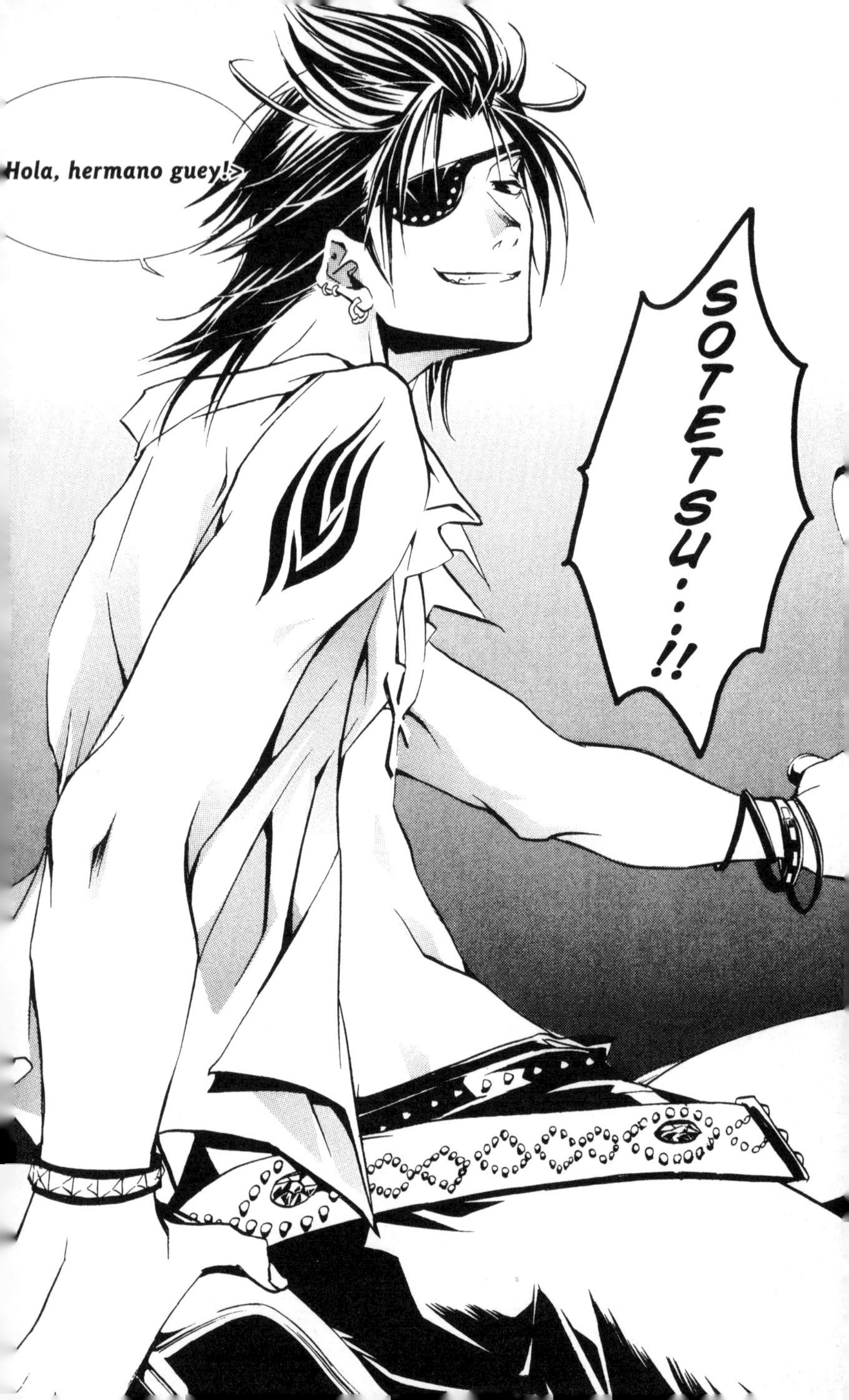
Hola, hermano guey!>
SOTETSU...!!

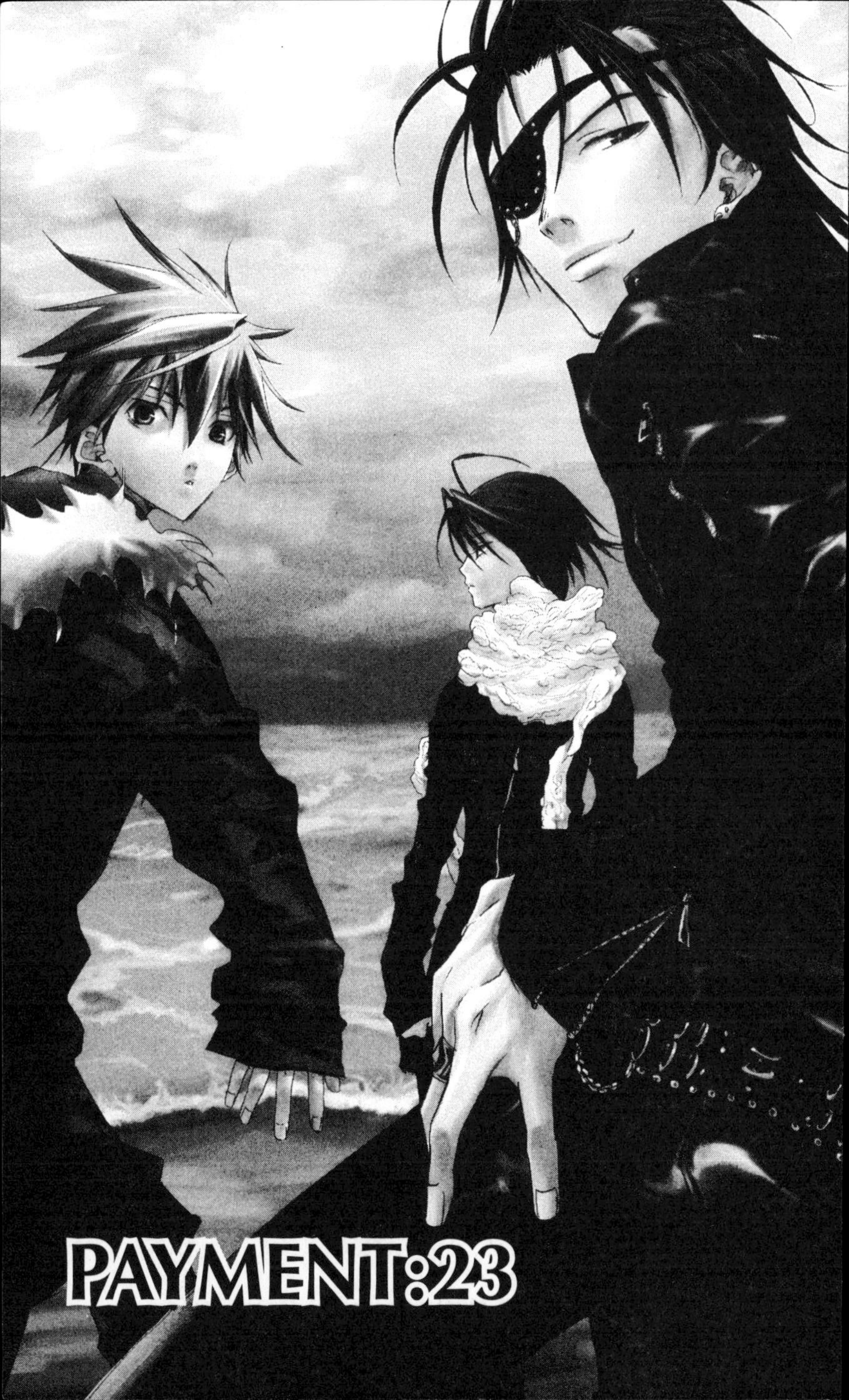

PAYMENT:23

MICHIRU KITA

5'2"/101 lbs
blood type: A
birthday: 2/22

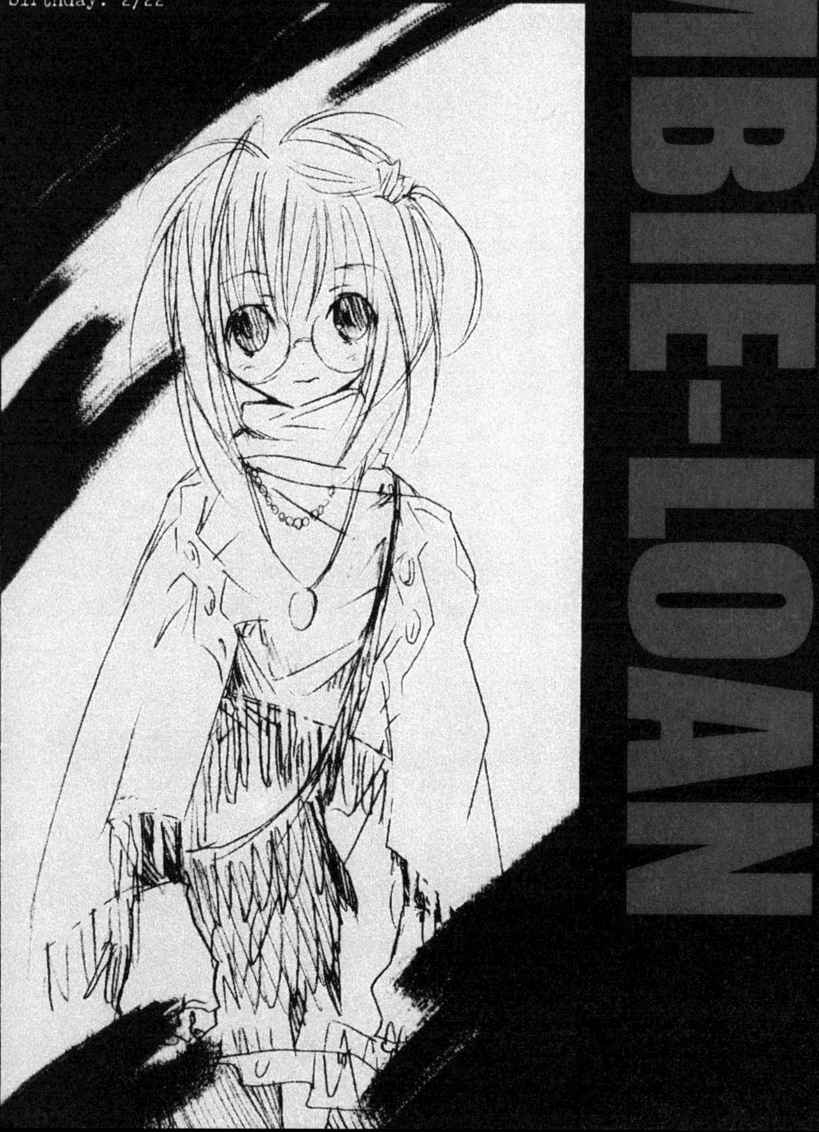
ZOMBIE-LOAN

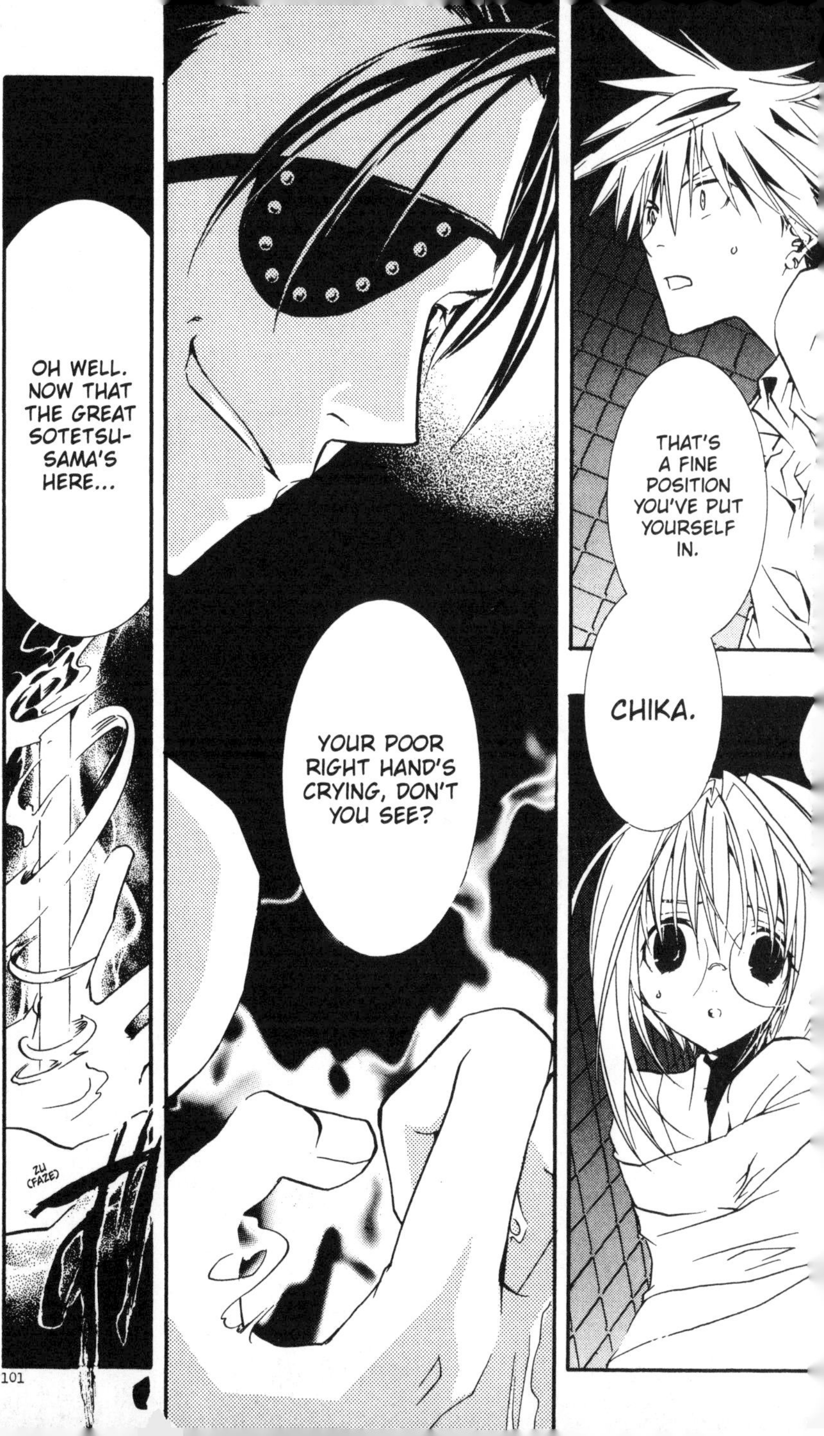

THAT'S A FINE POSITION YOU'VE PUT YOURSELF IN.
CHIKA.
YOUR POOR RIGHT HAND'S CRYING, DON'T YOU SEE?
OH WELL. NOW THAT THE GREAT SOTETSU-SAMA'S HERE...
ZU (FAZE)

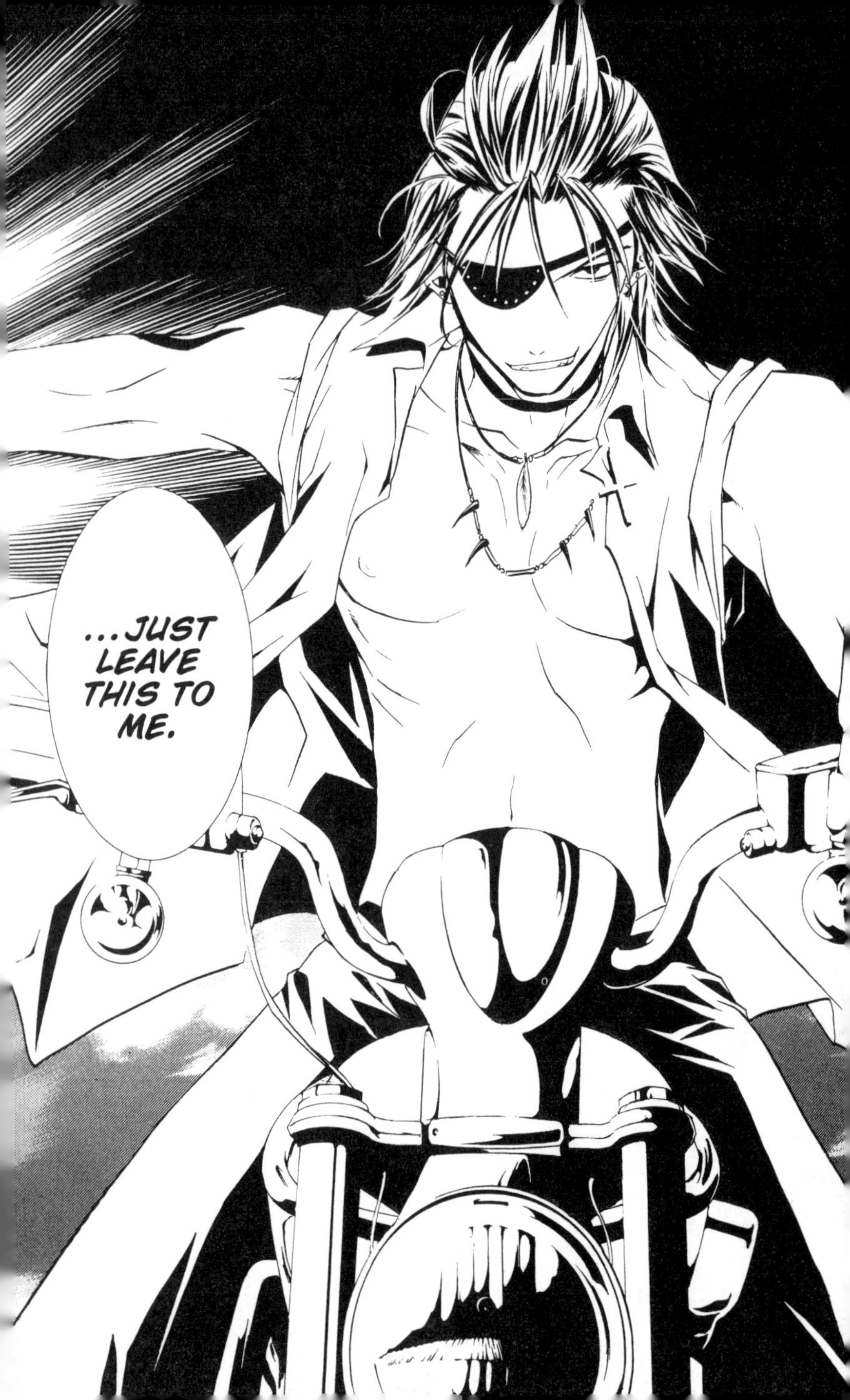
...JUST LEAVE THIS TO ME.

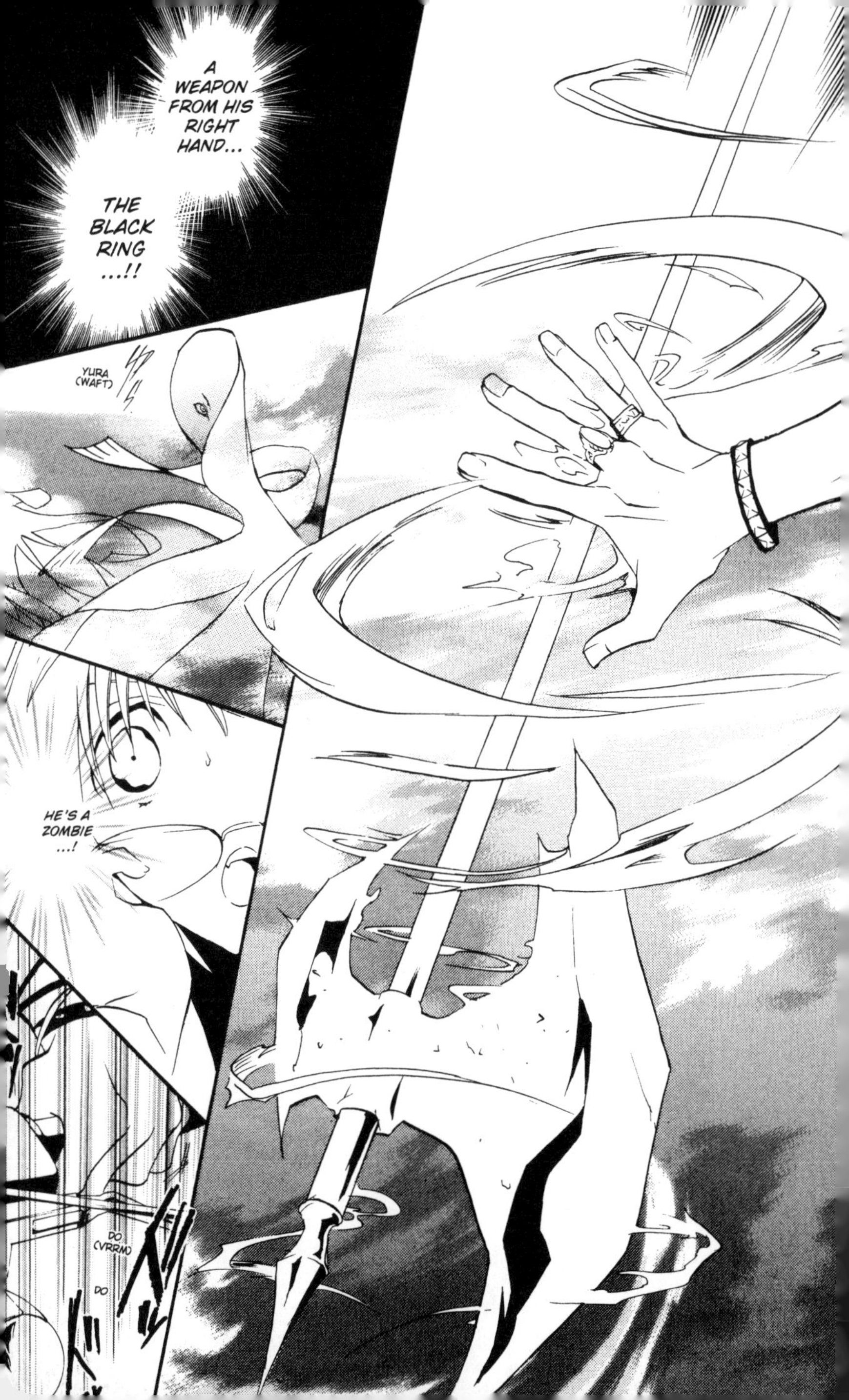
A WEAPON FROM HIS RIGHT HAND...
THE BLACK RING ...!!
YURA (WAFT)
HE'S A ZOMBIE ...!
DO (VRRM)
DO

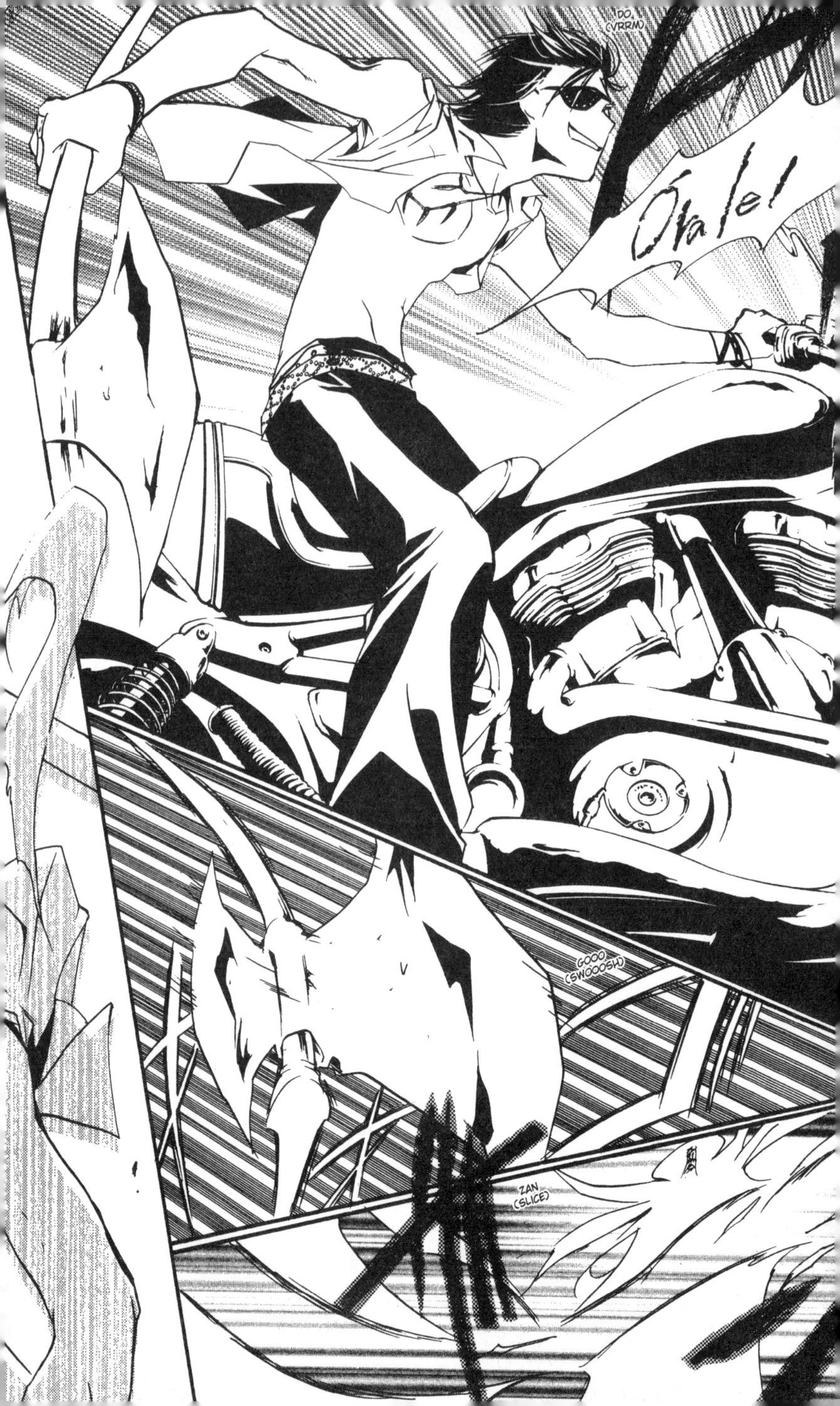
DO
(VRRM)
Órale!
GOOO
(SWOOOSH)
ZAN
(SLICE)

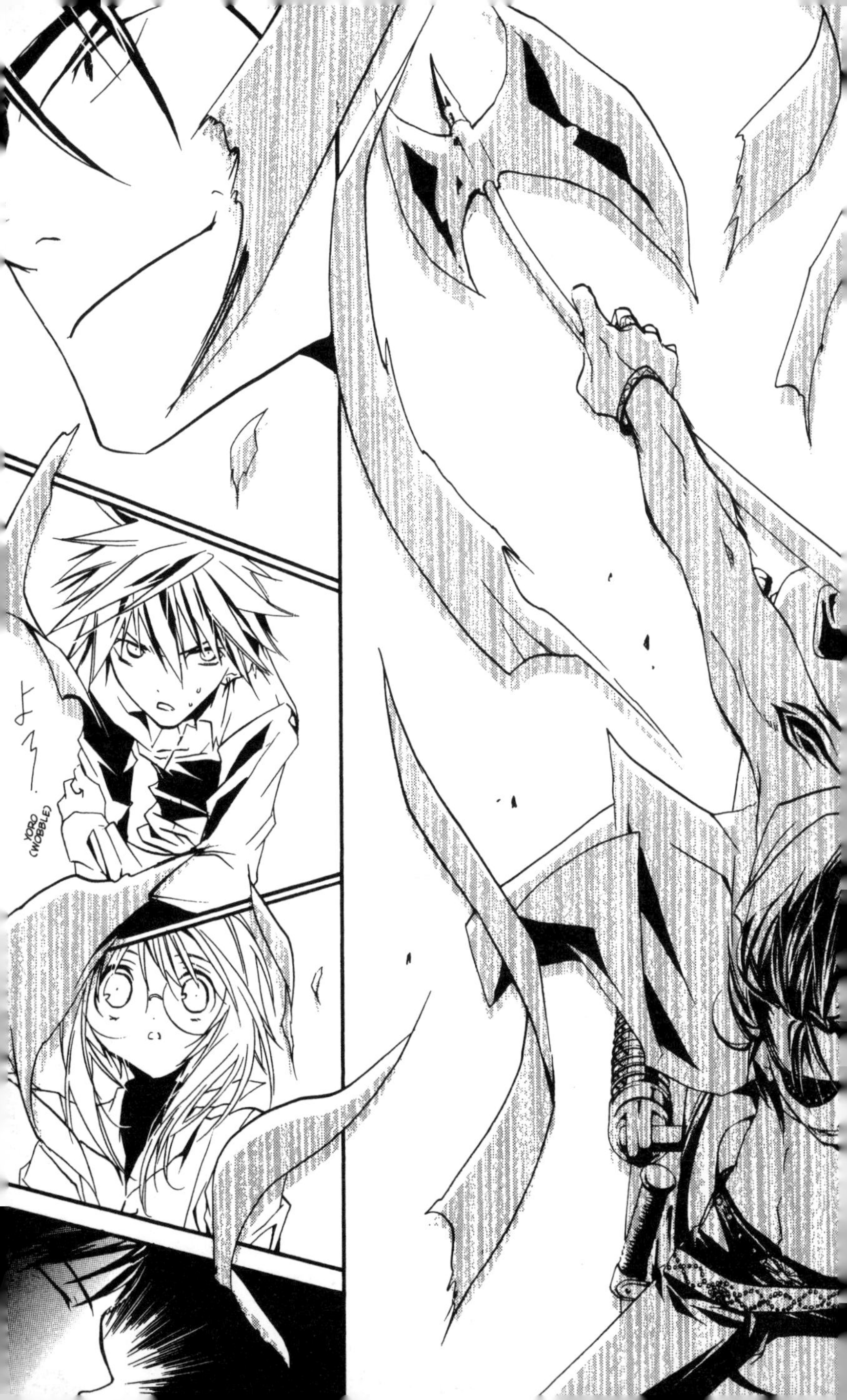
よろ
YORO (WOBBLE)

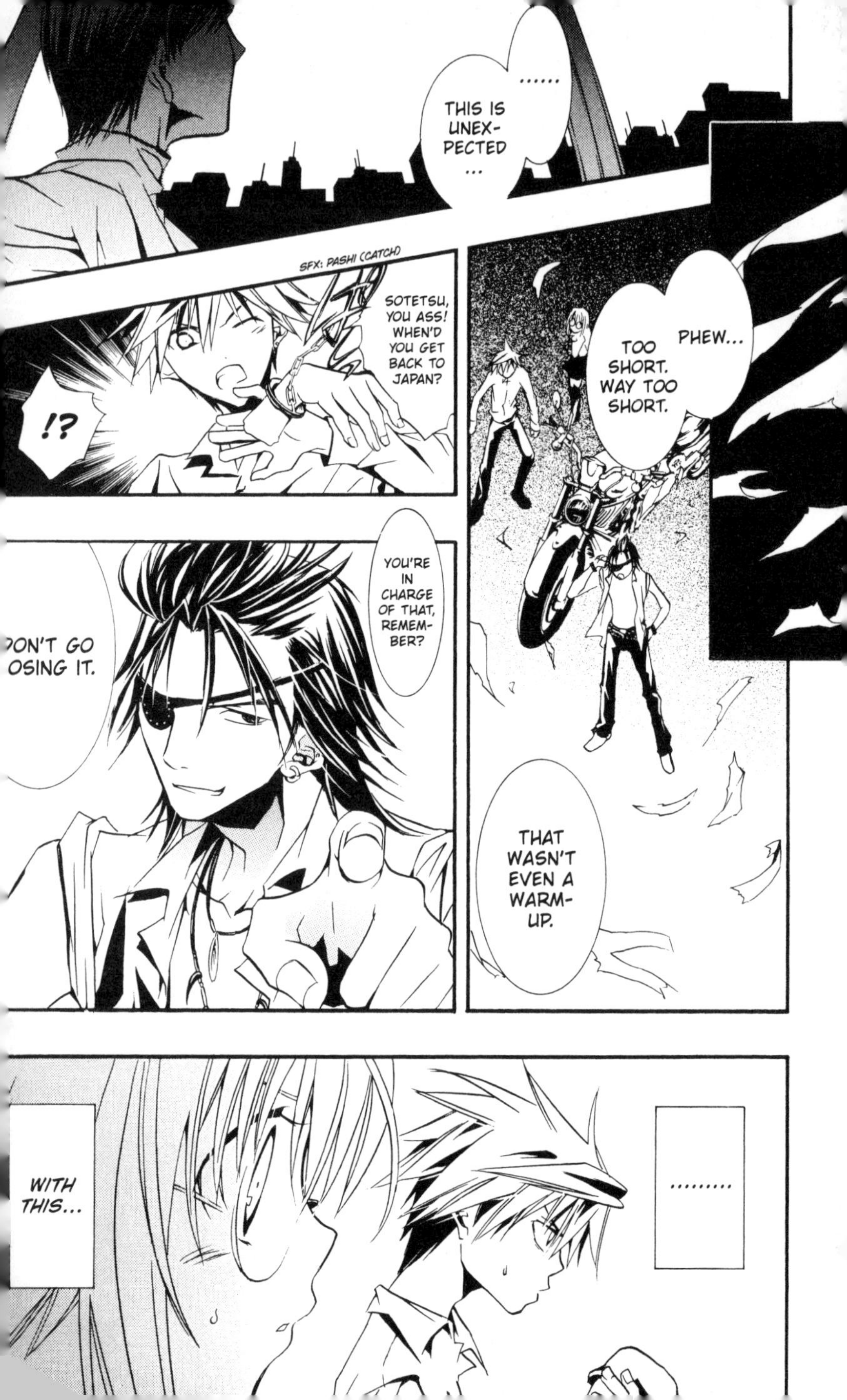
......
THIS IS UNEXPECTED ...
PHEW...
TOO SHORT. WAY TOO SHORT.
THAT WASN'T EVEN A WARM-UP.
SFX: PASHI (CATCH)
SOTETSU, YOU ASS! WHEN'D YOU GET BACK TO JAPAN?
!?
YOU'RE IN CHARGE OF THAT, REMEMBER?
ON'T GO OSING IT.
....
WITH THIS...

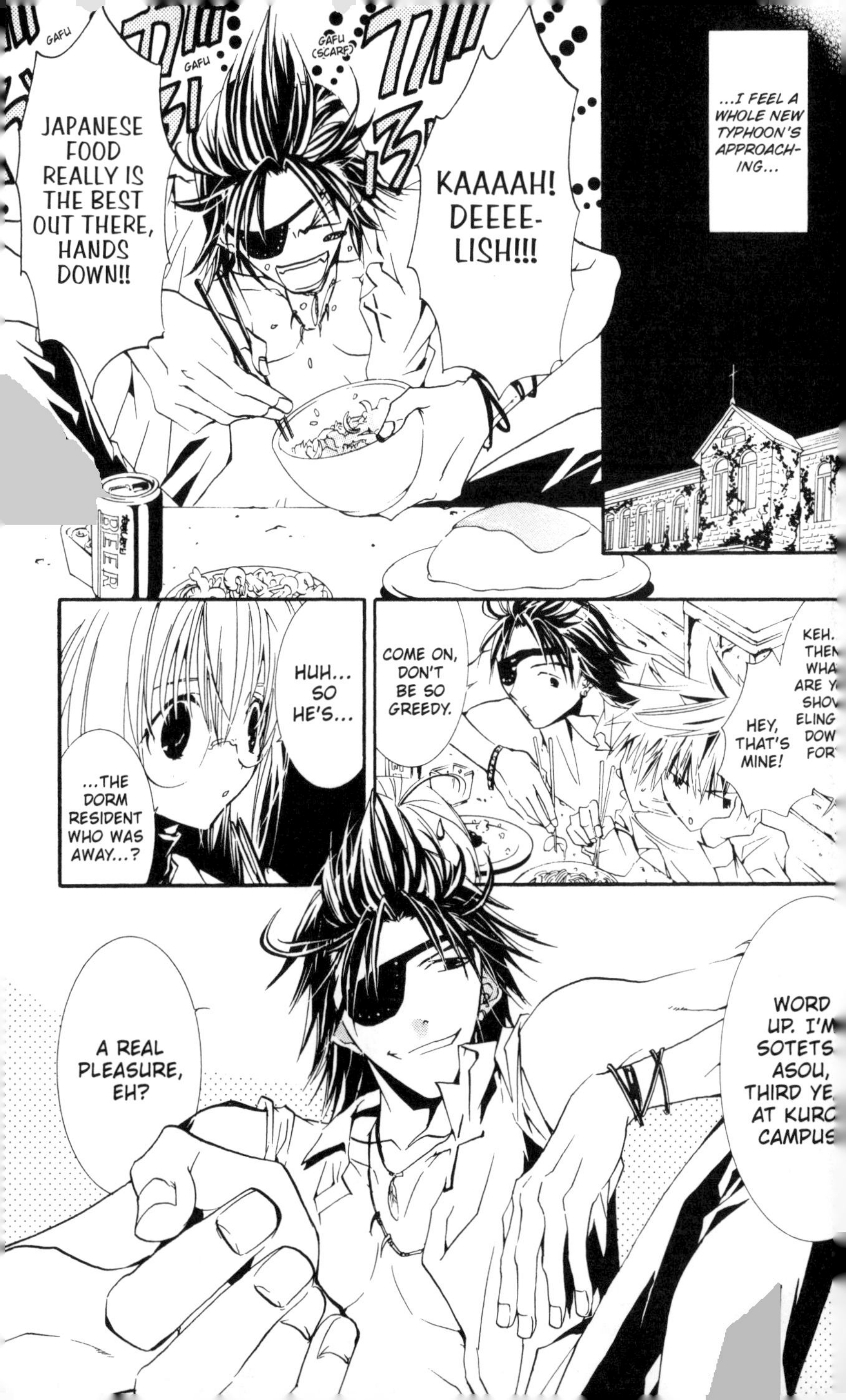
...I FEEL A WHOLE NEW TYPHOON'S APPROACH-ING...
GAFU (SCARF)
KAAAAH! DEEEE-LISH!!!
GAFU
GAFU
JAPANESE FOOD REALLY IS THE BEST OUT THERE, HANDS DOWN!!
KEH. THEN WHA ARE Y SHOV ELING DOW FOR
HEY, THAT'S MINE!
COME ON, DON'T BE SO GREEDY.
HUH... SO HE'S...
...THE DORM RESIDENT WHO WAS AWAY...?
WORD UP. I'M SOTETS ASOU, THIRD YE AT KURO CAMPUS
A REAL PLEASURE, EH?

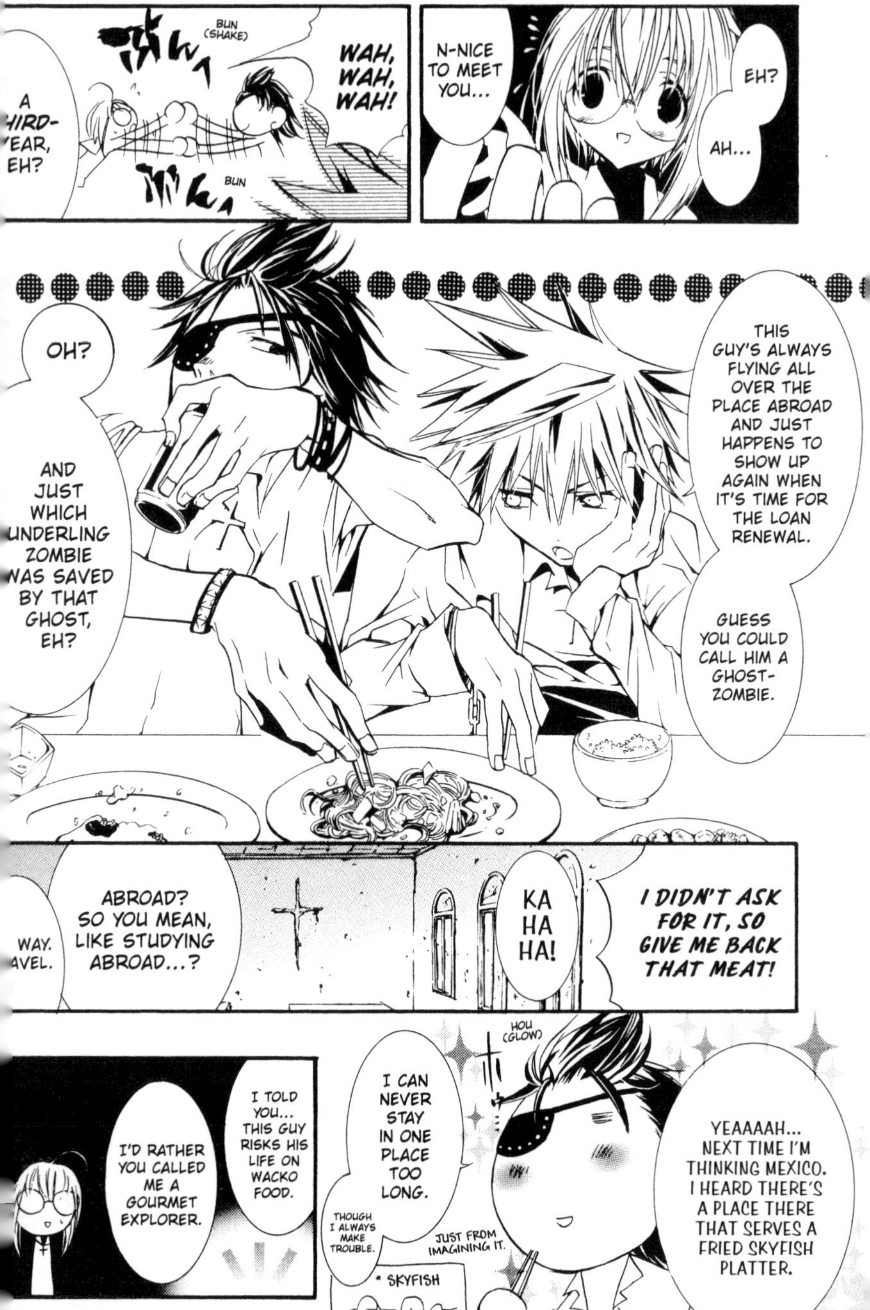
EH?
AH...
N-NICE TO MEET YOU...
WAH, WAH, WAH!
BUN (SHAKE)
BUN
A HIRD- EAR, EH?
THIS GUY'S ALWAYS FLYING ALL OVER THE PLACE ABROAD AND JUST HAPPENS TO SHOW UP AGAIN WHEN IT'S TIME FOR THE LOAN RENEWAL.
OH?
AND JUST WHICH NDERLING ZOMBIE VAS SAVED BY THAT GHOST, EH?
GUESS YOU COULD CALL HIM A GHOST-ZOMBIE.
I DIDN'T ASK FOR IT, SO GIVE ME BACK THAT MEAT!
KA HA HA!
ABROAD? SO YOU MEAN, LIKE STUDYING ABROAD...?
WAY. AVEL.
HOU (GLOW)
YEAAAAH... NEXT TIME I'M THINKING MEXICO. I HEARD THERE'S A PLACE THERE THAT SERVES A FRIED SKYFISH PLATTER.
I CAN NEVER STAY IN ONE PLACE TOO LONG.
THOUGH I ALWAYS MAKE TROUBLE.
JUST FROM IMAGINING IT.
* SKYFISH
UNIDENTIFIED MYSTERIOUS ANIMAL
I TOLD YOU... THIS GUY RISKS HIS LIFE ON WACKO FOOD.
I'D RATHER YOU CALLED ME A GOURMET EXPLORER.

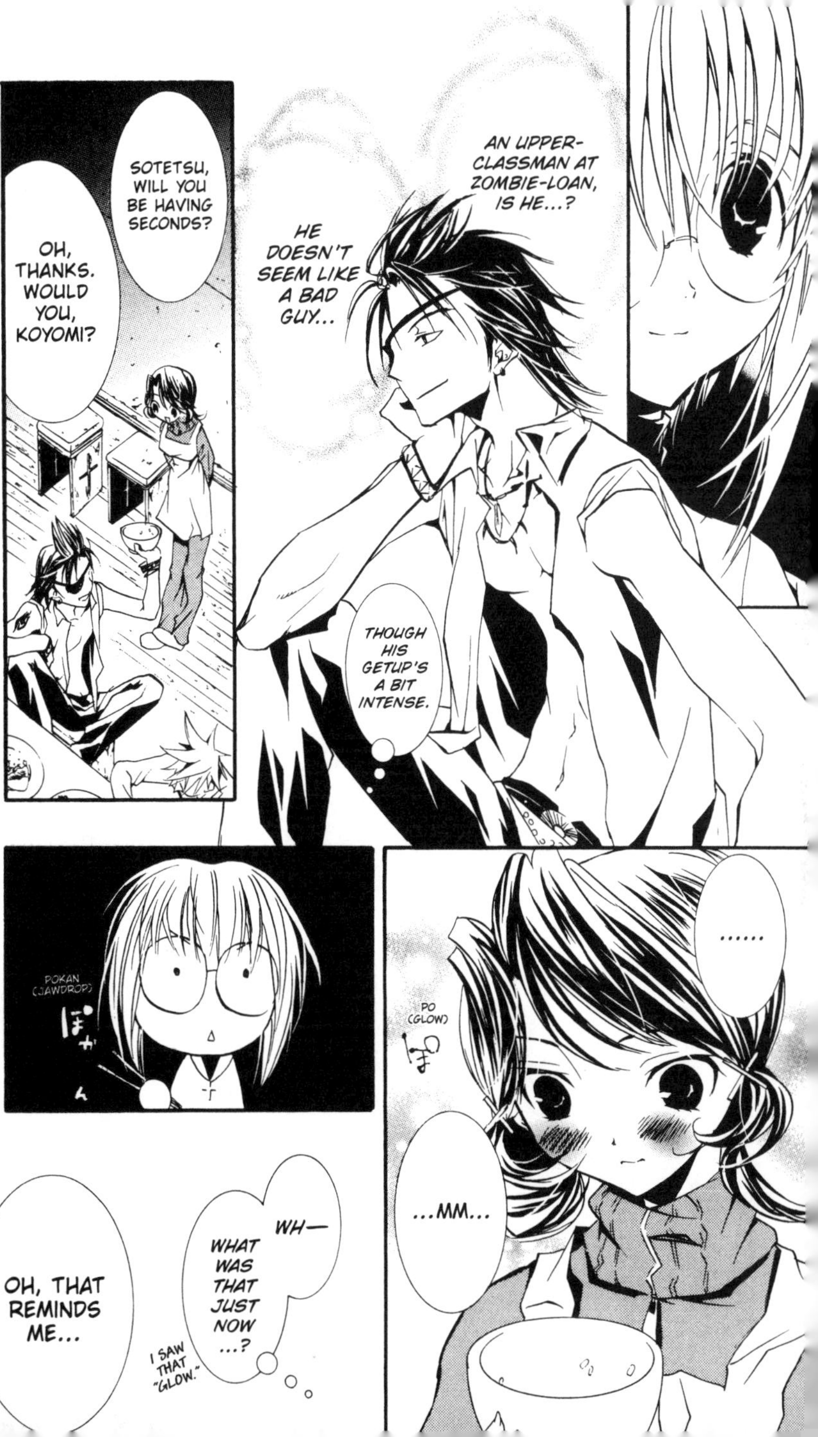
AN UPPER-CLASSMAN AT ZOMBIE-LOAN, IS HE...?
HE DOESN'T SEEM LIKE A BAD GUY...
THOUGH HIS GETUP'S A BIT INTENSE.
SOTETSU, WILL YOU BE HAVING SECONDS?
OH, THANKS. WOULD YOU, KOYOMI?
......
PO (GLOW)
ぽ
...MM...
POKAN (JAWDROP)
ぽかん
WH— WHAT WAS THAT JUST NOW...?
I SAW THAT "GLOW."
OH, THAT REMINDS ME...

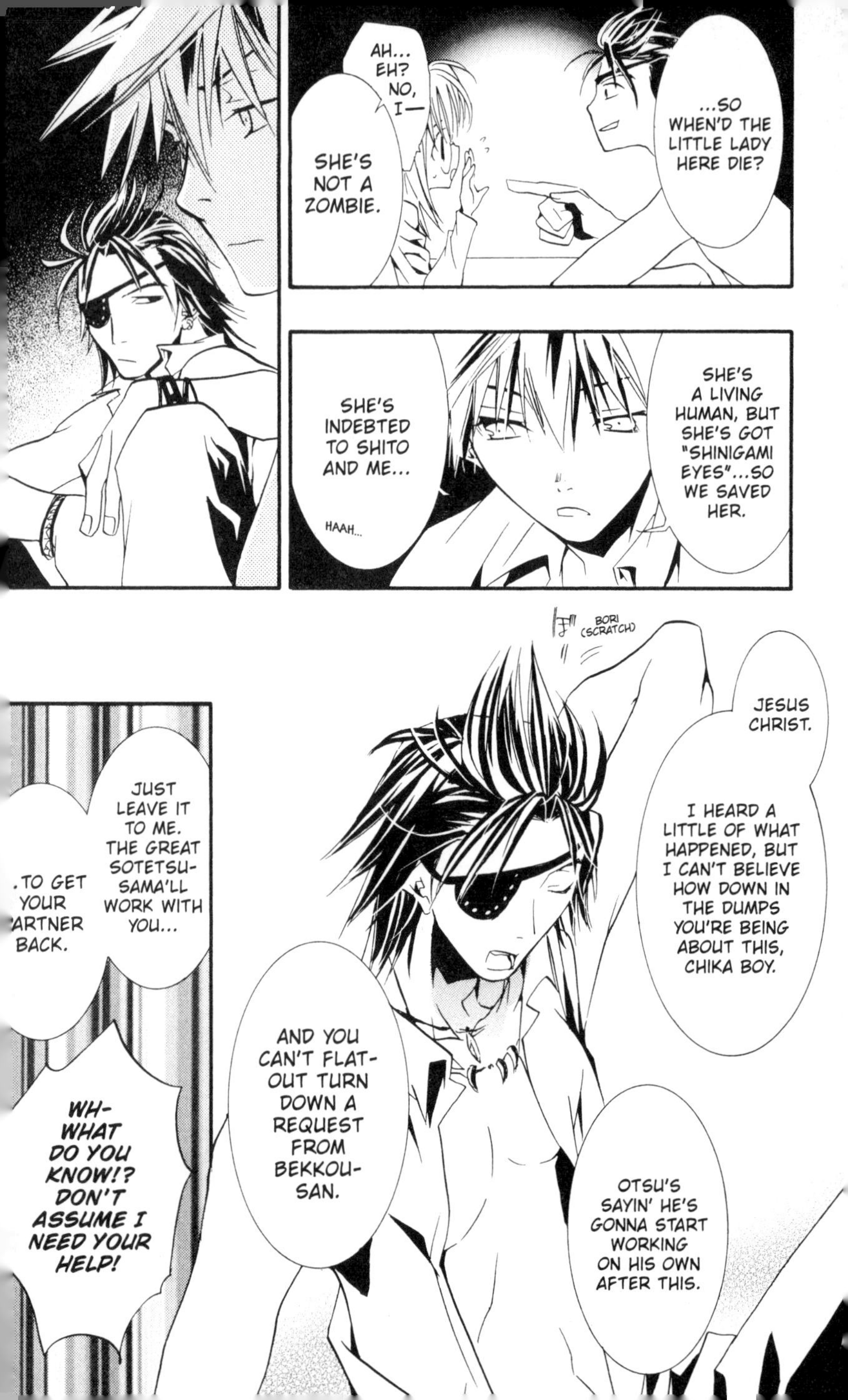
...SO WHEN'D THE LITTLE LADY HERE DIE?
AH... EH? NO, I—
SHE'S NOT A ZOMBIE.
SHE'S A LIVING HUMAN, BUT SHE'S GOT "SHINIGAMI EYES"...SO WE SAVED HER.
SHE'S INDEBTED TO SHITO AND ME...
HAAH...
BORI (SCRATCH)
JESUS CHRIST.
I HEARD A LITTLE OF WHAT HAPPENED, BUT I CAN'T BELIEVE HOW DOWN IN THE DUMPS YOU'RE BEING ABOUT THIS, CHIKA BOY.
OTSU'S SAYIN' HE'S GONNA START WORKING ON HIS OWN AFTER THIS.
AND YOU CAN'T FLAT-OUT TURN DOWN A REQUEST FROM BEKKOU-SAN.
JUST LEAVE IT TO ME. THE GREAT SOTETSU-SAMA'LL WORK WITH YOU...
.TO GET YOUR ARTNER BACK.
WH-WHAT DO YOU KNOW!? DON'T ASSUME I NEED YOUR HELP!

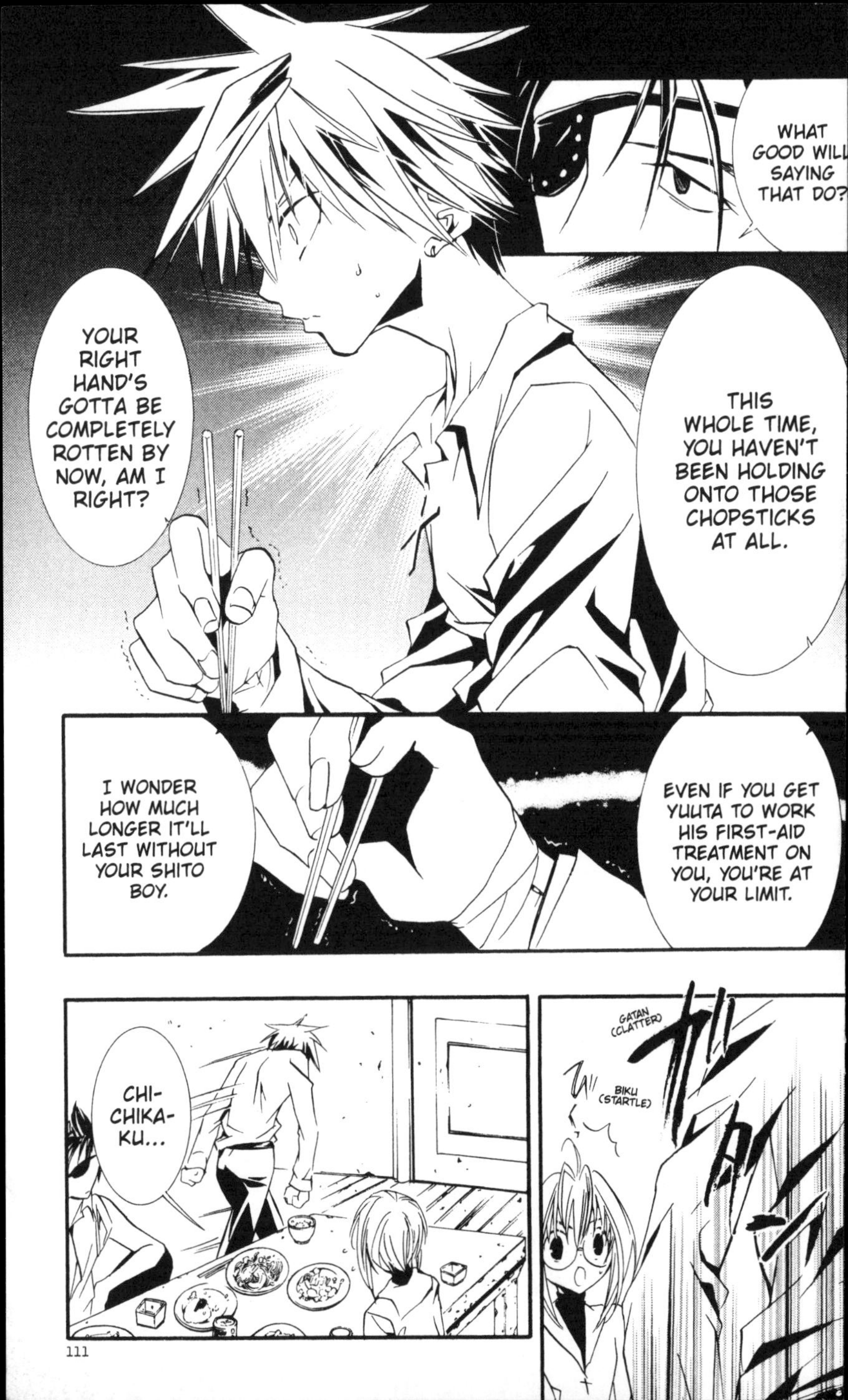
WHAT GOOD WILL SAYING THAT DO?
THIS WHOLE TIME, YOU HAVEN'T BEEN HOLDING ONTO THOSE CHOPSTICKS AT ALL.
YOUR RIGHT HAND'S GOTTA BE COMPLETELY ROTTEN BY NOW, AM I RIGHT?
EVEN IF YOU GET YUUTA TO WORK HIS FIRST-AID TREATMENT ON YOU, YOU'RE AT YOUR LIMIT.
I WONDER HOW MUCH LONGER IT'LL LAST WITHOUT YOUR SHITO BOY.
GATAN (CLATTER)
BIKU (STARTLE)
CHI-CHIKA-KU...

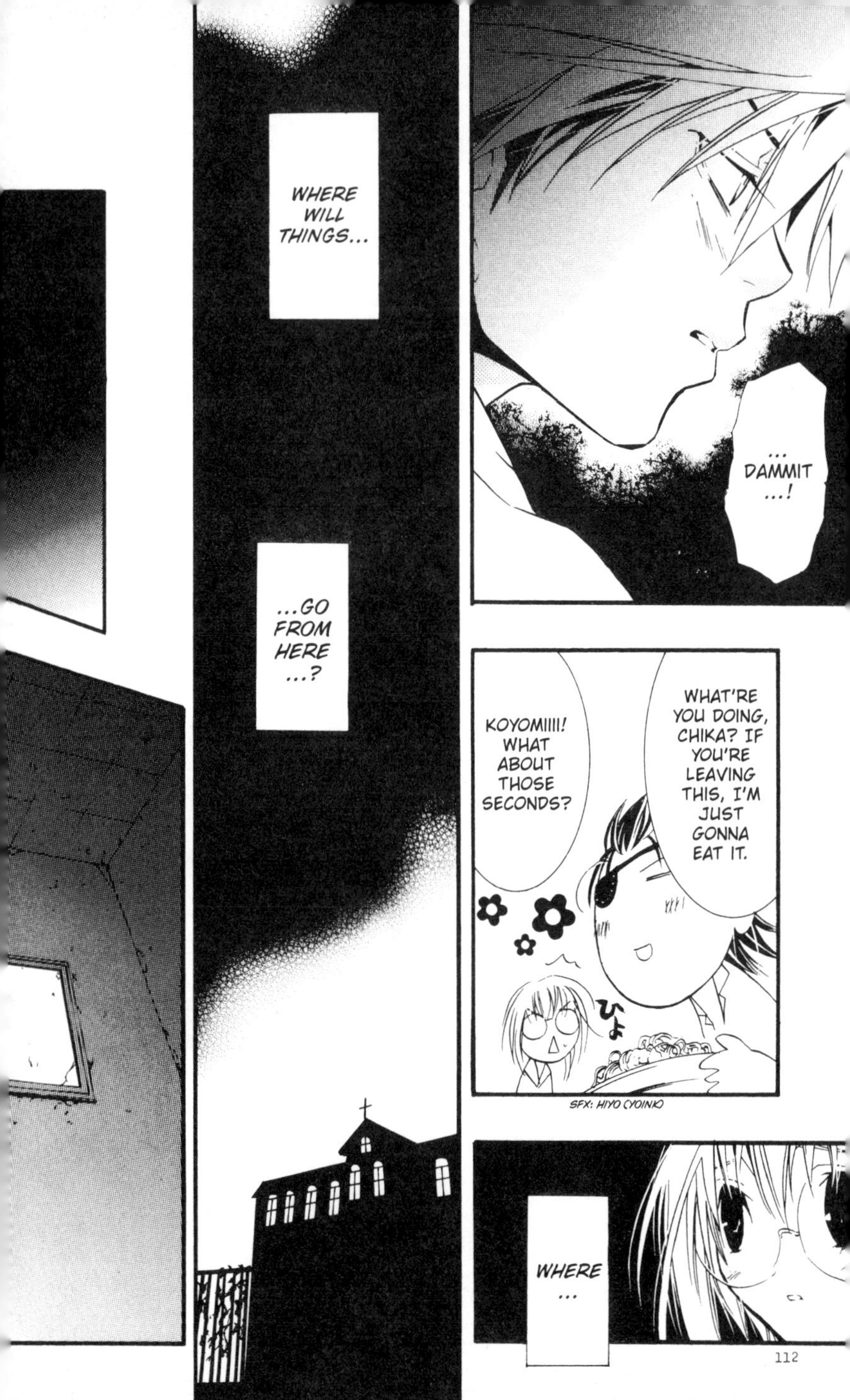
... DAMMIT ...!
WHAT'RE YOU DOING, CHIKA? IF YOU'RE LEAVING THIS, I'M JUST GONNA EAT IT.
KOYOMIIII! WHAT ABOUT THOSE SECONDS?
ひょ
SFX: HIYO (YOINK)
WHERE ...
WHERE WILL THINGS...
...GO FROM HERE ...?

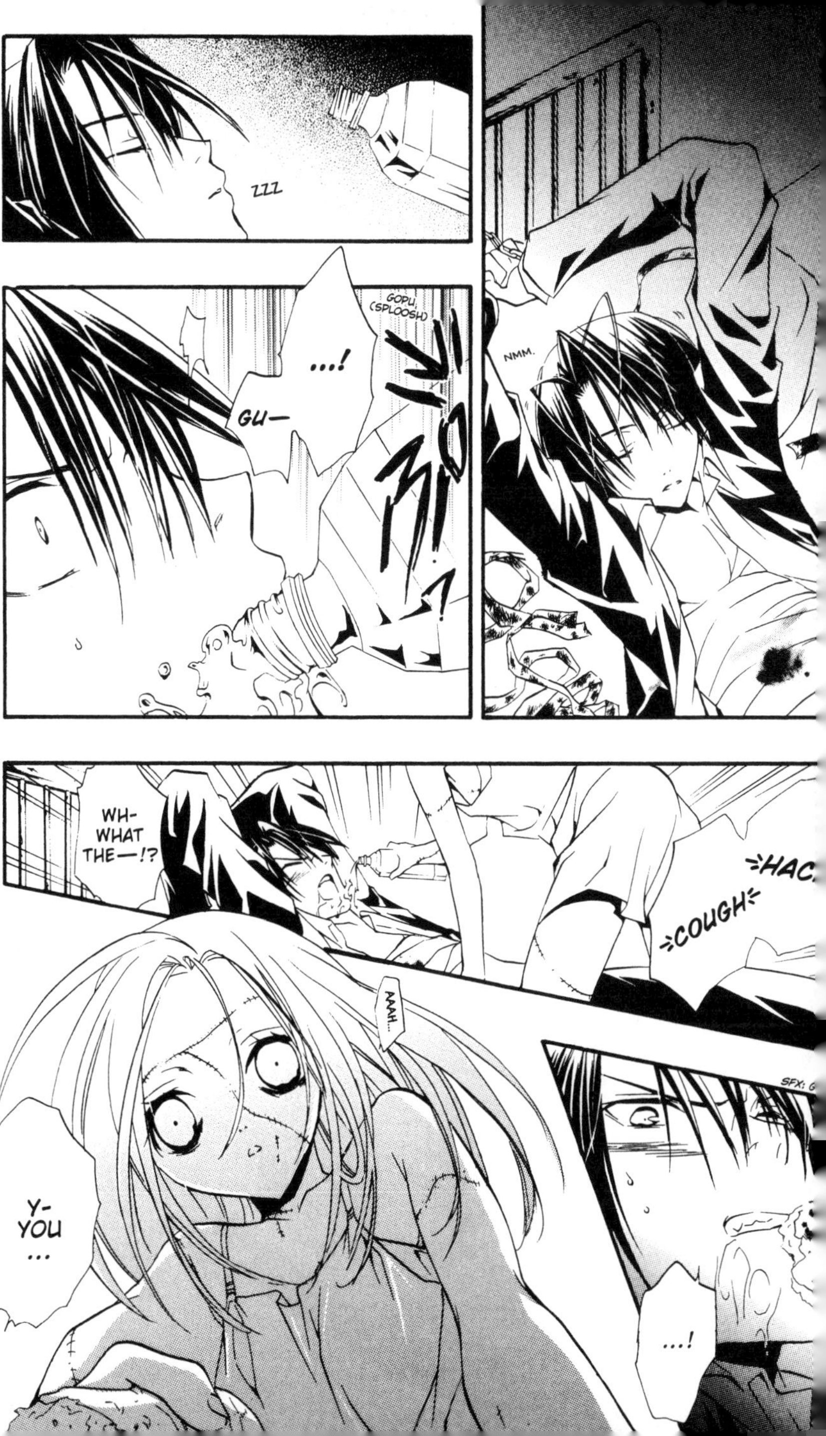
NMM.
ZZZ
GOPU (SPLOOSH)
...!
GU—
HAC
COUGH
WH- WHAT THE—!?
SFX: G
...!
AAAH...
Y- YOU ...

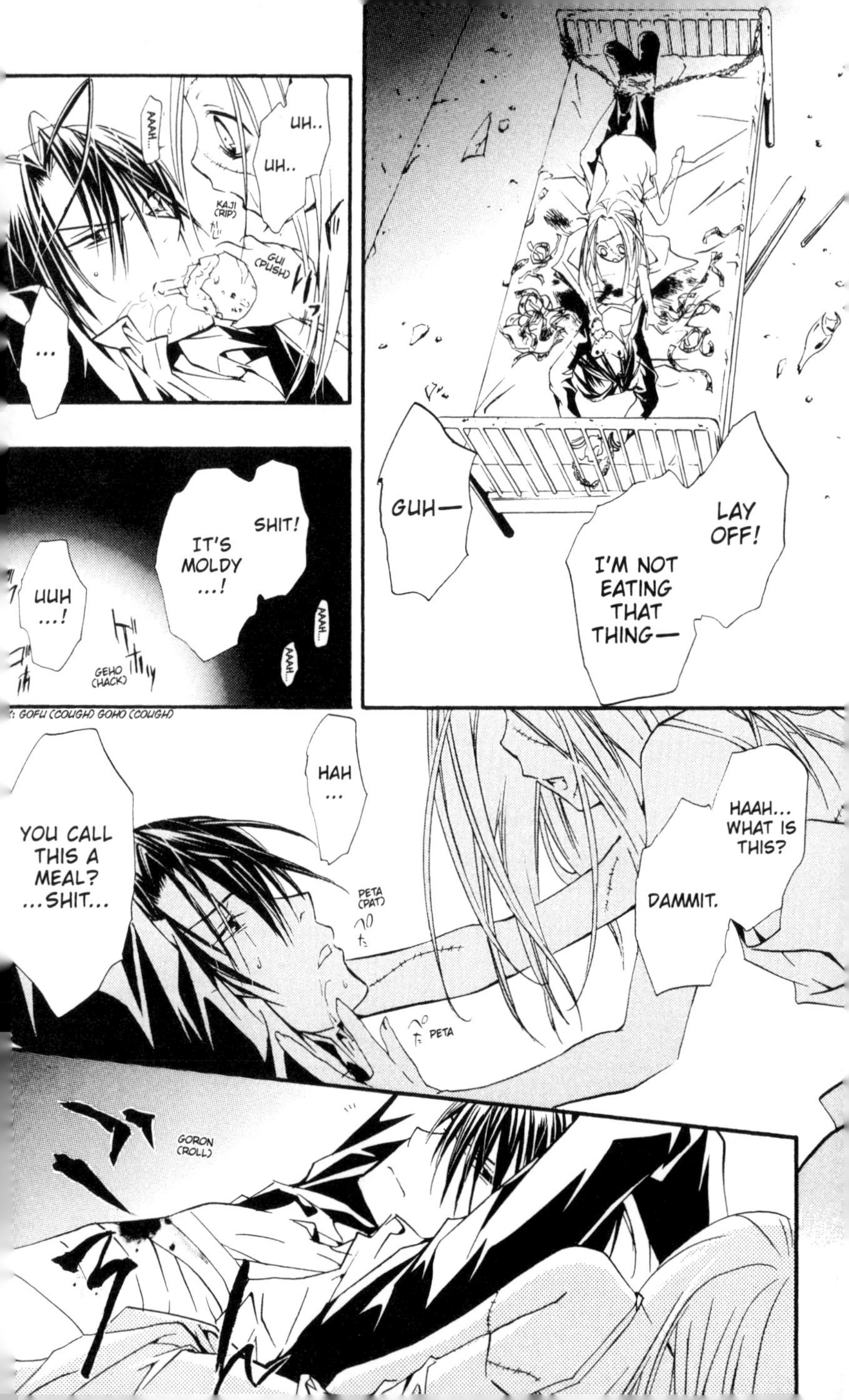
LAY OFF!
I'M NOT EATING THAT THING—
GUH—
UH..
UH..
AAAH...
KAJI (RIP)
GUI (PUSH)
...
SHIT!
IT'S MOLDY ...!
AAAH...
AAAH...
UUH ...!
GEHO (HACK)
*: GOFU (COUGH) GOHO (COUGH)
HAAH... WHAT IS THIS?
DAMMIT.
HAH ...
PETA (PAT)
YOU CALL THIS A MEAL? ...SHIT...
PETA
GORON (ROLL)

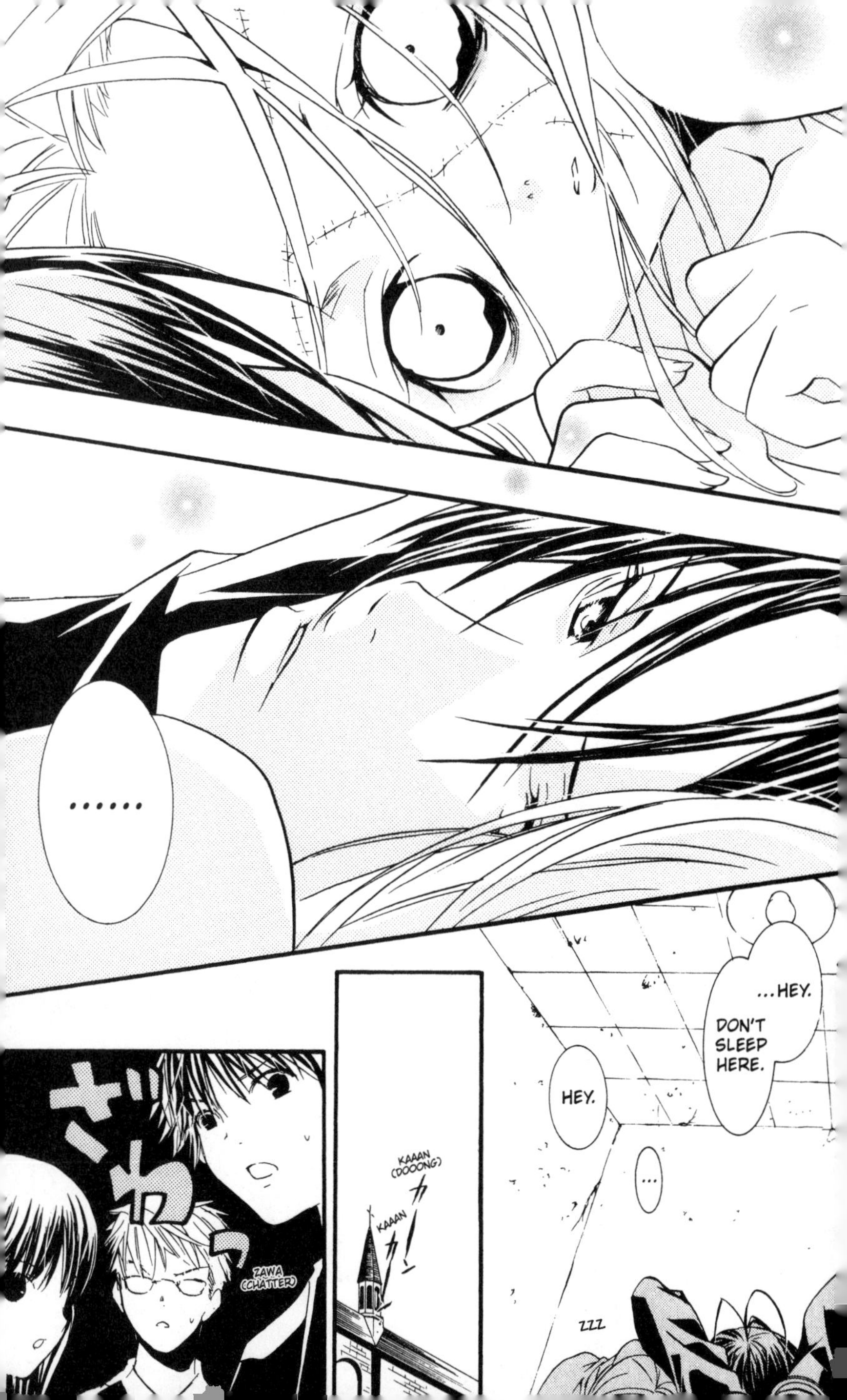
......
...HEY. DON'T SLEEP HERE.
HEY.
...
ZZZ
KAAAN (DOOONG)
KAAAN
ZAWA (CHATTER)

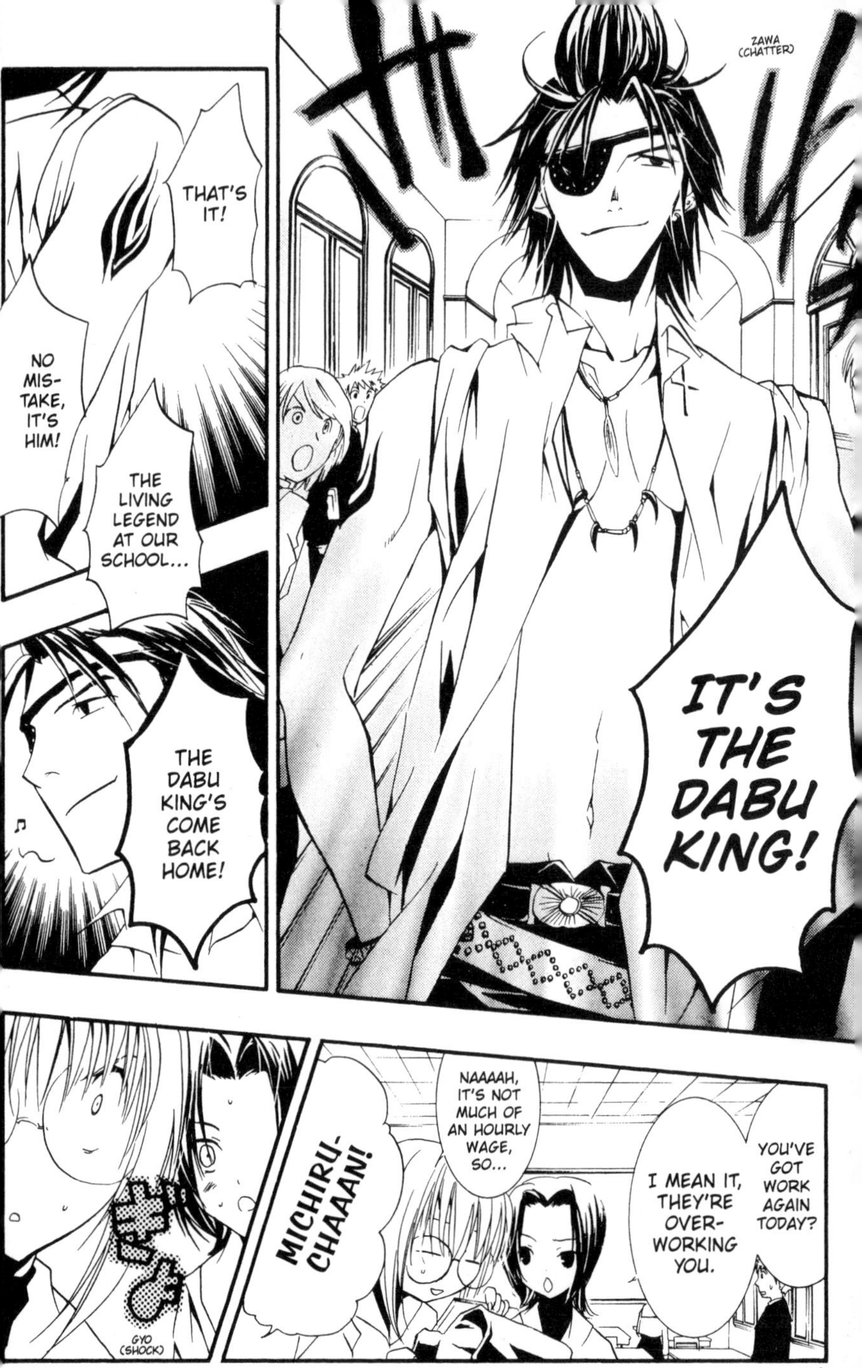
ZAWA (CHATTER)
IT'S THE DABU KING!
THAT'S IT!
NO MIS-TAKE, IT'S HIM!
THE LIVING LEGEND AT OUR SCHOOL...
THE DABU KING'S COME BACK HOME!
YOU'VE GOT WORK AGAIN TODAY?
I MEAN IT, THEY'RE OVER-WORKING YOU.
NAAAAH, IT'S NOT MUCH OF AN HOURLY WAGE, SO...
MICHIRU-CHAAAN!
GYO (SHOCK)

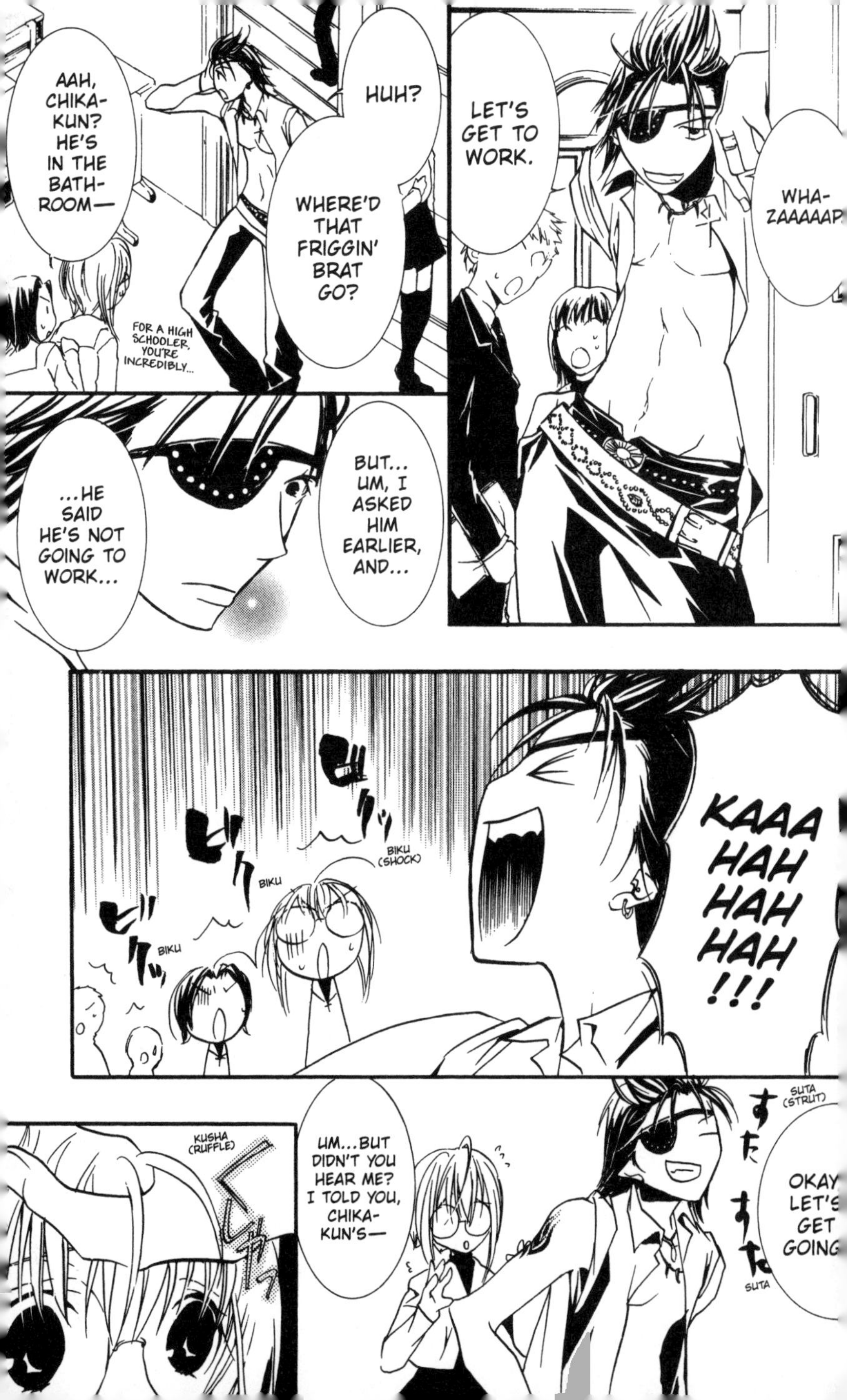
LET'S GET TO WORK.
WHA-ZAAAAAP
HUH?
WHERE'D THAT FRIGGIN' BRAT GO?
AAH, CHIKA-KUN? HE'S IN THE BATH-ROOM—
FOR A HIGH SCHOOLER, YOU'RE INCREDIBLY...
BUT... UM, I ASKED HIM EARLIER, AND...
...HE SAID HE'S NOT GOING TO WORK...
KAAA HAH HAH HAH!!!
BIKU (SHOCK)
BIKU
BIKU
SUTA (STRUT)
OKAY LET'S GET GOING
SUTA
UM...BUT DIDN'T YOU HEAR ME? I TOLD YOU, CHIKA-KUN'S—
KUSHA (RUFFLE)

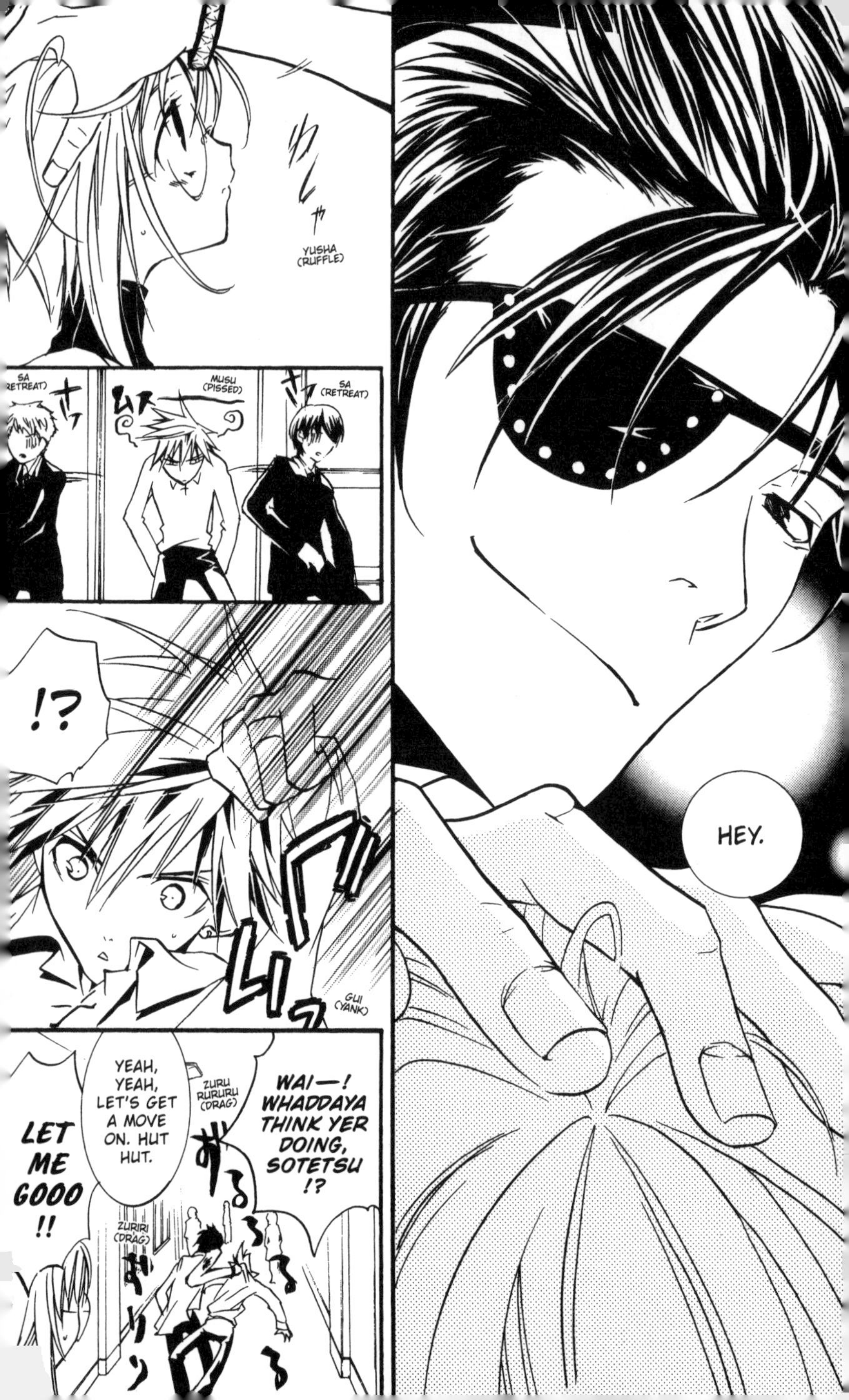
HEY.
YUSHA (RUFFLE)
SA (RETREAT)
MUSU (PISSED)
SA (RETREAT)
!?
GUI (YANK)
WAI—! WHADDAYA THINK YER DOING, SOTETSU !?
ZURU RURURU (DRAG)
YEAH, YEAH, LET'S GET A MOVE ON. HUT HUT.
LET ME GOOO !!
ZURIRI (DRAG)

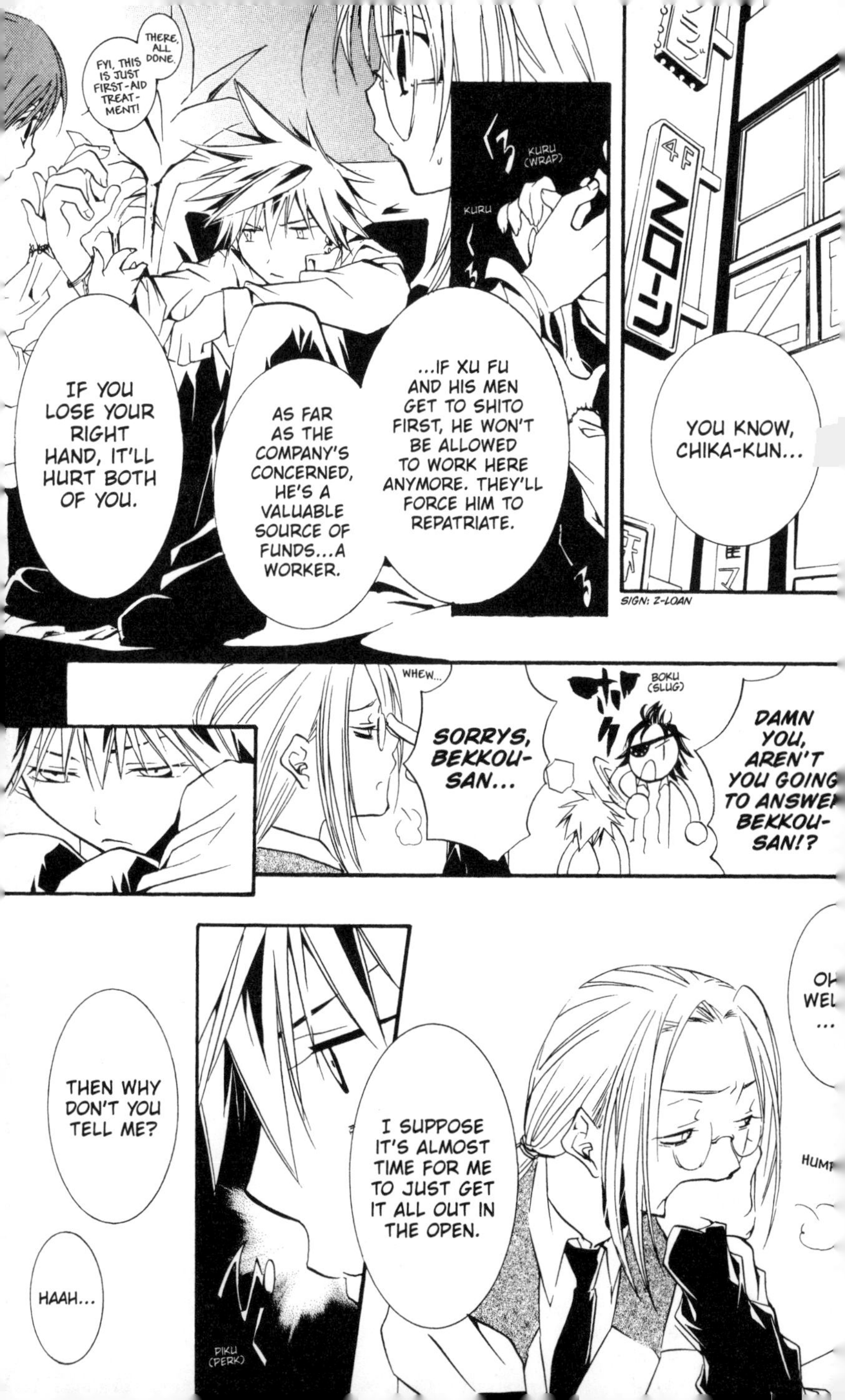
YOU KNOW, CHIKA-KUN...
SIGN: Z-LOAN
KURU (WRAP)
KURU
...IF XU FU AND HIS MEN GET TO SHITO FIRST, HE WON'T BE ALLOWED TO WORK HERE ANYMORE. THEY'LL FORCE HIM TO REPATRIATE.
THERE, ALL DONE.
FYI, THIS IS JUST FIRST-AID TREATMENT!
AS FAR AS THE COMPANY'S CONCERNED, HE'S A VALUABLE SOURCE OF FUNDS...A WORKER.
IF YOU LOSE YOUR RIGHT HAND, IT'LL HURT BOTH OF YOU.
DAMN YOU, AREN'T YOU GOING TO ANSWE BEKKOU-SAN!?
BOKU (SLUG)
SORRYS, BEKKOU-SAN...
WHEW...
OH WEL ...
HUMP
I SUPPOSE IT'S ALMOST TIME FOR ME TO JUST GET IT ALL OUT IN THE OPEN.
PIKU (PERK)
THEN WHY DON'T YOU TELL ME?
HAAH...

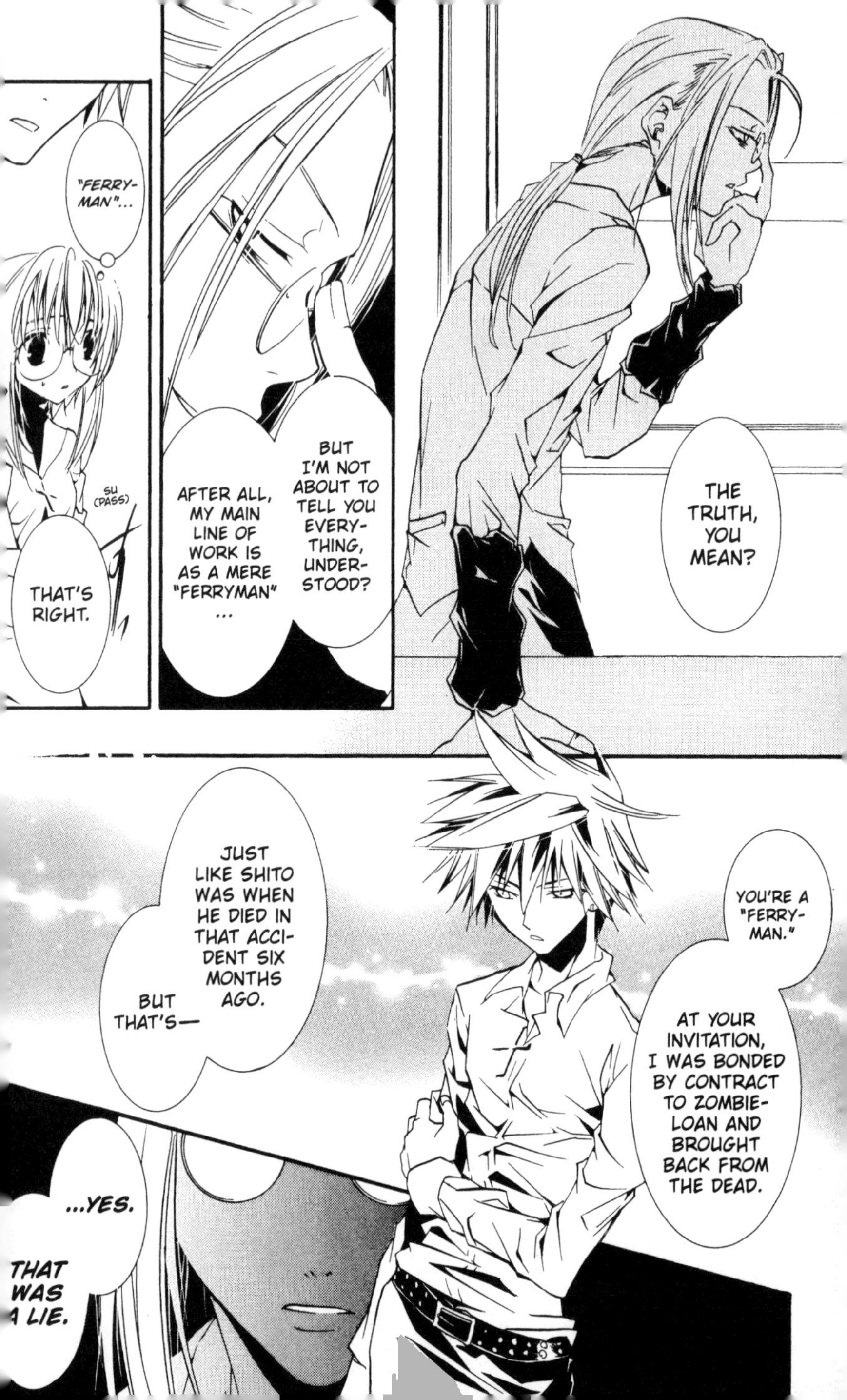
THE TRUTH, YOU MEAN?
BUT I'M NOT ABOUT TO TELL YOU EVERYTHING, UNDERSTOOD?
AFTER ALL, MY MAIN LINE OF WORK IS AS A MERE "FERRYMAN" ...
"FERRYMAN"...
SU (PASS)
THAT'S RIGHT.
YOU'RE A "FERRYMAN."
AT YOUR INVITATION, I WAS BONDED BY CONTRACT TO ZOMBIE-LOAN AND BROUGHT BACK FROM THE DEAD.
JUST LIKE SHITO WAS WHEN HE DIED IN THAT ACCIDENT SIX MONTHS AGO.
BUT THAT'S—
...YES.
THAT WAS A LIE.

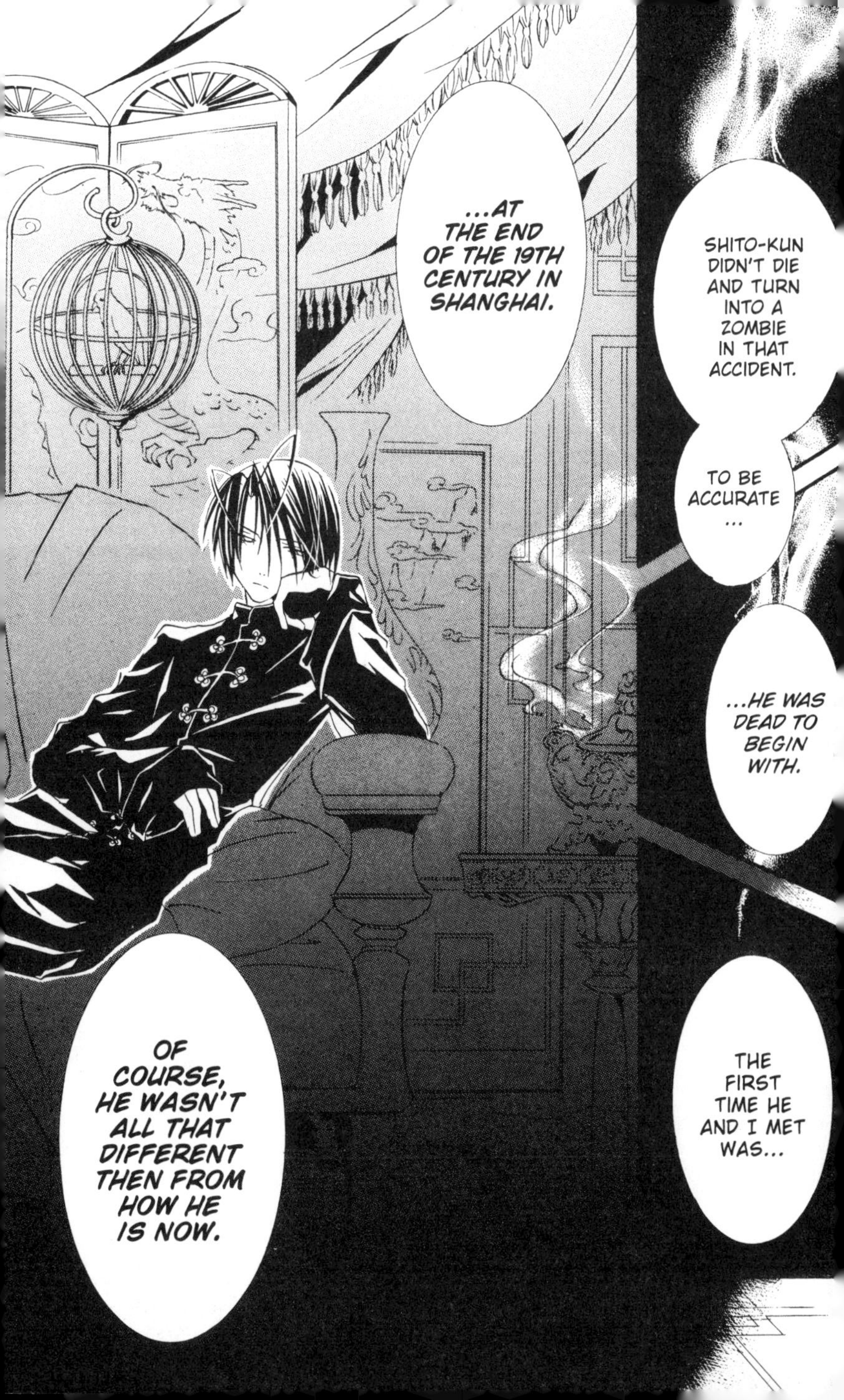
SHITO-KUN DIDN'T DIE AND TURN INTO A ZOMBIE IN THAT ACCIDENT.
TO BE ACCURATE...
...HE WAS DEAD TO BEGIN WITH.
THE FIRST TIME HE AND I MET WAS...
...AT THE END OF THE 19TH CENTURY IN SHANGHAI.
OF COURSE, HE WASN'T ALL THAT DIFFERENT THEN FROM HOW HE IS NOW.

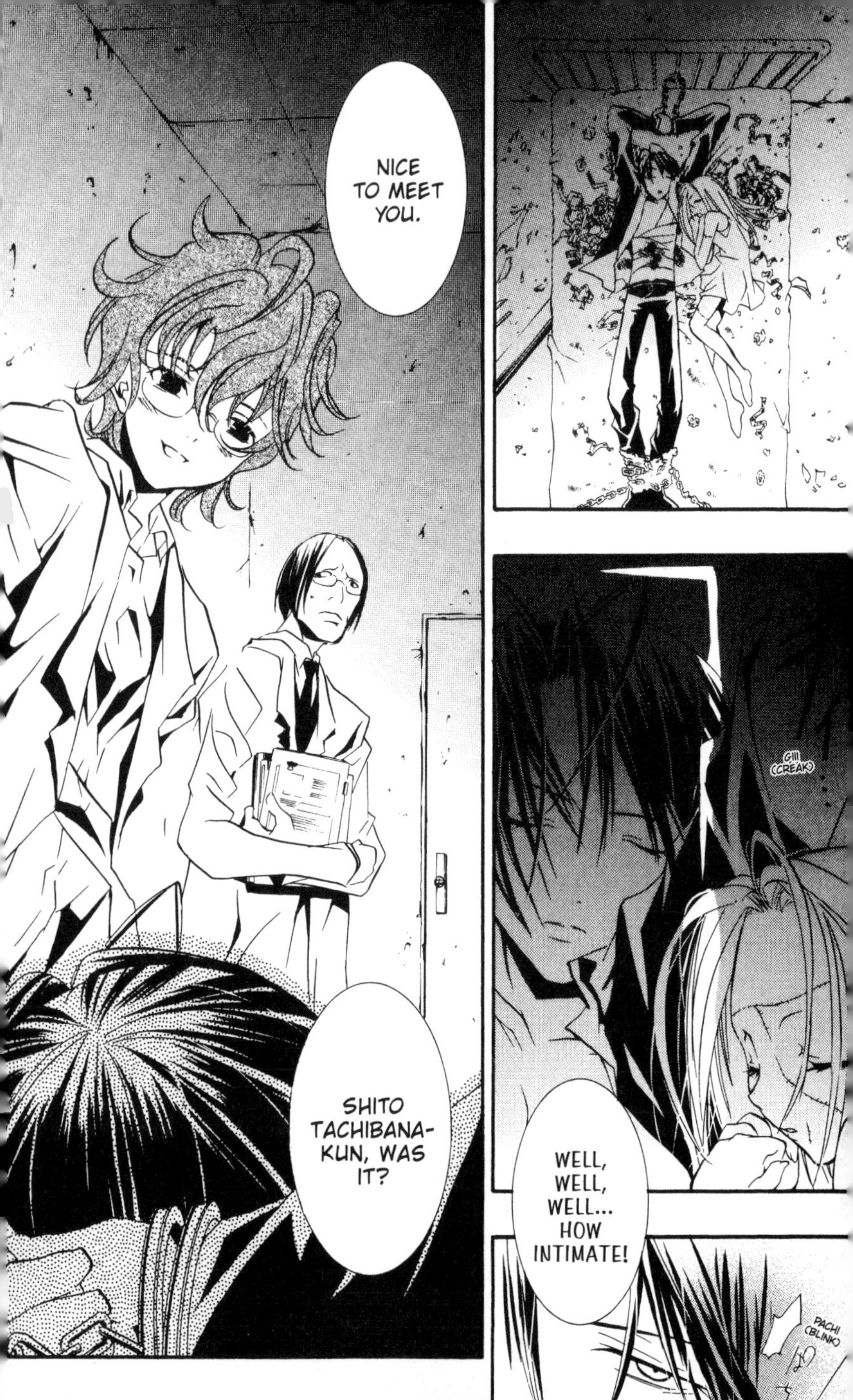
GIII (CREAK)
WELL, WELL, WELL... HOW INTIMATE!
PACHI (BLINK)
NICE TO MEET YOU.
SHITO TACHIBANA-KUN, WAS IT?

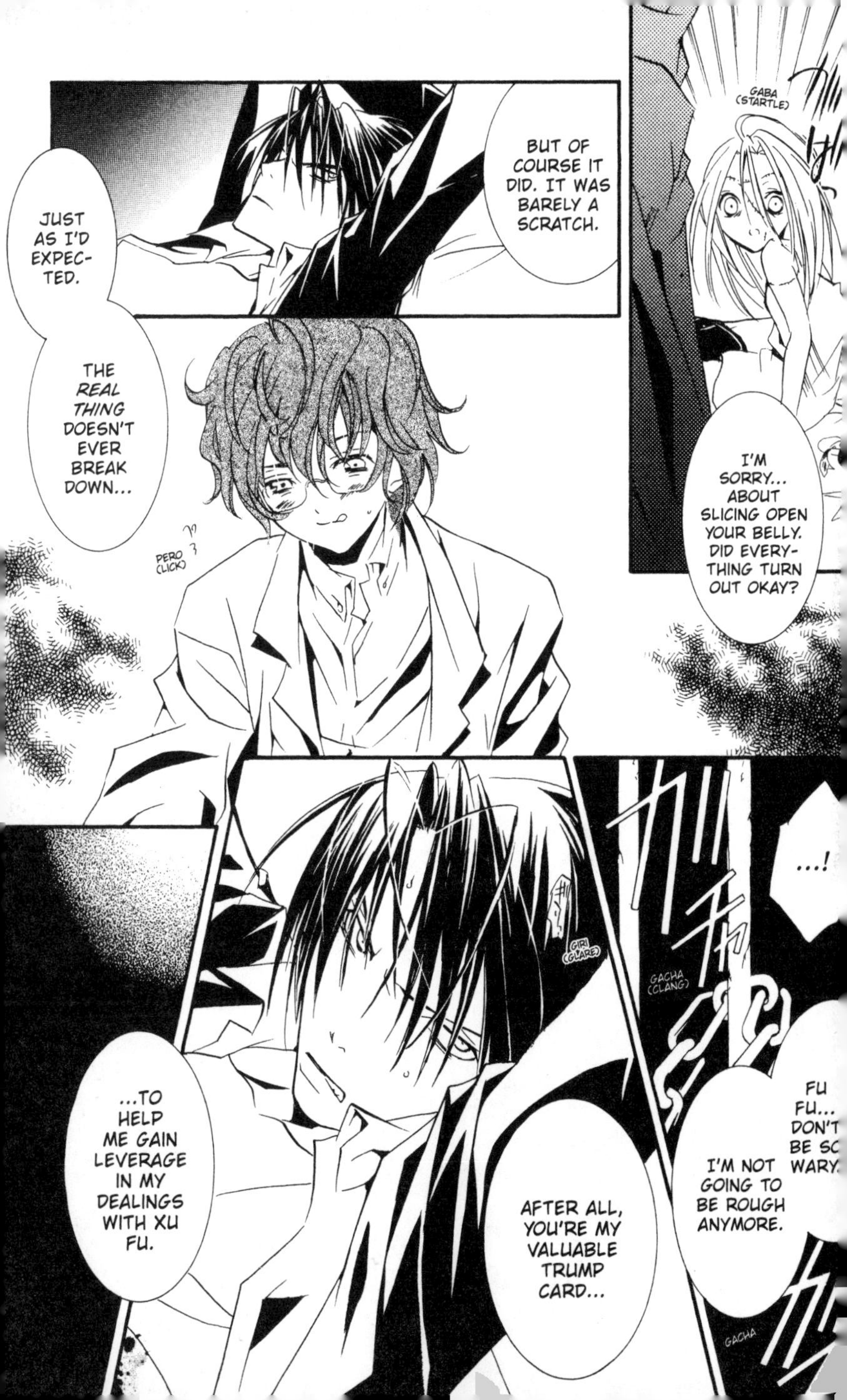
GABA (STARTLE)
I'M SORRY... ABOUT SLICING OPEN YOUR BELLY. DID EVERYTHING TURN OUT OKAY?
BUT OF COURSE IT DID. IT WAS BARELY A SCRATCH.
JUST AS I'D EXPECTED.
THE *REAL THING* DOESN'T EVER BREAK DOWN...
PERO (LICK)
...!
GACHA (CLANG)
FU FU... DON'T BE SO WARY.
I'M NOT GOING TO BE ROUGH ANYMORE.
GACHA
AFTER ALL, YOU'RE MY VALUABLE TRUMP CARD...
GIRI (GLARE)
...TO HELP ME GAIN LEVERAGE IN MY DEALINGS WITH XU FU.

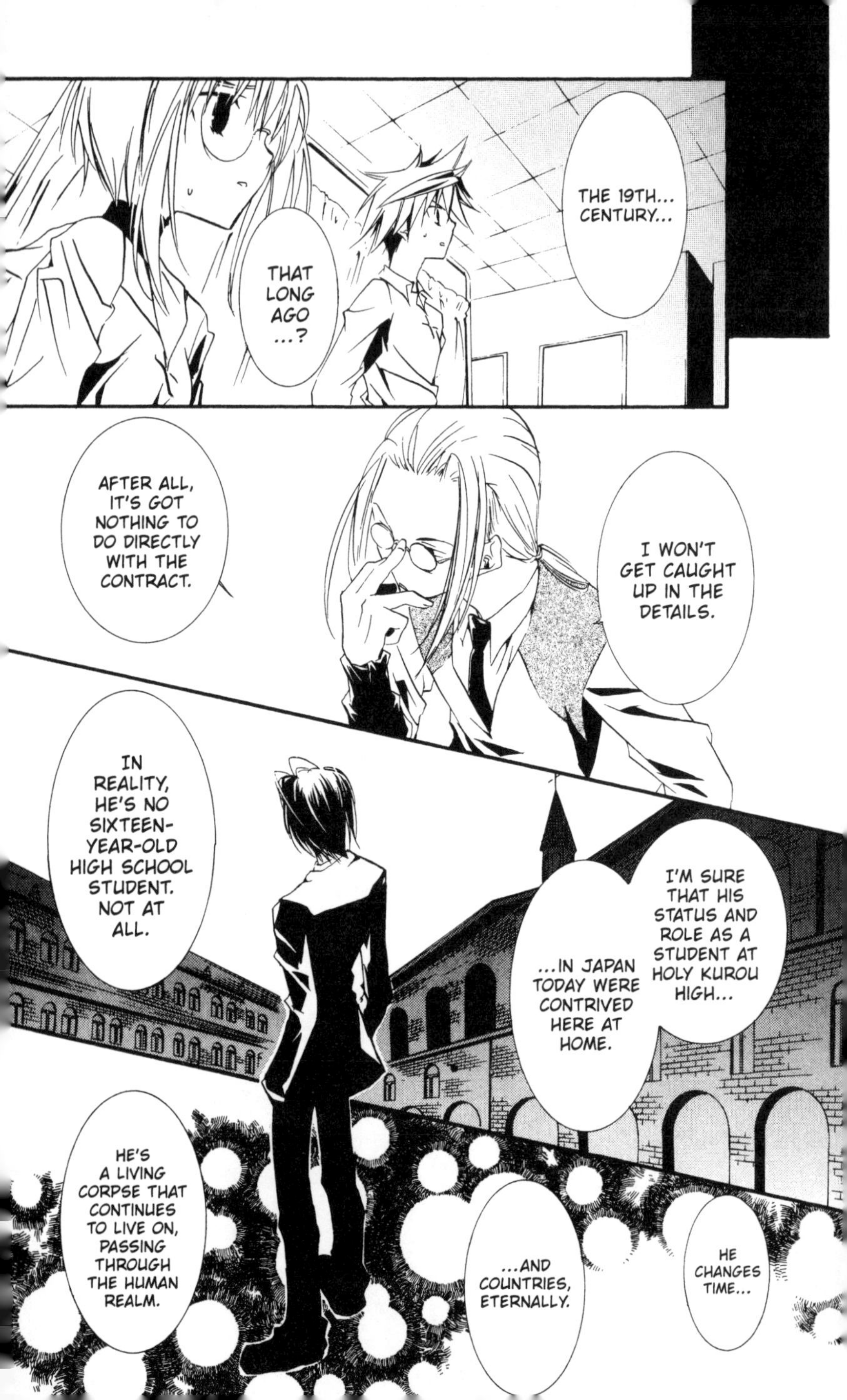
THE 19TH... CENTURY...
THAT LONG AGO...?
I WON'T GET CAUGHT UP IN THE DETAILS.
AFTER ALL, IT'S GOT NOTHING TO DO DIRECTLY WITH THE CONTRACT.
I'M SURE THAT HIS STATUS AND ROLE AS A STUDENT AT HOLY KUROU HIGH...
...IN JAPAN TODAY WERE CONTRIVED HERE AT HOME.
IN REALITY, HE'S NO SIXTEEN-YEAR-OLD HIGH SCHOOL STUDENT. NOT AT ALL.
HE CHANGES TIME...
...AND COUNTRIES, ETERNALLY.
HE'S A LIVING CORPSE THAT CONTINUES TO LIVE ON, PASSING THROUGH THE HUMAN REALM.

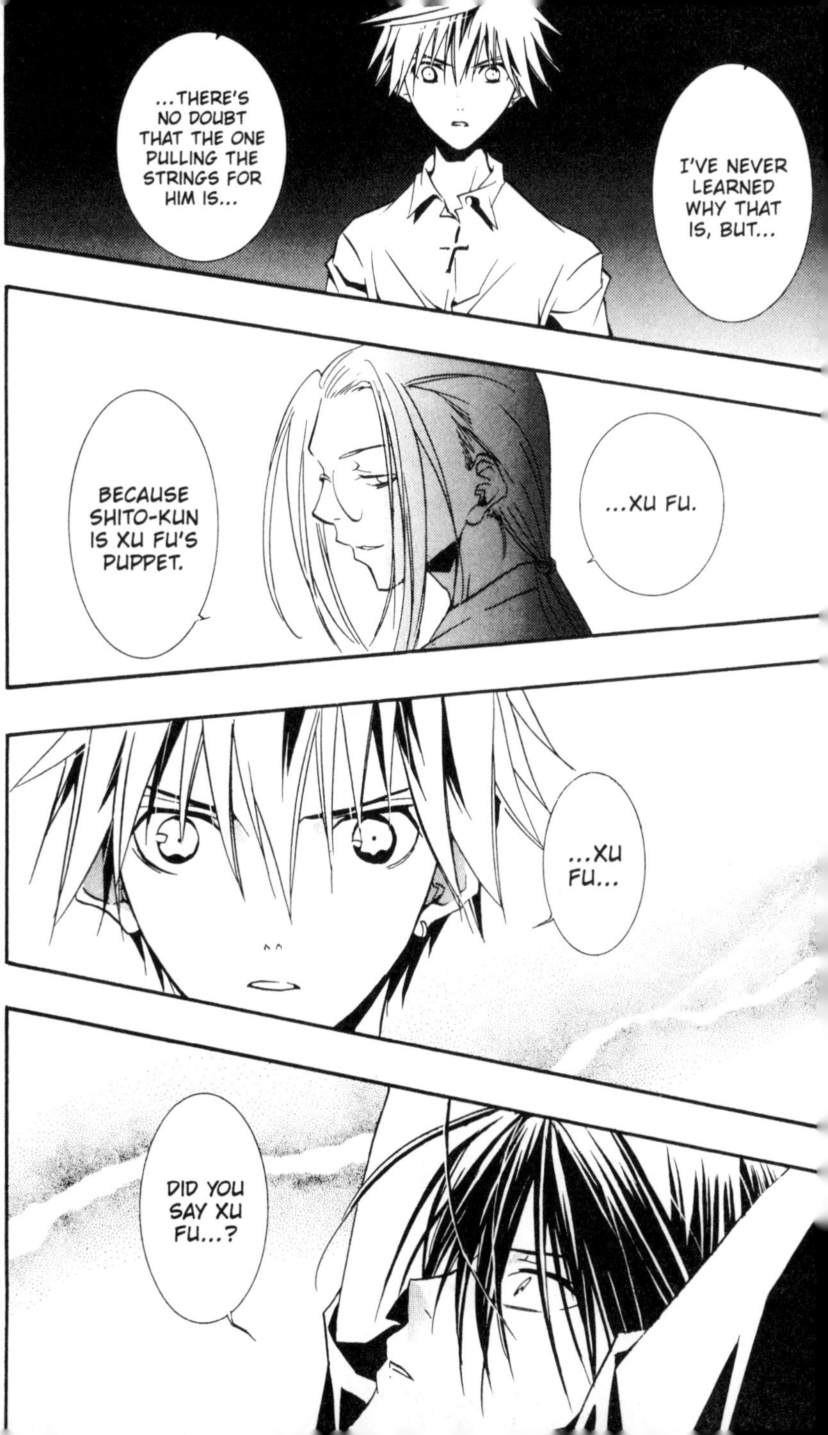
I'VE NEVER LEARNED WHY THAT IS, BUT...
...THERE'S NO DOUBT THAT THE ONE PULLING THE STRINGS FOR HIM IS...
...XU FU.
BECAUSE SHITO-KUN IS XU FU'S PUPPET.
...XU FU...
DID YOU SAY XU FU...?

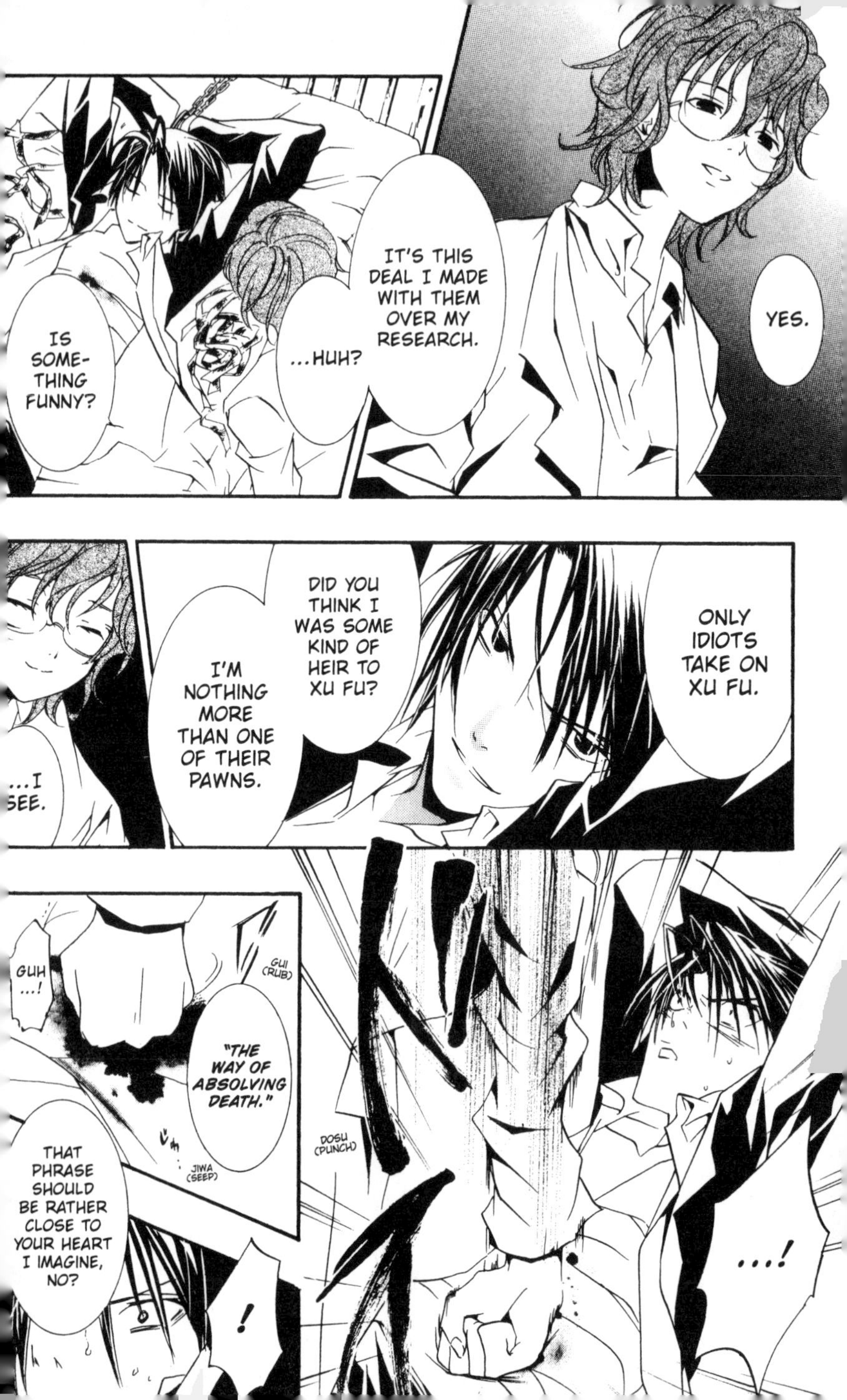
YES.
IT'S THIS DEAL I MADE WITH THEM OVER MY RESEARCH.
...HUH?
IS SOME-THING FUNNY?
ONLY IDIOTS TAKE ON XU FU.
DID YOU THINK I WAS SOME KIND OF HEIR TO XU FU?
I'M NOTHING MORE THAN ONE OF THEIR PAWNS.
...I SEE.
DOSU (PUNCH)
...!
GUI (RUB)
"THE WAY OF ABSOLVING DEATH."
GUH ...!
JIWA (SEEP)
THAT PHRASE SHOULD BE RATHER CLOSE TO YOUR HEART I IMAGINE, NO?
!

SFX: KACHI (TREMBLE) KACHI

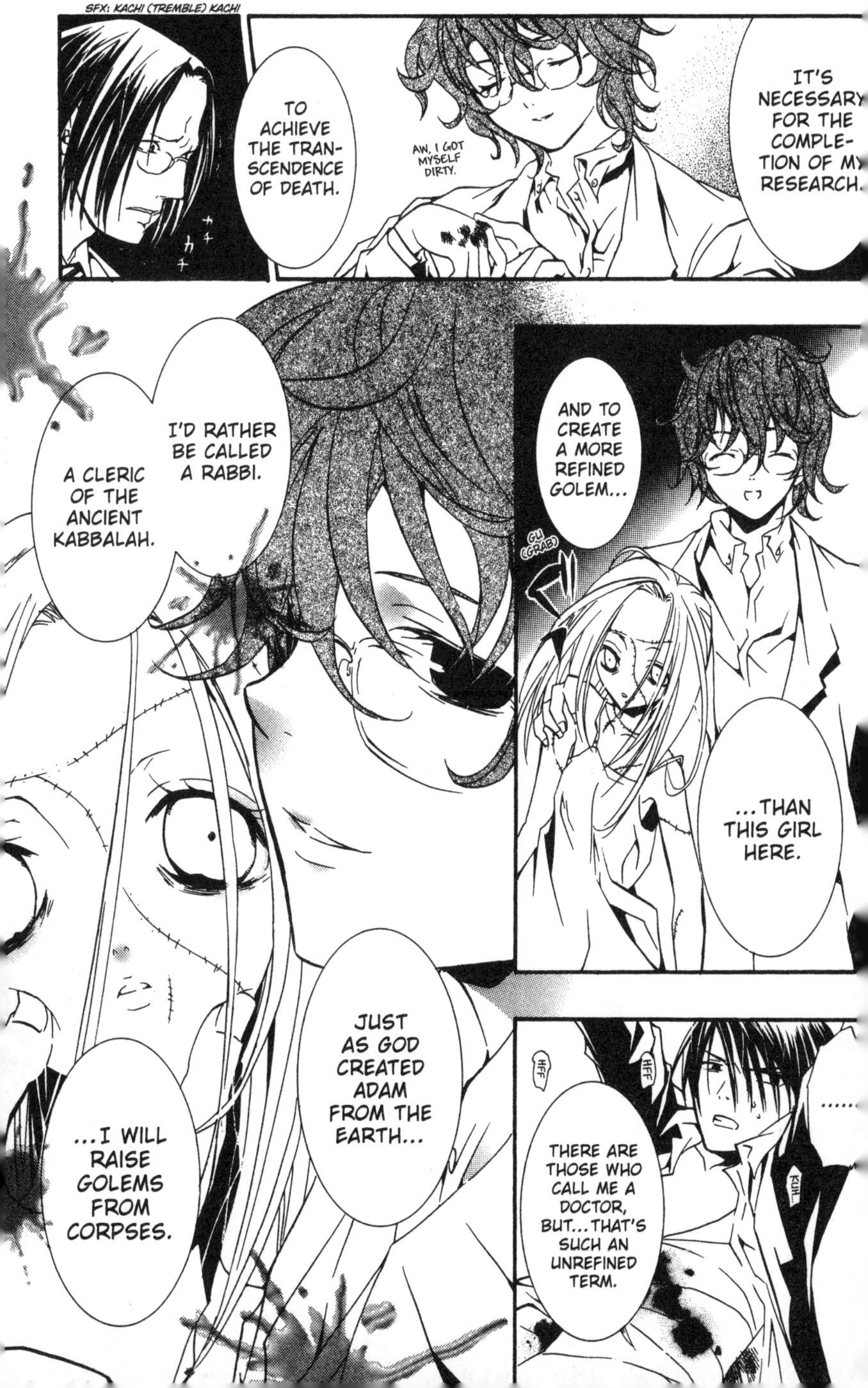
IT'S NECESSARY FOR THE COMPLETION OF MY RESEARCH.
AW, I GOT MYSELF DIRTY.
TO ACHIEVE THE TRANSCENDENCE OF DEATH.
AND TO CREATE A MORE REFINED GOLEM...
GU (GRAB)
...THAN THIS GIRL HERE.
......
KUH...
HFF
HFF
THERE ARE THOSE WHO CALL ME A DOCTOR, BUT...THAT'S SUCH AN UNREFINED TERM.
I'D RATHER BE CALLED A RABBI.
A CLERIC OF THE ANCIENT KABBALAH.
JUST AS GOD CREATED ADAM FROM THE EARTH...
...I WILL RAISE GOLEMS FROM CORPSES.

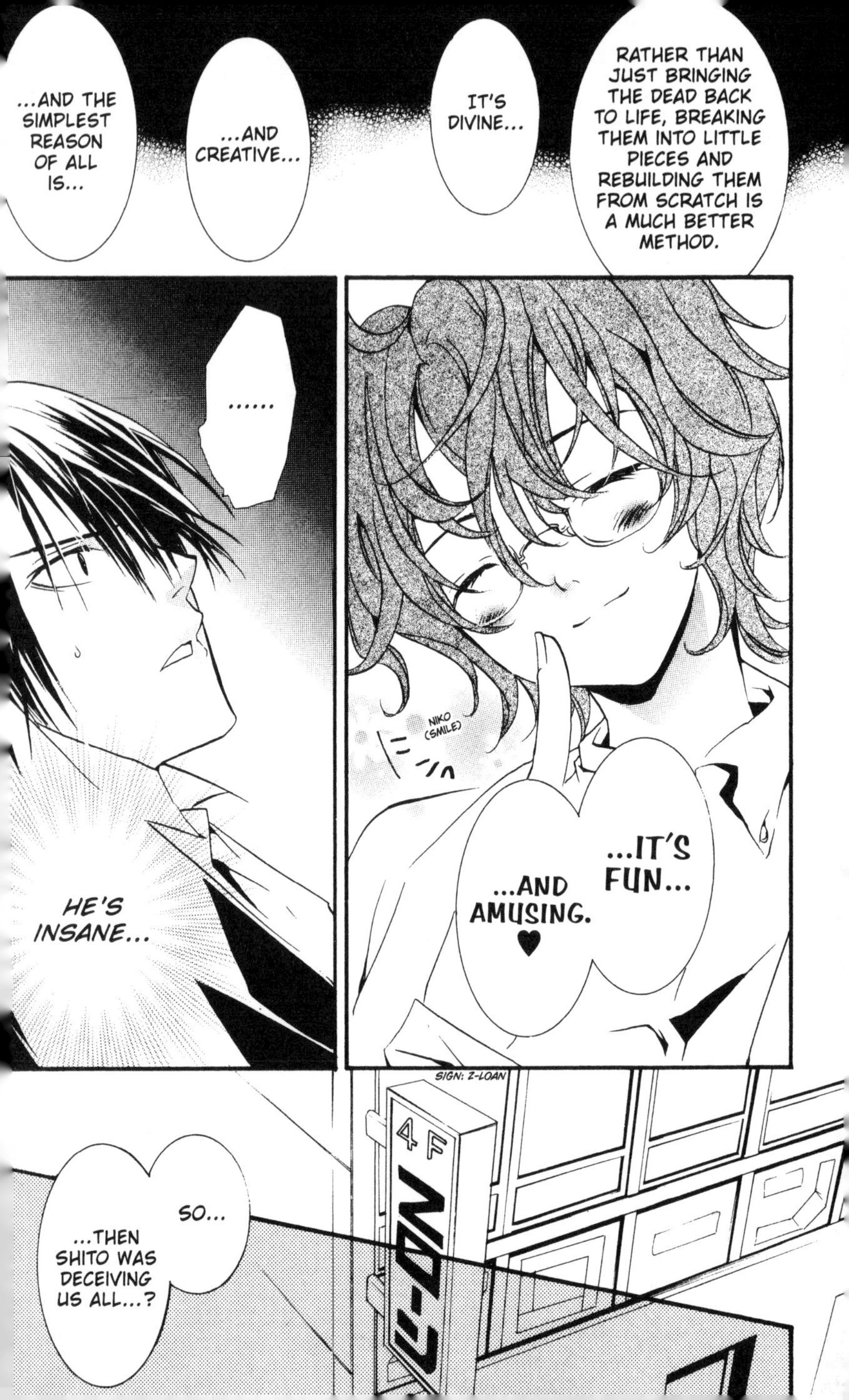
RATHER THAN JUST BRINGING THE DEAD BACK TO LIFE, BREAKING THEM INTO LITTLE PIECES AND REBUILDING THEM FROM SCRATCH IS A MUCH BETTER METHOD.
IT'S DIVINE...
...AND CREATIVE...
...AND THE SIMPLEST REASON OF ALL IS...
NIKO (SMILE)
...IT'S FUN...
...AND AMUSING. ♥
......
HE'S INSANE...
SIGN: Z-LOAN
4 F
SO...
...THEN SHITO WAS DECEIVING US ALL...?

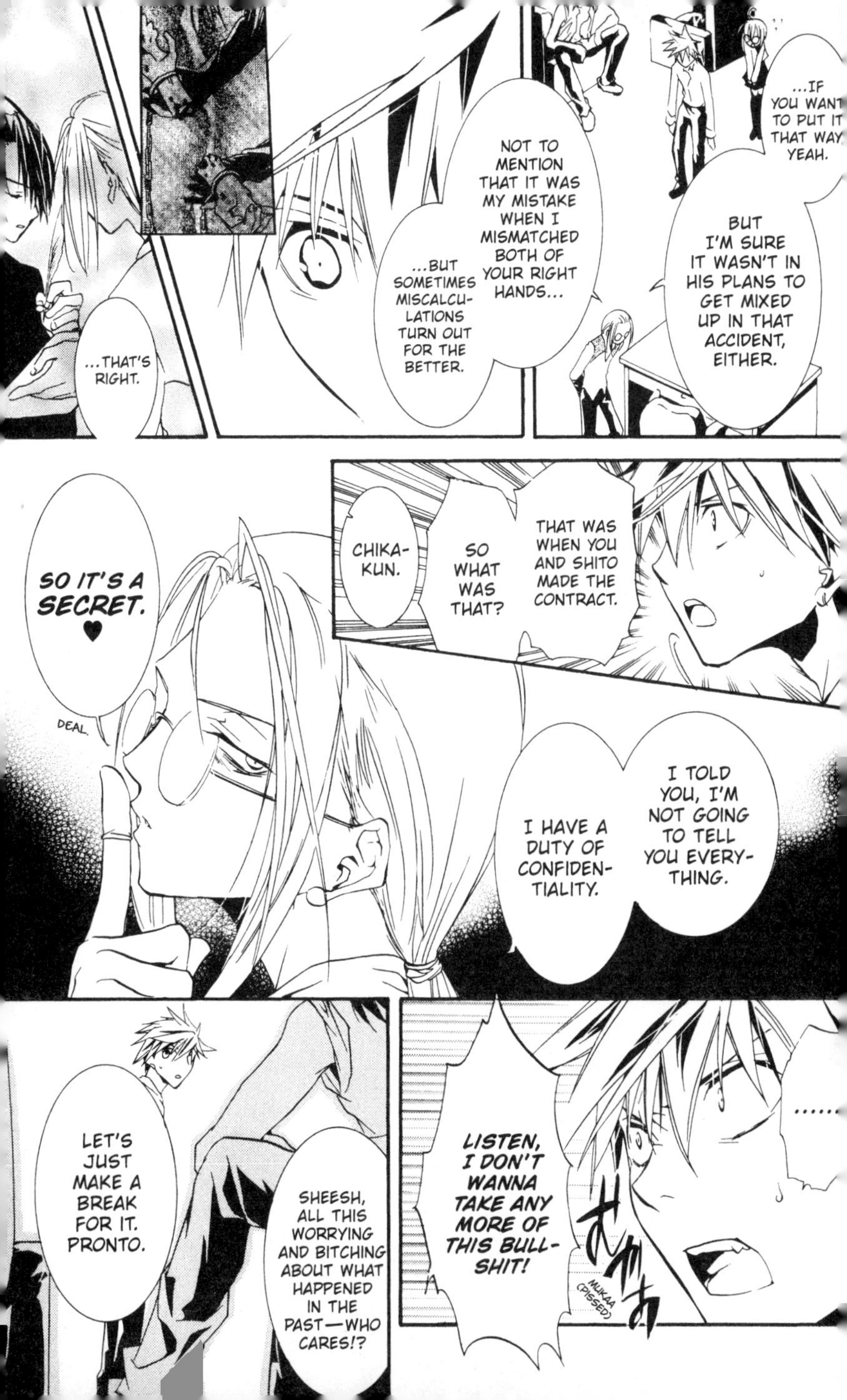
...IF YOU WANT TO PUT IT THAT WAY YEAH.
BUT I'M SURE IT WASN'T IN HIS PLANS TO GET MIXED UP IN THAT ACCIDENT, EITHER.
NOT TO MENTION THAT IT WAS MY MISTAKE WHEN I MISMATCHED BOTH OF YOUR RIGHT HANDS...
...BUT SOMETIMES MISCALCULATIONS TURN OUT FOR THE BETTER.
...THAT'S RIGHT.
THAT WAS WHEN YOU AND SHITO MADE THE CONTRACT.
SO WHAT WAS THAT?
CHIKA-KUN.
I TOLD YOU, I'M NOT GOING TO TELL YOU EVERYTHING.
I HAVE A DUTY OF CONFIDENTIALITY.
SO IT'S A SECRET. ♥
DEAL.
......
LISTEN, I DON'T WANNA TAKE ANY MORE OF THIS BULLSHIT!
MUKAA (PISSED)
SHEESH, ALL THIS WORRYING AND BITCHING ABOUT WHAT HAPPENED IN THE PAST—WHO CARES!?
LET'S JUST MAKE A BREAK FOR IT. PRONTO.

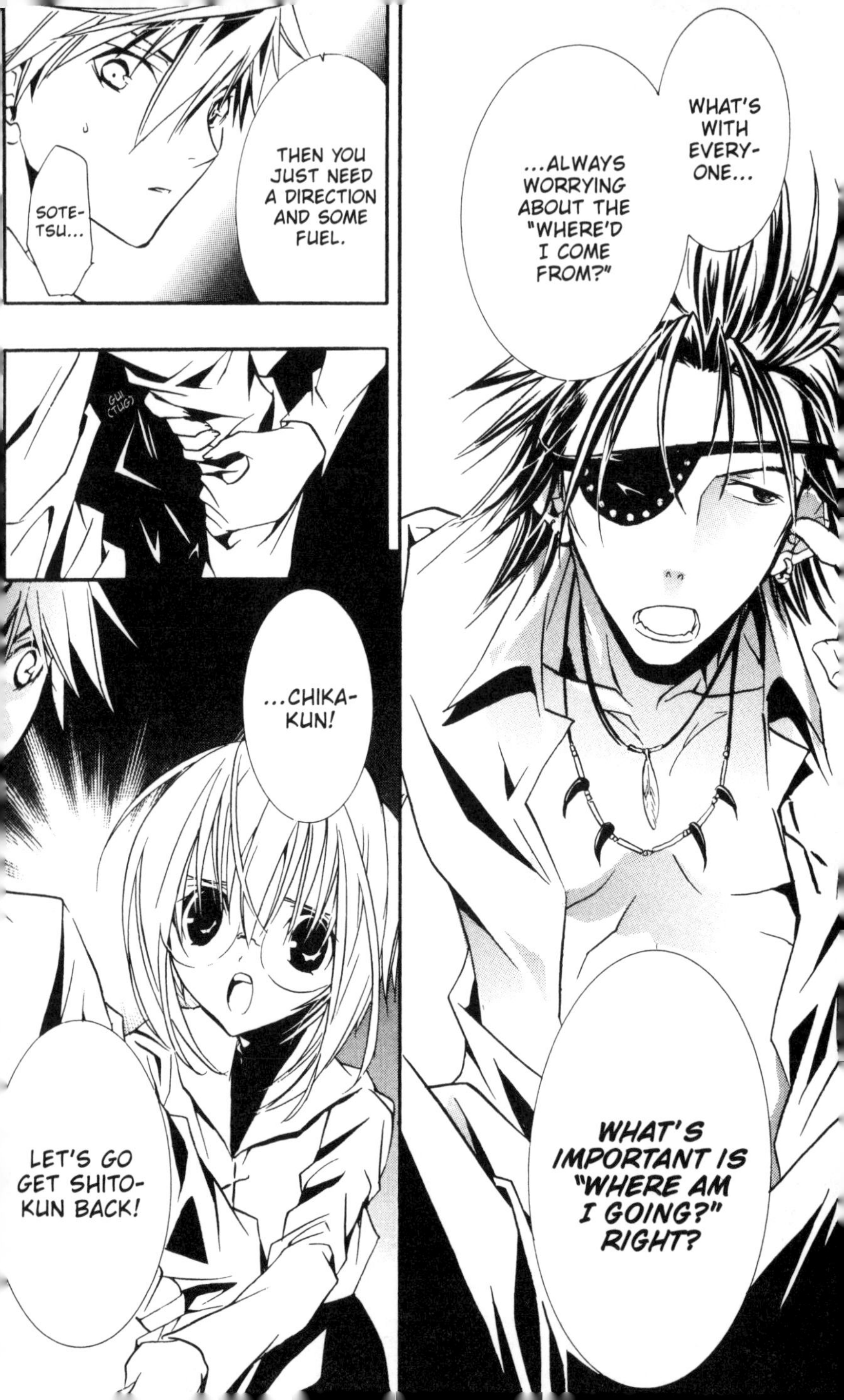
WHAT'S WITH EVERY-ONE...
...ALWAYS WORRYING ABOUT THE "WHERE'D I COME FROM?"
WHAT'S IMPORTANT IS "WHERE AM I GOING?" RIGHT?
THEN YOU JUST NEED A DIRECTION AND SOME FUEL.
SOTE-TSU...
GUI (TUG)
...CHIKA-KUN!
LET'S GO GET SHITO-KUN BACK!

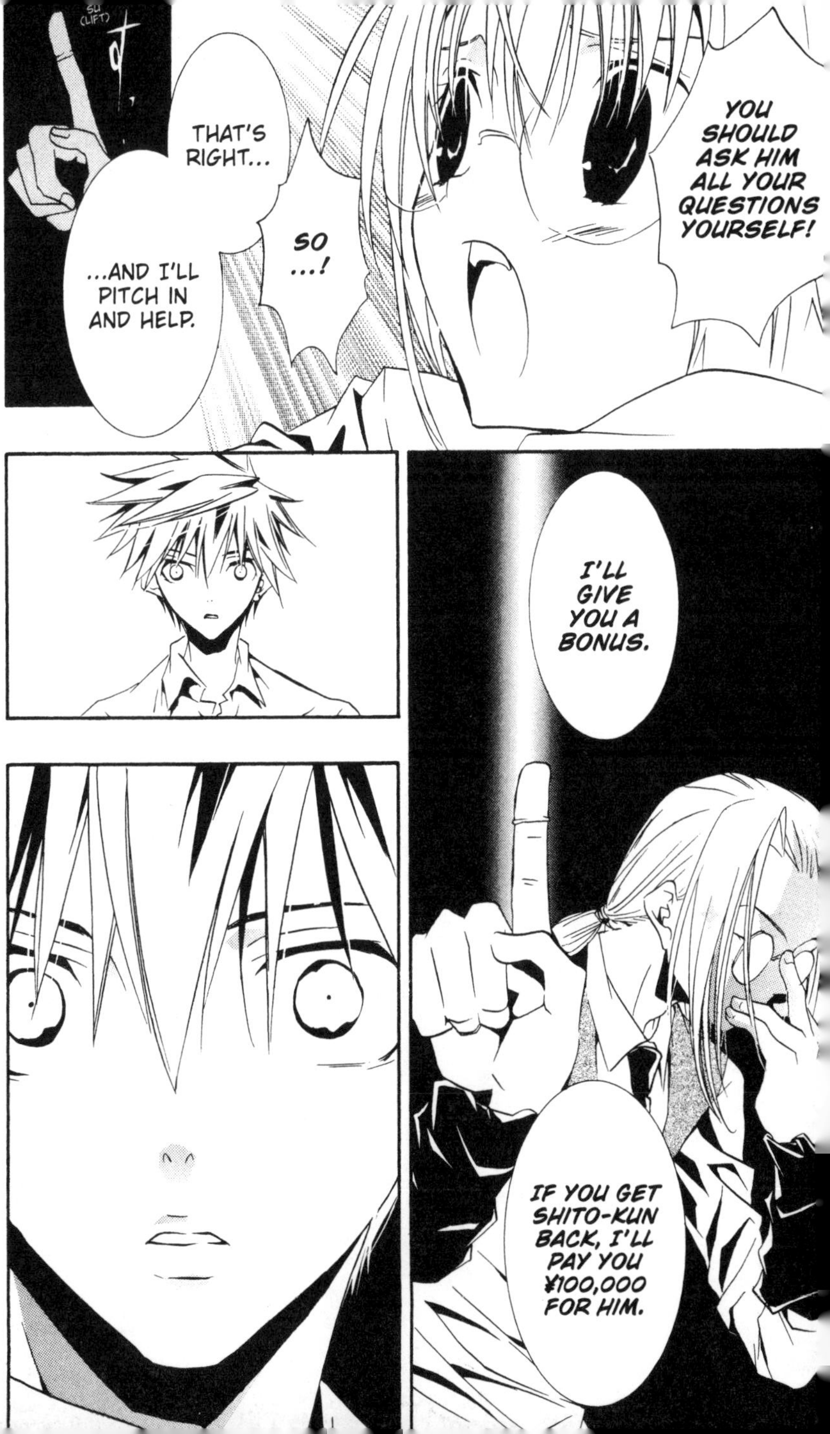
YOU SHOULD ASK HIM ALL YOUR QUESTIONS YOURSELF!
SO ...!
SU (LIFT)
THAT'S RIGHT...
...AND I'LL PITCH IN AND HELP.
I'LL GIVE YOU A BONUS.
IF YOU GET SHITO-KUN BACK, I'LL PAY YOU ¥100,000 FOR HIM.

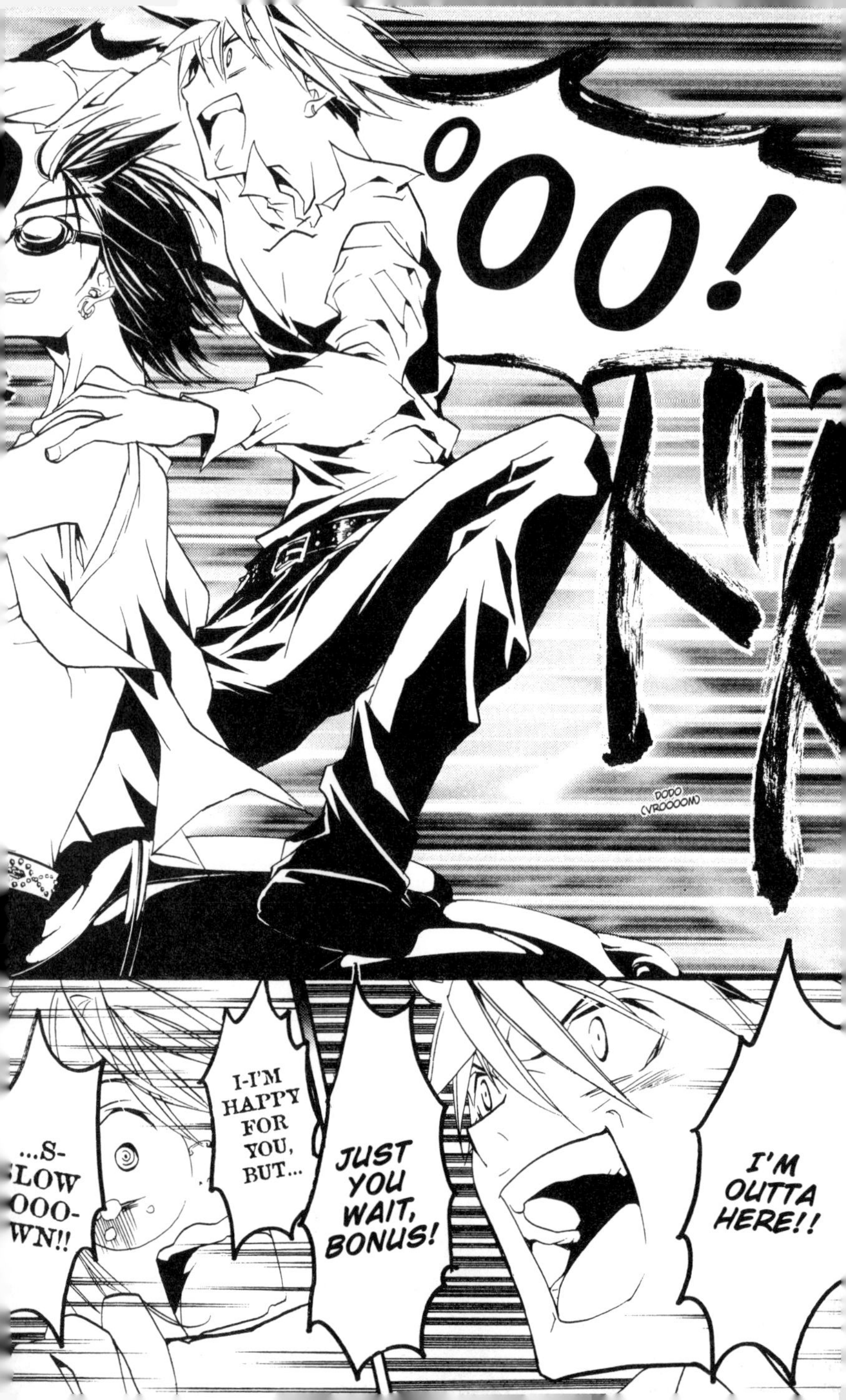
OOO!
DODO (VROOOOM)
I'M OUTTA HERE!!
JUST YOU WAIT, BONUS!
I-I'M HAPPY FOR YOU, BUT...
...S- LOW OOO- WN!!

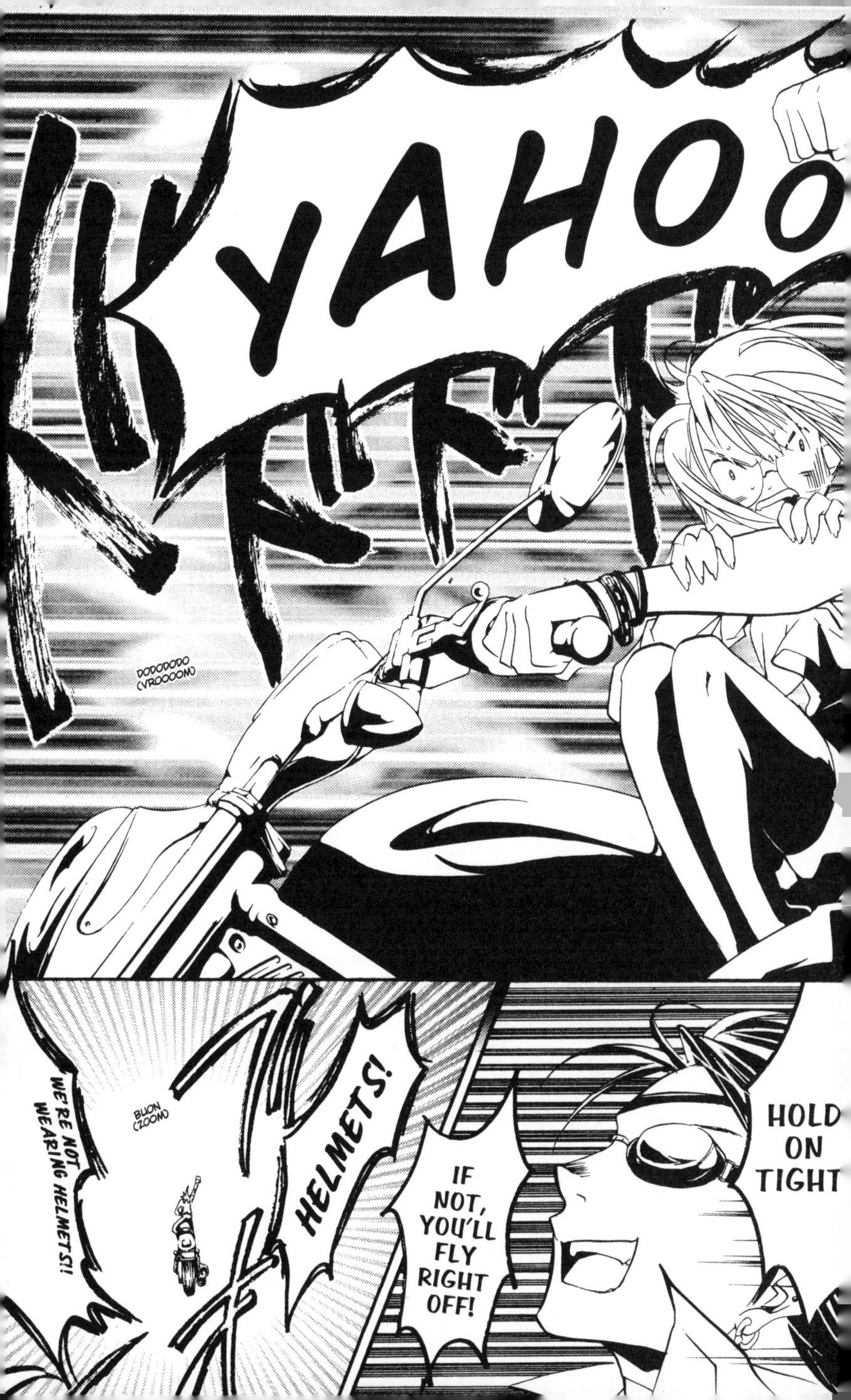
KYAHOO
DODODODO (VROOOOM)
HOLD ON TIGHT
IF NOT, YOU'LL FLY RIGHT OFF!
HELMETS!
BUON (ZOOM)
WE'RE NOT WEARING HELMETS!!

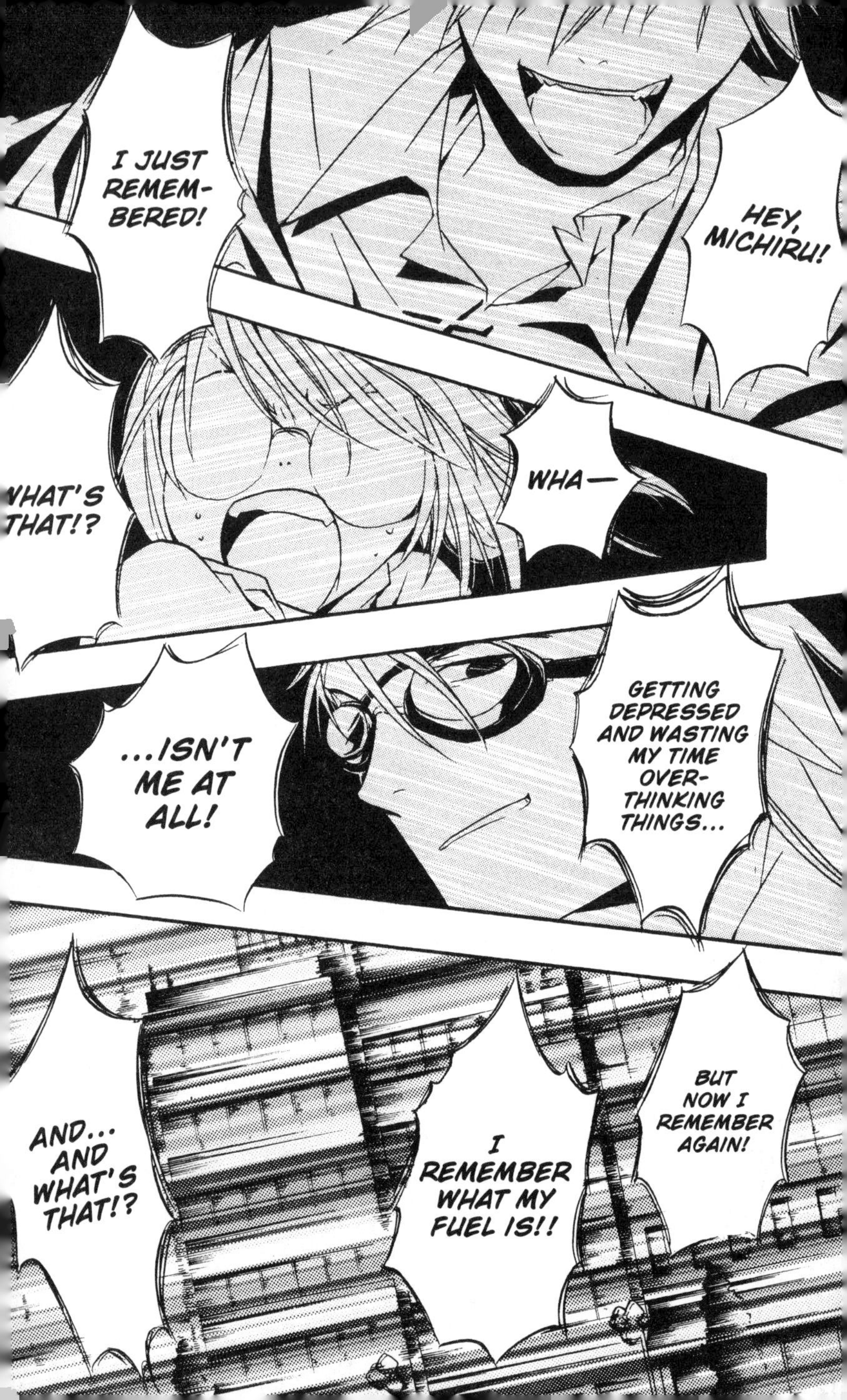
HEY, MICHIRU!
I JUST REMEMBERED!
WHA—
WHAT'S THAT!?
GETTING DEPRESSED AND WASTING MY TIME OVER-THINKING THINGS...
...ISN'T ME AT ALL!
BUT NOW I REMEMBER AGAIN!
I REMEMBER WHAT MY FUEL IS!!
AND... AND WHAT'S THAT!?

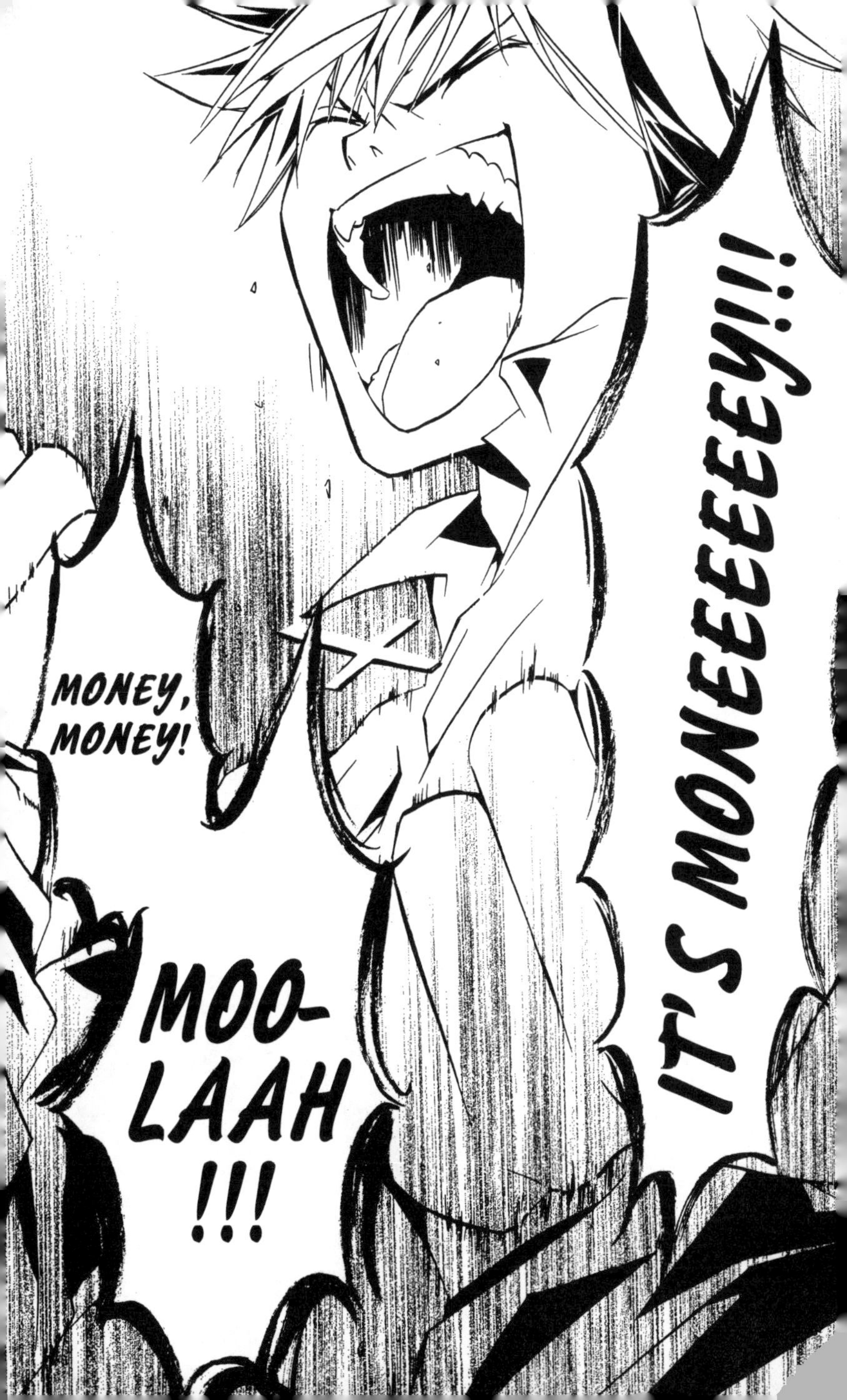
IT'S MONEEEEY!!!
MONEY, MONEY!
MOO-LAAH!!!

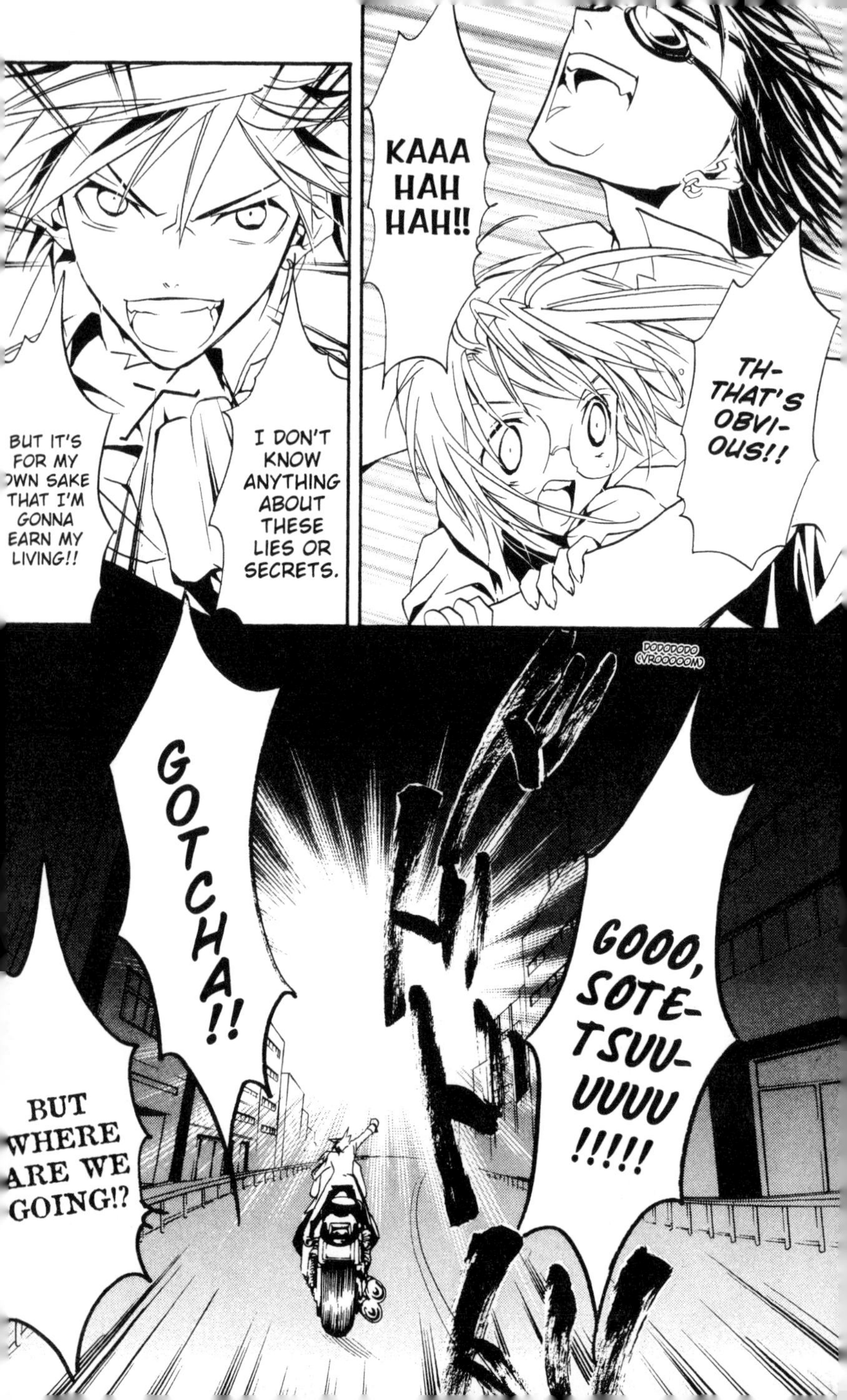
KAAA HAH HAH!!
TH-THAT'S OBVIOUS!!
I DON'T KNOW ANYTHING ABOUT THESE LIES OR SECRETS.
BUT IT'S FOR MY OWN SAKE THAT I'M GONNA EARN MY LIVING!!
DODODODO (VROOOOOM)
GOOO, SOTETSUUUUUU!!!!!
GOTCHA!!
BUT WHERE ARE WE GOING!?

PAYMENT:24

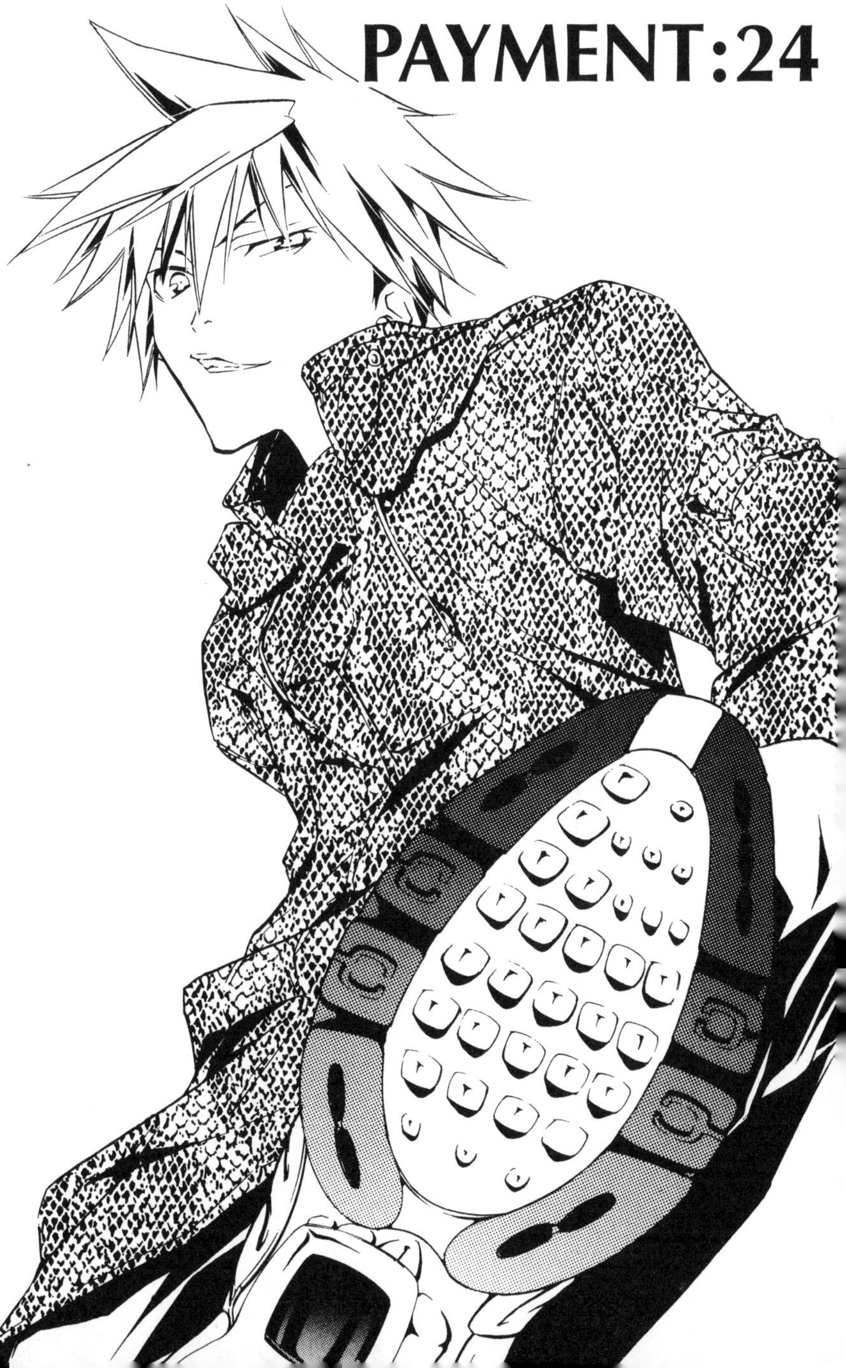

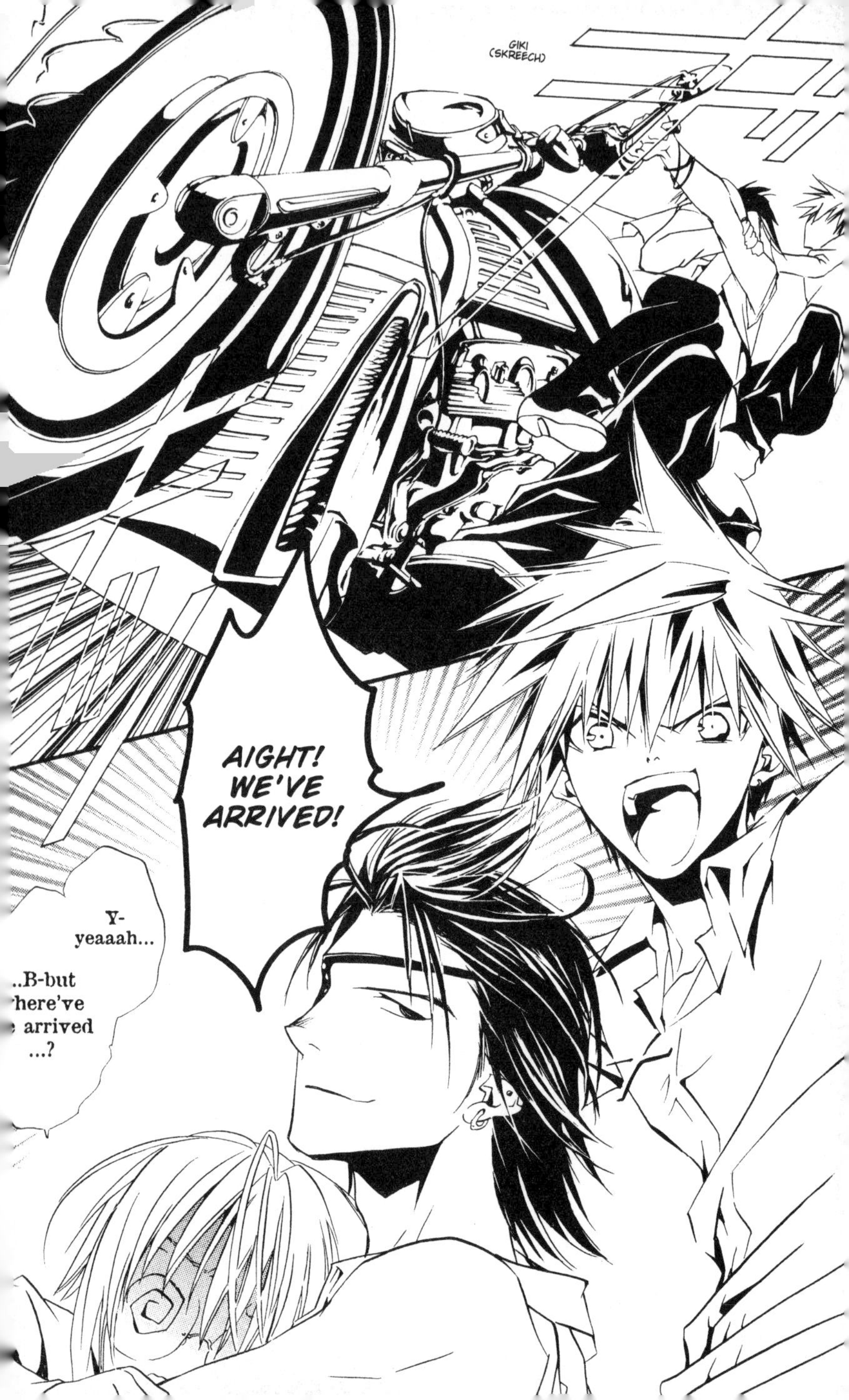
GIKI (SKREECH)
AIGHT! WE'VE ARRIVED!
Y-yeaaah...
..B-but here've arrived ...?

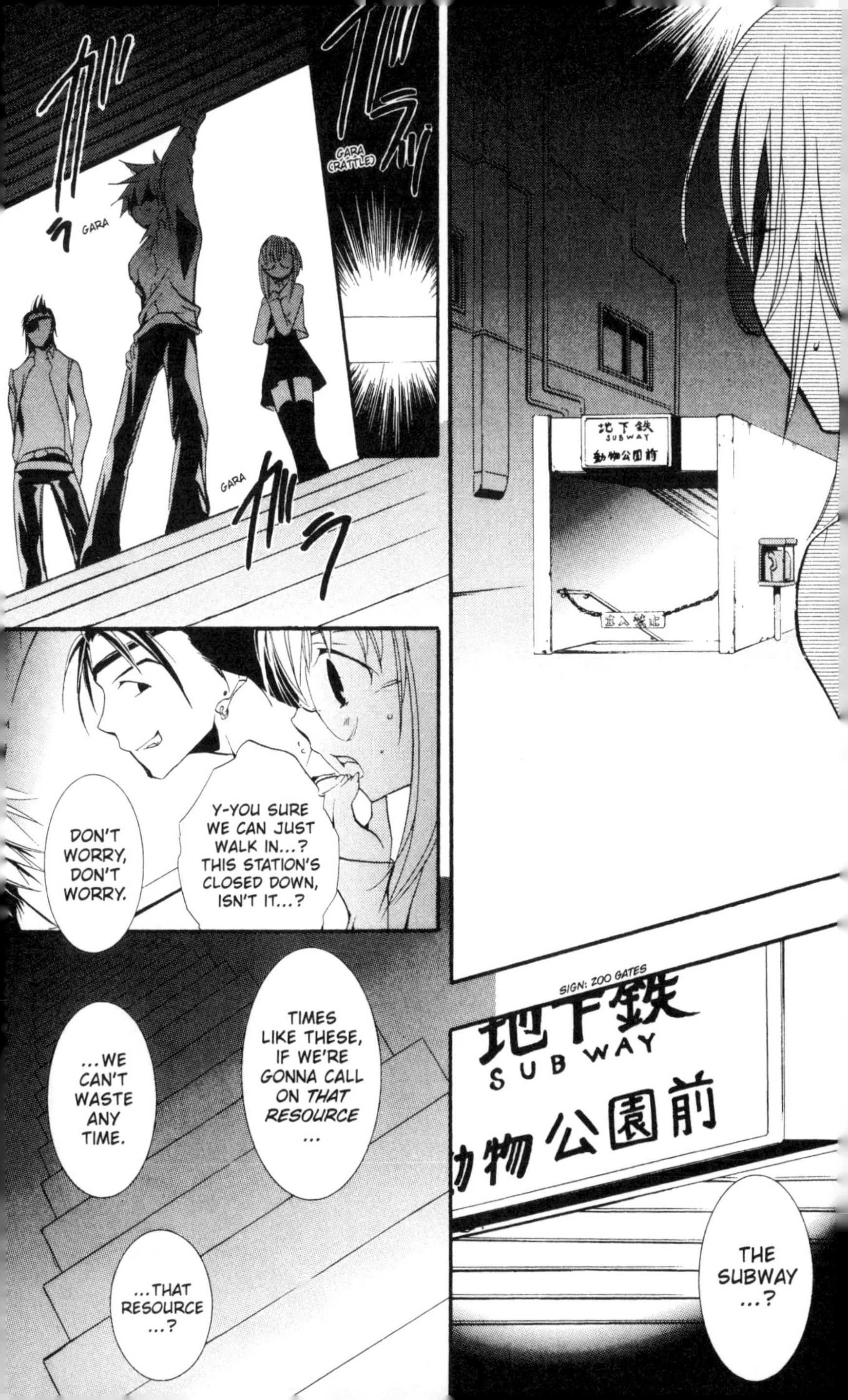
地下鉄
SUBWAY
動物公園前
SIGN: ZOO GATES
地下鉄
SUBWAY
動物公園前
THE SUBWAY ...?
GARA (RATTLE)
GARA
GARA
Y-YOU SURE WE CAN JUST WALK IN...? THIS STATION'S CLOSED DOWN, ISN'T IT...?
DON'T WORRY, DON'T WORRY.
TIMES LIKE THESE, IF WE'RE GONNA CALL ON *THAT RESOURCE* ...
...WE CAN'T WASTE ANY TIME.
...THAT RESOURCE ...?

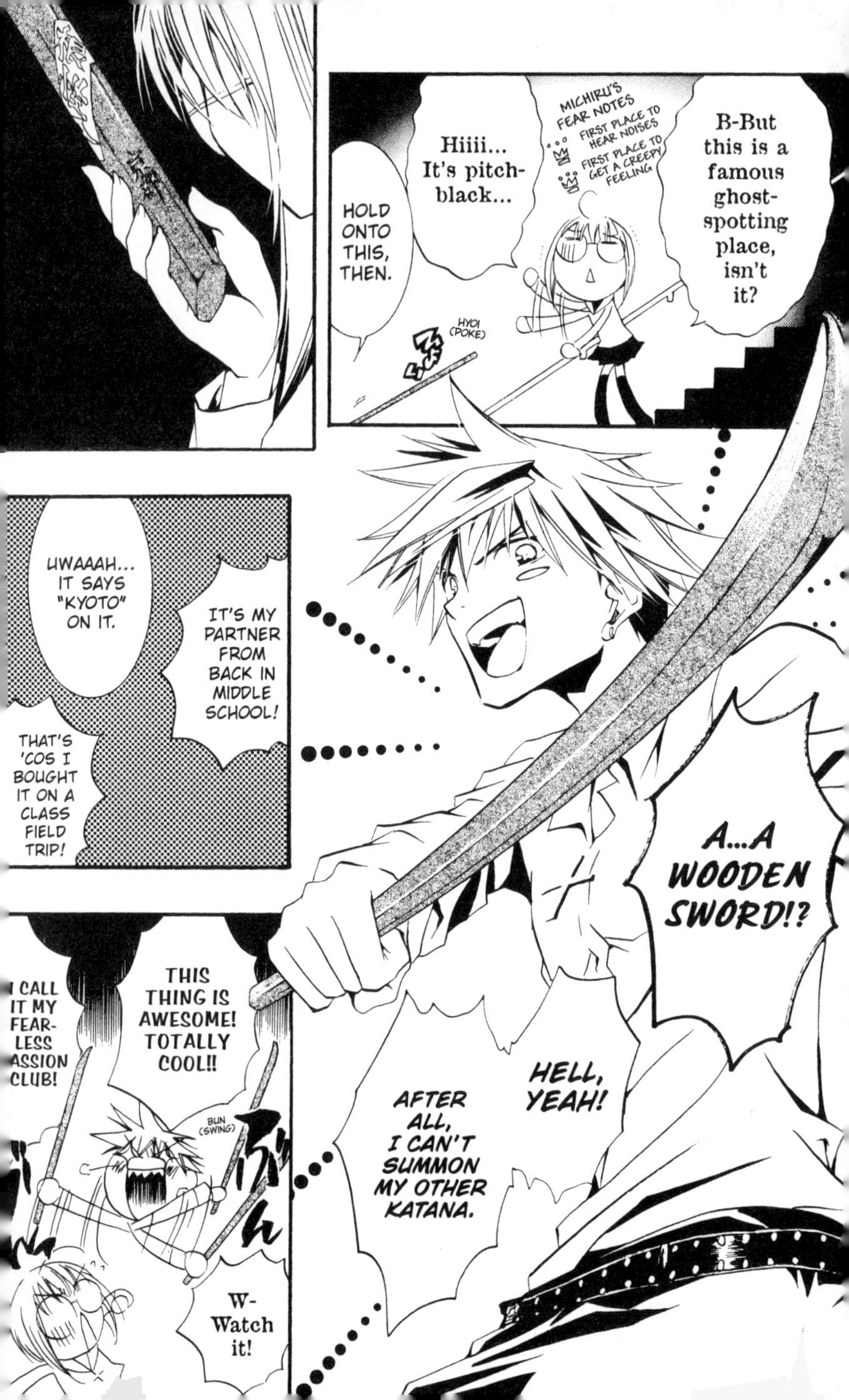
B-But this is a famous ghost-spotting place, isn't it?
MICHIRU'S FEAR NOTES
FIRST PLACE TO HEAR NOISES
FIRST PLACE TO GET A CREEPY FEELING
Hiiii... It's pitch-black...
HOLD ONTO THIS, THEN.
HYOI (POKE)
A...A WOODEN SWORD!?
HELL, YEAH!
AFTER ALL, I CAN'T SUMMON MY OTHER KATANA.
IT'S MY PARTNER FROM BACK IN MIDDLE SCHOOL!
UWAAAH... IT SAYS "KYOTO" ON IT.
THAT'S 'COS I BOUGHT IT ON A CLASS FIELD TRIP!
THIS THING IS AWESOME! TOTALLY COOL!!
I CALL IT MY FEAR-LESS ASSION CLUB!
BUN (SWING)
W-Watch it!

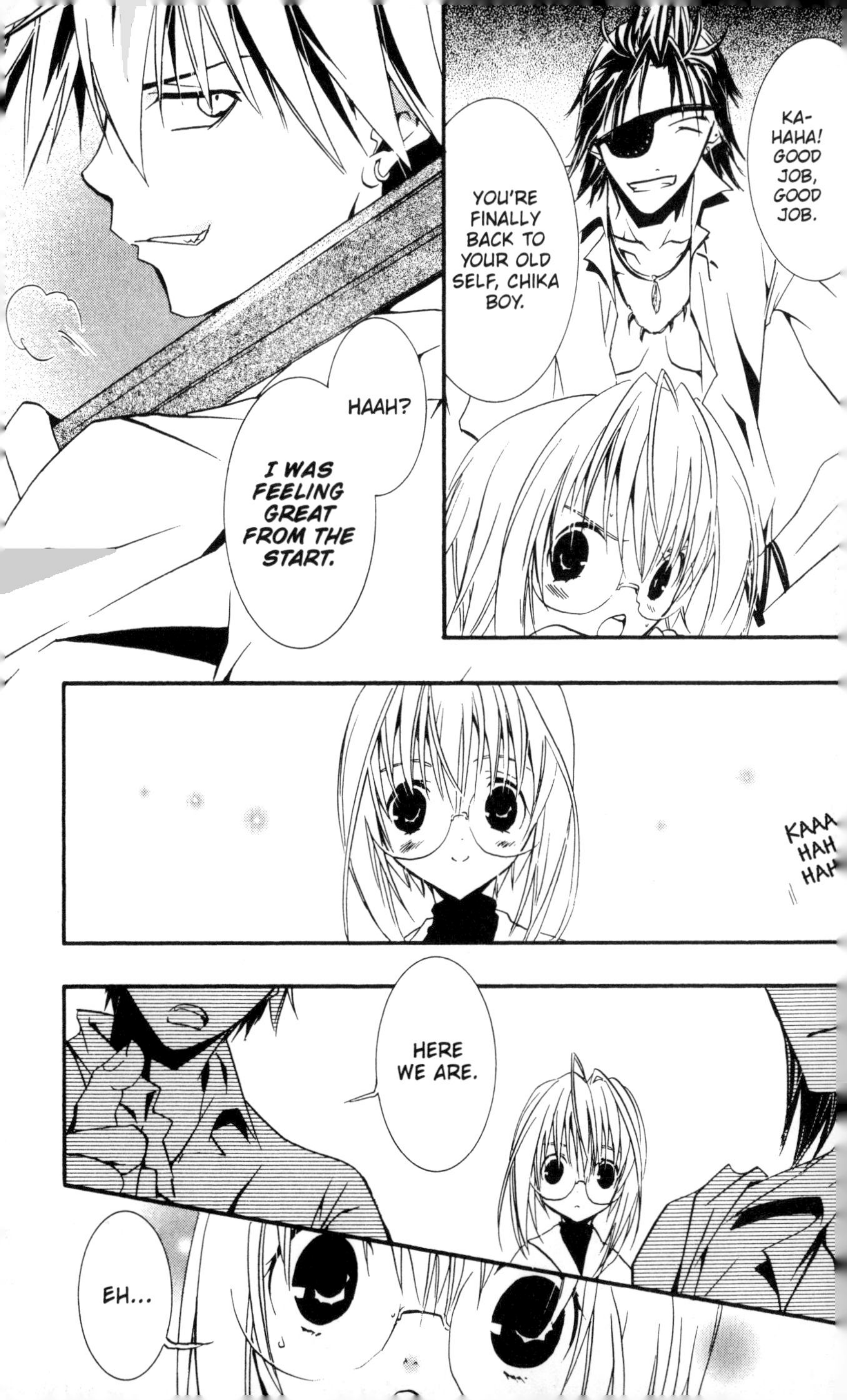
KA-HAHA! GOOD JOB, GOOD JOB.
YOU'RE FINALLY BACK TO YOUR OLD SELF, CHIKA BOY.
HAAH?
I WAS FEELING GREAT FROM THE START.
KAAA HAH HAH
HERE WE ARE.
EH...

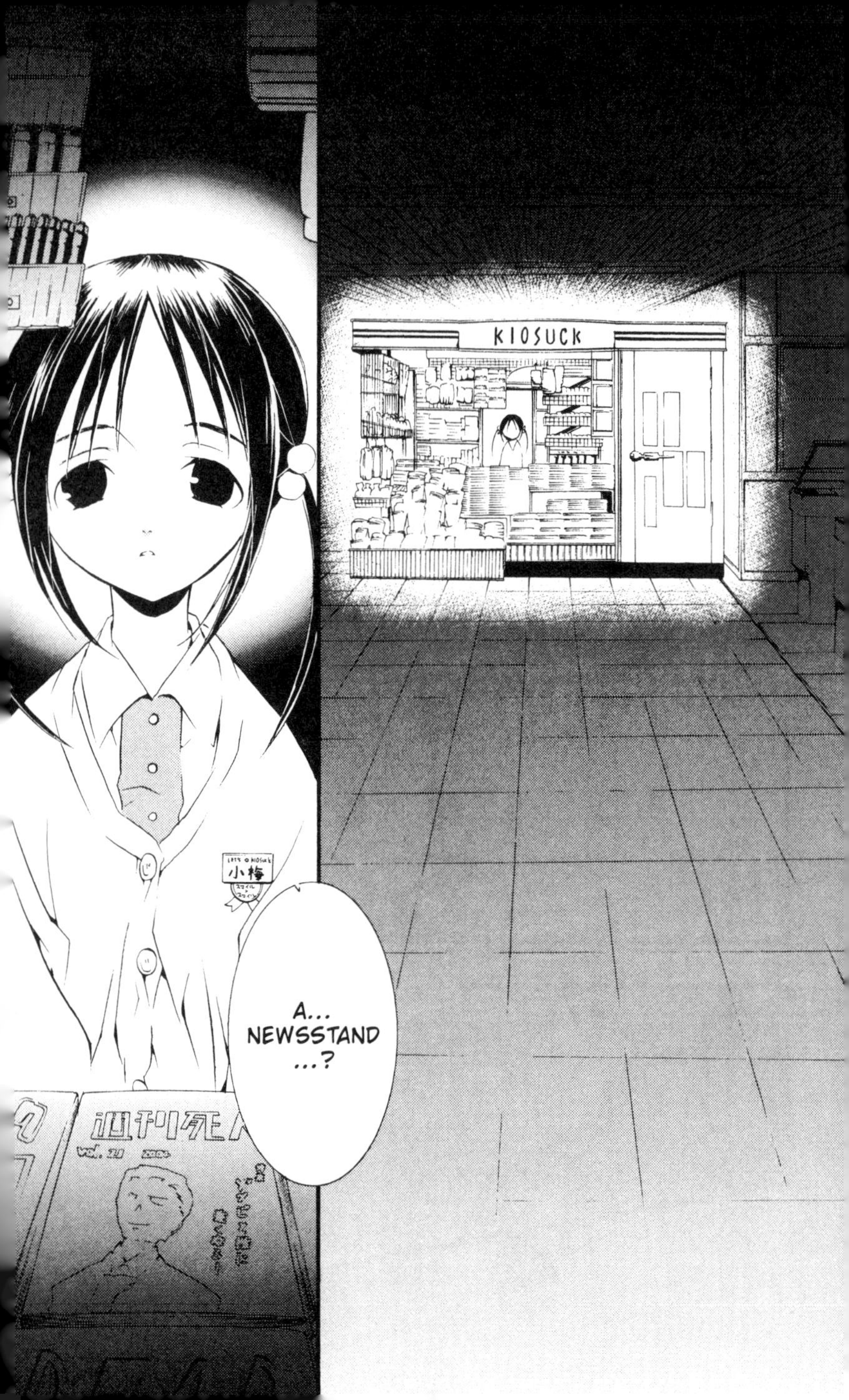
KIOSUCK
A... NEWSSTAND ...?
小梅

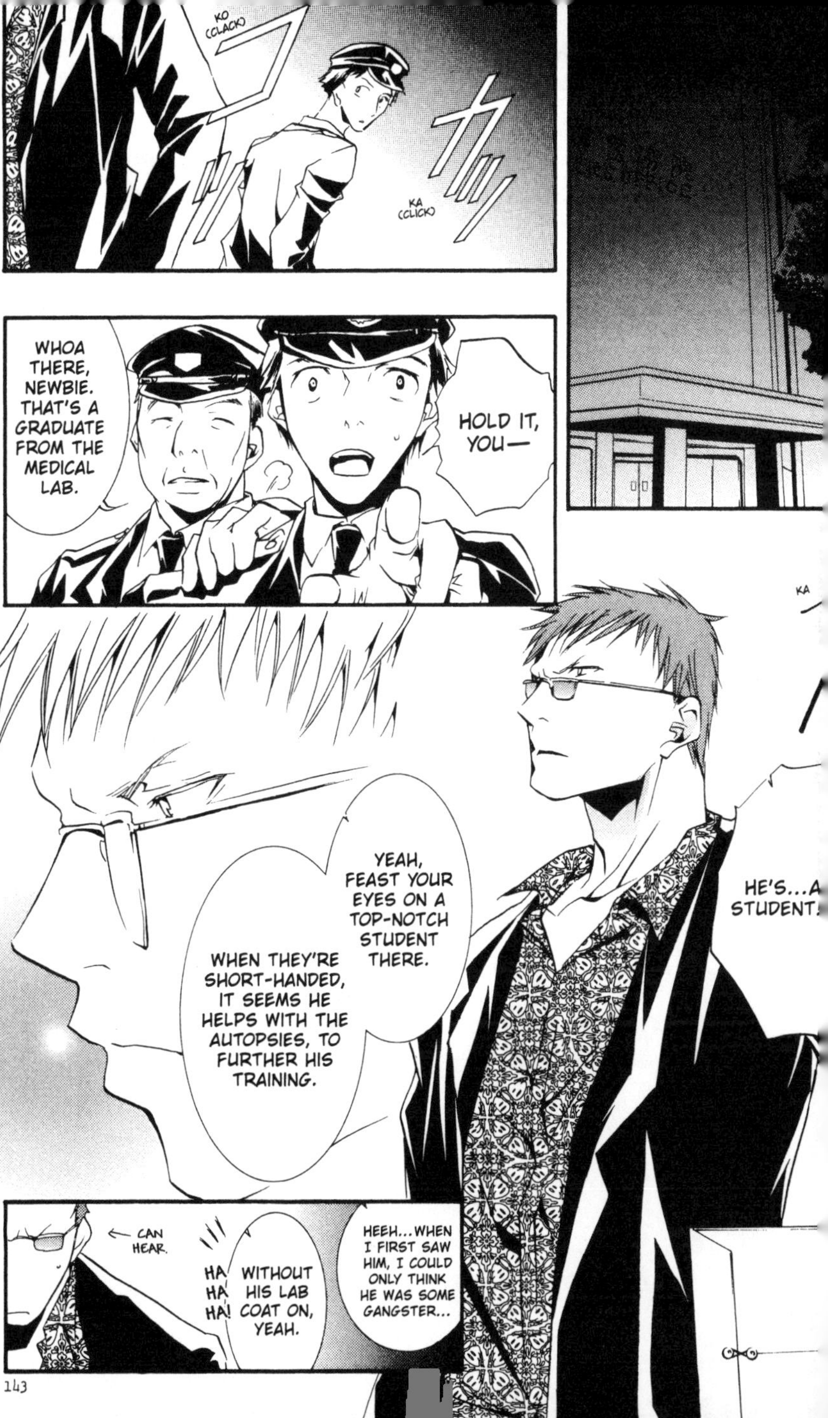
KO (CLACK)
KA (CLICK)
HOLD IT, YOU—
WHOA THERE, NEWBIE. THAT'S A GRADUATE FROM THE MEDICAL LAB.
KA
HE'S...A STUDENT!
YEAH, FEAST YOUR EYES ON A TOP-NOTCH STUDENT THERE.
WHEN THEY'RE SHORT-HANDED, IT SEEMS HE HELPS WITH THE AUTOPSIES, TO FURTHER HIS TRAINING.
HEEH...WHEN I FIRST SAW HIM, I COULD ONLY THINK HE WAS SOME GANGSTER...
WITHOUT HIS LAB COAT ON, YEAH.
HA HA HA!
← CAN HEAR.

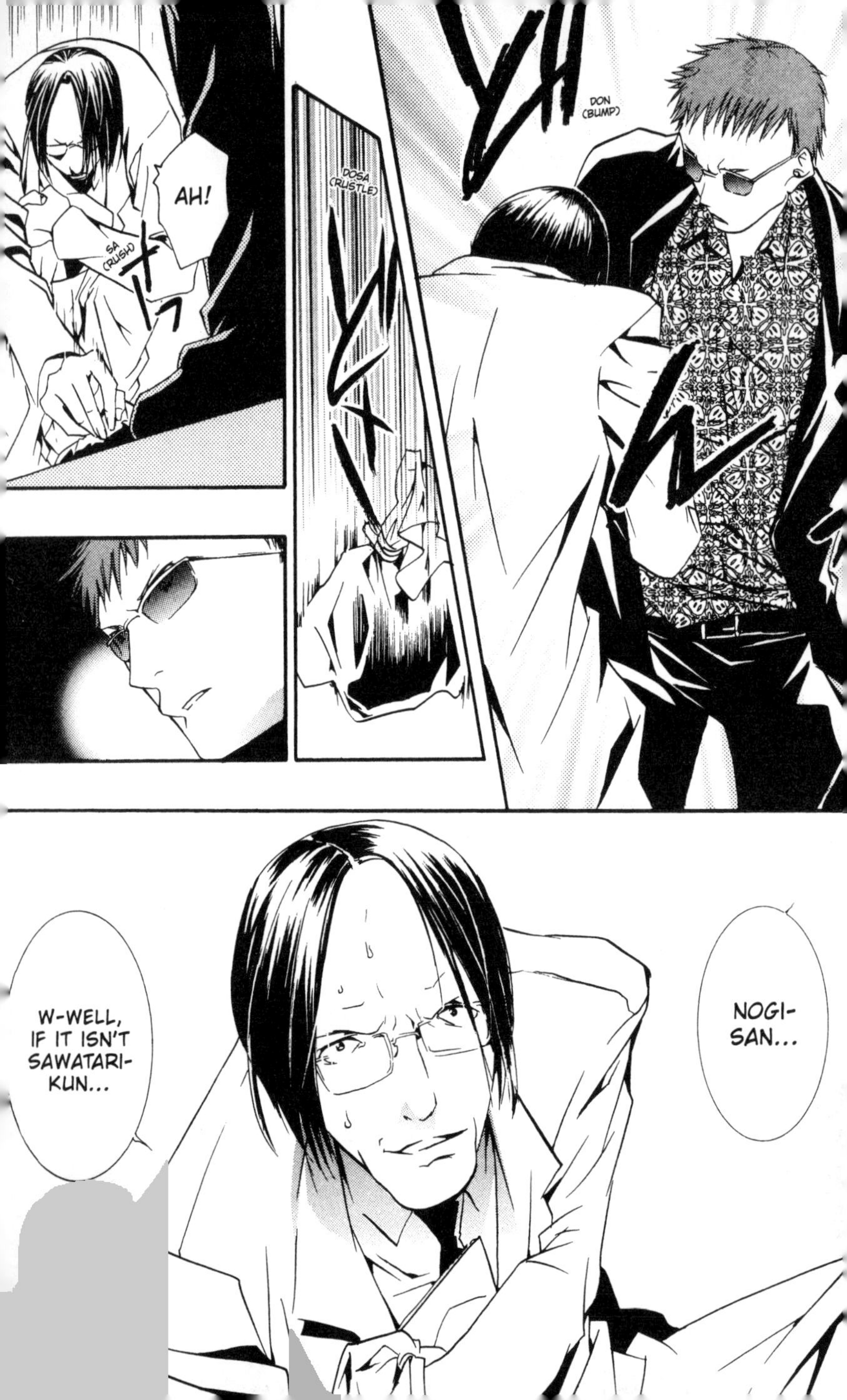
DON (BUMP)
DOSA (RUSTLE)
AH!
SA (RUSH)
NOGI-SAN...
W-WELL, IF IT ISN'T SAWATARI-KUN...

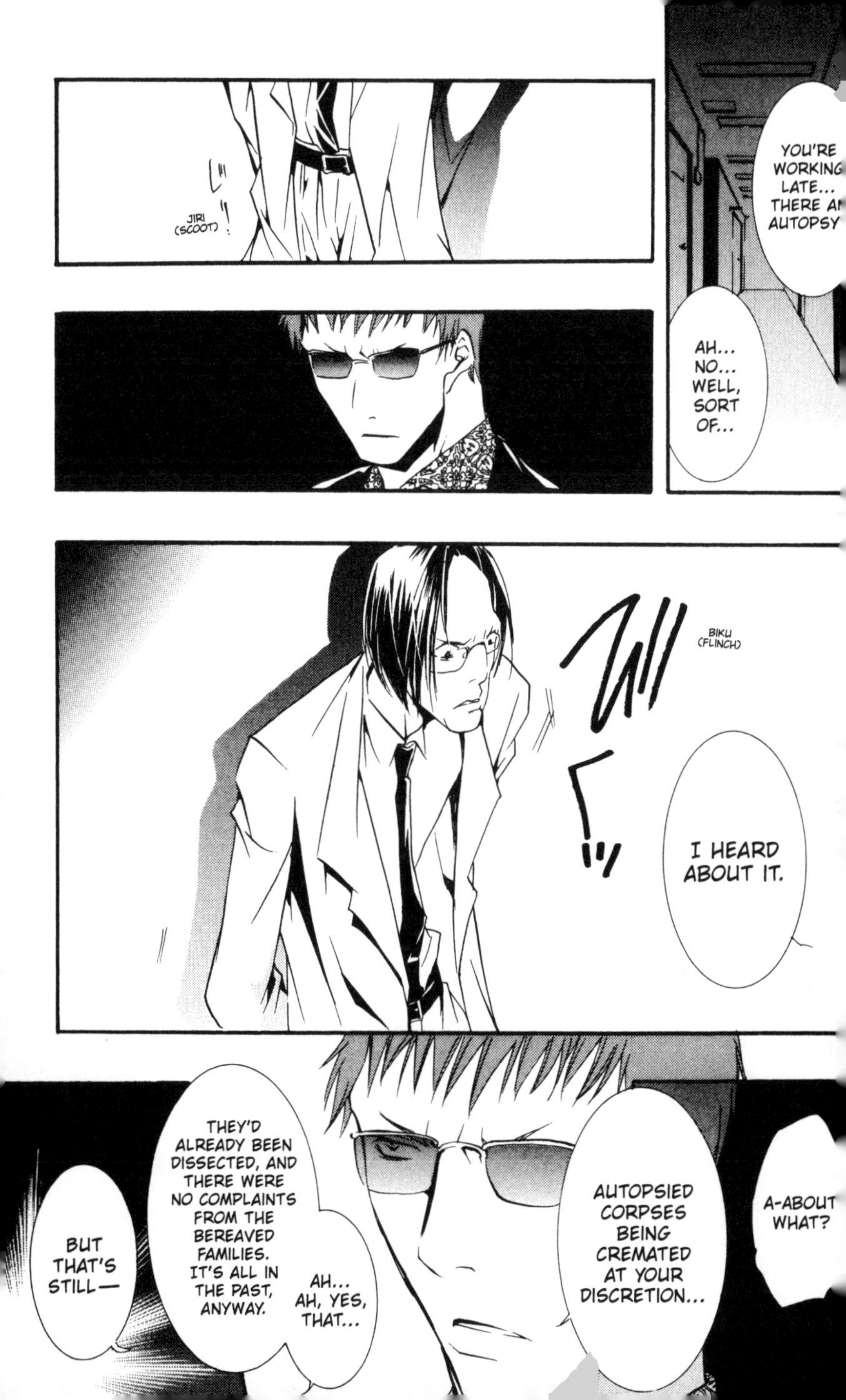
YOU'RE WORKING LATE... THERE A
AUTOPSY
AH... NO... WELL, SORT OF...
JIRI (SCOOT)
BIKU (FLINCH)
I HEARD ABOUT IT.
A-ABOUT WHAT?
AUTOPSIED CORPSES BEING CREMATED AT YOUR DISCRETION...
AH... AH, YES, THAT...
THEY'D ALREADY BEEN DISSECTED, AND THERE WERE NO COMPLAINTS FROM THE BEREAVED FAMILIES. IT'S ALL IN THE PAST, ANYWAY.
BUT THAT'S STILL—

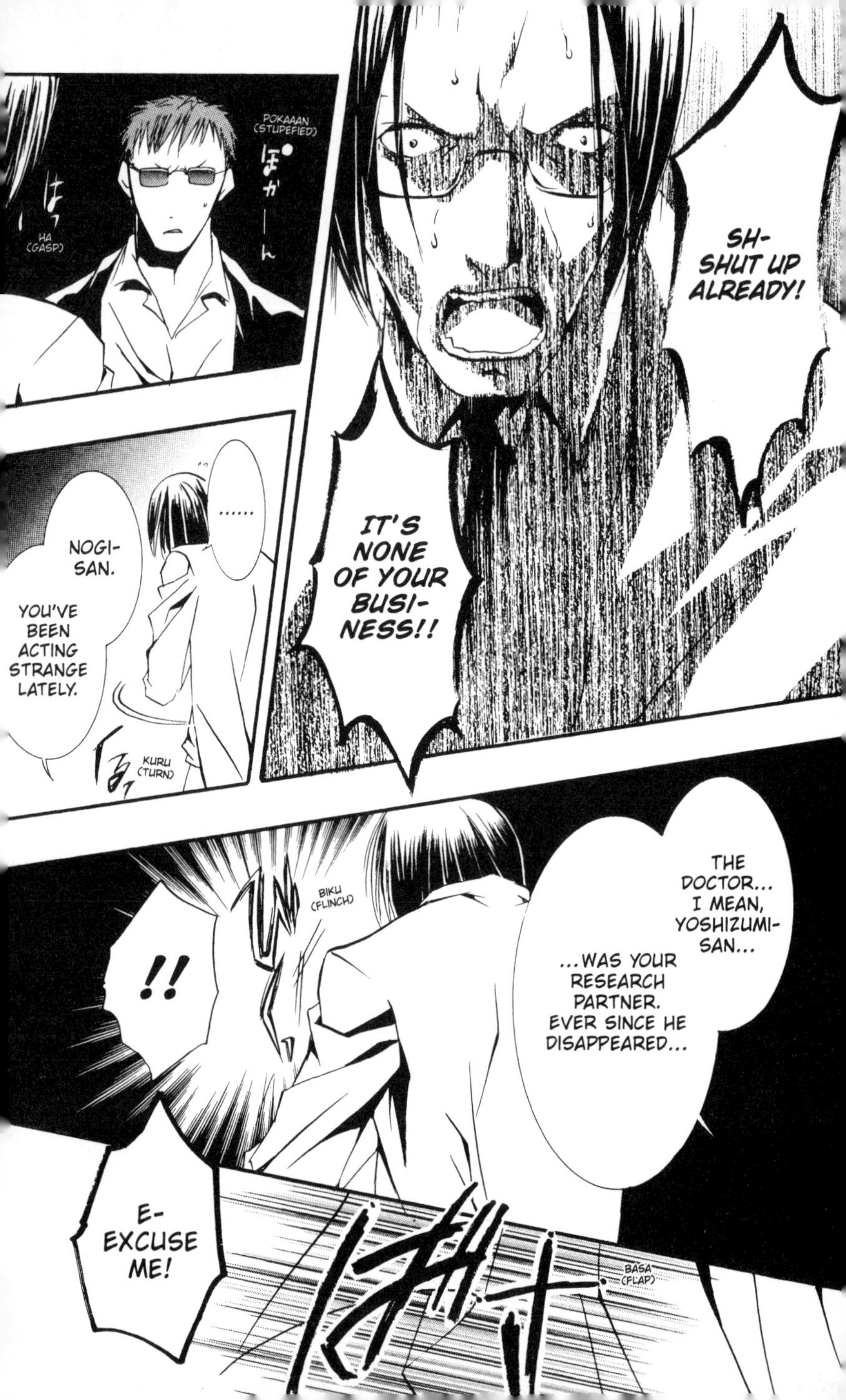
SH-SHUT UP ALREADY!
IT'S NONE OF YOUR BUSINESS!!
ぽかーん
POKAAAN (STUPEFIED)
はっ
HA (GASP)
......
NOGI-SAN.
YOU'VE BEEN ACTING STRANGE LATELY.
KURU (TURN)
THE DOCTOR... I MEAN, YOSHIZUMI-SAN...
...WAS YOUR RESEARCH PARTNER. EVER SINCE HE DISAPPEARED...
BIKU (FLINCH)
!!
BASA (FLAP)
E-EXCUSE ME!

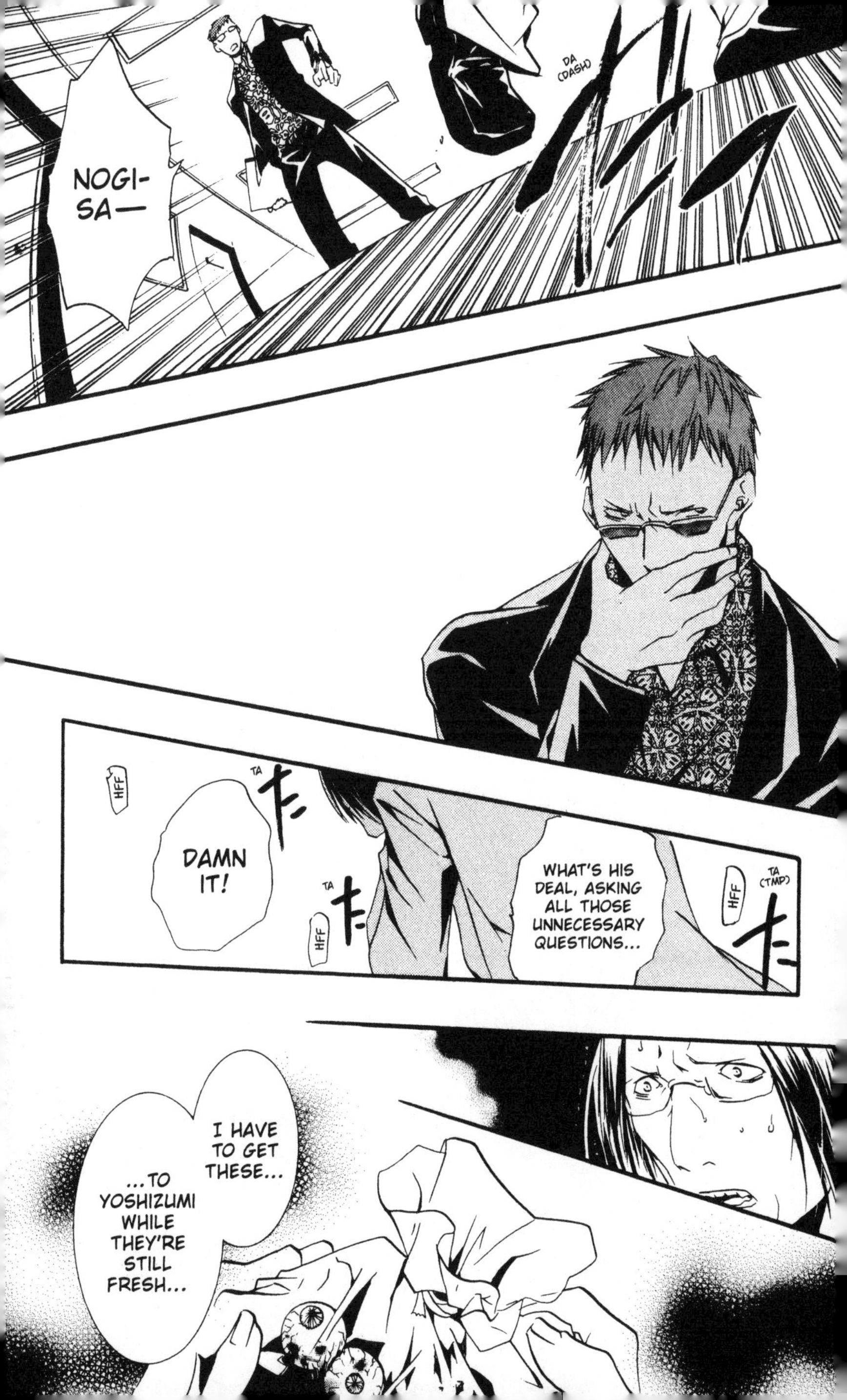
DA (DASH)
NOGI-SA—
TA (TMP)
HFF
WHAT'S HIS DEAL, ASKING ALL THOSE UNNECESSARY QUESTIONS...
TA
HFF
DAMN IT!
TA
HFF
I HAVE TO GET THESE...
...TO YOSHIZUMI WHILE THEY'RE STILL FRESH...

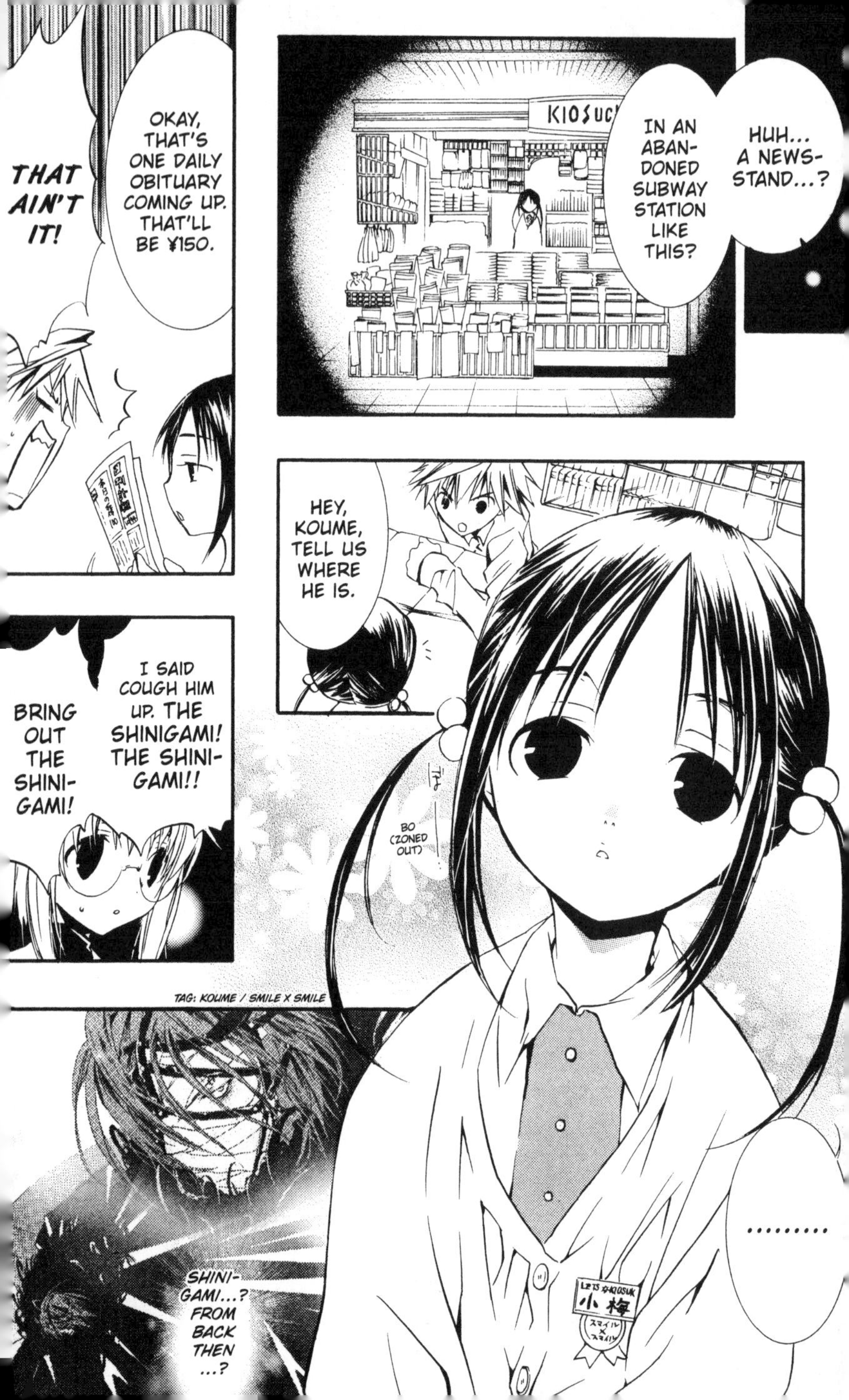
HUH... A NEWS-STAND...?
IN AN ABAN-DONED SUBWAY STATION LIKE THIS?
KIOSUCK
OKAY, THAT'S ONE DAILY OBITUARY COMING UP. THAT'LL BE ¥150.
THAT AIN'T IT!
HEY, KOUME, TELL US WHERE HE IS.
I SAID COUGH HIM UP. THE SHINIGAMI! THE SHINI-GAMI!!
BRING OUT THE SHINI-GAMI!
BO (ZONED OUT)
TAG: KOUME / SMILE X SMILE
....
小梅
SHINI-GAMI...? FROM BACK THEN ...?

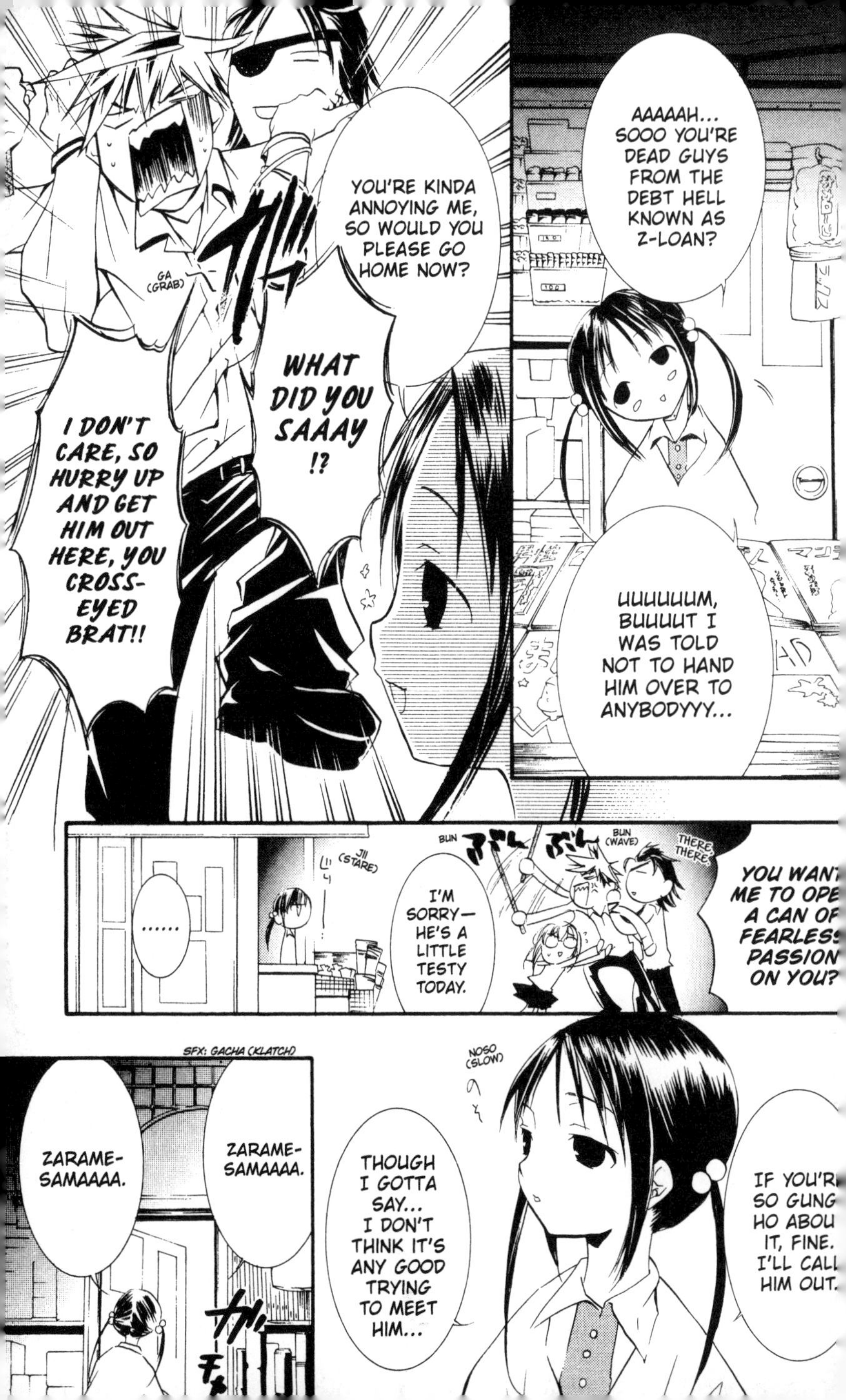

AAAAAH... SOOO YOU'RE DEAD GUYS FROM THE DEBT HELL KNOWN AS Z-LOAN?
UUUUUUM, BUUUUT I WAS TOLD NOT TO HAND HIM OVER TO ANYBODYYY...
YOU'RE KINDA ANNOYING ME, SO WOULD YOU PLEASE GO HOME NOW?
GA (GRAB)
WHAT DID YOU SAAAY !?
I DON'T CARE, SO HURRY UP AND GET HIM OUT HERE, YOU CROSS-EYED BRAT!!
YOU WAN ME TO OPE A CAN OF FEARLES PASSION ON YOU?
THERE, THERE.
BUN (WAVE)
BUN
I'M SORRY— HE'S A LITTLE TESTY TODAY.
JII (STARE)
......
IF YOU'R SO GUNG HO ABOU IT, FINE. I'LL CALL HIM OUT.
NOSO (SLOW)
THOUGH I GOTTA SAY... I DON'T THINK IT'S ANY GOOD TRYING TO MEET HIM...
SFX: GACHA (KLATCH)
ZARAME-SAMAAAAA.
ZARAME-SAMAAAAA.

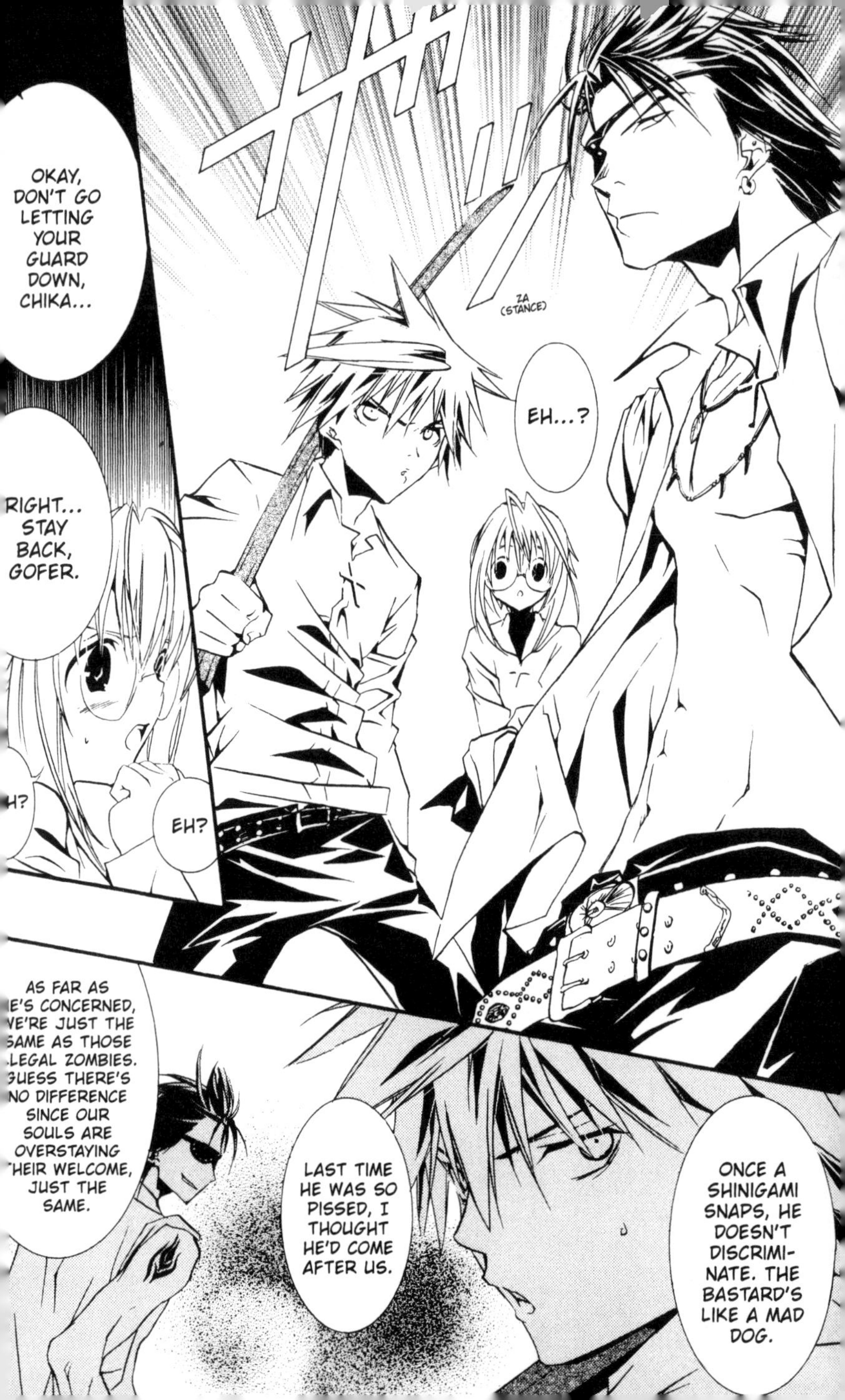

ZA (STANCE)
EH...?
OKAY, DON'T GO LETTING YOUR GUARD DOWN, CHIKA...
RIGHT... STAY BACK, GOFER.
EH?
H?
ONCE A SHINIGAMI SNAPS, HE DOESN'T DISCRIMI-NATE. THE BASTARD'S LIKE A MAD DOG.
LAST TIME HE WAS SO PISSED, I THOUGHT HE'D COME AFTER US.
AS FAR AS E'S CONCERNED, VE'RE JUST THE SAME AS THOSE LEGAL ZOMBIES. GUESS THERE'S NO DIFFERENCE SINCE OUR SOULS ARE OVERSTAYING THEIR WELCOME, JUST THE SAME.

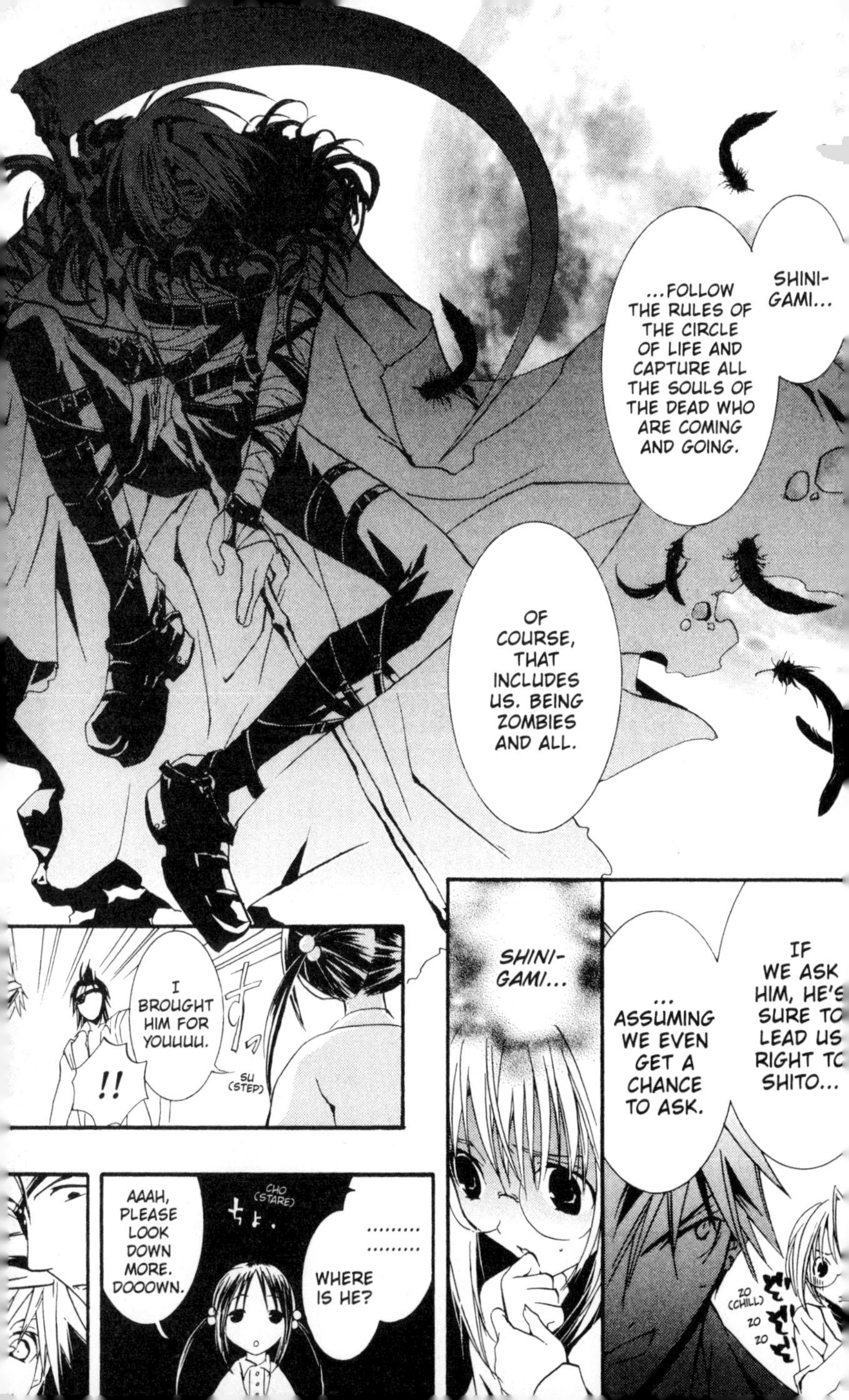
SHINI-GAMI...
...FOLLOW THE RULES OF THE CIRCLE OF LIFE AND CAPTURE ALL THE SOULS OF THE DEAD WHO ARE COMING AND GOING.
OF COURSE, THAT INCLUDES US. BEING ZOMBIES AND ALL.
IF WE ASK HIM, HE'S SURE TO LEAD US RIGHT TO SHITO...
...ASSUMING WE EVEN GET A CHANCE TO ASK.
ZO (CHILL) ZO ZO
SHINI-GAMI...
SU (STEP)
I BROUGHT HIM FOR YOUUUU.
!!
....
....
WHERE IS HE?
CHO (STARE)
AAAH, PLEASE LOOK DOWN MORE. DOOOWN.

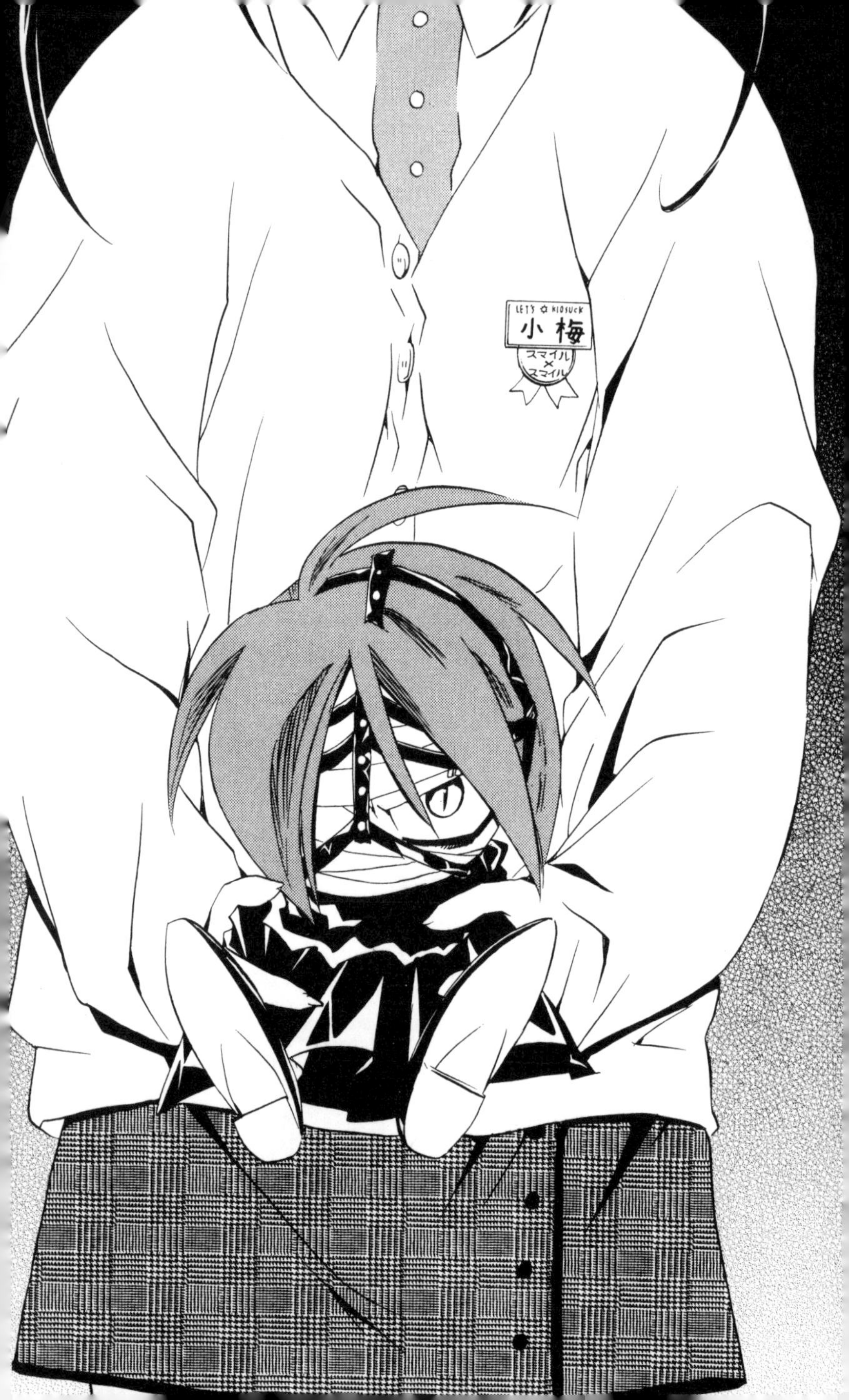
LET'S ☆ KIOSUCK
小梅
スマイル×スマイル

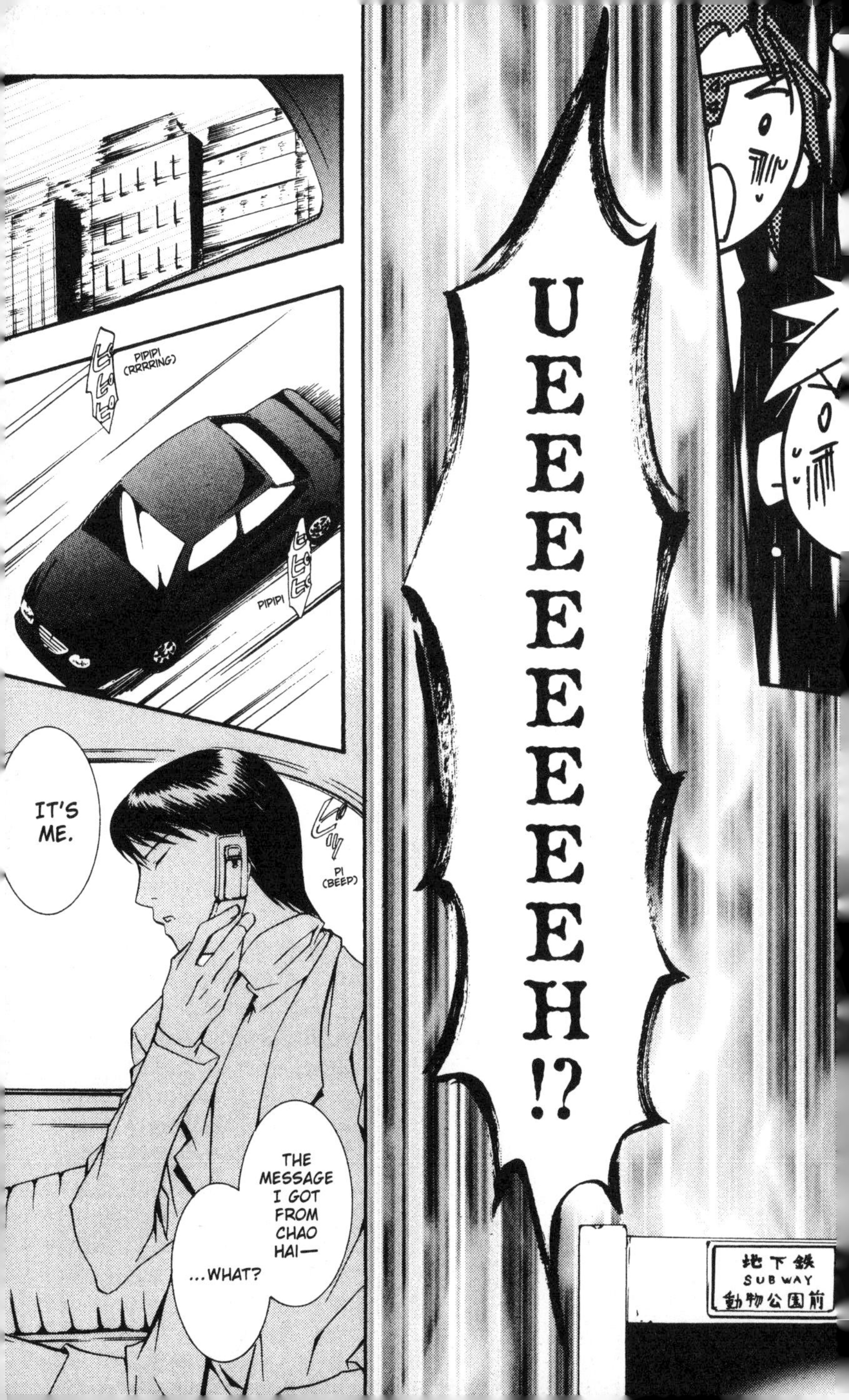
UEEEEEEEEEH!?
地下鉄
SUBWAY
動物公園前
PIPIPI (RRRRING)
PIPIPI
PI (BEEP)
IT'S ME.
THE MESSAGE I GOT FROM CHAO HAI—
...WHAT?

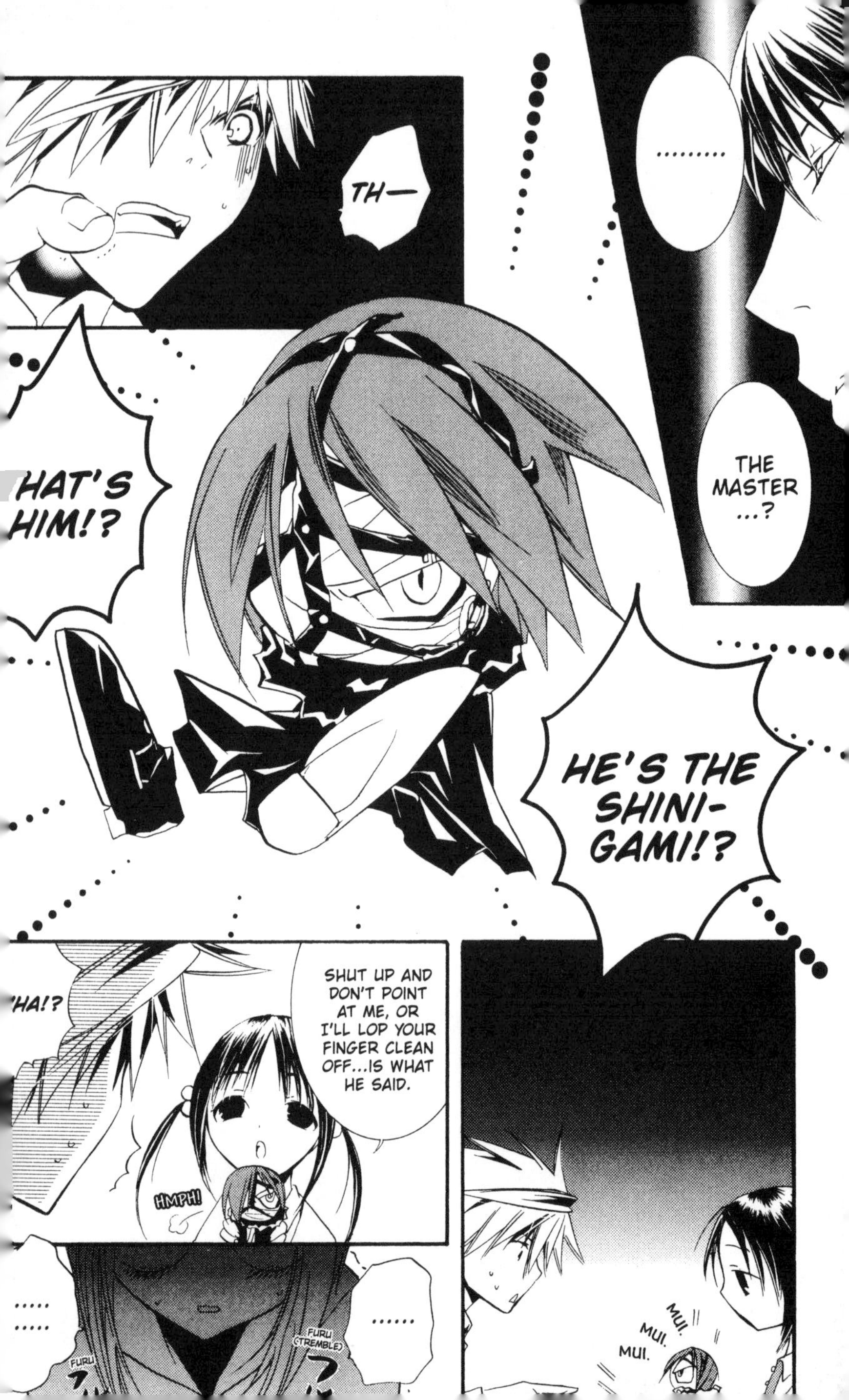

....
THE MASTER ...?
TH—
HE'S THE SHINI-GAMI!?
HAT'S HIM!?
MUI. MUI. MUI.
'HA!?
SHUT UP AND DON'T POINT AT ME, OR I'LL LOP YOUR FINGER CLEAN OFF...IS WHAT HE SAID.
HMPH!
......
FURU (TREMBLE)
FURU
....

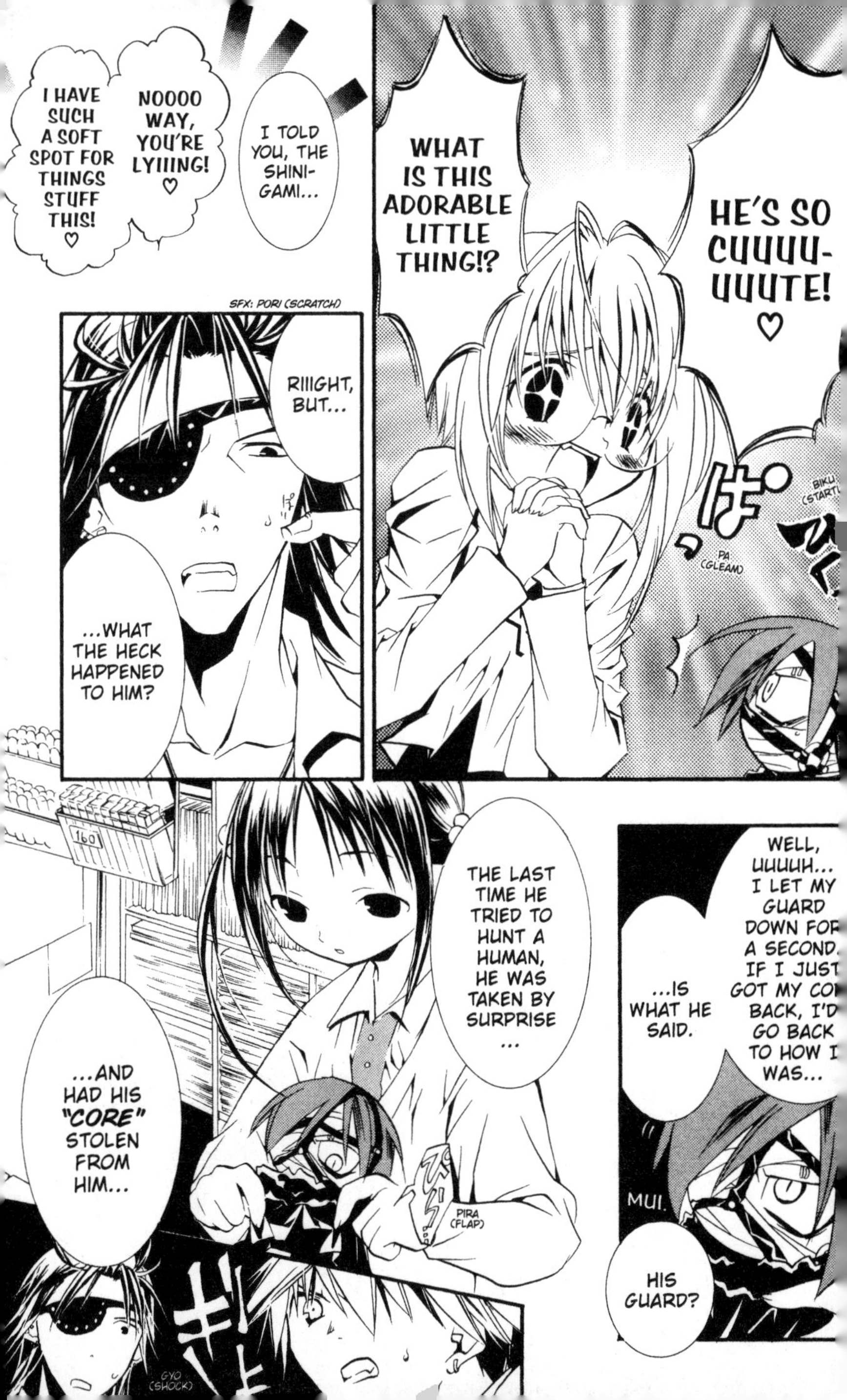
WHAT IS THIS ADORABLE LITTLE THING!?
HE'S SO CUUUU-UUUTE! ♡
BIKU (STARTLE)
PA (GLEAM)
I TOLD YOU, THE SHINI-GAMI...
NOOOO WAY, YOU'RE LYIIING! ♡
I HAVE SUCH A SOFT SPOT FOR THINGS STUFF THIS! ♡
SFX: PORI (SCRATCH)
RIIIGHT, BUT...
...WHAT THE HECK HAPPENED TO HIM?
WELL, UUUUH... I LET MY GUARD DOWN FOR A SECOND. IF I JUST GOT MY CO BACK, I'D GO BACK TO HOW I WAS...
...IS WHAT HE SAID.
MUI.
HIS GUARD?
THE LAST TIME HE TRIED TO HUNT A HUMAN, HE WAS TAKEN BY SURPRISE...
...AND HAD HIS "CORE" STOLEN FROM HIM...
PIRA (FLAP)
160
GYO (SHOCK)

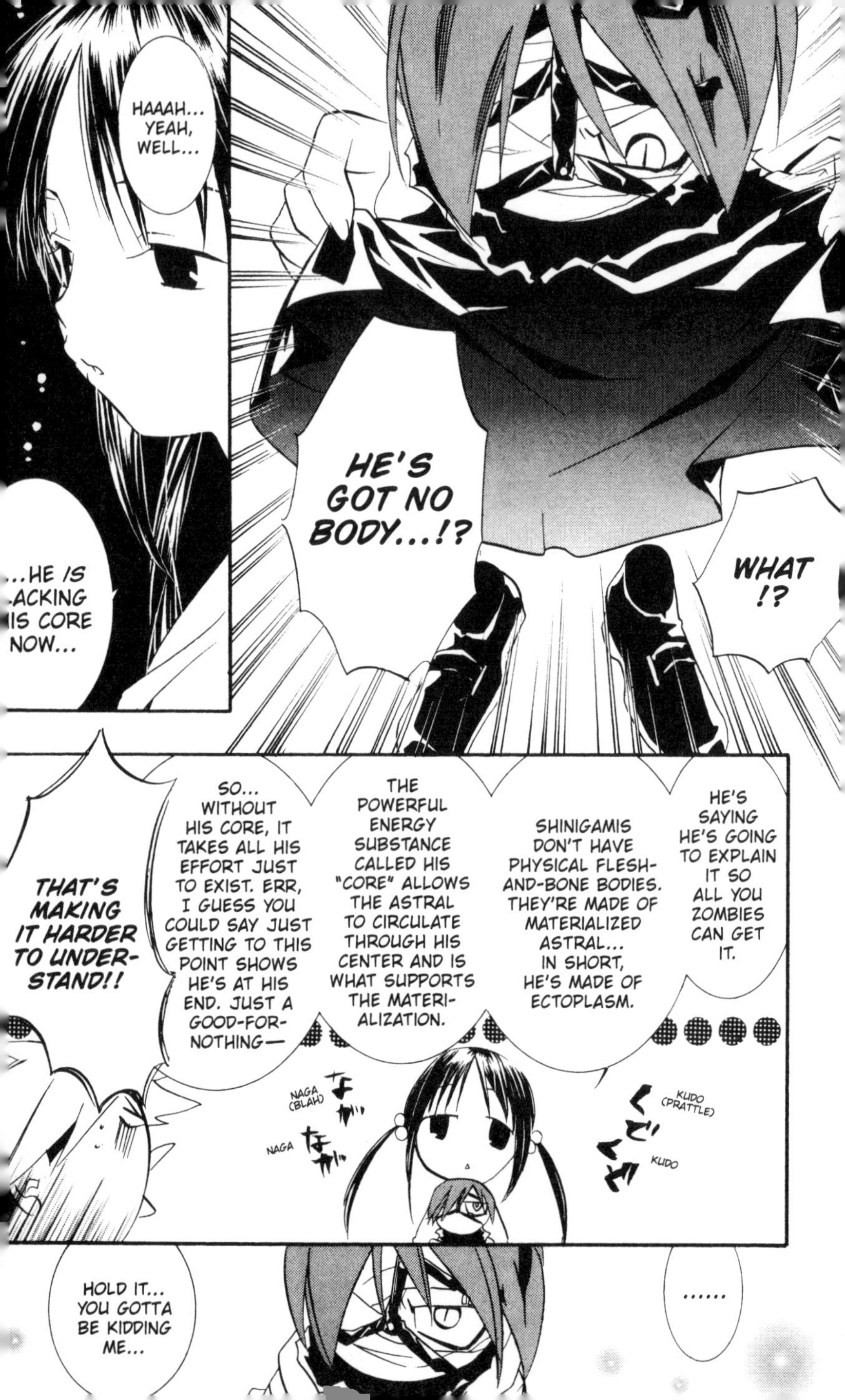
HE'S GOT NO BODY...!?
WHAT!?
HAAAH... YEAH, WELL...
...HE IS
ACKING
IS CORE
NOW...
HE'S SAYING HE'S GOING TO EXPLAIN IT SO ALL YOU ZOMBIES CAN GET IT.
SHINIGAMIS DON'T HAVE PHYSICAL FLESH-AND-BONE BODIES. THEY'RE MADE OF MATERIALIZED ASTRAL... IN SHORT, HE'S MADE OF ECTOPLASM.
THE POWERFUL ENERGY SUBSTANCE CALLED HIS "CORE" ALLOWS THE ASTRAL TO CIRCULATE THROUGH HIS CENTER AND IS WHAT SUPPORTS THE MATERIALIZATION.
SO... WITHOUT HIS CORE, IT TAKES ALL HIS EFFORT JUST TO EXIST. ERR, I GUESS YOU COULD SAY JUST GETTING TO THIS POINT SHOWS HE'S AT HIS END. JUST A GOOD-FOR-NOTHING—
THAT'S MAKING IT HARDER TO UNDERSTAND!!
KUDO (PRATTLE)
KUDO
NAGA (BLAH)
NAGA
......
HOLD IT... YOU GOTTA BE KIDDING ME...

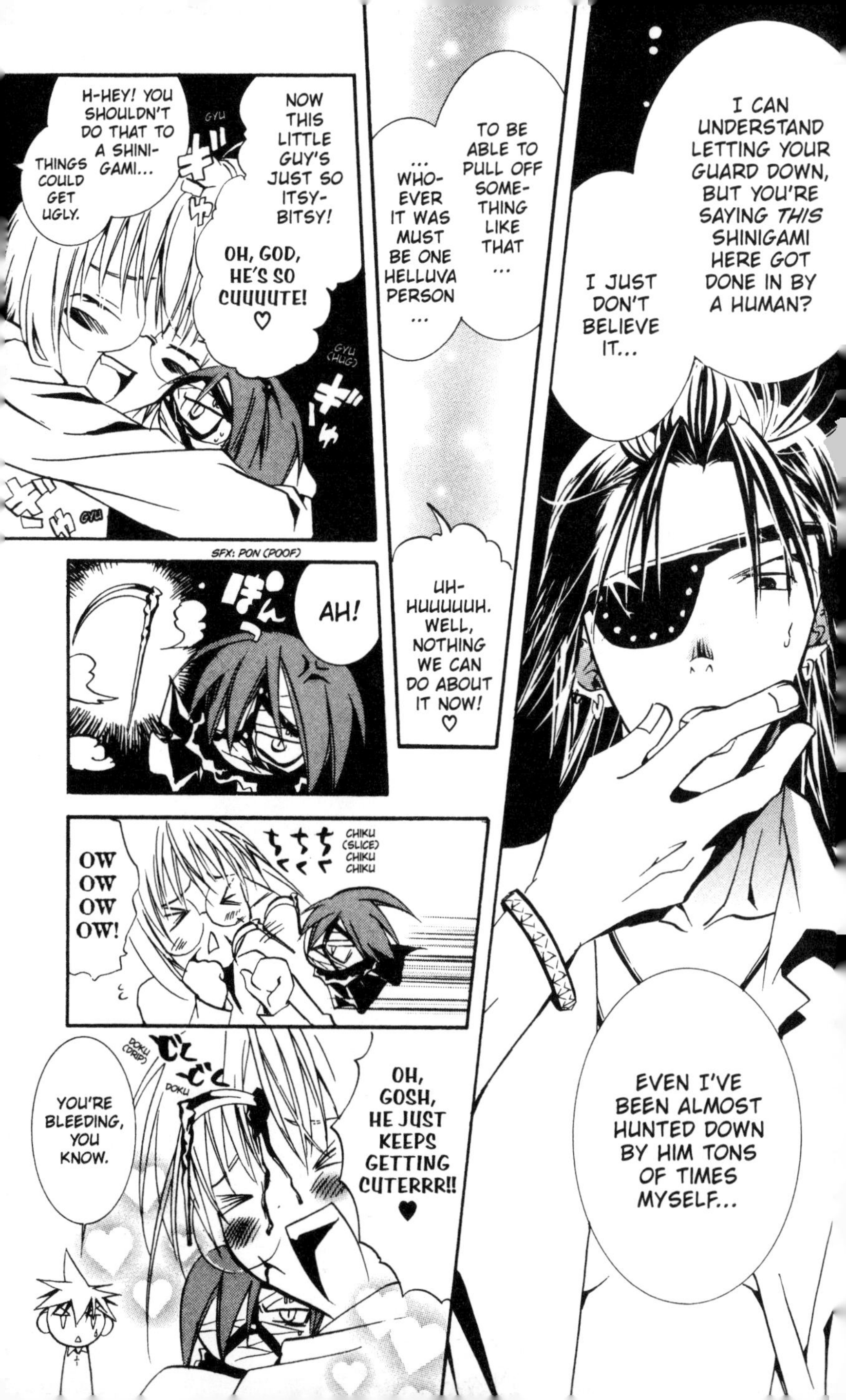
I CAN UNDERSTAND LETTING YOUR GUARD DOWN, BUT YOU'RE SAYING *THIS* SHINIGAMI HERE GOT DONE IN BY A HUMAN?
I JUST DON'T BELIEVE IT...
EVEN I'VE BEEN ALMOST HUNTED DOWN BY HIM TONS OF TIMES MYSELF...
TO BE ABLE TO PULL OFF SOMETHING LIKE THAT...
...WHO-EVER IT WAS MUST BE ONE HELLUVA PERSON...
UH-HUUUUUH. WELL, NOTHING WE CAN DO ABOUT IT NOW! ♡
GYU
NOW THIS LITTLE GUY'S JUST SO ITSY-BITSY!
OH, GOD, HE'S SO CUUUUTE! ♡
H-HEY! YOU SHOULDN'T DO THAT TO A SHINI-GAMI...
THINGS COULD GET UGLY.
GYU (HUG)
GYU
SFX: PON (POOF)
AH!
CHIKU (SLICE) CHIKU CHIKU
OW OW OW OW!
DOKU (DRIP)
DOKU
OH, GOSH, HE JUST KEEPS GETTING CUTERRR!! ♥
YOU'RE BLEEDING, YOU KNOW.

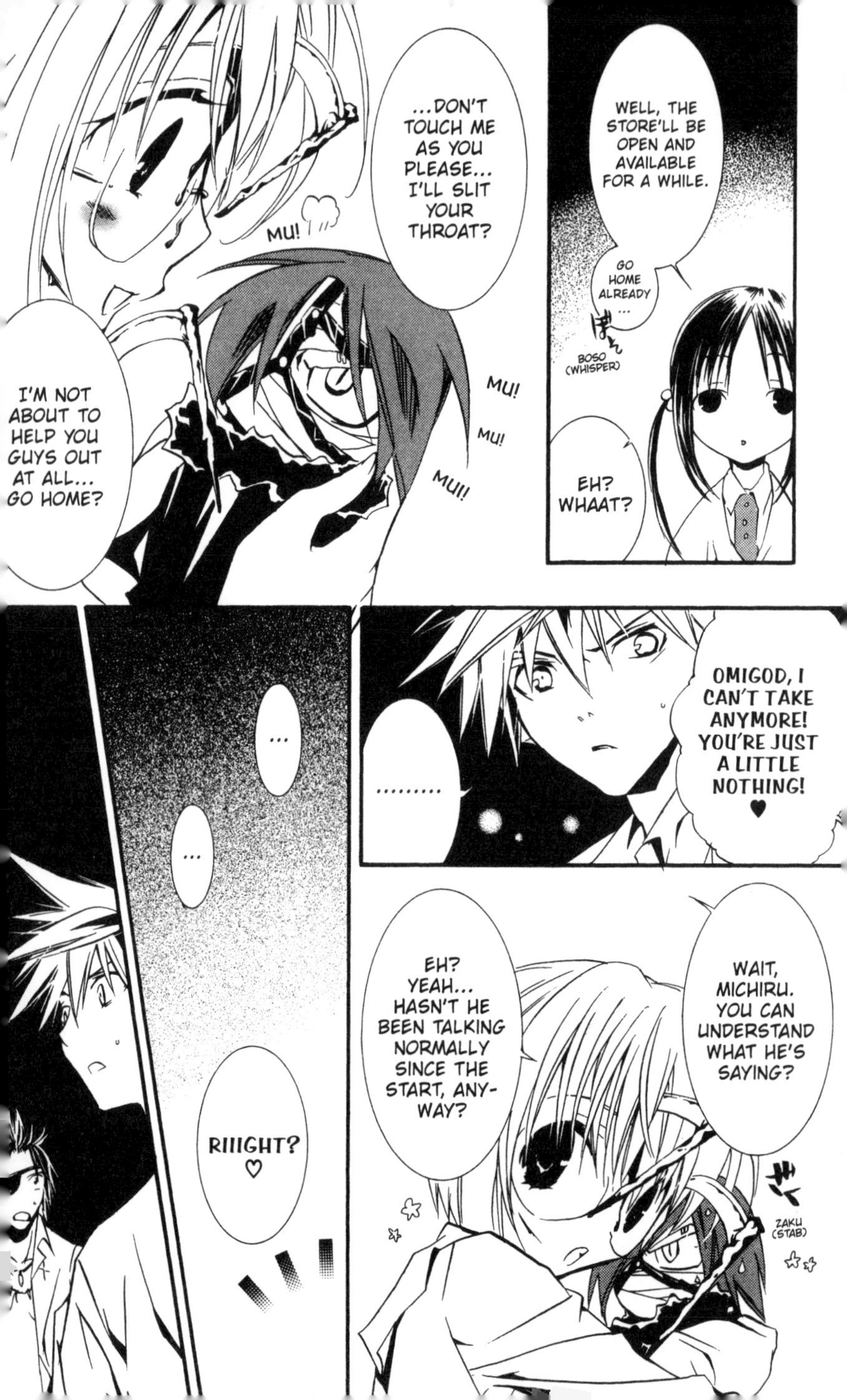
WELL, THE STORE'LL BE OPEN AND AVAILABLE FOR A WHILE.
GO HOME ALREADY...
BOSO (WHISPER)
EH? WHAAT?
...DON'T TOUCH ME AS YOU PLEASE... I'LL SLIT YOUR THROAT?
MU!
MU!
MU!
MUI!
I'M NOT ABOUT TO HELP YOU GUYS OUT AT ALL... GO HOME?
OMIGOD, I CAN'T TAKE ANYMORE! YOU'RE JUST A LITTLE NOTHING! ♥
....
WAIT, MICHIRU. YOU CAN UNDERSTAND WHAT HE'S SAYING?
ZAKU (STAB)
EH? YEAH... HASN'T HE BEEN TALKING NORMALLY SINCE THE START, ANY-WAY?
...
...
RIIIGHT? ♡

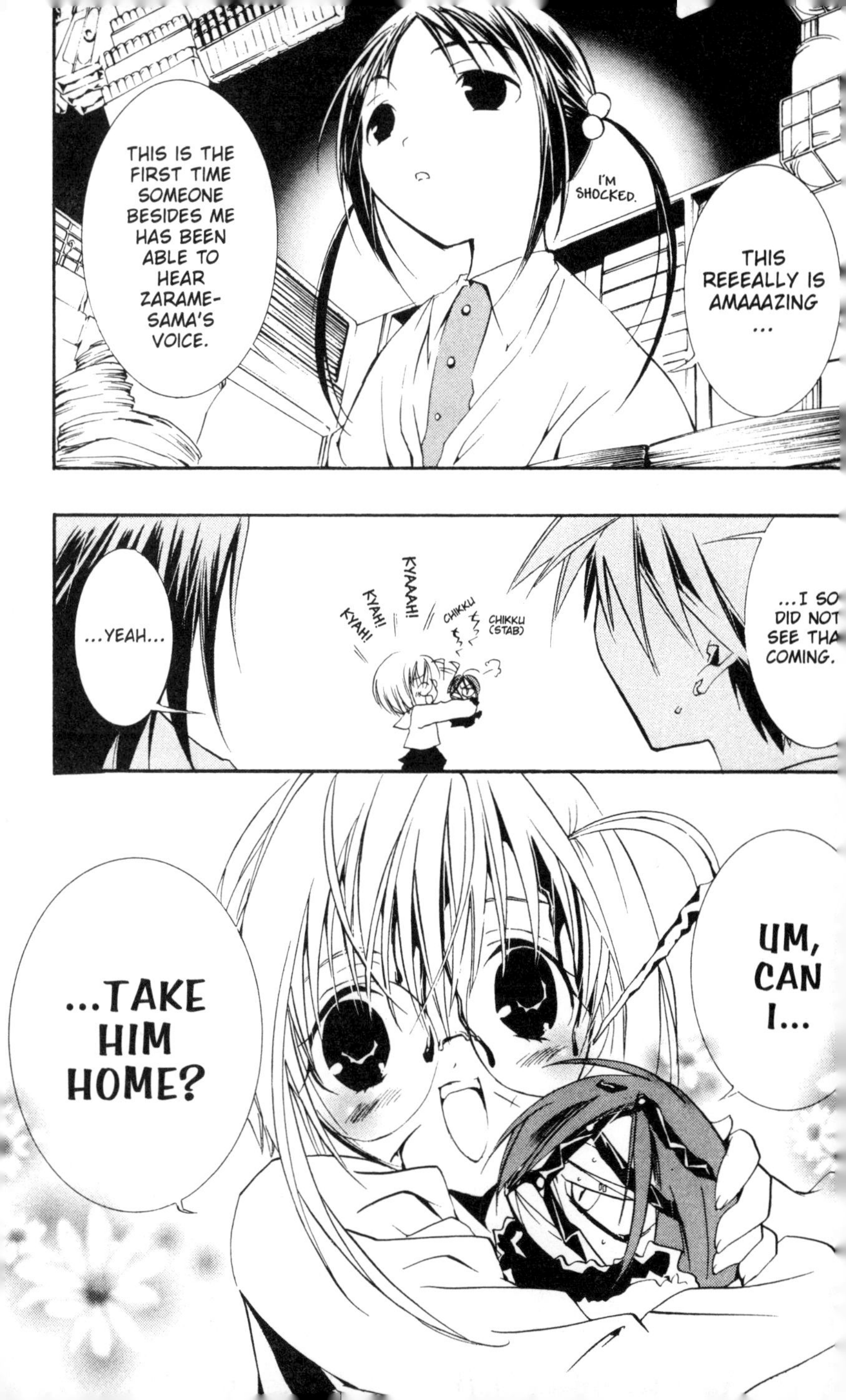
THIS REEEALLY IS AMAAAZING ...
I'M SHOCKED.
THIS IS THE FIRST TIME SOMEONE BESIDES ME HAS BEEN ABLE TO HEAR ZARAME-SAMA'S VOICE.
...I SO DID NOT SEE THA COMING.
CHIKKU CHIKKU (STAB)
KYAAAH! KYAH! KYAH!
...YEAH...
UM, CAN I...
...TAKE HIM HOME?

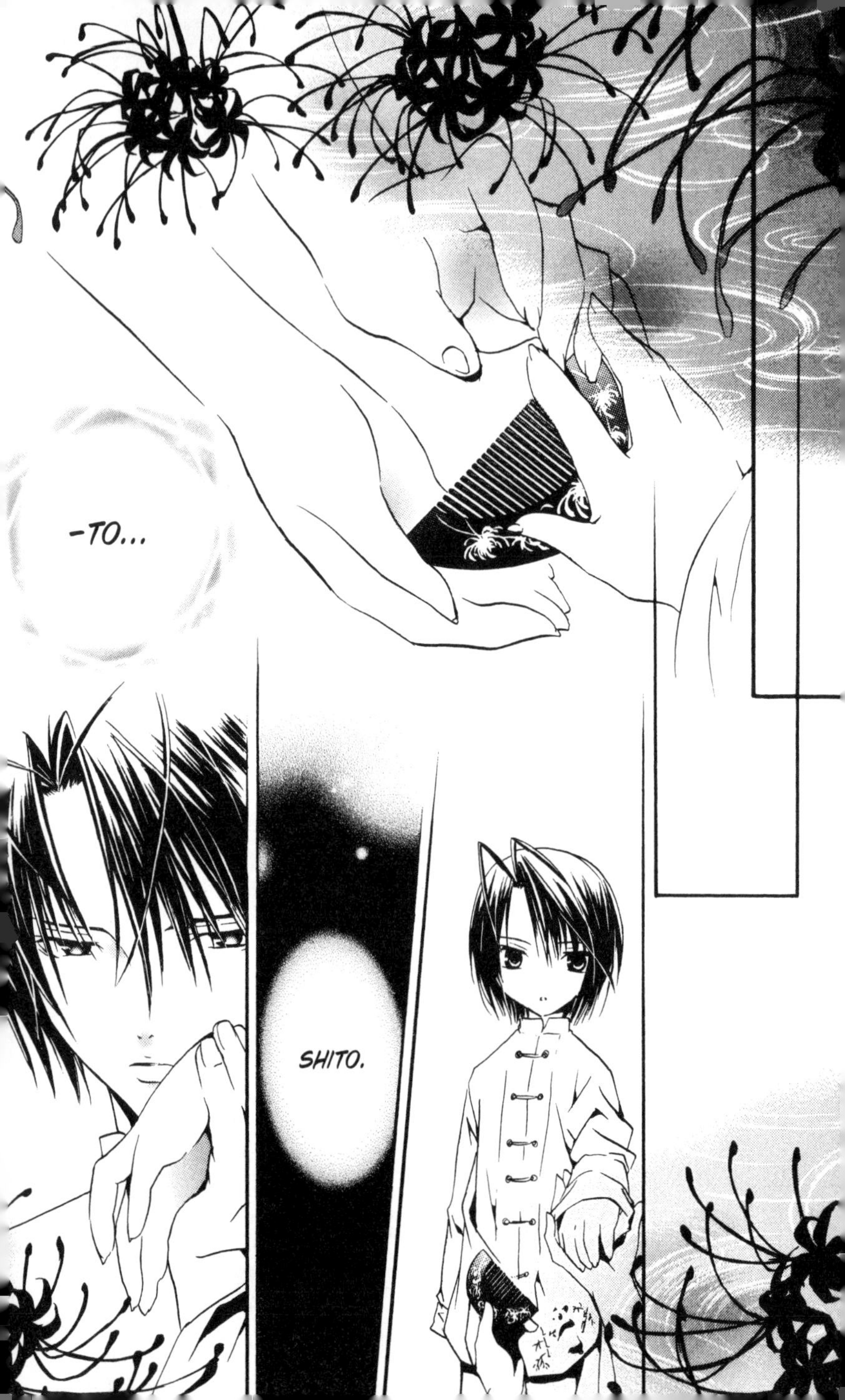
-TO...
SHITO.

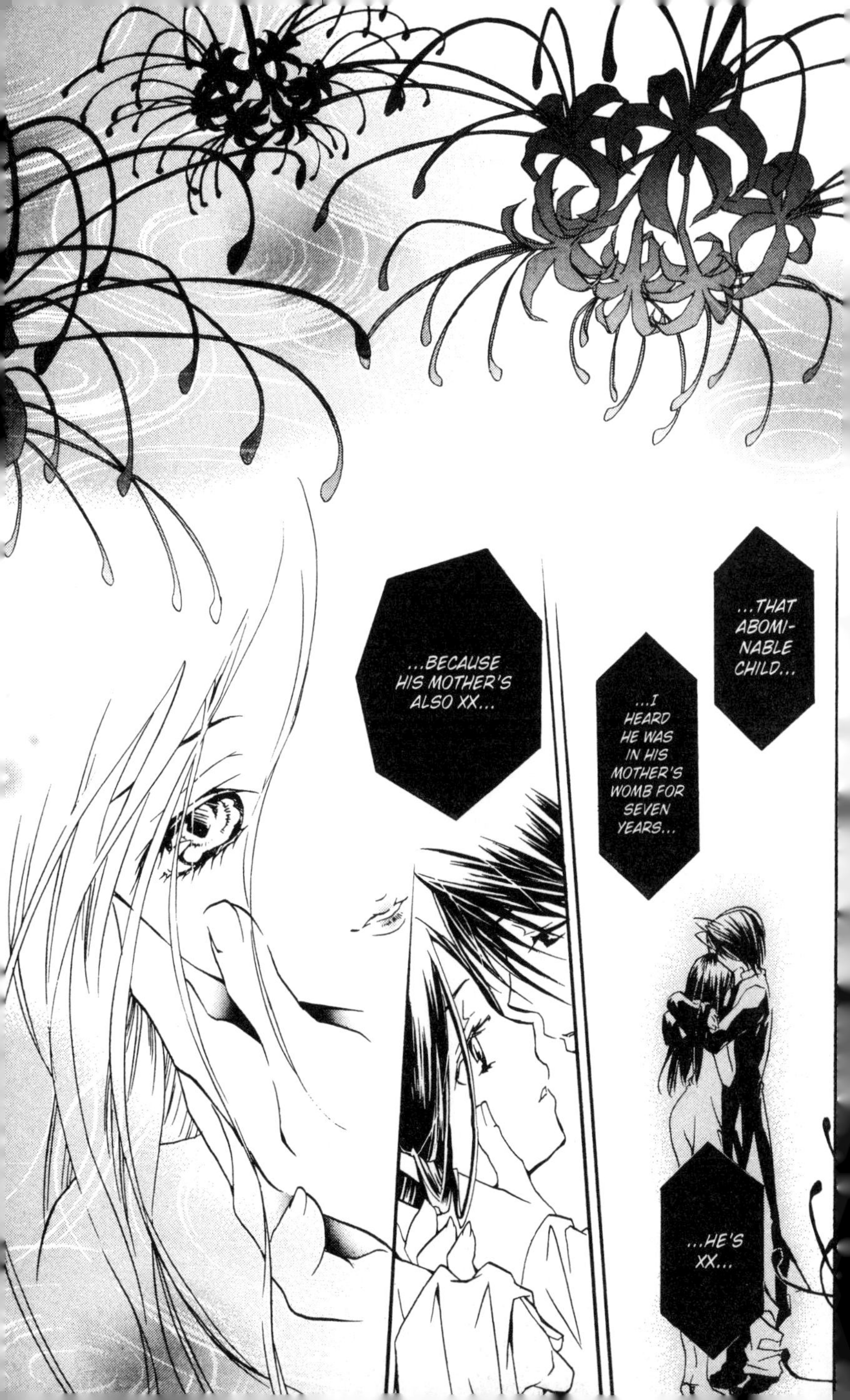
...THAT ABOMINABLE CHILD...
...HE'S XX...
...I HEARD HE WAS IN HIS MOTHER'S WOMB FOR SEVEN YEARS...
...BECAUSE HIS MOTHER'S ALSO XX...

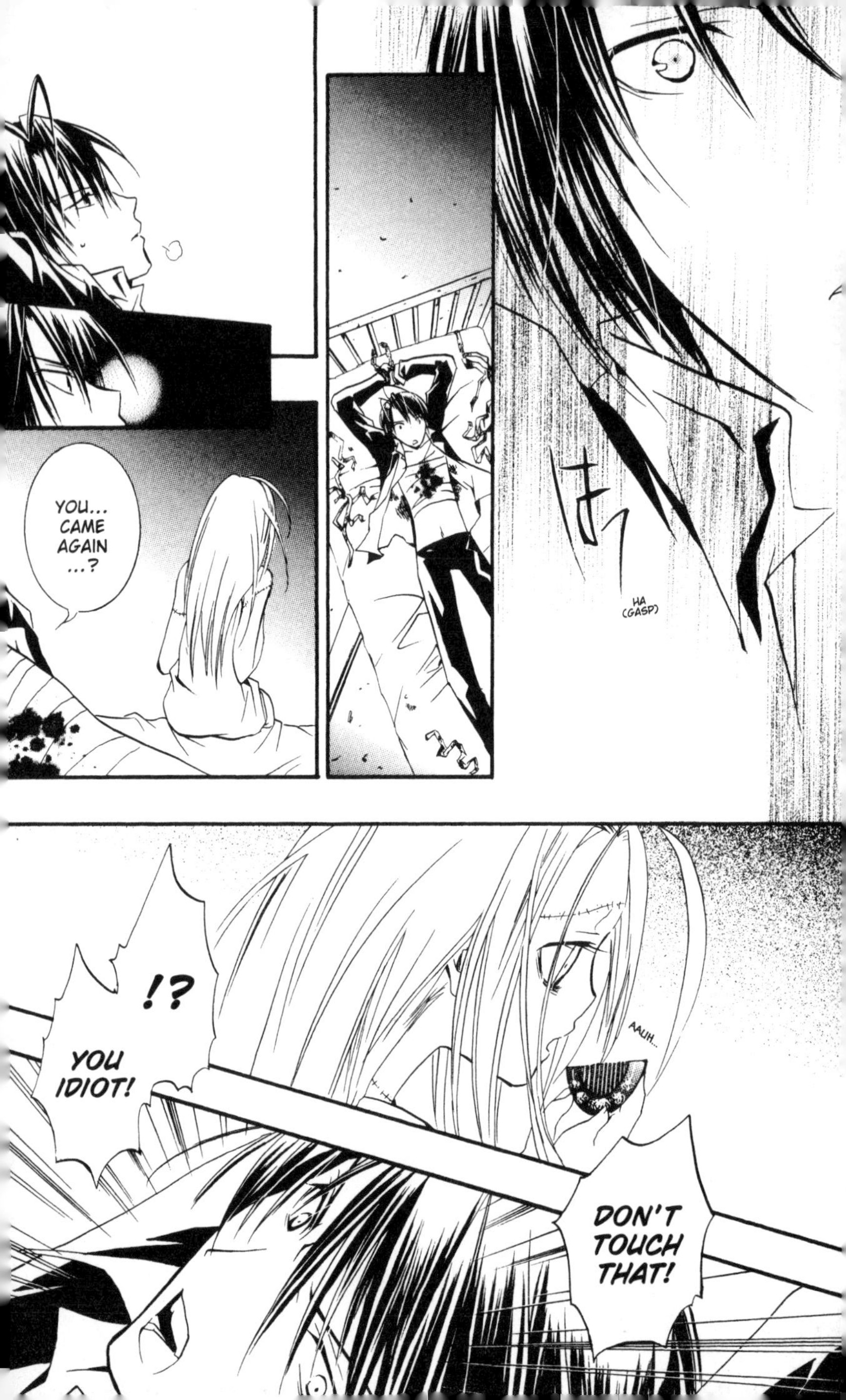
ほっ
HA (GASP)
YOU... CAME AGAIN ...?
AAUH...
DON'T TOUCH THAT!
!?
YOU IDIOT!

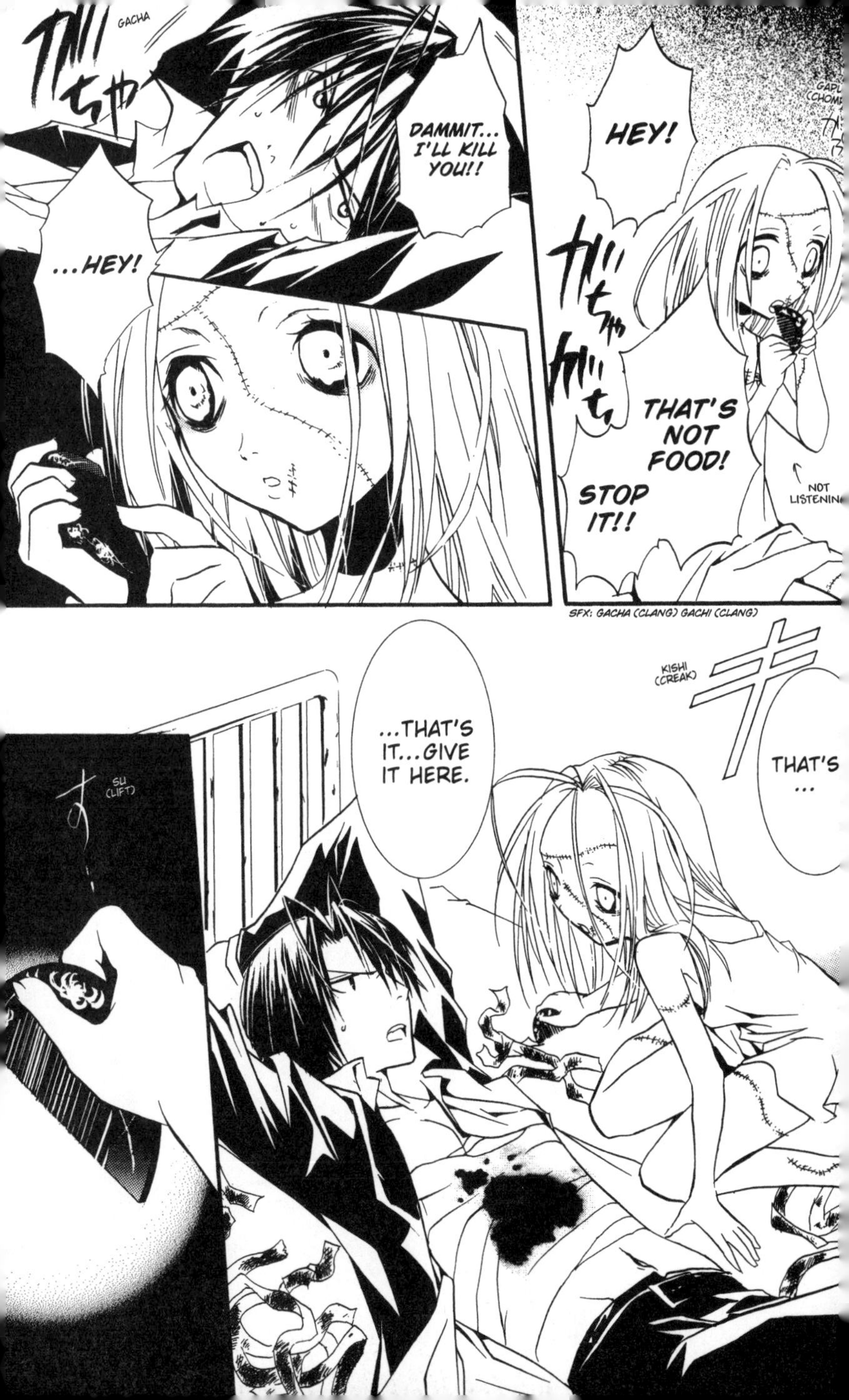
HEY!
GAPU (CHOMP
THAT'S NOT FOOD!
STOP IT!!
NOT LISTENING
SFX: GACHA (CLANG) GACHI (CLANG)
GACHA
DAMMIT... I'LL KILL YOU!!
...HEY!
KISHI (CREAK)
THAT'S ...
...THAT'S IT...GIVE IT HERE.
SU (LIFT)

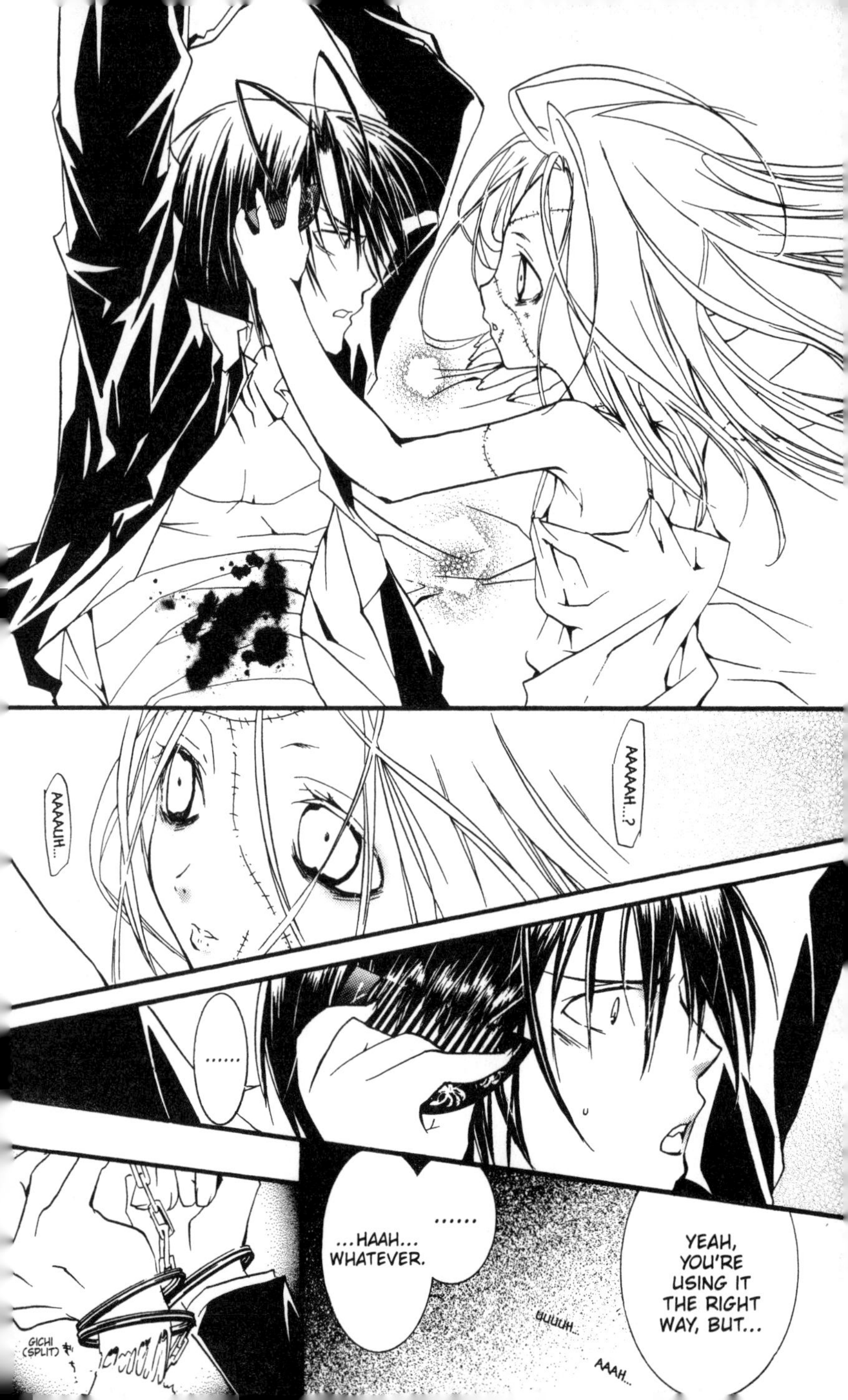
AAAAAH...?
AAAAUH...
......
YEAH, YOU'RE USING IT THE RIGHT WAY, BUT...
UUUUH...
AAAH..
......
...HAAH... WHATEVER.
GICHI (SPLIT)

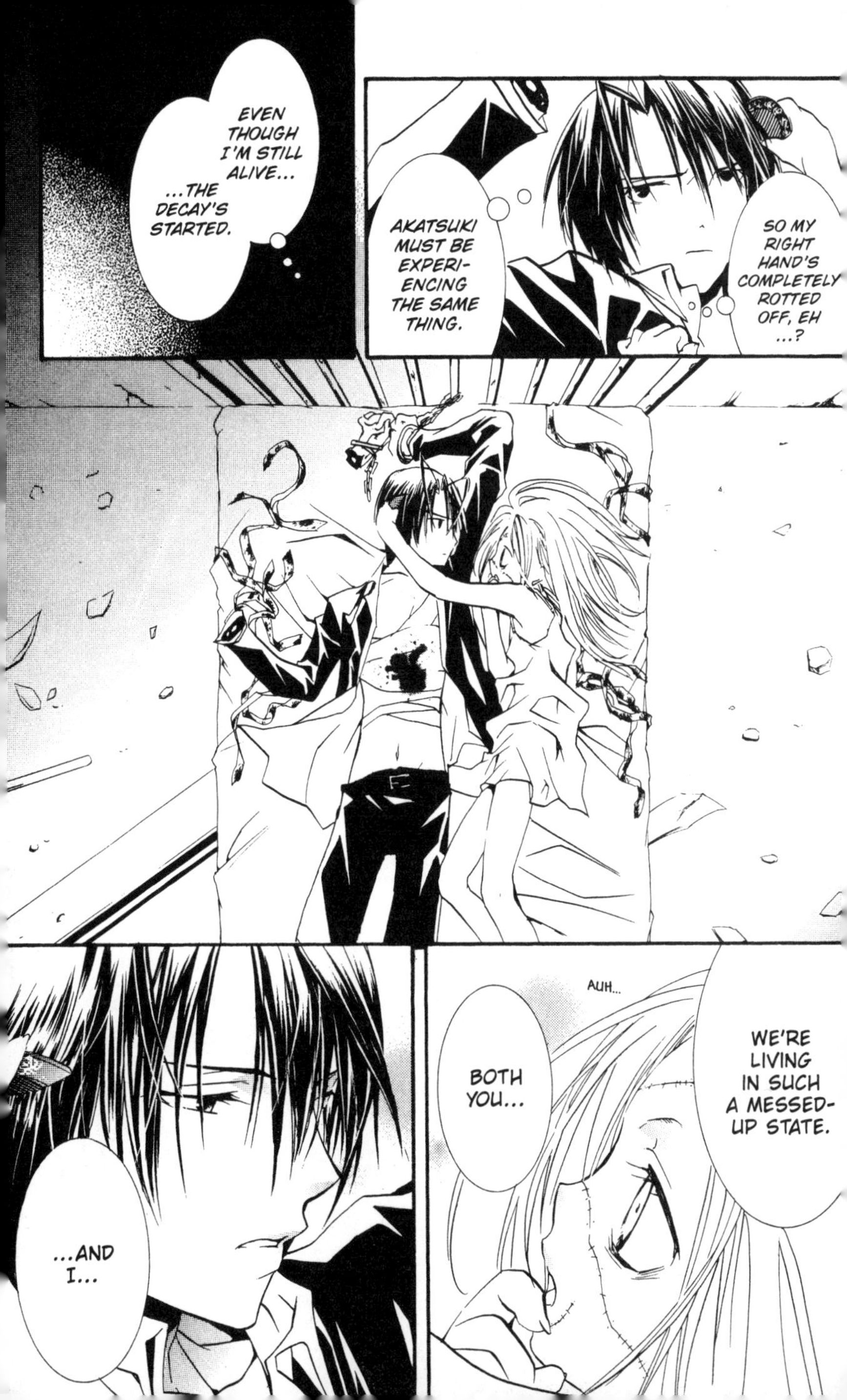
SO MY RIGHT HAND'S COMPLETELY ROTTED OFF, EH ...?
AKATSUKI MUST BE EXPERI-ENCING THE SAME THING.
EVEN THOUGH I'M STILL ALIVE...
...THE DECAY'S STARTED.
WE'RE LIVING IN SUCH A MESSED-UP STATE.
AUH...
BOTH YOU...
...AND I...

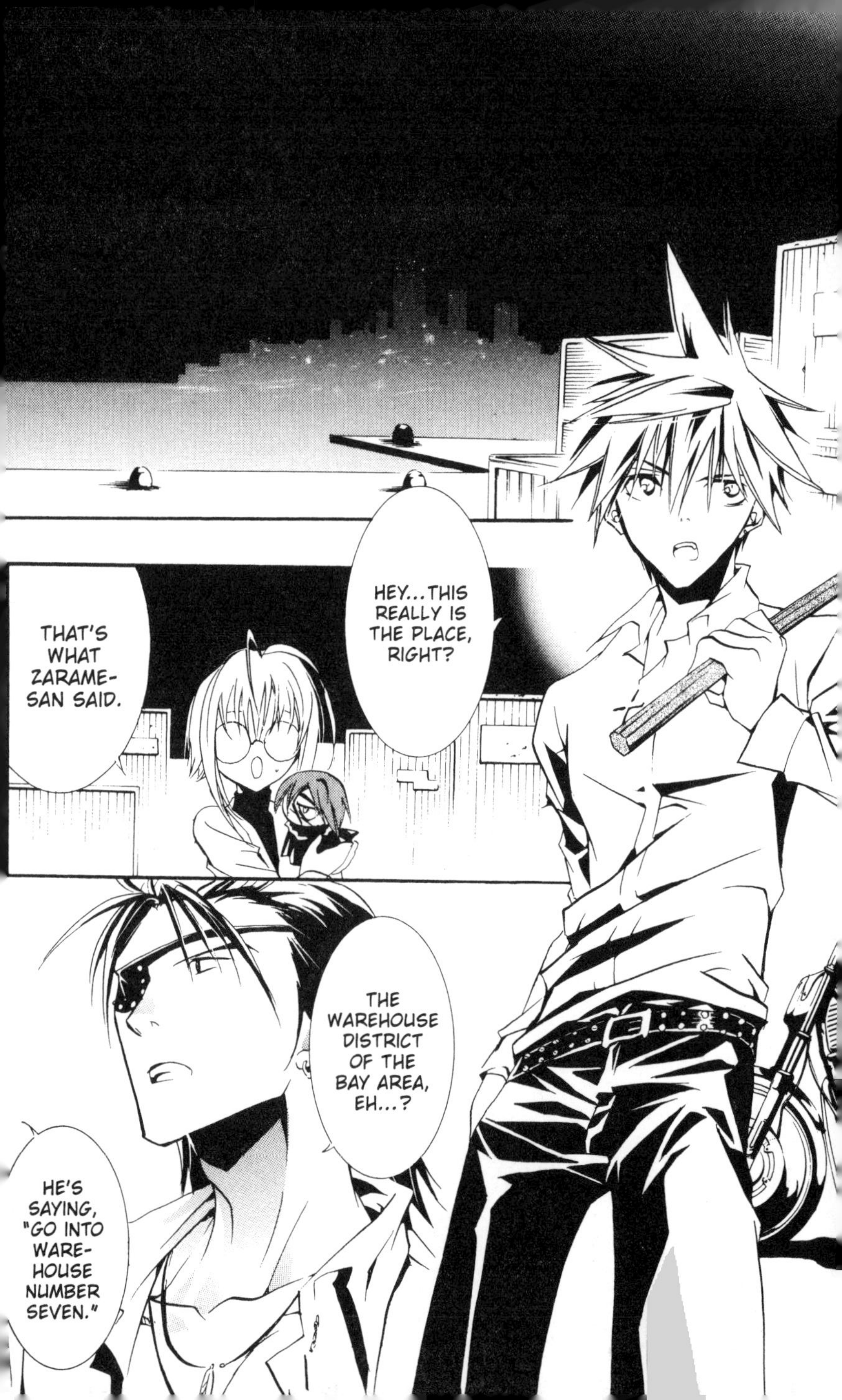
HEY...THIS REALLY IS THE PLACE, RIGHT?
THAT'S WHAT ZARAME-SAN SAID.
THE WAREHOUSE DISTRICT OF THE BAY AREA, EH...?
HE'S SAYING, "GO INTO WARE-HOUSE NUMBER SEVEN."

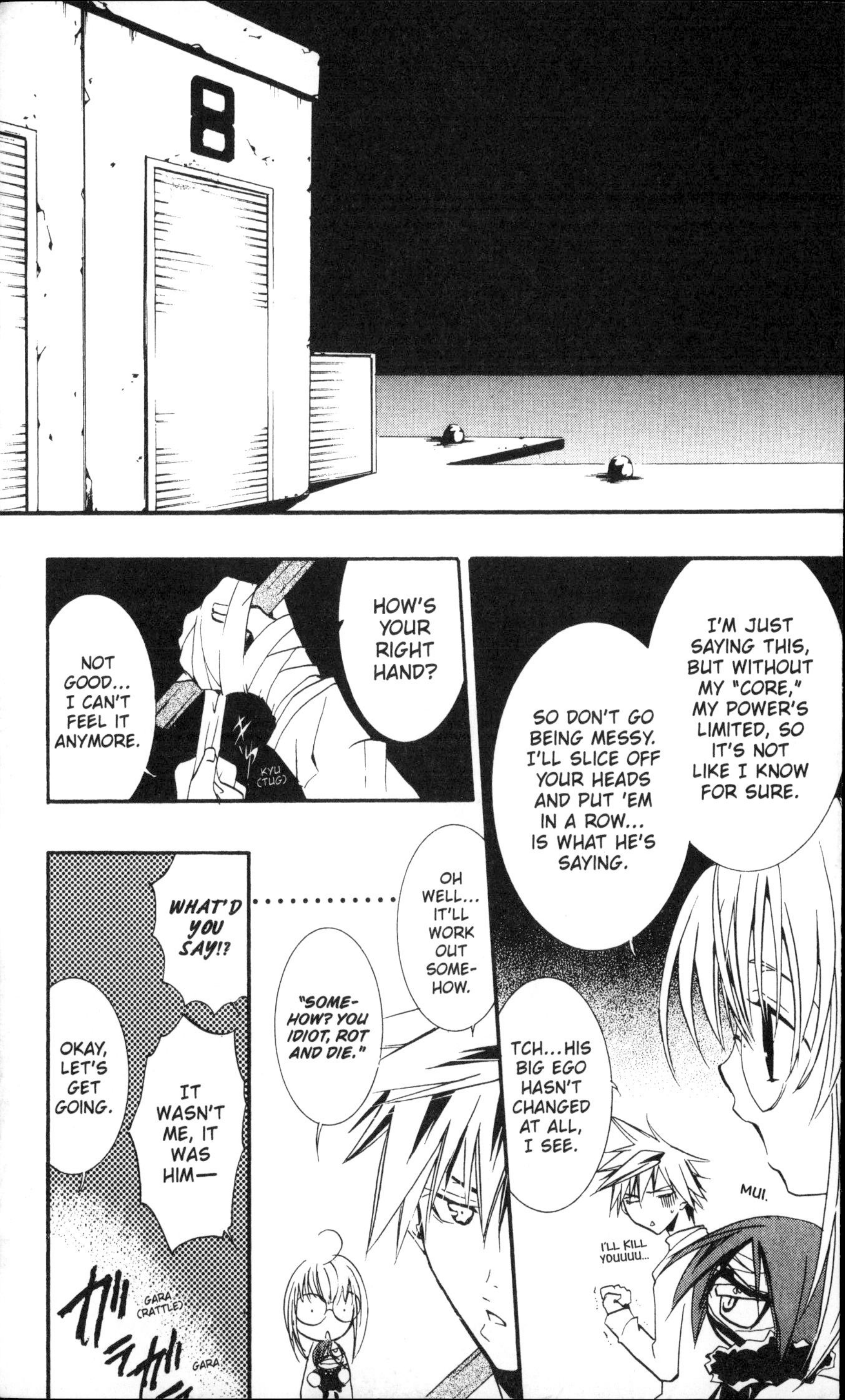

I'M JUST SAYING THIS, BUT WITHOUT MY "CORE," MY POWER'S LIMITED, SO IT'S NOT LIKE I KNOW FOR SURE.
SO DON'T GO BEING MESSY. I'LL SLICE OFF YOUR HEADS AND PUT 'EM IN A ROW... IS WHAT HE'S SAYING.
HOW'S YOUR RIGHT HAND?
NOT GOOD... I CAN'T FEEL IT ANYMORE.
KYU (TUG)
TCH...HIS BIG EGO HASN'T CHANGED AT ALL, I SEE.
MUI.
I'LL KILL YOUUUU...
OH WELL... IT'LL WORK OUT SOME-HOW.
"SOME-HOW? YOU IDIOT, ROT AND DIE."
WHAT'D YOU SAY!?
IT WASN'T ME, IT WAS HIM—
OKAY, LET'S GET GOING.
GARA (RATTLE)
GARA

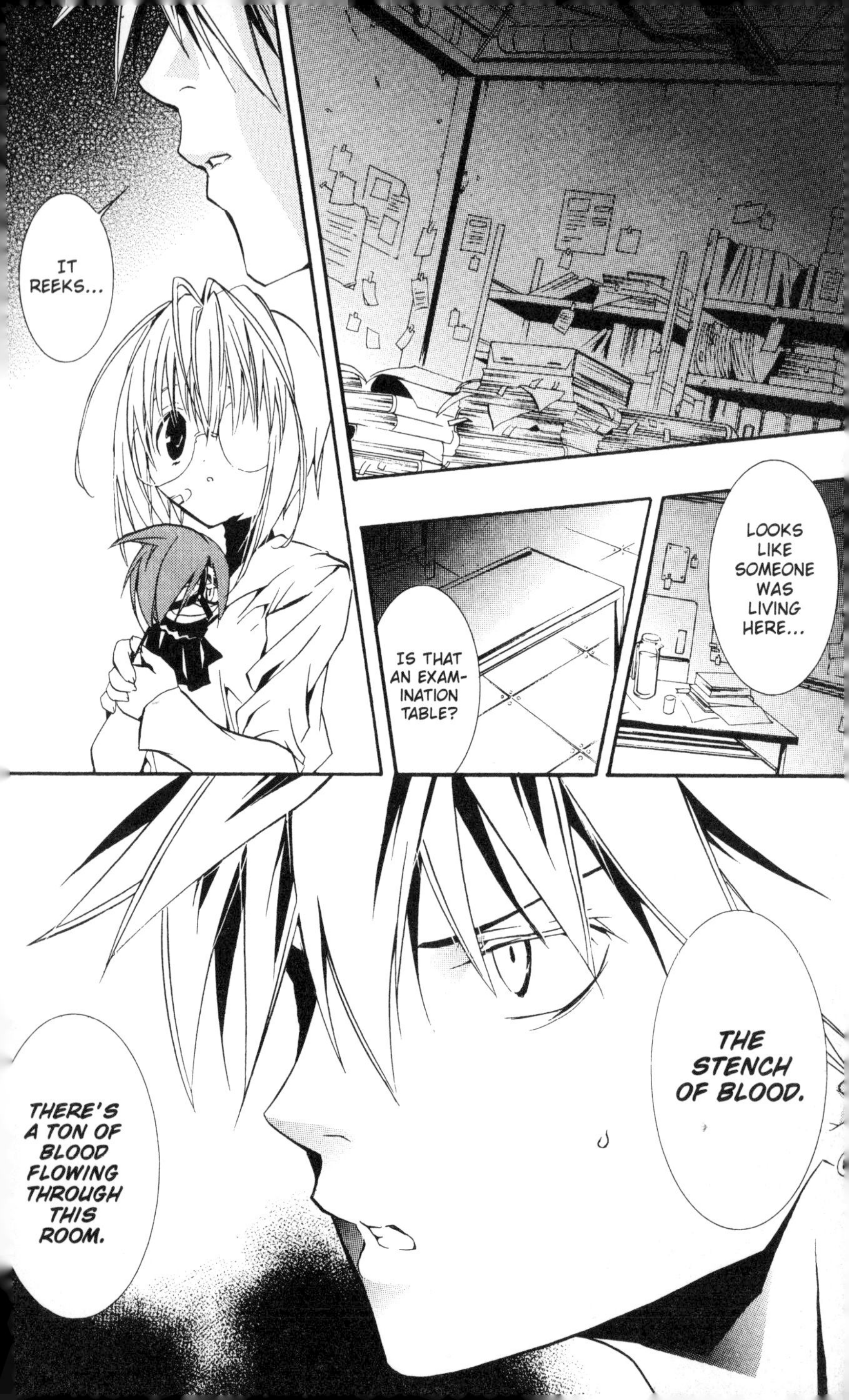
LOOKS LIKE SOMEONE WAS LIVING HERE...
IS THAT AN EXAMINATION TABLE?
IT REEKS...
THE STENCH OF BLOOD.
THERE'S A TON OF BLOOD FLOWING THROUGH THIS ROOM.

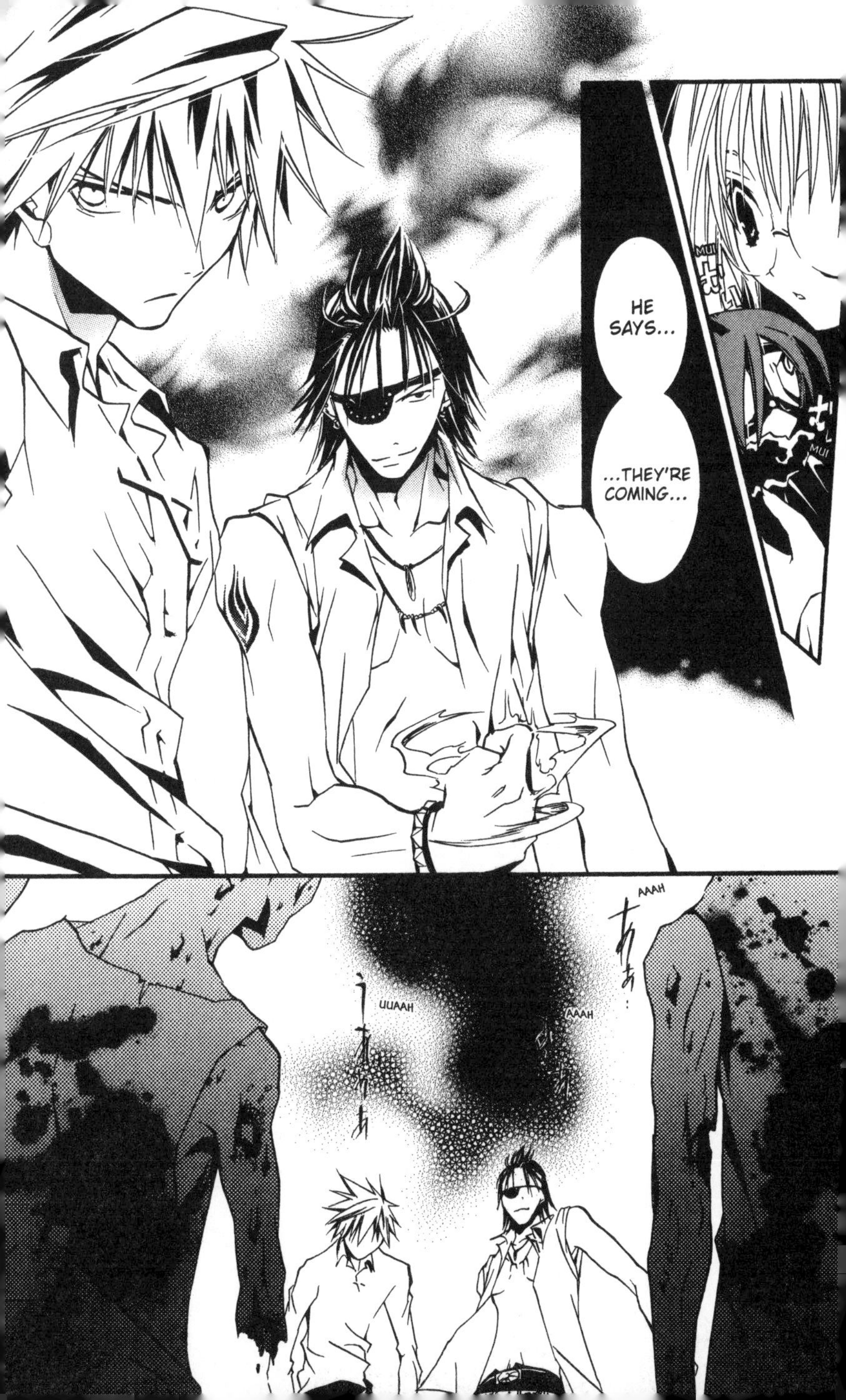
MUI
HE SAYS...
...THEY'RE COMING...
MUI
AAAH
AAAH
UUAAH

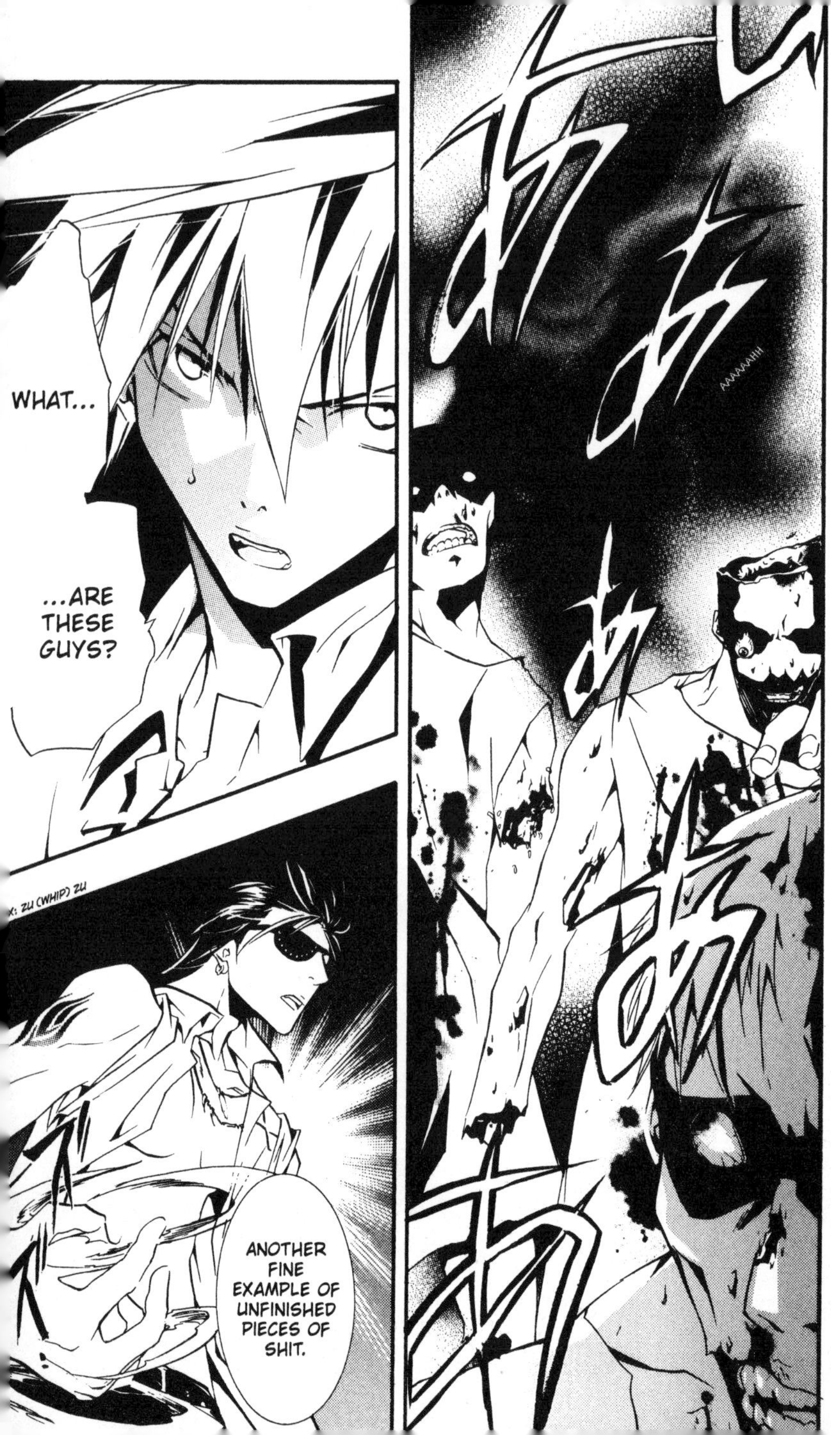
AAAAAAHH
WHAT...
...ARE THESE GUYS?
X: ZU (WHIP) ZU
ANOTHER FINE EXAMPLE OF UNFINISHED PIECES OF SHIT.

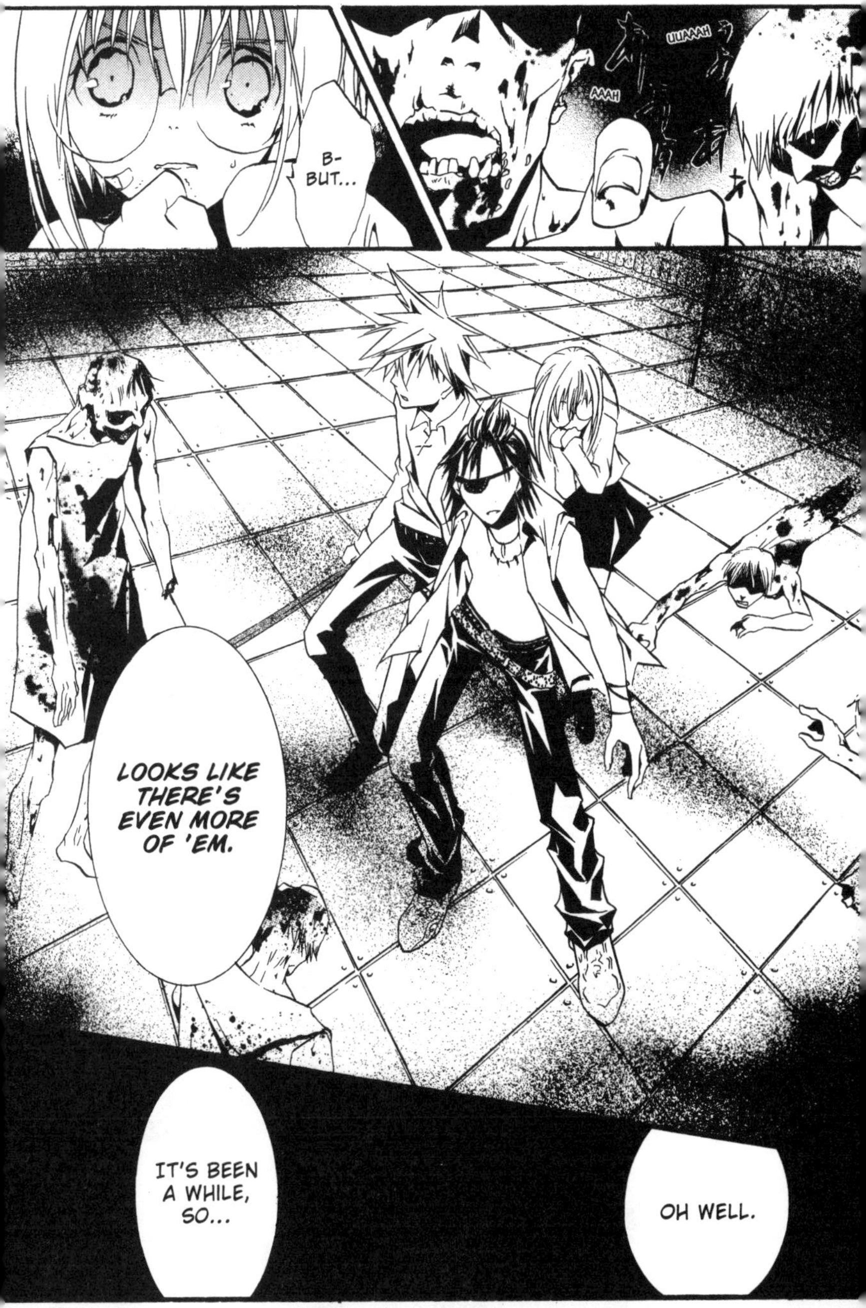
UUAAAH
AAAH
B-
BUT...
LOOKS LIKE THERE'S EVEN MORE OF 'EM.
OH WELL.
IT'S BEEN A WHILE, SO...

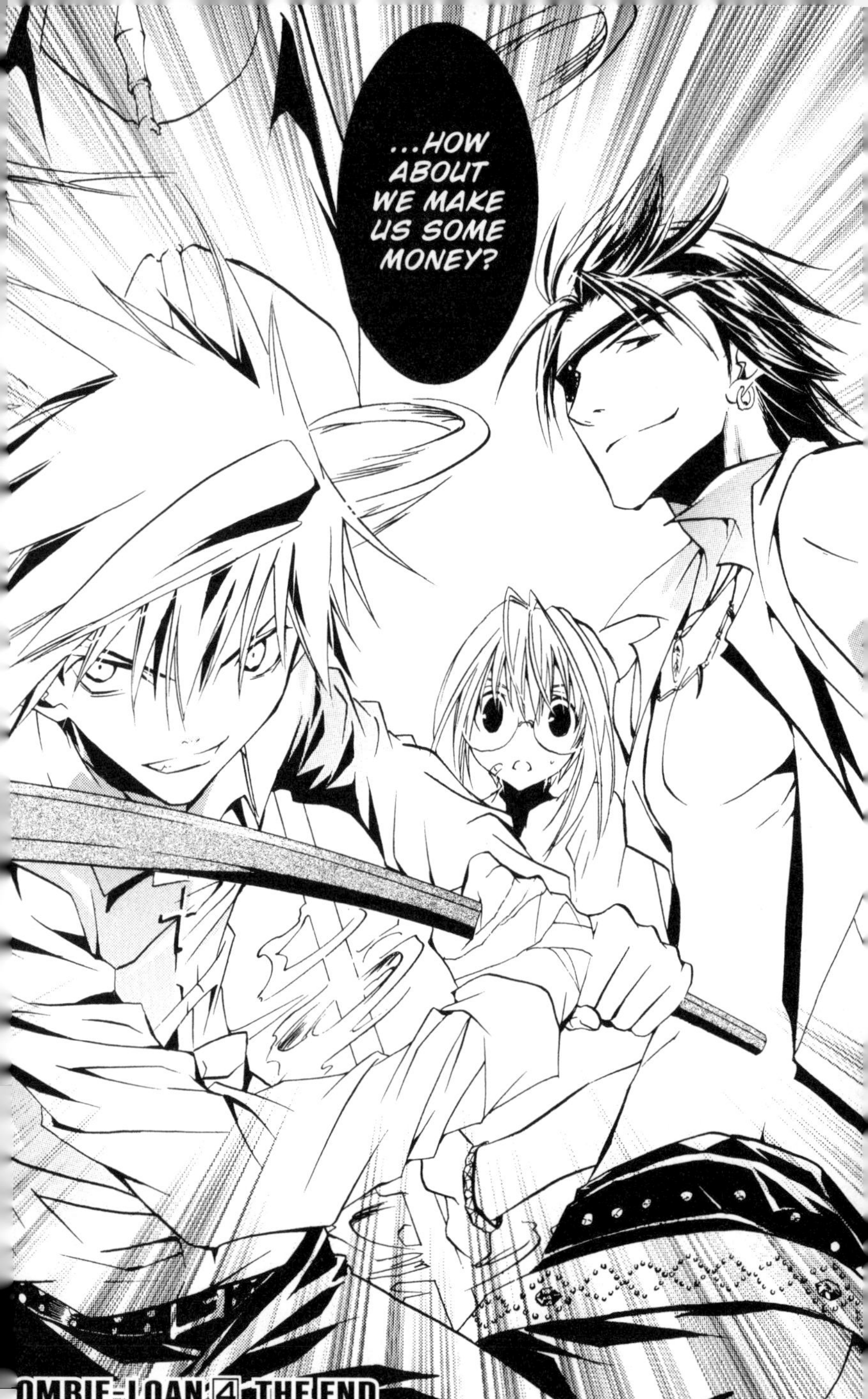
...HOW ABOUT WE MAKE US SOME MONEY?

OMBIE-LOAN 4 THE END

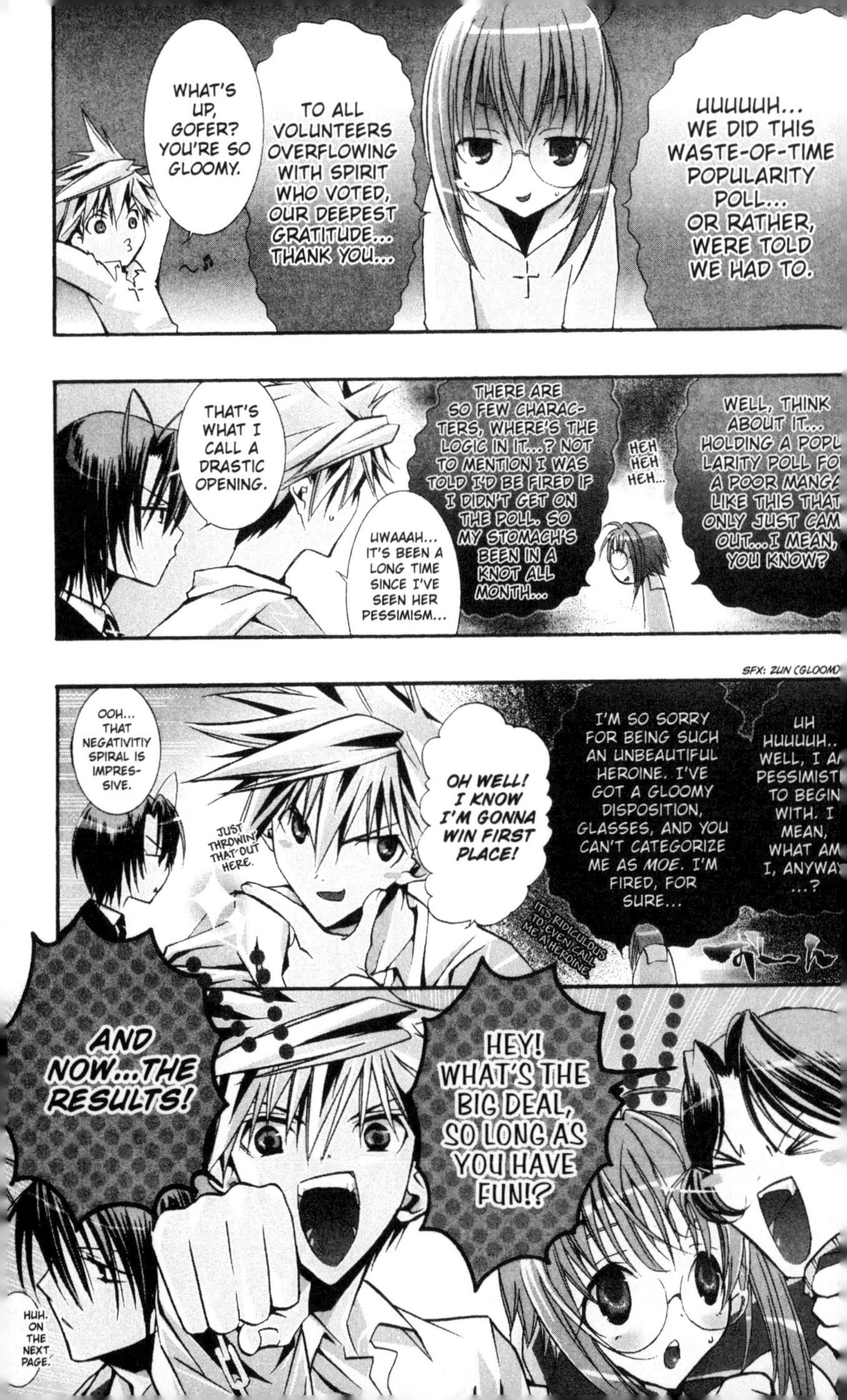
UUUUUH... WE DID THIS WASTE-OF-TIME POPULARITY POLL... OR RATHER, WERE TOLD WE HAD TO.
TO ALL VOLUNTEERS OVERFLOWING WITH SPIRIT WHO VOTED, OUR DEEPEST GRATITUDE... THANK YOU...
WHAT'S UP, GOFER? YOU'RE SO GLOOMY.
WELL, THINK ABOUT IT... HOLDING A POPU LARITY POLL FO A POOR MANGA LIKE THIS THAT ONLY JUST CAM OUT...I MEAN, YOU KNOW?
HEH HEH HEH...
THERE ARE SO FEW CHARAC-TERS, WHERE'S THE LOGIC IN IT...? NOT TO MENTION I WAS TOLD I'D BE FIRED IF I DIDN'T GET ON THE POLL. SO MY STOMACH'S BEEN IN A KNOT ALL MONTH...
THAT'S WHAT I CALL A DRASTIC OPENING.
UWAAAH... IT'S BEEN A LONG TIME SINCE I'VE SEEN HER PESSIMISM...
SFX: ZUN (GLOOM)
UH HUUUUH.. WELL, I A PESSIMIST TO BEGIN WITH. I MEAN, WHAT AM I, ANYWA ...?
I'M SO SORRY FOR BEING SUCH AN UNBEAUTIFUL HEROINE. I'VE GOT A GLOOMY DISPOSITION, GLASSES, AND YOU CAN'T CATEGORIZE ME AS MOE. I'M FIRED, FOR SURE...
IT'S RIDICULOUS TO EVEN CALL ME A HEROINE
OH WELL! I KNOW I'M GONNA WIN FIRST PLACE!
JUST THROWIN' THAT OUT HERE.
OOH... THAT NEGATIVITIY SPIRAL IS IMPRES-SIVE.
HEY! WHAT'S THE BIG DEAL, SO LONG AS YOU HAVE FUN!?
AND NOW...THE RESULTS!
HUH. ON THE NEXT PAGE.

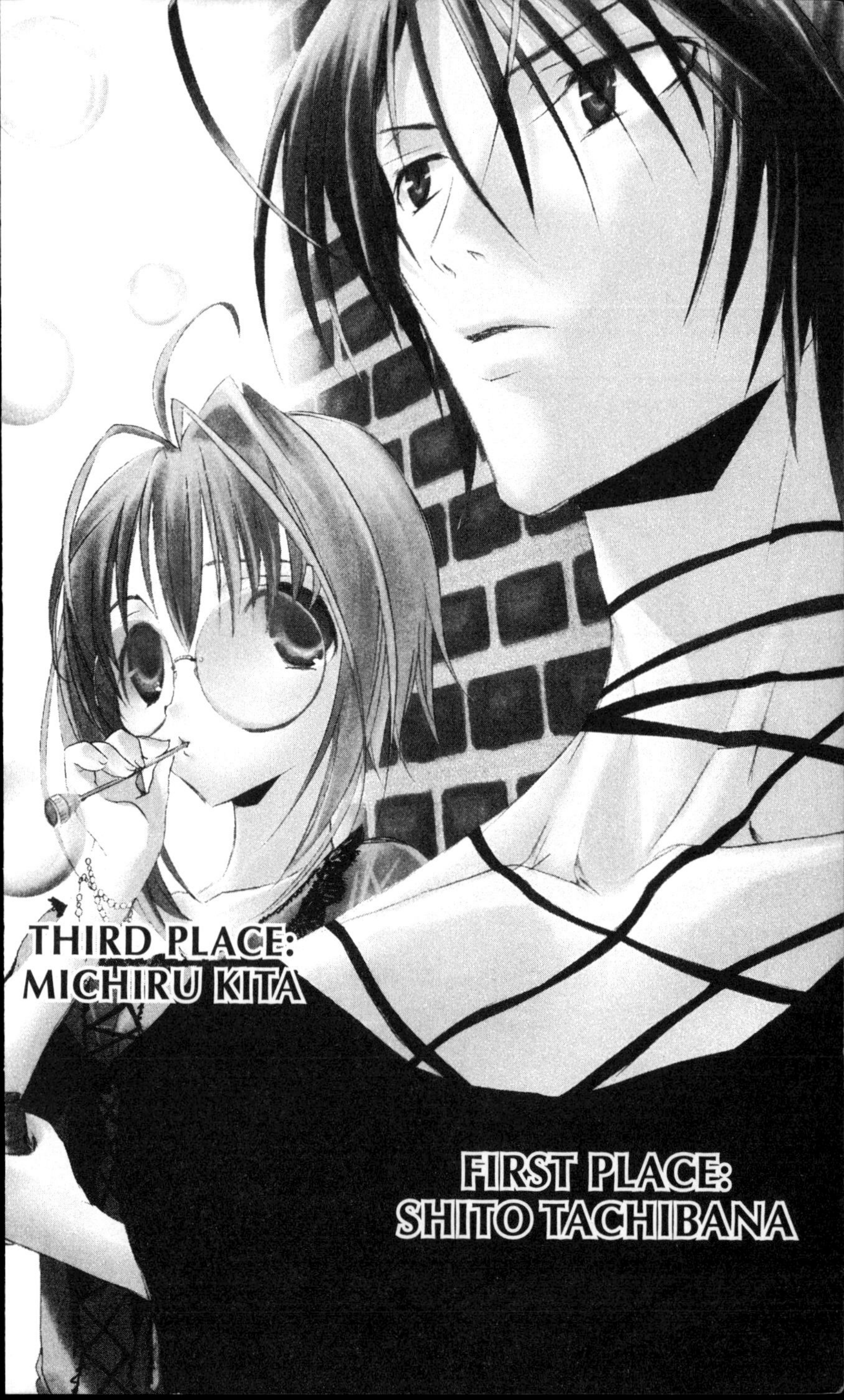
THIRD PLACE:
MICHIRU KITA
FIRST PLACE:
SHITO TACHIBANA

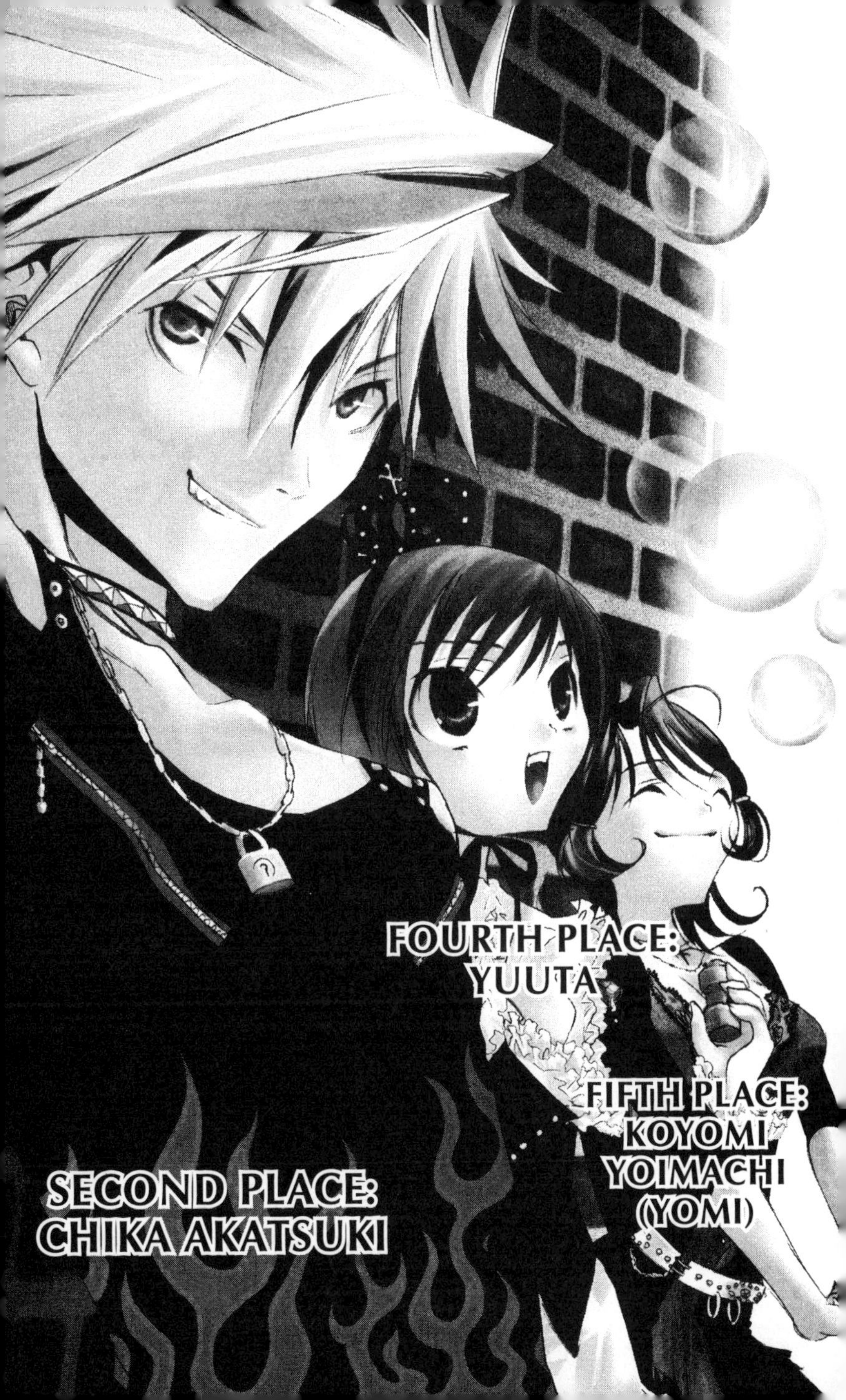
FOURTH PLACE: YUUTA
FIFTH PLACE: KOYOMI YOIMACHI (YOMI)
SECOND PLACE: CHIKA AKATSUKI

ZOMBIE-LOAN

ANNOUNCEMENT OF POPULARITY POLL RESULTS!!

*THIS POPULARITY POLL INVOLVED THE CHARACTERS THAT APPEARED IN VOLUMES 1 THRU 3.

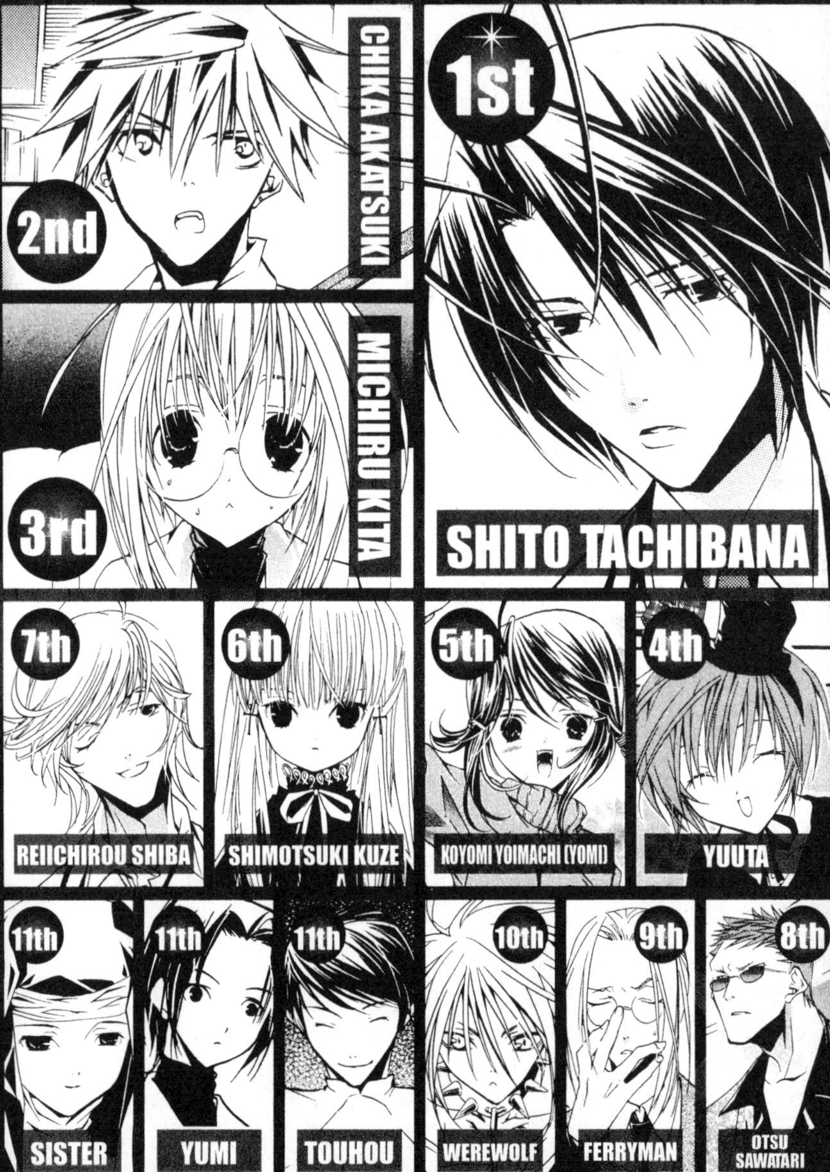

1st
SHITO TACHIBANA
2nd
CHIKA AKATSUKI
3rd
MICHIRU KITA
4th
YUUTA
5th
KOYOMI YOIMACHI (YOMI)
6th
SHIMOTSUKI KUZE
7th
REIICHIROU SHIBA
8th
OTSU SAWATARI
9th
FERRYMAN
10th
WEREWOLF
11th
TOUHOU
11th
YUMI
11th
SISTER

WE'LL BE DOING THIS AGAIN, SO KEEP YOUR EYE ON NEW CHARACTERS THAT APPEAR FROM HERE ON IN, TOO!

TRANSLATION NOTES

p15
Lao Ye is Chinese for "master," but it can also mean "father."

p16
-shao ye is a Chinese suffix meaning "young master."

p50
Baka means "idiot." *Kasu* means "shit."

p98
<*Hola, hermano guey!*> can be interpreted as a greeting along the lines of, "What's up, you bastard!" with "bastard" used here affectionately.

p104
<*Orale!*> is a Spanish word commonly used in Mexican culture to indicate enthusiasm or excitement, kind of like "Aww, hell, yeah!"

p116
Dabu is mostly likely taken from the adjective *dabudabu* which can mean "loose" or "sloppy" and probably refers to Soutetsu's slacker status at school.

p126
"The Way of Absolving Death" is the art of breaking the curse of the "corpse insect" (*shichuu*) that decides the length of one's life.

General note:
There are many mentions of various sums of money (in ¥) throughout this volume. Since exchange rates fluctuate daily, equivalent sums printed here would most likely be inaccurate. At the time this volume went to print, $1 USD was approximately equivalent to ¥115 JPY. In general, a rough estimate to use is $1 USD to ¥100 JPY.

all produced by
PEACH-PIT
Banri Sendou : Shibuko Ebara

main staff
Nao
Zaki
Chie
Kinomin
Tama

special thanks
T. Kuma A.Kitamura

...and your reading

ZOMBIE-LOAN

tO be cOntinued vOl. 5

ZOMBIE-LOAN

4

by PEACH-PIT

Translation: Christine Schilling
Lettering: Alexis Eckerman

Yen Press
Hachette Book Group USA
237 Park Avenue, New York, NY 10017

Visit our Web sites at www.HachetteBookGroupUSA.com and www.YenPress.com.

Yen Press is an imprint of Hachette Book Group USA, Inc. The Yen Press name and logo are trademarks of Hachette Book Group USA, Inc.

First Yen Press Edition: October 2008

ISBN-10: 0-7595-2838-1
ISBN-13: 978-0-7595-2838-3

10 9 8 7 6 5 4 3 2 1

BVG

Printed in the United States of America